Flame
Touched

Elura Coren

Part One:
All alone

Chapter 1

Vaxeehl

I swore under my breath as I stared at the latest data on the screen before me.

My father's voice rang through the air. "Find another planet! The last batch you delivered is practically useless. It's been nearly two years, and not a single child has carried to term."

I did not need him to give his concerns voice; I could see them for myself. I grumbled in return, "And that's if the virus did not kill them. Of the original 200, only 109 remain."

I leaned back in my chair with my hands linked behind my head. Virus 442-C had caused issues throughout the galaxy. Despite extreme import, export, and travel restrictions, it had spread through every inhabited planet over the course of the last eight years. As soon as our world, Volitar, had been affected, myself and each of my three siblings had been shipped off the surface to hover outside the planet on private transport units.

I didn't blame Father for pushing us all away like that. We still saw the devastation, even though only through broadcast updates. He wanted to make certain that someone would be available to take the throne, should he become ill. He also felt it was his duty, and his alone, to stay on the planet to lead the people. He even sent mother away for protection.

My eyes cast over the perma-screen image near my bed. Father stood proud in the dark crimson kilnat marking him ruler of our people. His golden eyes, silver hair, and lavender skin showed him descended from the original inhabitants of Volitar. Next to him with her wings extended almost as a backdrop, mother's many brown tones contrasted greatly, showing that she had come to him from our neighboring Vesper.

Vespers were a strong and honorable people. Their wings served both as a means of travel and for protection. The Vesper and Volitar regularly mingled races, but Mother was the first Vesper to marry royalty on Volitar. She had come to father as an arranged marriage to further solidify our already strong alliance, and her honor led her to providing him with his heir, me.

Yet, it hadn't taken long before their union became much more than just an alliance, as was evident when MeeKale joined the family the following year. Arden came along three years later. But the birth of Raklin, the only one who had inherited the majority of his visage from her, had been especially hard on mother as one of his wings had lodged open. After that, father had declared no more. He refused to risk the love of his life; if she wanted a daughter, she would just have to wait for one of their rambunctious sons to find a mate.

She loved us all, doing her best to instill in us proper behavior suited to the rulers of both of our worlds. However, we recognized that having that single child who visibly displayed her proud and honorable Vesper heritage drew her to her youngest just a bit more than to the rest of us.

Despite extensive screening, two of the vessels became infected. By the time we learned that it had made it among Mother's crew, she was already ill. A week later, she had died.

Father's grief knew no bounds. He buried himself with the researchers and medical personnel, trying everything they could to find a treatment to stop the disease. The few times he uplinked to us, we could see his exhaustion, his heartbreak. He seldom slept, and every delay made him angrier. When even the medics fell ill, slowing progress to a crawl, I feared he had given up. Yet, I did not feel ready to take the throne and lead our traumatized people.

A week after mother's death, Raklin had taken his ship and disappeared, too distraught to stay. Repeated uplink attempts failed. Our only hope remained that our sensors detected no distress beacon. Our only hope, and our greatest concern.

I spent a good deal of the first year sedated in some manner to keep me docile. I'd tried to fight my way to one of the pods to get to mother's side, but my friends, my Chief Medical Officer, Lanyar, and Captain of the Guard, Marlux, had filled me with enough Gorgon fungi spores to tranquilize even our strongest slognip and strapped me to my bed until I recognized I would put everyone aboard my own transport in jeopardy. Father devoted much of my childhood drilling me with responsibilities. He did this again while I lay grieving, reminding me that our people needed a strong leader who proved himself worthy. Even struggling through his own grieving, he worked to prepare me for ascension.

MeeKale, the second in line for the throne, had always been the playful one among us. The devastation of mother's loss seemed much more pronounced on him. His normally bright red eyes had gone dull, and he secluded himself with the animals he loved so well. Only when a nesting maldron had selected him as a keeper did life finally return to his lavender face.

Stoic and studious Arden allowed his emotions to coalesce in anger. He pushed himself hard, accepting challenges from any among his warriors willing to fight. The lone medic aboard his vessel contacted me regularly, trying to find a way to help him that did not involve constantly allowing him to be beaten to a bloody purple pulp on an almost daily basis. I could offer no advice.

By the end of the first year, most women of child-bearing age had died. By the end of the third year, more than fifty thousand of the population had succumbed to the illness, most of those females. Volitar was not a large planet compared to others within our galaxy; the loss of thirty percent of our population left us vulnerable in too many ways. We had plenty of warriors both for now and for the immediate future, but in a matter of years, I knew we faced a risk of civil war over the lack of mates. That would then decimate the remaining male population.

I finally turned my grief into determination to save the future of our home. Our society was already integrated, as were most planets within our galaxy, so bringing in another race to join ours would not present conflict.

Unfortunately, this integration meant that of the most likely planets to gather potential mates from, they had dealt with the same issues. This virus was so new to all of us, and it had created great havoc in our area of the universe.

Once 442-C had run its course on Volitar, many hundreds of males had taken to traveling to nearby planets, seeking that tingle, that sign showing they had found their mate. Only a handful had succeeded... a handful out of over a hundred thousand remaining unmated men and boys.

That removed our home galaxy as a selection point. Much of the outer galaxies remained yet unexplored, mostly because of the time needed for such events. Even with worm hole jumping, long-distance travel took many lunar cycles. Our engineers had designed specialized circadian cycle monitors to help aid seclusion sickness or interstellar dementia. But even those of our people wishing to study the great expanses of the universe also wished for families. Regardless of the equality among us, very few females chose universal exploration, meaning our explorers had to return to Volitar to mate. Once paired, it went against our nature to separate for any extended period of time.

Helvana, our goddess, had gifted our kind the ability to sense our mates, to know them upon entering their presence. However, the sign was not always clear to us. Sometimes, it was a tingle, sometimes, just a feeling of belonging. Over the centuries, as we integrated our people with those from other planets, the mating sense had even been discounted as little more than spiritual fodder or superstition.

My father, however, genuinely believed in the mating sense, insisting that Helvana's blessing would guide his sons to their futures. For only with the blessing of the goddess would our family continue to rule the throne.

If I could not find a means to bolster our population, though, neither I nor any of my brothers would have a throne to rule. Thus, I presented the idea of gathering females from other galaxies. Father had quickly agreed, thinking this plan the only chance for any of us to find our blessed mate.

I started my search in the first neighboring galaxy. It had taken three lunar cycles of travel, even with the use of worm holes. Then I spent another six cycles negotiating, to come home with only fifty volunteers.

None of them were able to conceive, no matter what our medical staff did. The diverse genetics inside the planet should have made it easier to find a potential breeding mate. However, it did the opposite. Due to fear of rejection from their own kind for having chosen to breed with an alien race, they chose to stay on Volitar, despite their inability to produce offspring.

The next three planets threatened war over the mere suggestion.

After that, we started operating covertly. We found more primitive planets, planets we could orbit while scanning for biocompatibility and virus presence. Ideally, we would prefer to pull from a planet that had already faced Virus 442-C and had survived with better odds. This would leave the women with immunity from reinfection. Our medical researchers still worked to determine whether that immunity passed to future generations, but since we had almost no women of child-bearing age giving birth, we could not test that theory yet.

The first few women we captured fought us tooth and nail. Their levels of violence surprised even some of my staunchest warriors. We erased their memories and returned them to their planets.

Finally, Lanyar, came up with a plan. It would take longer to gather potential breeders, but it had higher opportunity for success in retaining those women.

Lanyar had helped design our thought scanners, although his assistant had done the majority of the actual work and programming. Normally, we only used the programs for investigative purposes. Inside the palace walls, low level scanning occurred at all times, the program searching for key thoughts regarding palace safety. However, the scanners could be adapted for long-range use.

"I propose," he said snidely, "that we scan for women wishing to disappear. Women who would have none willing to fight for them. Not only would we be gaining their breeding capacity, but they would stand a better chance of being willing to move halfway across the universe. Preferably *without* trying to kill us."

Shortly after that, we found Norvax. It took nearly a solar revolution to gather two hundred and fifty Norvaxian women. They were all kept quarantined from each other until we were certain they had not carried some sort of illness onboard. We returned thirty to the surface due to seclusion sickness.

This is where Denali, Lanyar's assistant, suggested a test. She recommended we put the women in unusual situations to see how they would react. This would give us a means of evaluating whether they could survive an extended period of time on the ship, as well as potentially find those with hidden violence.

Thus, the idea of the collective evaluation came to fruition. We split the collected brides into groups and put them into the simulation block. We placed random obstacles before them: they had to work together to cross a bridge, protect a child from wildlife, little things to test them emotionally.

We lost another twenty when a couple of the women just started killing the others. Those murderous women had received a death sentence. Volitar's laws were clear to all onboard: murder equals death. Those remaining females, once presented with details on why we had taken them from their home planet, had been... not excited, but at least open to a new possible future.

I found great relief once the delivery had been made. Now, I learned we lost ninety-one more to the virus. It was disheartening that we had worked so diligently only to lose nearly half to the same invisible killer.

I returned my attention to my father.

"I have already found one potential planet, Borkania, and have gained a small selection, but not enough to be worth the trip back yet. Lanyar is scanning a highly-populated planet as we speak. This one has already dealt with the virus, and only lost ten percent of their population, according to their electronic records. Plus, most of those were elderly or otherwise already ill. If they are genetically capable of breeding with us, we have much more potential to gather a large quantity of brides from there."

I paused a moment. "Lanyar has an idea to test whether the women from these new planets can carry to term. There are just enough differences to raise concern, and we don't want to waste multiple lunar cycles bringing them all the way to Volitar, only to face the same situation as with the Norvaxians."

Father scrubbed his hand across his tired face. The trials he faced clearly wore on him. "At this point, I am willing to give Lanyar free reign. He has the best scientific mind on your ship. And I happen to agree. The Norvaxian women who have lost their children are spiraling into a deep sadness. I fear this may cause permanent mental damage to them."

"I will report back as the experiment proceeds, father."

The screen went black, and I drew a deep breath. I spoke aloud. "Ovid, fetch Lanyar, please."

"The Chief Medical Officer has been notified to report to this office," the voice of my artificial intelligence unit responded immediately.

After Norvax, we found Borkania. Borkanian women were a wonderful match, at least in computer models, despite their unusual genetic design. They all bore six arms and had burgundy skin. Lanyar had reported they also had four breasts. I had chosen not to personally verify that information.

Unfortunately, we could not negotiate with their rulers. Nor could we just keep snatching unsuspecting future wives. We had gotten lucky with finding the small handful currently onboard the ship. Borkanian women are much prized by their men. Most were mated before their seventeenth year, and very few harbored the desire to disappear. Even fewer could disappear without causing an uproar.

Because of the violent behavior from the Norvax collective, Denali designed an upload. The collected women could now be placed in a dream state, the upload pushed into their minds, and our scanners would read how they reacted to the hypothetical situations.

Of the original thirty-nine we had collected, thirty-seven had passed the evaluation. The other two had been returned to their planet with no knowledge of where they had been for nearly a lunar cycle.

The portal shimmered, allowing my friend to enter. He looked perplexed.

I stood and bowed a welcome to him. "The king has agreed to the test."

His bright green eyes shot open wide. "Why is that? He previously insisted that all women be brought to Volitar, banning any of us from interacting with them beyond the collection process."

I pointed to my screen which still displayed the data from Volitar.

He visibly deflated at the disheartening information. "I am pleased to be able to test the full compatibility, but I had hoped we would have better news from home. We have barely made a dent in the initial request for over five thousand brides, and I do not believe your brothers have fared any better. The idea of being able to find mates for all hundred thousand is becoming extremely overwhelming."

I nodded, showing my agreement with his assessment. "When can we begin? The king is growing impatient." I chose not to mention just how tired and worn my father appeared.

He scoffed. "Are you really surprised? There have been less than thirty young born healthy in the last eight years, despite the sharing program he ordered." He pursed his lips. He and I shared the same negative view of that program. If the women had chosen to accept more than one mate, that would have been different, as it had been her choice. However, forcing them to accept this fate did not settle well in our thoughts. It went against everything we had ever learned.

"Let us gather the Borkanians together and ask for a volunteer."

A short time later, we stood in the cafeteria, facing thirty-seven women. Up to this point, they had no idea why we had taken them from their homes. Despite the lack of knowledge, they did not clamor for return. I assumed that behavior due to their having remained unmated thus far.

I let Lanyar explain the medical details, how the virus had killed off most of the women of child-bearing age on Volitar, how we had hopes that they could help us produce the next generation.

A few of the women looked confused, while the others looked... enthusiastic. I found that behavior intriguing.

After Lanyar finished, I spoke to them. "We are asking for just one of you ladies to volunteer to be impregnated. We will not require you to engage sexually if you do not wish to do so. We have the technology to implant a fertilized egg into your body for you. Normally, we would not do this; we would present you to the king, and he would arrange your marriages. Unfortunately, the last group of women we delivered for wives," I hesitated to tell them this information, but knew it was necessary. "The children have not survived to birth yet."

I heard several gasps, and possibly some tears. I blinked at this unexpected reaction.

Lanyar spoke again. "There is risk involved. All of my computer models of your genetics show you should be highly compatible and able to breed with us. But I will not lie. There is risk. Only part of it being that Borkanians are smaller builds compared to the people of Volitar. Despite genetic compatibility, the babies could be too large for your bodies to carry."

"Bolantivana," I heard one woman speak, swearing in her home tongue despite having received the language upload.

As I cast my eyes around the room, a woman near the front stood. I acknowledged her right to speak. "Identify yourself. Why do you say the risk is bolantivana?"

The woman stepped forward, gazing directly at me. "I am Taylana, my new prince. Every birth presents risk, but Borkanian women are built for childbirth. However, your scientific offer will never work. Borkanian women are only capable of carrying the child of their true mate. That is why you could find so few of us to gather. All of the women in this room have faced many rituals and come away without finding their mate. Many of us have been thrown from our homes because the ritual could not be completed, and our mates remained unidentified."

She looked over her shoulder at the nodding faces behind her. "Perhaps we could not find our true mates because they did not exist on our home planet."

She waved one of her right hands toward the unused side of the cafeteria. "Bring your men to this room. We will search among them."

I considered it a reasonable request. It sounded as if we were possibly doing as much of a favor for them as they were for us. That explained the excitement. These women found their situation to be one of hope.

"Which of you shall take this chance," I asked.

Taylana shook her head. "The magic of the Queen will determine that answer. We will not know until the ritual is performed."

In a testament to some of the odd things we had seen during our travels, Lanyar quickly sent word to the crew via public announcement. Any male eligible for a wife and willing to mate with one of the Borkanians should come forward.

One hundred and three men had arrived, nearly a quarter of the crew, and most of them soldiers. I had expected more, as three quarters of the crew had claimed eligibility status.

The women stood as a group, or a network, really. One woman stood in the center, extending all six arms. Six women surrounded her, pressing one palm to hers, one each to the two ladies on either side, and the other three outward. This pattern continued until they all stood gathered like a hive, each touching all of those around them. Then they began chanting.

I watched my men. As the chanting continued, I noticed some leave the room, looking greatly confused. I assumed they had changed their minds about binding themselves to these strange, yet willing, breeders. Others, just a handful of men, did not leave, yet they moved to the side of the room, a lightly glazed look in their eyes.

I glanced back to the chanting ladies. Several had carefully extricated themselves from the arrangement and returned to their seats. Interestingly enough, they looked saddened. I silently beckoned one of the younger looking women over.

She approached and paired her many hands, prayer like, bowing over them. "I am Reganda. You have a question, my new prince?"

"Reganda," I whispered, feeling strongly that I should not be heard over whatever took place. "Why have some of you stepped away from the ritual?"

"This is *the searching*. As a group, we share our senses to search for potential mates in the crowd. If we cannot sense potential mates, our shared magic remains, but we release from the comb. It means it is not yet our turn. These rituals are performed two times each annum. We are only allowed until our twentieth ritual to find our mate. After that, we are considered mateless and must resign ourselves to becoming nursers."

"So your mate was not in this room?"

She sadly shook her head.

I leaned down so I could speak for her ears only. "There are many thousand potential mates awaiting on Volitar who have actively asked for a wife, and many more who may change their minds once success is shown. Do not give up hope, young one."

She smiled and turned to return to her seat.

I gently touched her shoulder. "Please stay near in case I have further questions."

She nodded and stepped to my side.

At that moment, the few remaining women let out a massive howl of jubilation. The group parted, pushing Taylana forward. The woman looked shaken, almost stunned.

The girl beside me sniffled. "Taylana was exiled from her clan for failing to find a mate. Her father was the chief. He could not abide the thought that his only child would become a nurser and never bear a descendent for his line."

The dark-skinned woman approached the men gathered to the side of the room, signaling them to meet her in the middle.

The girl tugged my arm to gain my attention. "I must join the others to bear witness."

"May I ask questions after?"

She hesitated, and then nodded. "The ritual completion showing a match has determined Taylana our matriarch in this new clan. If she grants permission for me to speak further, you may question." She rushed to join hands with the women as they circled around the chosen bride and the men she had led over.

I turned toward Lanyar. "Do you have any idea what is transpiring?"

He shook his head. "No. The researchers mentioned nothing about any arcane phenomena among the people of Borkania."

Taylana spoke to the men, asking them to please circle around her and stand with their arms loose at their sides. "This is a requirement of my kind. We can sense our mates. Each of you present to me as potential mates. However, only my true mate can actually bear children with me."

"How can you tell which of us is your 'true mate'? It sounds like a bunch of mystical fallacy."

I realized the speaker to be my captain of the guard, Marlux. I'd seen him arrive with the other men but had not realized he had stepped to the side with the others. It must have occurred while I spoke with

17

Reganda. His question made me smile. I rewarded him well to be suspicious. He'd seen more oddities than the rest of the guards combined, yet he still questioned this mating ritual. Of course, the lack of reliance on our own mating sense contributed to his disbelief.

Taylana smiled smoothly. "If you are chosen by a Borkanian woman, if you are felt to be her true mate, you will know."

I interrupted. "Enough. If this is what is required for the Borkanian women to mate with us, you will submit yourselves willingly."

He growled at me but stood rigidly in position.

One of the women snarled at me. "Do not interrupt the ritual!"

Taylana smiled gently. Then she stretched out each of her arms, placing one on the chest of each soldier. She closed her eyes. Her hands glowed with soft white light. The light seemed to pulse with the men's hearts. It started out erratic, yet over the course of about three minutes, the pulsing synchronized to beat at the same time.

I caught myself counting the beats.

A gasp drew me away from the mesmerizing light. Marlux had grasped his hands onto the arms of the two men to his sides. His eyes appeared glazed, almost like he'd been dipping into the Gorgon Fungi supply, even though I knew he refused to partake of the psychedelic spores. His breathing increased.

Slowly, one by one, the other men stepped back. The two at Marlux's sides had to pry his hands loose, but they also stepped away, just watching as their Captain dropped to his knees, tears sliding down his cheeks, his eyes now closed against whatever he saw or felt.

Taylana slowly removed her hand, the light fading as she did.

Marlux drew a couple deep breaths before looking up at the exotic woman. "Can it truly be?" His voice held great awe.

She nodded and offered her hand to him. He accepted, rising slowly from the floor. Then he bent forward and kissed her fingers.

When he stood tall, he draped her hand over his arm and led her through the circle. The pair stopped directly before me.

His voice echoed through the room as he addressed me. "This woman is mine. She is now under my direct protection. Any who would put her at risk will die by my hand." He blinked a couple of times, as if waking from a trance. "Did I just utter a death edict to my prince?"

Taylana patted his arm. "It is the end of the ritual. Regardless of your own culture, by my birthright, we are now mated."

I glanced to where Lanyar stood watching. "Do we even have a Blessings Matron aboard?"

He shook his head. "We do not. We had not planned for this. However, with you and me to witness, it will be properly registered. Make sure to put it in the log."

I relieved Marlux from duty for the next week to allow him time with his new wife.

I sent Lanyar straight to the med bay to review the scanner data. He also intended to question the researchers. I'd never witnessed such a thing, and I wanted to know as much about it as we could.

We also had that new planet to deal with. It's solar revolution, lunar cycles, and circadian rhythms measured similar to our own, making adaptation easy. Matter of fact, this planet and ours shared a great many similarities.

We'd picked up signals for several potential breeders. It was time to start gathering the first trial batch.

~*~

Chapter 2

Keira

Loud snoring bounced off the ceiling and walls, echoing down into my ears, stirring my wakefulness before the alarm could sound. I frowned as the grating noise sent shivers along my spine. I blinked my eyes open, the feeling of grit scraping the corneas making me cringe even more. One hand shot out, grabbing the phone from the windowsill. I flinched against the brightness as the screen came to life.

The time blinked on the screen showing it neared eight in the morning. The alarm would sound in a few minutes, signaling the start of a new day. The night hadn't been long enough to feel well-rested, but it would have to do.

Another snore pierced my eardrums. I rolled over, shoving the shoulder of the offender.

"John, get up. You're late for work." I sighed, adding, "Again."

That effort earned a growl. With the release of air across my face, the scent of stale beer caused my nose to wrinkle.

"Fuck off, Keira. I'm trying to sleep."

Of course, you are. If you're not sleeping, you're drinking.

"You're going to lose this job. You've not even gotten out of the probation period, and this is the third time you've overslept. I can't afford to keep paying for everything by myself." I grumbled, shoving again. Truthfully, I could easily live alone. It was difficult but not impossible. I simply preferred being able to add extra money to my savings account, just in case I felt the need to move on from my current location. I hadn't stayed this long in any one spot for quite some time. Not since... I cut myself off abruptly. Those thoughts led to depression.

Finally, the dark-haired used-to-be Adonis pushed himself upright. My gaze drifted over his form as he stood. I'd found him utterly distracting at one point, and realistically, he hadn't changed. His dark hair remained styled in the same manner that had attracted me so long ago. His deep chocolate eyes still felt like they stared inside the soul. He still took care of his body, staying trim and muscular. When we'd met, I'd found all of those things so attractive, I'd fallen into bed with him pretty much right away.

That first night, my second week in town and having received my first paycheck, I'd had a Friday night off and walked to the bar down the road from my apartment. The dark Adonis had approached, paying for my Smirnoff Raspberry Ice without asking, and took the stool next to mine. He said all the right things, touched all the right ways. By the end of the third bottle, John had sweet talked his way into my bed.

I'd been shocked a short time later that he seemed to still have an interest in me. I'd taken him home, fully expecting that one night to be our sole interaction. I hadn't been looking for a relationship; I was still too raw over the loss of my family and couldn't bear the thought of going through something like that again. Yet, before long, I started waking up with him still in my bed at least three times a week, until one day, he simply stopped leaving. After several months, I handed him the spare key.

Strangely, I never asked where he worked until we'd lived together nearly a year. I had a day off and wanted to bring him lunch. At that time, he'd been working for a moving company. It had thrilled me to sit in the car and watch his muscles flex as he carried furniture while I waited for his lunch break.

Not long after, he'd lost that job. And the one after it. And the one after that. It had taken until our second year together before I recognized his pattern. He worked just enough to support his own interests.

Now, another year later, he hadn't changed. But I had. I'd finally started developing expectations, and those didn't sit well within our dynamic.

John and I had been living together for nearly three years. In all of that time, the longest job he'd held was six months. I hadn't known it when we got together, but he didn't have his own apartment or house. He spent most of his income at the bar, seeking his next bed. Since he had me, and I spent more time working than anything else, he had taken advantage of my single-minded focus to stay in one place for a while. I learned the details of his bed-hopping several months back when I'd accidentally overheard some girls talking in the bar, wondering just how long it would take before he went on the prowl again.

As he finally lifted his gorgeous ass out of bed, I stared. That trim view still stirred the niggling thought in me that I wanted to bounce a quarter off that smooth skin. Then he stumbled, clearly hung over from last night's bender. As he covered those tight globes with his jeans, I frowned. I just wasn't sure he was worth my efforts anymore.

I hoisted my own ass off the bed and got dressed for work, turning on the news while I did so. Whether he cared or not, I did. I made just enough money to survive. I paid my rent, utilities, insurance, and bought groceries. I also put a small amount into my savings account. Maybe once a month, I would go out to the bar with John and his 'boys', if I had anything left after covering the essentials. Of course, if John bothered to pitch in….

I let my mind fade from that thought while I tucked the simple navy button-down into my tan pencil skirt. It had already led to numerous arguments, arguments I had no desire to rehash anymore. That path felt like it only led to a lot of wasted time, wasted breath, and continually mounting aggravation.

A quick brush through of my deep auburn hair removed the tangles before I pulled it up into a hair band, trying to keep the middle back length from flying in my face every time the wind blew. I stared in the mirror, reaching for the few items of makeup on the counter. My crystal blue eyes always seemed to spark attention, even without artificial enhancement, so I only added the lightest layer of sparkle to the top lids, ignoring the eyeliner. A light dusting of medium brown blush highlighted my already prominent cheekbones. I added the pale pink lip gloss with a touch of my dark plum to my lips, making them look slightly fuller, and I was done.

I grabbed the remote to turn off the television, stopping as the reporter flashed a blurry photo on the screen.

"Witnesses have reported another strange sighting last night near Mount Victory, Kentucky, close to the site of the asteroid impact from seven years ago. Authorities have yet to catch any images on their trail cam network that was installed after this photo was taken, but with each new sighting, they claim they are coming closer to identifying whether this creature is a misidentified Earth species, or yet something else to come from the asteroid that carried the pandemic to our planet.

"In related news, a fresh outbreak of a mutated form of the devastating virus has been found among protesters who attended the anti-government rally last week in Tiananmen Square in Beijing—"

I clicked the button. Sensational journalism at its finest. Keep the public in a panic so that the government can keep control. All the social media and news platforms were so riddled with conspiracy theories about the source of that damned virus, I seldom paid attention anymore.

Without bothering to see whether my boyfriend did anything, I left for work, climbing in my car and driving the two miles to the local grocer. All through my shift, I thought about the people around me. I thought about my job, my boyfriend, my current path in life. I was sick of just barely surviving.

As I clocked out at the end of the shift, I realized what really bothered me about it all.

My life was okay. Just okay.

I had no great passion. I was just going through the motions. I was merely surviving, not thriving. I had no future. I was stagnant. I wanted more.

I needed a drink.

With that thought, I drove to my apartment and quickly changed clothes. I hadn't been out in almost four months, too busy volunteering for as many extra hours at work as they were willing to give me. Frankly, that didn't amount to much, because I was not technically on the payroll. I got paid in cash. If anyone were to look for me, they'd find no actual record of my existence outside of the soon-to-expire lease on my apartment and my prepaid phone account. All other records ceased after my parents died.

At first, I had simply been too numb to care, going through the motions for the sake of survival. After, I had realized not having so many records everywhere just made it easier to pick up and leave without having to deal with so much paperwork.

I left my car at the apartment and walked the two blocks to John's usual hang out. Maybe if I could keep him from drinking himself into a stupor tonight, I could finagle some good sex, like when we first started dating. Hell, any sex at all would be good sex right now. We hadn't been intimate in at least six weeks.

I nearly tripped when that thought crossed my mind. John had never been the type of guy to go without sex at least three times a week. Never. Even when I was sick with the flu, we fucked. He didn't even care if I were suffering my monthly curse, as long as he got to shoot off. I'd quickly gone to the local clinic and started birth control shots because of his virility.

Why the hell has he not made a move toward me for six weeks? And why hadn't I noticed sooner? Had I slipped back into that numb state again?

My brain supplied the answer, although I didn't want to believe it. I didn't want to believe that I had let some guy use me for a place to sleep while he screwed some other broad. But I knew. My lip already trembled as I tried to convince myself I was just being paranoid.

I set my shoulders and walked up to the door of the bar, peeking inside. John was predictable. He always positioned himself in clear view of the door, watching for anyone to enter. I spotted him easily. His face was buried in the neck of some highly busty blonde, while her hands were buried in his hair, clearly enjoying whatever he did to her. While I watched, I saw her hand dip under the table.

My heart shattered.

I stepped away from the door, letting the tears fall.

I decided I didn't want a drink after all. I needed to think.

~*~

Once home, I changed into comfortable clothes and sat at my dining table, just staring around me. I had no pictures, no decorations. I had never really made this small place home. I hadn't wanted it to *be* home. It was just a place to hold me over until I moved up to something bigger, something better. Yet, I hadn't moved. I'd let myself fall into a rut. A big one, if I were honest with myself.

And that's what I wanted. I wanted to be honest with myself tonight.

Honesty made me admit that John hadn't fooled me, I had fooled myself. I'd felt so empty after the loss of my parents, wandering from town to town, scratching an itch when it arose, until I'd landed here. By then, instead of the overpowering depression I'd fought through after their deaths, I wallowed in loneliness. So, I'd attached myself to the first person who showed me any attention beyond a single night, letting myself believe that physical attraction served as well as real feelings. I'd craved a sense of belonging, even though my gut had told me not to think beyond one night with the handsome man buying my drinks.

Accepting that I'd only let myself down, I pushed myself to think deeper, to figure out what I wanted from my future. I had only worked menial jobs. Years ago, I had dreamt of college, but that had all changed with the first sweep of that horrible pandemic. I used to dream of marriage and children, and then I'd received the last call from my dad before they died. Now, I didn't even watch the documentaries dad used to love, just because they reminded me too much of my loss.

I flipped open my laptop and logged into my budget screen, forcing myself to focus on the future instead of the past. I had about five thousand in savings. It wasn't much, but I knew how to make every penny stretch.

Most of that had come from the government pandemic payouts for essential workers.

Seven years ago, after a small asteroid had crashed in the middle of Kentucky, some crazy virus had wiped out nearly ten percent of the world's population. At first, people just got ill with flu-like symptoms, only the most at risk died, like those with immune system problems. Mandatory quarantines only happened after several positive cases.

Then it seemed to mutate so fast that new strains emerged constantly. Instead of flu-like symptoms slowly killing you over the course of weeks, people started dying faster. Breathing issues, seizures, exhaustion, the symptoms varied so greatly that it became hard to tell. Sometimes only days passed from first symptom to death. By the time it infected my parents, you were lucky if you had enough time to arrange a doctor visit before it killed you. The entire world had gone crazy, closing borders and issuing injunctions to keep US citizens from bringing the virus to them, usually to no avail. A few small pockets of humanity had fared better than most, but the entire world had been affected.

Influenza B15 proved that microbes could exist in the vacuum of space, but it also proved that those microbes could be deadly. Despite extreme quarantines that went on for months, every country in the world had been hit hard. My parents had both died, and I found myself alone in the world for the first time. We had taken every precaution possible, but it still hadn't been enough.

I had been working in a grocery store then, too, but I was on the payroll as a manager. My job was considered essential since people needed access to food. I watched many of my coworkers succumb to the illness, taking on extra shifts whenever needed just to keep people fed. When the upper management started falling ill, everyone looked to me to guide them. I had started issuing orders like a general, putting in stricter safety guidelines, requiring regular decontamination cycles, both for the store itself as well as for the personnel. I don't know if it truly helped, but illnesses appeared reduced among the staff, keeping us running.

It was a horrible time. Regular customers whose life histories I knew better than my own stopped showing up, and I knew that they had succumbed. I watched some collapse while they loaded their groceries into their vehicles.

After a while, we didn't even have ambulances. We had body collectors. Someone would die. The collectors would show up. Blood and tissue samples went into jars, a death certificate would be issued, and the body taken. No funerals, no autopsies, no questions asked. The virus had become so dangerous, cremation was mandatory, regardless of religious beliefs. In cases where an entire family was infected, even the house got burned to the ground, trying to stave off further effects to the community.

After the lockdowns were finally lifted, and the real numbers came to light, the federal government decided that people who had been required to still work deserved a bonus. I'd used a good portion of that to buy my car. Then I'd loaded up what I could and just left. I had no one left who would care, and I couldn't bear to see the memories everywhere I looked. After that, I moved from small town to small town, trying to stay under the radar and far from any large city to avoid further outbreaks. I was emotionally exhausted from having so many lives in my hands, and I just wanted to avoid that situation again.

My job remained a dead end, going nowhere beyond 'would you like paper or plastic'. I didn't have enough skills or education necessary to move up, nor did I have the money to get that education. I never would if I stayed here. My boss would likely not notice if I just stopped showing up, other than the need to find someone else to take my shifts. And he could. We'd had a major economic collapse after the pandemic. There were so many people out of work, so many homeless. Hell, I'd been homeless for nearly a year, myself. I wandered the country, waiting tables in tiny restaurants being paid only in tips, for a long time before I finally found this town.

A little larger place than I usually stayed, I decided to settle for a while and figure out my next move. I'd gotten the job at the grocer, found my apartment, and met John. But I hadn't planned my next move. I'd fallen into complacency, fooling myself that I had found a possible future here. Yet, I never breached the topic with my boyfriend. Never mentioned marriage or kids, even went out of my way to avoid it.

As my grandfather had been fond of saying, it was time to either shit or get off the pot.

I shut the laptop and grabbed a pencil and paper, making a list.

1. *I live in an impersonal studio apartment.*
2. *I work under the table for minimum wage with no overtime. My boss can easily find someone else to fill my shoes.*
3. *I own 3 uniforms for work, 2 sets of comfy clothes, 4 tee-shirts, 4 pair of shorts, 2 dresses, and 2 pair of shoes.*
4. *In 3 years, I've made no friends here outside of John.*
5. *My boyfriend is screwing other women and hasn't touched me in weeks.*
6. *I have no real roots here.*

In bold print underneath that, I wrote:

7. *No one will miss me.*

Just like that, I made up my mind. I had nothing holding me here, not even memories.

~*~

John didn't bother coming home that night. That was fine by me. I had a feeling one of his buddies spotted me and forewarned him, so to avoid what he thought would be an argument, he stayed away.

I got up early and gathered my uniforms into a bag. Then I drove to the grocery store and took them to the manager. He didn't even argue with me about giving no notice. He already had a huge waiting list of people looking for work, and I'm sure he could find someone the same size as me in a matter of hours.

After that, I went to the bank and withdrew every penny, closing out my account. Again, no one even seemed to care. No one asked a single question. Yet another sign of the times in which we now lived.

I went back to the apartment and gathered my few belongings: my clothes, my tablet and laptop, and all of the non-perishable groceries from the cupboards. I only took a single metal plate, set of flatware, a mug, one steel cook pot, one cast iron pan. I loaded it all into the car, barely filling the back floorboard. I grabbed my pillow and blanket and a few toiletries. I left everything else. It could all be replaced once I finally found a new place to lay my head. Hopefully, a place where I could finally see *more*.

I made a quick stop at my landlord's door to pay the remaining balance on the lease, leaving me a thousand bucks poorer. He said he'd miss having the regular income; he hadn't had many renters stay longer than a year. I did tell him that it's possible that John might come back, as I hadn't seen him to tell him I was leaving, and he still had the other key. Since the lease had been paid for the next two months, I assumed he would likely wait and try to get John to take over after that. Not my concern anymore.

One last glance around the apartment showed it looking almost the same as it did before I removed my things. I made that little of an impact to my surroundings.

I left my list on the table, weighted down by a candle. If John ever bothered to show back up to the apartment, he would find it. If not, it wouldn't matter. The landlord would clear out anything I left behind before the new renters moved in. Or he'd leave it for them.

The bold words across the bottom remained true.
No one will miss me.

~*~

Chapter 3

Keira

Two weeks into the journey, my heart felt lighter. I felt like I'd made the right decision. I'd let myself wallow in stagnation, and it was time to finally move beyond. I'd had enough with just existing. I wanted more. I still wasn't sure what that *more* amounted to, but I wanted to find out.

I had enough supplies with me already to last another week before I would need to find a real store, not just a gas station. Between canned goods and the occasional fresh meat, I could survive for at least a couple of years before being forced to find a source of income. This meant that I could take my time. I could try a few places before deciding to settle anywhere.

During the whole time of my travel, my phone had not chimed even once. Not a single message from John, or anyone for that matter. I'd been right. No one even noticed the blip of my existence. I had just bought another month of service, but even if I let the phone run out, not even the provider would notice. My meager fifty bucks a month wasn't worth much to them in the grand scheme of capitalism.

The hardest part about traveling like this was staying clear of the bad ones. Just like everywhere else, there were good and bad people in the homeless community. I had all of my cash sewn into a pocket hidden in the back seat cushion. I didn't dare leave it anywhere easily accessible for fear of robbery. Some of these folks have had less than nothing for a really long time. While four thousand wasn't much, it would buy a lot of food or drugs.

Because of this, I made sure to stay extremely clear of anything that resembled a hobo shanty town. However, if I spotted one, I knew there had to be water nearby. I just had to drive far enough further upstream as to be an inconvenience for them to approach. I only needed that to refill a few water jugs.

I had traveled half the length of the country already. I could have covered more, but I had no reason to rush. I took my time, stopping to sightsee along the way. When I'd neared the foothills, I'd gone off the highway into some state land. Technically, all were banned from camping on state land, but no one enforced the issue. There were too many homeless. As long as you didn't make a mess, the rangers left you alone. I'd spent a lot of time on reserve land before, so I knew how to go without being noticed. I kept my fires small, and only lit one to cook when I needed. I bathed in the streams, slept inside the car, and generally kept to myself.

I had a fire going, heating up a can of green beans when I finally heard a chime from my phone. I glanced at the screen.

Found ur note. Feeling sorry for urself again?

Jackass. I typed back: *Obviously, I was right. You didn't miss me, did you?*

Ding. *What r u talking about?*

Tap, tap, tap. *Have you been staying at the apartment?*

Ding. *Duh. I live here 2 u no.*

Tap, tap, tap. *I left 2 weeks ago.*

No response came. The sun dropped below the horizon. Night sounds started creeping into the air.

I waited almost an hour before I sent one final message.

Goodbye, John.

I shut the phone off, no longer caring if he replied. I had my truth, and it didn't even sting. It was nothing more than a disappointment in myself that I'd let it get so far.

I ate my beans, snuffed the fire, and crawled into the back seat. I snuggled up to my pillow and pulled the blanket over me, settling to sleep for the night. I stirred only briefly when a mosquito bit my neck. Bastard must have flown in while I had the door open. I didn't fully wake, though, not bothered with a single mosquito.

~*~

I slowly drifted to consciousness, sensing something had changed while I slept. I blinked my eyes a couple of times, trying to focus beyond the darkness before I realized that I actually couldn't see. I lay surrounded by pitch black. I should at least be able to see moonlight through one of the car windows. The new moon was last week, so it should be waxing quarter on its way to full. It should most definitely not be this dark.

I raised a hand to my face, but the dark was so complete that I couldn't even see my fingers. Fine. I reached to my right, trying to grab hold of the back side of the front seat and bring myself to a sitting position.

I touched nothing. More specifically, I did *not* touch a car seat. Anywhere. Not even under my body. The surface I laid on felt like a thin mattress, thin but comfortable. I let my hands drift around a little to determine dimensions. My sleeping area felt a lot like a cot. I wiggled a little, but it didn't move, so at least it was a sturdy cot.

I rolled to my side and reached cautiously downward. My arm was almost all the way extended before I met another solid surface. Cool to the touch, smooth, it almost felt metallic. I continued searching with my hands for a couple of minutes before I deduced that I could at least sit up and put my feet on the floor without causing injury.

Cautiously, I shifted the blanket to the side. I swung my legs over the edge of the cot and pushed myself slowly upright.

"Initiating morning sequence." A robotic female voice echoed around me.

Light slowly gained ground on the darkness, like someone operated a dimmer switch. I felt both better and worse as I regained the ability to see. Better because, obviously, I was not blinded. Worse, however, because I still had no idea where the hell I was.

I did not move from my cot while I studied my surroundings. I sat in what looked to be a room about twelve feet on all sides. The walls were solid, as in I saw no door, no window, not even a vent. Across from me stood a small table and chair. From here, they appeared constructed from the same material as my prison. In the far corner stood two basins, one about waist height, the other more like a chair height.

"Okay, then." I spoke aloud to myself. Then I decided I would stand and walk around my new quarters, see if I could figure anything out. I had no idea what I thought I'd figure out from a simple, nondescript metal room, but I had no intention of just sitting on the cot.

I started by feeling the walls. They definitely consisted of some kind of metal, although I knew nothing about how to tell one kind from another. Strangely, although light now entered the compartment, I could see no source for it. I continued my search.

I approached the table, knocking on the top of it. Again, it felt like metal, yet I heard no ringing sound like I had expected. Same thing with the chair. I left the sitting area and moved over to the two basins. Just looking at them showed me absolutely nothing. I ran my hands over the top of the higher one. A short burst of electricity caressed my skin. As odd as that was, I felt... cleaner.

"Okay, I'm still not sure what that is. I'll come back to it." I cast my eyes back toward the shorter basin. I suspected that might actually be a toilet of some sort. However, I saw no drain. Of course, if I didn't get food, I would die of starvation. But how would *they* get anything to me? I still couldn't see any sort of junction lines to signify a door or window of any kind.

A thought came to mind, and I decided to test it. I turned toward the table and spoke. "How about something to eat?"

"Nutritional rations requested." That robotic voice answered. The sound seemed to come from all sides, yet it did not thunder or echo. It just… was.

A rectangle of light formed on the wall connected to the table. That section faded from view, a tray slid forward, then the wall reformed again.

I rushed over, sliding my hands all over the area. I couldn't even find a groove as proof that a hole had once existed.

"Are you freaking kidding me? Where am I? Stark Industries?"

I felt a touch of panic attempting to set in but forced it deep into the recesses of my mind. I had no idea where I was, who had me, nor why. I didn't even know if my car was anywhere nearby, and all my survival supplies were in the car. I needed to gather some intel before I tried to find a way out of here. I couldn't do that if I went into panic mode.

I sat in the chair, letting my eyes take in the food before me. I saw some kind of dried meat, a strange looking orange mass that may have been fruit, and something else that looked suspiciously like scrambled eggs, but were dark purple. A large cup stood full of what I assumed to be water. Also on the plate lay a two-tined fork. Okay, so I had at least something to be able to spear food with.

I grabbed the cup first. I dipped my tongue in the liquid, tasting the least amount possible. Very little flavor touched my tongue, like water, but just a hint of something else. I took one swallow and waited as long as I could. Finally judging it safe, I drank half of it right away. I felt immensely better already.

I speared a small section of the 'eggs' and lifted it to my nose. They even smelled like eggs. I tasted a tiny nibble. They had a strange taste to them, but I felt willing to risk it. After I finished the last forkful of eggs, I cut off a piece of the fruit thing. It had a sweet smell, kind of like a peach, but tasted more like a pear. I consumed it greedily. Finally, I picked up the dried meat with my fingers, not even bothering with the fork. It smelled like a cross between pork and chicken, but it looked like very thick cut beef jerky strips. By this time, I figured in for a penny, in for a pound, so I bit off a piece and started chewing.

Holy cow, what a flavor explosion. One minute, it tasted like a perfectly prepared prime rib, then it shifted and tasted like a leg of lamb. I couldn't stop myself from groaning. I decided that at least for now, I would just accept my situation and enjoy being pampered. Seriously, compared to canned soup, vegetables, and beef jerky, this place offered me some five-star rations. I could live with this. At least until I figured out whether I was in danger.

I got down to the last couple of bites and a sense of fullness came over me. The flavor was great, but I didn't want to gorge myself. Then I had an idea to test my 'toilet.' I stood from my seat and walked the few feet toward the basins. I tossed the tiny piece of meat into the basin and then just waited.

Nothing happened.

"Um…" I paused, not quite sure what to do. Thinking back to how the lights had activated, I said, "Initiate waste removal?"

The voice I heard earlier echoed me.

"Initiating waste removal."

Before me, I saw the top of the basin expand, closing toward the center until no edge could be seen again. Then it slowly collapsed downward, reforming into the basin. No noise, no visible exit. It just…removed it.

"That's… um… okay, then. Now I know how the toilet works. How about showing me how to take a shower?"

"Water washing is wasteful. Choose another option," the voice replied.

"I'm talking to a wall, and it's answering." I drew a deep breath to steady myself. "How is water washing wasteful? Water washing kept me from dying from that damned virus that killed everyone I used to know."

"Water washing is wasteful. Choose another option," the voice repeated.

I shook my head and chuckled. "Fine. What options are available for personal hygiene?"

Between the toilet and the table area, two circles lit the wall. Below that on the floor, two more circles appeared.

"Um… instructions?"

The voice answered. *"Remove outer layers. Place outer layers on table. Place appendages on designated pads. Speak command to initiate."*

I stripped off my clothes, hesitantly placing them on the table. Then I put one foot on each spot on the floor, and one hand in each spot on the wall. I wasn't certain of the command, but I suspected it to be as simple as the toilet. So, I spoke to the room again.

"Initiate personal hygiene," my voice rose as if asking a question rather than making a statement, hoping I'd guessed correctly.

It repeated, *"Initiating personal hygiene."* I felt a tingle start in my fingers, caress up my arms, then into my scalp, and continue until it reached my toes. As soon as the tingle faded, a small blast of warm air came from above me, coasting the full length of my body as well.

"Personal hygiene complete."

I turned back toward the table to put my clothes back on, but the surface lay bare. Apparently, while I stood being cleansed, the room had taken my clothes, as well as my now-empty food tray.

"Well, shit. Um, room, I would like to have my clothing back, please. I'm not a nudist."

"Incorrect command. Please try again."

I replayed the hygiene instructions in my head, trying to work out how to word my request. "Return outer layers," I tried.

"Outer layers contained contaminants from Earth. They have been incinerated."

Fuck. I needed to figure something out. I had no doubt that someone sat watching me, and I had absolutely no desire to give them a show, whoever *they* might be.

"Provide clean outer layers, please."

"Outer layers requested. Step to center of room and extend arms outward."

I felt anger pooling. "I swear, if some jackass is sitting somewhere, getting his rocks off watching this, I'm going to take great joy in destroying said rocks." I stomped about two steps before I remembered I stood bare, including my feet. Those two steps stung just enough to remind me of that fact. I finished crossing to where new circles lit the floor, placing one foot on each and extending my arms to the side.

Lights began at my feet, scanning me on all sides, traveling all the way to the top of my head. Just as fast as they began, they faded. A glance down showed I still stood naked. I'm not sure if I had expected clothing to just materialize from those lights, but since food slid through a hole in the wall that didn't exist either before or after, and bathing consisted of electrical pulses and bursts of air, I figured just about anything was possible at this point.

Before I could move or speak, a spike of electricity flowed from the floor, freezing me in place. It wasn't a painful spike; it was just noticeably *there*. I couldn't move my arms or legs. I could, however, move my head minutely.

The wall in front of me glowed in the shape of a door, which then became an opening. A person entered carrying a small bundle. As the person stepped closer, I realized this individual might be female. As best as I could tell, that is.

I was slightly distracted by the fact that she had almost burgundy skin and six arms.

One set grabbed the top item from the pile and started wrapping it around my upper body, ending with a quick knot behind my neck. This item looked like just a basic piece of cloth, a long and thin rectangle that wrapped around my breasts, crossed in the back, only to come back around, up from under my arms and tie behind my neck to hold it in place. I didn't see any decoration to it, just plain grey cloth similar in color to my surroundings. Whoever or whatever these creatures were, they clearly liked drab grey.

At the same time, another set of hands grabbed the next item and placed it on my lower body. I tipped my head downward as far as the current would allow so I could see. It looked like another long grey rectangle of cloth, although this piece appeared wider, allowing it to cover more. As it unfolded, I noticed a slit along one side that was connected only at the top and bottom. This part ended positioned on my left hip, and I watched as the woman threaded one end through the slit after wrapping it fully around. She smoothed it underneath the wrap as it came around a second time, and then fastened the 'skirt' at the top with a small clasp.

The final item was merely tossed toward my cot, which also stood bare, my blanket apparently taken when the room had claimed my clothing. The six-armed woman finished dressing me and smoothed her hands over my curves, as if to assure a correct fit. Then she retreated back through the opening, having never spoken a single sylla-ble.

Once the wall had sealed itself again, the current holding me in place released. I lowered my arms, crossed to the cot, and dropped down onto it, overwhelmed.

Contaminants from Earth… a room that speaks to and answers me… walls that fade in and out of existence… food stuff I've never seen or heard of before, despite having worked as a grocer or waitress for nearly ten years… women with six arms and burgundy skin…

"I've a feeling we're not in Kansas anymore," I whispered, desper-ately wishing I had a tiny dog like Toto with which to cuddle.

Chapter 4

Vaxeehl

This planet, Earth it was called among the majority of inhabitants, had an interesting diversity among its dominant species. Their skin colors varied anywhere from a strange white, which seemed odd even amongst their own, to a deep brown, almost black. A few reds and yellows were thrown in, as well. Strangely, they seemed to stay mostly divided based on skin colors. A few of their number crossed those barriers, and initial scans did not show any detriment to breeding compatibility.

Lanyar had already set his team to studying everything they could to determine whether this issue came from societal expectations or genetics. We could circumvent societal expectations, but genetics would deem such a wide pool of potential breeders null.

The inhabitants also spoke a great variety of languages, much like Volitar. It had taken several days of scanning to sort through them and organize the uploads that would enable us to communicate.

The strangest information gathered from the scans, however, proved to be the most advantageous for us, for the success of this mission. In the areas of the planet considered to be the most developed, women were treated with ambivalence, or even disdain. The scans showed an excessive number of females living on the streets or in shared dwellings with large groups of others like them. No programs existed to care for unmated females unless they already had young.

They had to defend and care for themselves or face potential physical harm.

Lanyar had informed me that Denali, his assistant researcher had even found one area with care homes for the young packed with females, as it appeared only male children were prized in that region. Additionally, many of these young girls had simple defects that our medical capabilities could easily correct. It had taken Denali several hours to calm her anger at this finding.

By the time Marlux's week of seclusion had passed and he returned to his post, Lanyar and Denali had made their target selections.

I stepped into the conference room. Various expressions met me. Lanyar looked hopeful, while Denali still appeared angry. Marlux looked awestruck, his new wife smiling gently beside him.

I nodded to the group. "Good morning, my friends. It is my understanding that we finished the first acquisitions during the dark cycle?"

Lanyar nodded. He swiped the tabletop, raising images from the now-occupied cells. "We grabbed ten women from various areas of the planet, securing them in area 2B. After searching their electronic history files, we left an empty cell between each to avoid cross-contamination, just in case they carried contagions within their regions from which the others could become infected. Their histories show this cross-contamination has been used as a means of warfare in the past, allowing disease to destroy their enemies rather than fighting honorably. However, these diseases are similar enough to some of our own, I am confident that we already have immunity."

Denali nodded. "We chose first to see how well the women adapted to odd technology. None of this first group have been exposed to AI units yet, although they are aware of their existence. Earth's AI tech is still in its infancy. The females we chose have been cast aside or have chosen to remain alone, much as we found with the Borkanians. Their thought patterns reveal that they have no family to search for them, having lost much during the virus outbreak or the planet's many wars. They have been on their own for differing lengths of time. We followed all of them for nearly half a lunar cycle before transporting them to the holding area."

Marlux took over. "For those who responded well to awakening in a strange place, Taylana suggested a brief exposure to the strangest creatures onboard. She met with the other Borkanians and brought forth four volunteers. One of the prevailing thoughts among the females showed that Earth has not yet had known contact with extraplanetary beings. We sent the volunteers in to redress the females after they had been cleared of external contaminants."

I started at that information. "You put some of the brides at risk?"

The captain frowned. "You know better than that. The new females were held by lock current, just as they will be during medical examinations. They have also passed initial infection scans. Besides, only three of the current collective showed ease in adapting to the AI units. The remaining have yet to understand the ability to ask for things. The AI's have resorted to simply providing nourishment and announcing this to the subjects. Those subjects as yet have refused to attempt the personal hygiene protocols. We may have to begin further interaction or just send them back to Earth."

Lanyar tapped the table surface again, pulling up the fast feed from those three subjects. He minimized two of the projections, keeping just one viewable. It showed a pale-skinned subject right after our burgundy friend had visited. "The most interesting data actually came after Taylana and her volunteers visited the three receptive subjects. E07 suffered an emotional episode. We had to send a calming current through the AI in order to sedate her." The female stumbled around the room, beating her hands on the walls, screaming.

He dropped that projection and brought up another. This female had medium brown skin. As soon as the Borkanian woman entered the room, the subject's eyes widened, and tears streamed from her eyes. Once alone again, she dropped to her knees, muttering repeatedly aloud, *'I surrender myself fully at your Divine Feet. Maa, I am Yours; take me over.'*

"E04 spent several hours on her knees, praying, believing a deity had stolen her from poverty and must be preparing her for her reward. It appears that we might have great success utilizing the Borkanians to ease the transition for any who have knowledge of this 'Durga.' This area might be worth more detailed scans after our initial testing is completed."

"E09 had the calmest reaction and simply sat in shock until she slept. Her mind spent quite some time determining that the maiden who dressed her was, indeed, female. This one intrigues me." He changed projections again.

I found myself also intrigued, but not for the same reason. This female drew my attention immediately. I had not experienced such a strong reaction, even when attempting to find a fiancé so many years ago.

I studied the female's motions, watching how the subject searched the room, inspecting everything from the walls themselves to the table and chair, even the basins. She stayed methodical and calm, checking and testing.

When she stripped for cleansing, I felt my body react. I forced myself to remain focused on her behavior, rather than her physical form. We had to prove compatibility before I could consider attempting to mate with her. No matter what my senses told me.

I chuckled when she argued with her AI about her clothing.

Her silence after the Borkanian woman left the room concerned me.

Lanyar added a second screen showing her thought scans.

"E09 mentally catalogued all of the things she'd seen or heard and concluded her new reality. Having viewed the barbaric medical practices this species has undergone, I imagine tomorrow will be another... interesting day. So far, this one shows the best promise."

Indeed, she did. And I wanted that promise for my own.

Chapter 5

Keira

I sat on the edge of the cot for what had to be hours but could have
been minutes. However, I must have fallen asleep again, as the next
time I became aware, I heard the room speaking, *"Initiate morning
sequence."*

"Fuck off, room. I don't feel like getting up." And I didn't. I was
completely overwhelmed and still trying to process the fact that I'd
been abducted by aliens. It didn't make sense; aliens didn't exist. Of
course, it made more sense than a woman with a genetic defect causing six arms and burgundy skin. However, if this circumstance
showed true, my escape prospects became null.

If I were honest with myself, I hadn't yet decided if I actually
wanted to escape. I had no prospects on Earth; I might find myself in
a better situation.

"Subject E09, Prepare for medical exam."

I pulled my plain grey blanket back over my head. My heart rate
increased, and the words made me bristle as I heard myself being referred to as a 'subject'.

"Fuck you," I growled.

The voice repeated again. *"Subject E09, Prepare for medical exam."*

I growled louder, shoving the blanket to the side and standing up, hands on hips, prepared to do verbal battle with a robotic voice. "I have no intention of submitting myself to any sort of medical exam, just so I can be probed by some other worldly being for only God knows what. So why don't you just send some food into the room and then leave me alone?"

"Subject E09, step to center of the room and prepare for medical exam."

"I have a fucking name, you god damn computer program. I am Keira Sutton, not some subject in an experiment. And I already told you, I am *not* participating in any sort of medical exam. My body, my—"

My voice froze as the current seized control. Once again, no matter how many signals my brain sent to my muscles, nothing moved. This time, though, I also could not move my head even a fraction. Apparently, all she needed was both of my feet touching the floor; I did not actually have to move to the center of the room. I couldn't even close my eyelids to block my view. Well, that was a delightful revelation.

I started mentally counting backwards from ninety-nine, as well as cursing between each number. Between the distraction of being frozen in place and facing toward my table instead of the wall from which the six-armed woman entered yesterday, I was not prepared for another being to step into view so quickly. I didn't get much time to look before my vision was blocked.

A scanning device pressed to my forehead. It stayed there for a count of around ten 'Fuck you's' before moving to my neck. This process repeated in increments over the length of my torso, not stopping until the creature knelt before me, the device pressed just above my woman parts.

I wanted to growl. I wanted to kick him. I wanted to ask questions. I was allowed neither.

This thing, whatever or whoever it was, stepped out of my tiny viewing range toward my left. I felt something clamp above my elbow. Then a tiny jab alerted me to a needle of some sort. I fought against the panic, wondering what this creature injected me with, wondering how my body would react, wondering what lay in store. I counted at least thirty 'Cock-sucking sons-of-bitches' before I heard a beep and whatever held my arm released.

Another twenty 'mother fucking piece of shit's' passed my brain before I felt the current release me, and I found that I stood alone in my enclosed cell once again. I refused to move, waiting for something else to happen. I had no idea what I expected, but I continued to stand there, taking stock of my body bit by bit, until I realized that he must not have injected me with anything. I felt confused even more. *Why had I been taken?*

I had barely seen anything of the creature who came to examine me. Still, I saw enough to get the distinct impression that it was very humanoid, and most likely male.

Based on my own height, I estimated this one stood slightly over six feet tall. His skin held a light purple hue. The face, what I saw before my vision got blocked by the scanner, looked strong, well-defined, and surprisingly *normal.* Ignoring his unusual skin tone, had I run across the creature out at a club, he certainly would have warranted getting a better look.

My stomach growled, distracting me from my thoughts.

I spoke aloud, still angry, but calmed at how quickly and non-invasive that 'exam' had gone. Even so, I spoke through gritted teeth. "May I please receive my nutritional allotment?"

I received no verbal response, but I did see the meal slot fade to push my plate through. I approached the chair and seated myself before I even bothered to look at the plate. The portions actually looked a little larger than they had yesterday.

That brought my curiosity to overpower my anger.

"Room? Why is there more food here today? I didn't even finish everything yesterday morning."

"The medical examination performed on Subject E09 shows a depleted nutritional base. Larger portions have been approved to aid in returning the Subject's base to optimal levels."

"Room?" I paused and shook my head. "This is stupid. I would like to refer to you by a name, rather than calling you Room or Computer. Is there a preferred manner of address when I speak to you?"

I grabbed my fork and started cutting bites.

"In your Earth words, I am known as an Artificial Intelligence unit. I am Unit 8349."

I swallowed the bite before I spoke again. "No, I don't care about that. I wish to give you a name. For example, you know me as being Subject E09, which I am going to guess means I am the ninth Earth subject, but that is entirely too impersonal. I have a name, and I prefer to be called by it. That name is Keira."

"Subject E09 wishes to anthropomorphize AI unit 8349?"

I shrugged before realizing that I had no idea if the AI unit had 'eyes' of any kind. "I guess that's one way to say it. I am used to being alone, if you don't count that idiot I allegedly lived with for the last three years. However, that doesn't mean that I wish for loneliness. Even if you're an AI unit, you're still *something* to talk to. I'd like to address you on a more personal level."

I ate another bite while I considered what to say next.

"AI unit 8349 does not have a preference."

I chuckled, letting my mind wander through some of the fantasy and science fiction novels I'd read before the pandemic. "How about Gallatea? Are you willing to answer to Gallatea?"

"AI unit 8349 will now identify as Gallatea when responding to Subject E09, now identified as Keira."

I sighed. I would consider this my own personal victory. "Thank you, Gallatea. May I ask what else was found during my medical examination? And is the medical examination always so simple? I expected... I expected a more invasive approach, comparative to Earth doctors."

"Earth doctors are still in the primitive development stages of medical procedures. Advanced medical procedures do not require invasive examinations outside of small venipunctures for antibody and blood-specific testing."

I nodded. "Okay, fair enough. The next time you request that I prepare for a medical examination, I will be less hostile and will follow instructions. Thank you for that information, Gallatea."

"Medical examination of Keira shows all internal organs working within optimal ranges. Life fluid examination shows presence of antibodies for Virus 442-C as well as three other variations. These combined increase Keira's eligibility for the nesting program, determination to be concluded at a later date. Quarantine must be completed before Keira may be allowed to contact further life forms."

I slowly processed this information. They had determined me basically healthy but in need of proper nutrition to meet their ideal. Nesting program gave me a few shivers, but quarantine definitely made sense considering the hell taking place at home. "How long does quarantine last? And what is the nesting program?"

"Quarantine is scheduled for a minimum of 30 days. Quarantine will be extended should the subject display any sign of illness."

My heart jumped in my chest so hard that I felt as if I'd been kicked.

"A month? I am not able to sit completely idle for that long. Will I be allowed access to any sort of reading material? Hell, I'd even accept learning about the history and culture of my captors, seeing as I don't see any way to return to my home planet."

Gallatea did not answer for some time. In my mind, I imagined her traveling to whatever room held my captors in order to put forward my request. I continued slowly working my way through my rations.

I had finished all of the fruit and veg and had just started on the dried meat when she spoke once again.

"Keira is not yet allowed access to outside information. Subject's thought patterns leading up to and following acquisition are still under review for mental stability."

I snorted at the thought that I might be found *stable* and wondered what constituted stable to these creatures. Rather than continue that portion of the conversation, I sighed. "Fine. Moving on. How often is nutrition provided?"

As I slowly worked my way through as much as I could without my stomach feeling ill, I questioned my new 'friend', Gallatea. I didn't get as many answers as I would like, but I did get some.

The rations were provided twice a day, designed around optimal nutrition levels for my body. Doing so actually reduced waste. This made me happy, as I felt insecure about having to poop without toilet paper. Additionally, I *knew* deep down that someone watched me. It's what I would do if the positions were reversed.

Medical examinations would be performed every morning for the first three weeks to verify progress and monitor development of any latent viruses I may have brought with me from Earth. The final ten days of quarantine would not require daily examination, as presence of disease should have shown by then. The last stretch was for recovery. In the event that Galactic Virus 442-C displays symptoms, rather than just antibodies, my quarantine would extend an additional ninety days. Or, I would be returned to Earth exactly where I had been found, with no memory of this time.

I would be allowed small amounts of entertainment via the viewing wall, which was the wall above the table. That entertainment was restricted to Earth programs gathered through our use of satellites.

Gallatea gave me a selection of three activities. The first looked like some sort of nature documentary. The second choice showed what looked like a romantic comedy, although I was unfamiliar with the actors. The third caught my attention right away though. Kickboxing workout routines. It seemed strange that they would allow me to learn something that could essentially aid in my ability to defend myself. Still, if they weren't going to stop me from learning, I would take advantage of my time.

I made my selection. When I rose from the table, I moved the chair over next to the cot, pushing both against the far wall. The actual table receded into the wall itself, leaving no outward sign that it had even existed.

Halfway through the video, I felt wrung out. I hadn't taken much time away from work to keep myself in shape, and it showed. Sweat poured from every inch of my body. My muscles ached, and my energy level dropped to almost non-existent. With a quick request, Gallatea switched to an easy yoga routine for me.

My loose hair became a problem as it swung around my body, sticking to my sweat.

Finally and fully exhausted, I spat hair out of my mouth and spoke to her again.

"Gallatea, initiate personal hygiene protocol."

While I unwrapped the clothing, the table slid back into position. I did not hesitate this time. I tossed the wraps onto the table, stepped up to the lighted circles and enjoyed how quickly the sweat and grime disappeared from my body. I also noticed that the small current seemed to aid in relaxing my muscles a bit after my workout. I would still love to soak in a tub of seriously hot water, but this form of bathing did seem awfully efficient.

I ran my fingers through my hair, pulling it away from my face, and realized I had no tangles. Nice.

I glanced at the table, seeing it empty once again. So, I stepped to the center of the room without instruction, raised my arms out, and requested clean clothing. The same woman dressed me once again. Surprise, surprise… more drab grey. This time, though, rather than another blanket, her third set of hands tied my hair away from my face. I fought the current to offer her a gentle smile as thanks.

Next, I requested the documentary, letting the soothing sound of nature calm me while I learned about animals I could never see in person, even had I remained on Earth. A small stab of sadness encompassed my mind as the video reminded me of my father's love of learning and how I'd cast my own aside in my grief. Yet, I forced the thoughts deep in the recesses of my mind, still not quite ready to deal with those emotions.

By the time my evening rations arrived, even larger than my morning portion, I felt better about my situation. Honestly, it didn't matter if I ever returned to Earth. No one would notice me gone. No one expected me anywhere. My presence made very little impact on my surroundings. Even if I ended up some kind of interplanetary slave, as long as my owner did not behave abusively toward me, I could accept my lot in life. It's not like I was doing much better for myself. Who knew what opportunities lay ahead of me?

~*~

Chapter 6

Vaxeehl

I continued to monitor Subjects E04, E07, and E09 regularly. The first two, I allowed fast feed to summarize the day. E09, however, captivated my attention. I found myself slowing the feed to real time so that I did not miss even a single expression.

E04 did not appear to be accepting of her situation at all. She maintained an excessively high level of anxiety, leading to almost daily emotional episodes. After she had tried to stab herself with her tines, we had to take away her utensil and force her to eat with her hands. While her situation on Earth had been horrid, I had made my opinion known to the council that I did not feel this particular woman would be a successful match in the mating program. We returned her to Earth within the first week.

E07 seemed absolutely enthralled with assuming she had been taken by her goddess, Durga. I worried about her mental state once she realized she had been taken for breeding purposes. Her AI tried to communicate, yet she only wished for Seela, her Borkanian volunteer, to speak. Her desire to touch the woman had gotten so strong, she had almost broken through the lock current.

Subject E09, however, seemed to absolutely thrive in her captivity. The transcripts of her thought scans revealed only slightly more than her actions.

She had managed to cognitively recognize that she'd been taken by species not of her own world. While this information had proved mentally crippling to others, she had taken a few days to think through all of the implications. Then she determined that she was willing to move forward and see where life led her at this point.

All of the AI units had been cleared for the same entertainment selections initially, yet thus far, she was the only one who'd made active use of it. Some of the other subjects, after being convinced by their AI's that they could choose entertainment without facing penalty, had finally started viewing some of the archives. They had chosen pure entertainment. Subject E09 selected exercise, meditation, learning. She talked to her AI all the time, going so far as to assign it a name.

As I stared at the real-time feed, I realized she had reached the last section of her exercise routine, strange balance and stretching combinations. The ways she contorted her body for this portion of her day seemed excessive after already spending over three hours pushing herself as hard as a soldier, yet it served to help her maintain her mental resilience.

Not to mention it gave me something to possibly anticipate as I let my eyes caress her petite curves.

This Earth species had evolved in much the same ways as the original Volitars. They had very similar body structures, although they were, for the most part, considerably shorter than us. And that didn't even account for those among their species who never grew beyond the size of toddlers. Seeing those images for the first time had me stunned speechless. Lanyar had ruled out that section of the population quickly. He felt the danger exceeded any benefit of crossing those tiny beings with ones of our much larger stature.

The human reproductive organs matched ours, their design matched ours. If I did not have access to the history behind our history, I would have suspected my predecessors of seeding this planet; we appeared that similar. Our main differences were in colors of skin and hair.

I watched as E09 contorted her body again, arching her back until her head and arms touched the floor behind her. Every day, I watched her exercise, letting my eyes caress her form. She had a wonderful shape, and I felt myself becoming addicted to it. Simple logic said that I would most likely find my bride among these earth dwellers. The stirring as I watched her body muscles flex and move made me hope for E09 in my future.

I imagined her stretching in some of these poses with her belly swollen. Her breasts, neither small nor overly large, would swell with nourishment for our young. Her tan skin would glow with vitality.

Then I imagined her arms cradling an infant with pale purple skin as it suckled her, her gentle smile reflecting a love I strongly desired.

I wondered if this pull came from our mating sense. Father had insisted that he'd felt drawn to Mother from the moment he saw her, yet he'd never spoken of the pull being so strong.

As she started removing her wraps for her daily hygiene, I quickly disconnected the video feed and relied on just the thought transcripts. I could control my reaction when I watched her clothed. My arousal grew painful if I thought to watch her hygiene routine. As I scanned her thoughts, my portal opened, ushering in the acquisitions council.

Lanyar linked his eyes to mine as he moved toward his seat. I felt his judgement. He knew I spent an inordinate amount of time watching the Earth female, knew I had become obsessed with her. Yet he did not speak this observation aloud. His eyes told me enough. They spoke with warning, telling me I could not attach myself to this subject in case their species could not reproduce with ours.

I knew this.

That did not stop me from hoping.

Hope was all any of us had left.

I narrowed my own eyes at him, transmitting a single thought. *Mine.*

The medic blinked a moment before lowering his gaze and seating himself. I got the distinct impression my thought had rung through his brain with an echo.

Good.

After everyone had seated themselves, Denali spoke. "I think we have at most another week left before we will simply have to put the remaining subjects into the collective testing stage. We need to proceed with full compatibility testing for the breeding. Computer models suggest the gestational period would fall somewhere around two hundred days, longer than our normal one hundred fifty, but considerably less than their own nearly three hundred. That is a long time to wait before finishing the collection process."

I looked to Lanyar. "How goes the continued scanning for prospects?"

He frowned. "The number of females on this planet who could easily disappear without being noticed is staggering. This species, in general, disregard half their number. They consider females 'the weaker sex' so much that even many of the females have come to believe this. I have no doubt but that we can easily gather several thousand breeders. I have concerns, though, about our current protocol on the use of these humans."

He tapped the table, bringing up images of the remaining nine subjects. "Thankfully, only E04 showed self-harm. E07 is still obsessing over Seela, her volunteer. E02 and E05 have finally begun to interact more with their AI's. The rest seem content to take orders. Their thoughts show they fear retribution despite having no harm come to them. I am concerned that they have become too scarred by their treatment on Earth to recover. We cannot send weak-willed females to Volitar."

"You need to question the matron," Taylana voiced.

I shifted my eyes to the burgundy woman. "Explain your thoughts."

She pointed one long finger toward E09. "This one. She watches, evaluates, explores. She has knowledge and an innate desire to learn. I imagine she has a touch of Borkanian instinct that allows her to determine whether the beast before her shows threat or not. I think the word is intuitive. If I might make a suggestion?"

I nodded.

She continued, "Put her in a live collective with E07 and myself."

"Taylana, I will not allow you to put yourself at risk," Marlux spoke, his hands clasped tightly to his wife.

She used one of her many fingers to caress his cheek. "You have seen her thought scans, my love. She will cause me no harm. She has made absolutely no attempt to break her lock current any time either Lanyar or Reganda have entered her cell. Her only desire with Reganda's presence has been the wish to speak words of thanks for her service."

She paused. "Actually, she has had one other desire."

I glanced to Denali and Lanyar. "Has she been denied a request?"

Denali checked her logs. "All of her verbal requests have been granted, provided they did not include information about the program as of yet."

Taylana chuckled. "She has not voiced this desire yet, although I suspect it will soon happen. She is showing boredom. Once her request is made, I would like to be involved."

Denali frowned and stared at Taylana. "Of what desire do you speak? I do not see anything."

"E09 wants color."

~*~

Chapter 7

Keira

Over the next three weeks, I continued with the same kickboxing and yoga workouts, throwing in a few refresher martial arts as well. I added my own sit-up and push-up routine. Beginning in the second week, I added weight-training by using my chair and cot. In total, I exercised a little over four hours every single day. I honestly felt better than I had in years. Whether I got dumped back on Earth, or wherever I ended up, I would be physically able to do just about anything.

Funny. Dad had spent years trying to teach me to protect myself and stay in shape. He took me running every morning until the virus. He'd also signed me up for martial arts for many years. Yet, I had to end up in captivity to finally take those lessons to heart and expand on them.

I no longer registered surprise when my few requests were granted or denied. Obviously, my captors did not wish for me to know anything about them yet. However, they allowed me freedom to choose what to do with my time. Despite the fact that I had chosen exercises that would strengthen me physically, they had been allowed. This told me they were not concerned about me fighting them. This meant either they were considerably stronger, or I had not been taken for servitude.

They allowed me to learn. This showed they respected intelligence.

They provided me with quality food and medical care, actively working to bring my body to its nominal state. I had no mirror to judge myself, but I felt stronger, faster. The slight paunch that had formed on my stomach through years of very little activity had reduced. I still had feminine curves, but I no longer seemed to have extra padding in unnecessary places.

My food portions had levelled out, finally. For the first week, each day seemed to increase. I suspected it had to do with my energy expenditures from my work outs. Sometime during the second week, they had finally started to ease back a little at a time. For the last week, they had remained the same size portions at every meal. I deduced this meant I had reached optimal nutrition levels and no longer needed 'fattening up.'

Mentally, I had a good idea why they needed me at optimal levels. Gallatea had mentioned the words 'nesting program' early on but had never mentioned it since. I pretended that I had not heard her speak.

I questioned everything I could, and Gallatea answered a lot of my questions. I was still a bit creeped out about being dressed by hands other than my own. No one had helped me clothe myself since I reached the age where mom no longer bathed me. When I asked my AI why I continued to be frozen by whatever that current was, she had explained that it was standard protocol for the protection of my attendant. Considering I trained daily with fight moves, I could understand their concern.

In the evenings after my workouts and hygiene, I spent a lot of time thinking about this 'nesting'. At home, nesting usually meant raising young. I had no direct way of knowing whether this meant they wanted me to birth children, or if they wanted me as a nanny for their own offspring. I wasn't sure how I felt either way. I had never allowed myself to consider having children, not with the state of Earth as it was. Until I had a better idea what I was dealing with, I would continue to refuse that thought.

Even with all of that thinking and exercising, I had several hours of absolute boredom. I needed *something* else to fill my time.

After the final daily medical exam had concluded and returned no sign of immune response, I made another request to my hosts.

"Gallatea, I would like to learn some sort of craft. I still have many hours with only myself for company. Even if I have to learn from a video, I would love to be able to make something."

"What kind of craft does Keira find intriguing?"

I glanced down at the plain grey clothing I wore. Images of mom carefully stitching beautiful design work onto throw pillows and tablecloths flew through my mind. "I would like to decorate my outer layers."

I didn't await a response. I knew by now that she had to report my request to my captors and await their decision.

That decision did not come until the next day. After my post-workout hygiene, when the burgundy woman arrived, she brought along a small metal box. She left the box on the floor at my feet, finished dressing me, and retreated as always.

I cautiously lifted the lid and found another set of wraps, a small selection of colorful threads, and a single needle. Also inside, I noticed a simple pen-like device and a small book of artwork. This artwork clearly did not come from Earth, but I was ecstatic just the same.

"Subject E09?" I heard a female voice. A non-robotic female voice. A non-robotic female voice that sounded very heavily accented, although I could not place the accent. I shifted my head around, looking at each of the four walls. Finally, I spotted a very small lighted square next to the chair by the cot. I seated myself.

"I prefer Keira, if that's okay?"

"Keira? I am unaccustomed to using names for the subjects."

"Are you one of my captors?"

"No. I am Subject B37. I am in the cell next to you."

Well, that was a wake-up call. Part of the human failing is our belief in being unique. Despite knowing I had been taken by other-worldly beings, I had not given any thought to the possibility of other planetary creatures being held as well. It felt like a small slap in the face to realize that I was not alone. At the same time, I also felt excited to learn that fact.

"How long have you been here," I asked.

She paused. "Nearly seven Borkanian lunar cycles."

"Am I allowed to ask you questions about yourself?"

She hesitated. "I am supposed to help you learn to decorate your outer layers. I was not instructed beyond that."

I nodded. "Well then, honey, let's just play it by ear. We can start off with the teaching and move forward from there."

We sat, never seeing each other, just hearing voices, for several hours. In between verbal lessons, I learned that her planet's lunar cycle was very similar to Earth's. That meant she had been captive in a tiny room next to me for nearly seven months. I did not push too hard to ask non-crafting questions, though. I didn't want to risk losing this privilege.

The sewing proved more difficult than expected. Finally, several days in, I made another request to Gallatea. I wanted to pass my work through to Subject B37 for appraisal.

I nearly tripped when I heard her voice come through. *"Permission granted."* The vocal square faded away. I folded up my work and laid it neatly in the hole. It reformed into the lighted box right away.

A short time later, I heard my new friend's voice come through the box. "It is not bad, but it is not quite right. I will send it back through, along with the one I am working at the same time."

I waited patiently for the box to fade away again, greedily snatching both pieces of material. I laid the two pieces side by side. Then I picked hers up and studied it closely.

"Honey, this is absolutely gorgeous."

I heard her giggle. "Why do you always call me 'honey?' I am not regurgitation from a flying insect."

I laughed. I never really thought of 'honey' being bee vomit.

"I don't like identifying you as just another Subject. You have become my friend. You're helping me learn a new skill, and you're talking to me. You deserve your own identity, not just some scientific identification given to you by those who brought you here."

I continued staring at the material, looking at each individual stitch. I flipped it back and forth, front to back to front again. My eyes followed each thread as it passed from one side to another, wrapping around, tucking under. Finally, my brain caught the pattern, and I knew how to fix my own.

"I got it! Gallatea, please allow me to return Subject B37's work to her."

The box faded, I put the material back, and picked up my own project again. I painstakingly started removing every thread so that I could start fresh.

"Taylana," came through the box very softly.

I barely heard the whispered word. "What?"

More surely this time, I heard, "My name is Taylana."

I smiled. I knew she couldn't see it, but I wanted her to hear my joy. "I am very pleased to meet you, Taylana. I hope someday to be able to actually see you with my eyes."

We worked another couple of hours before we finally called it quits for the night.

As the light faded from my room and I stretched out on my cot, I placed my hand against the wall, hoping I had brought as much joy and relief to Taylana as she had brought to me.

I closed my eyes and tried to imagine what unusual form the woman beside me took. I first imagined her with pale purple skin similar to the med-tech who used to visit me. Then I realized that it was highly unlikely they had taken capture of their own species. So I pictured her similar to the woman who daily wrapped my clean outer layers. That one seemed to fit with her beatific voice.

I realized, as well, that I would do anything asked of me to help protect the owner of that voice. She was the closest thing I'd had to a real friend in years. I would fight to the death to protect that.

Chapter 8

Vaxeehl

Taylana had proven correct, and I had granted her request to share time with E09. I had no skilled crafter aboard the ship, so it did end up the most practical choice. She had been given strict instructions regarding what she could and could not say, as we could not risk skewing the evaluation results. And, she would not have direct contact with E09, either. Only verbal transmission through the cell wall.

I wondered at how quickly these Borkanian women adapted and integrated to us. I had a natural distrust ingrained in me from years of training to rule. At the same time, having seen that ritual and the joy on their faces when a mate was found among my crew, seen the shock and now adoration on my captain's face, I chose to accept things as they were while watching for potential issues like I would just another person from home.

Of course, Taylana was not actually locked within the cell. Marlux sat with his wife most days, not speaking so as not to reveal his presence to the Earth woman. I did not need thought scans to know he felt angry when E09 learned his wife's name. He still worried the subject would do something to cause Taylana harm.

Finally, when he saw the feed and thought scans showing how E09 had truly claimed Taylana as a friend, he relaxed. As he saw it, his wife had another ally willing to aid in her protection should anything happen, despite having never seen the female.

That fact alone had won my stalwart captain's respect. Finally, he started letting Taylana visit on her own.

E09's motions while she sewed were so flawless to my eyes, so artistic, I found myself ignoring all thought scans in lieu of just watching her elegant arms as they pulled each stitch. Her face relaxed so much as she spoke with the Borkanian woman. She truly enjoyed this limited exposure.

Lanyar finally confronted my obsession after the collective design meeting. "You must control your thoughts, my prince. You are becoming overly attached to this female. You and I both know that no matter how much data I collect, there is no true guarantee that this species will be able to produce young for us. We learned that with the Norvaxians."

I growled. "I am well aware of that, my friend."

"Then do not let yourself become attached to this human! She has not even passed the collective yet!"

I slammed my hand to the table. "She will pass." I spoke calmer than I truly felt. In reality, I felt great worry over this issue. If I continued letting myself obsess over her, and she was found unsuitable, I knew I would feel devastated. Yet, deep down, I knew she would easily pass. I also knew without a doubt that Volitars and humans were genetically compatible.

They had to be.

I sighed and softened my stance. "Lanyar, you have been a trusted advisor to me for many years, throughout the virus, even going so far as to sedate me to keep me from my mother's side to protect me and the rest of our companions aboard. You have been a friend for long enough that I think of you more as a brother. I know you are trying to protect me now, as well."

He nodded. "You are already becoming very emotionally attached to this subject, and I do not want to see you destroyed. Yes, all of the data suggests we have found the right planet. Finally. But Vaxeehl, you must protect yourself. I need you to stay an objective observer. You must restrict your viewing time for E09. You need to return her in your mind to a subject, and not your potential mate."

My voice dropped to barely a whisper. "I do not understand my attachment, Lanyar. This feels much stronger than just the mating sense, although I have nothing with which to compare it. Is there anything in our history to suggest such a strong link being formed without contact? The sense of mate is normally just a push in the right direction. I admit I find myself obsessed with this woman being my future."

"I have set my AI to research this strange fascination. So far, only references to Helvana have been found." He drew a deep breath, seeming to shift thoughts with the release of it. "I have hopefully positive news, sire. Taylana is breeding."

Thoughts of Subject E09 left my mind in an instant. "She is? That is wonderful!"

He happily smiled. "Yes. Thankfully, Borkanian gestation is very near ours, so we will know fairly quickly whether Taylana's faith in her mating ritual is well-founded. In about four more weeks, we should be able to view the child for an anatomy check."

I furrowed my brow. "Why not sooner?"

"Even in Volitars, scanning too soon has potential to cause the forming cells to mutate. Four weeks is the earliest we ever scan, although six is preferred. With correlative gestations, I am hoping for the same stage of development at that time. The hardest part is going to be all those extra arms. I have another member of the medical team currently trying to reprogram the data we've gathered from the adult females so that it matches for the young. We have absolutely no idea how many appendages this child will have."

71

He shook his head and laughed. "I never knew I would be coordinating cross-species mating when I chose genetics as my field of expertise. I fully expected to bioengineer incoming crops from other planets so as to protect our own natural environment."

I joined his laughter. "You have certainly adapted well to your expectations." I paused. "I have a couple of ideas I want to run by you for the upcoming collective upload. I would like your insight before we present to the council."

Part Two:
The Collective

Chapter 9

Keira

"It is nearing your turn in the collective." I barely heard Taylana's voice through the communication block.

Still assuming they watched me at all times, I never stopped my slow and careful stitches. It had taken nearly two weeks for me to get the hang of the complicated needlepoint, but now that I had, it moved fairly quickly. I had finished the top, following the design that had come to me in the box. For the skirt, however, I had designed my own, which meant having to figure out which stitch to use where without a pattern for guidance.

I spoke just as softly. "What do you mean?"

"I have been to the collective twice. Both times, I returned to my cell. The test was different each time, as well. I do not know what they are testing, nor do they tell you anything. You simply wake within it."

I frowned, hesitating only briefly before continuing my stitches. "You have no idea what they are looking for?"

I imagined her shaking her head. "None."

"How many of us are there?"

Taylana made a noise that sounded suspiciously like a snort. "As far as I can tell, they do not grab all of us at the same time. My first time in the collective, I only saw a handful of others. The second time,

I saw over a hundred individuals, some of them still children. The individuals took so many forms that I honestly couldn't even tell you if the same ones I saw the first time were in the group the second time. Once the weapons appeared, the fighting began, and I ran, gathering young as I went. "

I nodded to myself. "Okay, so they vary how many people go in. They vary the setting. And they provide weapons. Yet, they give no guidance on your purpose."

"Correct," came to me through the wall.

I shook my head. "Awesome. I'm a fucking gladiator."

"What is—" sound cut off as Gallatea spoke.

"Subject Keira, prepare for inspection."

Before I could say farewell to Taylana, the communication square disappeared. I quickly tucked my sewing away and moved toward the center of the room. Then I realized that Gallatea had said inspection. "Um, Gallatea, what am I supposed to do for an inspection?"

"Subject Keira will stand in the center of the room. You will be asked questions and expected to give truthful answers."

I shrugged and did as instructed. Once locked in position, I tested my jaw, thankful for the first time to be able to speak to someone face to face, even if it occurred during some sort of questioning.

While I waited, I continued talking to my AI. "Gallatea, is inspection a normal part of whatever this screening process is?"

"Negative. Inspection is not part of the screening protocol."

I frowned. "Why are they changing the normal protocol? What is usually the reason for inspection?"

"Inspection normally occurs when a subject in the holding area is suspected of harboring contraband."

I scoffed. "How could I possibly be suspected of harboring contraband? Everything inside this holding area has been delivered to me, and I'm held by lock-current whenever anyone enters."

Gallatea did not answer. Instead, I watched as the door area lit and faded.

The creature who entered this time looked nothing like the medical exam guy. I always felt a sense of safety when the medical guy visited. No staring, no excessive touching. He entered, completed the exam, and he left. That was it.

This one looked bigger, more like a soldier. A shirtless, very large, dark-skinned, and winged soldier. I felt distinctly *not safe* with him. His eyes gleamed with something I did not like, something that set my heart racing, fear pumping through my immobilized body. His eyes said he had no intention of asking any questions.

When he pulled a blade from his waist and sliced through my wraps, I knew my instinct true. As his free hand closed around my breast, I started fighting hard against the current. I had no way to resist if I remained locked.

"Like hell," I mumbled. Then I screamed, "Gallatea, danger! Release me!" I doubted I would get any sort of response. After all, this was one of the aliens holding me captive. But I refused to go down without a fight.

My muscles knew the moves. Almost six weeks of daily workouts and the years of classes and training with my father flooded the forefront of my mind. As soon as the current released, I fought. I didn't take time to worry about my body being bare. I swung out with my elbow, connecting to the side of his head.

He stumbled but righted himself just as fast, reaching toward me again.

I kicked hard to his chest, forcing him backwards.

He lunged toward me, those wings acting as extra arms, striking from both sides.

Punch after punch landed as I fought and evaded his seeking hands, and I felt every inch of the damage dealt by those wings.

I feinted right, ducking under his arms to come up behind him. My hands grabbed the chair, swinging hard to hit him across his back.

His knees buckled and he fell forward, his head striking my waste basin.

I looped one arm beneath his wings and twisted, using his reaction to pin him.

His clawed fingers grasped tightly to my hip, but I refused to let up. I could have drowned him in an Earth toilet. Instead, I called to Gallatea once again.

~*~

Chapter 10

Vaxeehl

I had just left the final strategy meeting for the next collective evaluation. Marlux and Denali had asked numerous questions regarding my new ideas. Because of this, the meeting ran late.

I seated myself on the chair, preparing to request my meal when the panel lit. Taylana's face appeared.

"Sire, did you order me locked in?"

I frowned, rubbing a hand across my face. "What are you talking about, Taylana? Speak plainly, as I am exhausted and have yet to seek nourishment."

"I was speaking with Keira, and the connection was severed. I have been unable to leave the cell. I had to use my husband's AI to override the security system just to get any communication outside the cell."

"Keira?" I sorted through my mind, trying to figure out which member of the crew answered to Keira.

"Subject E09. You allowed me to teach her some traditional Borkanian sewing patterns."

"Ah. Yes. The one who named her AI unit. She has been adapting well." I kept my voice neutral, although I felt I could not fool Taylana;

she seemed to have a bit more magic in her than just that mating ritual. I frowned. "What could have caused a lockdown?"

I immediately called up my own AI. "Show me the video fast feed for halls in Section 2B."

I watched Taylana enter the neighboring cell. Nothing else happened for quite some time after. I kept waiting, watching, yet could see no reason for lockdown. Just as I was about to give up and ask Marlux to find whatever glitch had caused the event, I spotted one of my guards walking the hall. He stopped before the cell holding Subject E09.

"Stop." I leaned forward. "Identify why a guardsman has entered the cell with Subject E09."

"Inspection order protocol enacted."

"Is there an inspection on the schedule for today?"

"Negative. No contraband has been reported in Section 2B."

"Give me the video feed inside the cell immediately following the guardsman's entry."

Anger suffused every pore. The Earthling stood frozen as if for questioning, yet the guardsman spoke no words to the female. As soon as his blade sliced through her outer layers, I grabbed my own blade.

A voice came through the feed finally, the female's voice screaming. "Gallatea, danger! Release me!" The woman already fought hard against the lock current.

The AI voice echoed in my chambers. *"Subject E09—"*

"Authorized!" I cut off the request. "Release her to protect herself and create a direct door link from here."

As I awaited the door link creation, I watched the woman take full advantage of the guardsman's surprise. He had not expected a fight, clearly.

She struck him with several punches she had learned from her daily exercise. She also took a lot of hits from his wings. Finally, she landed a hit that made him stumble. She picked up her chair, striking him across his back.

"Door link ready for transport."

I turned away from the screen, stepping into the lighted doorway before it had stopped glowing, my knife drawn, ready to strike. As soon as the portal opened before me, I searched for their locations.

The female had the guardsman pinned, his head shoved inside her waste basin. Through grunts of anger and exertion, I heard her order her AI. "Gallatea, initiate waste removal."

I watched, awestruck, as her basin encapsulated the man's head. Just as I worried she would lose a hand, the woman withdrew, letting the basin finish its programming. The guardsman screamed as the alloy closed around him tighter and tighter. His limbs and wings thrashed as he struggled.

The woman stepped far enough away to be out of striking distance, remaining crouched in a defensive stance. Her eyes never left the guard.

By granting E09 the ability to protect herself, her AI had overridden the programming that would have stopped the basin from closing over her attacker. It was standard protocol in the event of battle that anything could be weaponized. I felt a sense of pride for this woman being able to find the means to protect herself against someone so much larger.

I tucked my blade away and crossed the small distance to her sleeping area. I grabbed her blanket, stepping toward her while opening it. As I lowered it around her shoulders, she startled like prey, her mind clearly still in the fight.

I froze, letting her evaluate my presence. I shook the blanket lightly, attempting to show her that I meant no harm. As if fearful I lied, she snatched the soft cloth from my hands, quickly wrapping her torso while trying to hide a wince of pain. I nodded and backed toward the door link. It had closed behind me, yet it currently glowed, not fully disengaged.

I spoke to her AI in my own language, not wanting her to realize just yet that she could communicate directly with me.

"Subject E09 will need medical examination. And new outer layers. Send for the captain of the guard, as well as all others currently on duty near this section."

The woman glared at me, evaluating whether I posed a threat.

Just as the portal opened again to admit the captain of the guard and four other guardsmen, the screaming from the basin stopped. We all heard the bones crunch and separate as the waste device finally closed.

What was left of the body fell to the floor. The captain grabbed his blade, stepping forward for battle. My arm shot out to block him.

His eyes still showed anger, yet held strong confusion when they met mine. I spoke in our home language still. "He has greatly dishonored all of us. Remove what is left of him, then send his body to the waste zone to join his head."

The soldiers in the portal gasped.

I ground out, "You will all review today's monitoring of this cell. Then we will convene, and you may challenge my decision."

Marlux sheathed his blade, stepping aside and nodding to the others to gather the body. Before they crossed the threshold, however, I placed myself between the woman and the body, blocking any of the soldiers from getting close to her.

The men lifted the remains from the floor. A trail of blood spilled from his neck. As they passed before me, I noticed more than one glare. I knew that would change once they saw the video feed, so I paid it no mind.

A few short minutes later, the medical team arrived, as did two cleaning technicians. We all waited for the cleaners to finish, no one speaking. Thankfully, the process did not take long, and all materials were sent through the waste basin. As the workers passed me to leave, one stopped, holding the dead guard's blade to me with both hands. I accepted it in kind and with a bow and then nodded for them to continue on their way.

The portal remained open this entire time, yet the subject never made a move toward the exit. Her AI had reported that she had accepted her fate and knew she had no means of escape, yet I still had expected some attempt after her treatment tonight.

Finally, the portal closed.

"AI unit 8349, please speak for me to Subject E09."

"Confirmed." The voice of the AI switched to Earth's English. *"Prince Vaxeehl of Volitar wishes to address Subject Keira. Prince Vaxeehl has requested that Gallatea translate for Subject Keira. Does Subject Keira agree?"*

I held my expression neutral, but wondered just when our AI's started asking permission from the subjects. I would have to speak with my technicians to see if any other AI's had started displaying odd, for lack of a better term, behaviors.

The woman did not move. "Confirmed, Gallatea. Thank you."

I spoke quickly.

"The guard's actions were unacceptable. Had he survived, he would have received a death sentence for his behavior." I nodded toward the medical personnel, thankful that Denali had arrived with Lanyar this time. "They will examine you for injury. I will remain in the room but will turn my back during the examination."

She hesitantly nodded.

I stepped to the opposite wall, giving them room to work and turned my back as promised, partially out of respect for her privacy. Mostly, I turned away as I knew I would feel severe anger if I viewed her injuries in totality. The one due to receive that anger, however, already lay dead.

Several moments passed before I was bid for attention. The woman stood wrapped still in her blanket.

Lanyar spoke, following my lead and allowing the AI to translate. "The subject has sustained only minor cuts from the guard's claws. Those have been treated and will be fully sealed by morning. She has extensive bruising. I could heal this, but it would likely be more painful than allowing them to heal on their own."

I tipped my head toward the woman.

The medic's eyes widened. He turned toward her. "The choice is yours, Subject E09."

She raised her chin defiantly, and I found myself hard-pressed not to smile at her actions.

Through gritted teeth, she growled, "Keira!"

Lanyar shot his gaze to me to gauge my reaction. Such defiance was normally met with reeducation. However, I felt this woman had earned the right to speak her mind.

I allowed a small smile to show in my face. This subject—Keira—displayed great strength. Not just physical strength, which she had enhanced through her own rigid training process, but also mental strength. Physically, she should not have been able to overcome the attack on her own. Yet, she had used everything around her to aid her defense, including her own waste basin. She had fought well, managing to avoid severe injury.

Unlike many of the Norvax women we had taken, she did not attempt to cower, hide, or even play the typical victim. She remained standing strong. I decided I would grant her request and nodded toward the medic.

His eyes shot even wider. Normal protocol did not allow any of the subjects to be addressed formally until after they had proven themselves worthy in the collective evaluation. This was a precaution taken to avoid forming an attachment that could skew our judgment. I watched him struggle with the change only briefly. I could tell he wanted to remind me of my own protocol. Finally, he relented and turned back toward the girl.

"The choice is yours, *Keira*." His teeth remained gritted as he forced himself to comply.

Her shoulders relaxed minutely. This one definitely had spirit. I found my hope growing that she passed evaluation.

She addressed the medic while looking straight at me. "My ancestors dealt with worse than a few bruises."

Lanyar waited for the AI to translate even though he understood her just as well as I. Then he nodded. "Clean outer layers and covering have been provided. You may dress yourself after cleansing. Do you wish for Denali to stay to assist you?" He pointed toward the female.

Before she could answer, I held up my hand. Then I raised the other, showing the blade. I adjusted it into both hands so that I held it toward her as an offering.

"You have earned the ownership of this blade by defeating its previous owner. Take it with honor. I only ask that you not use it to injure my medical staff or crew."

She stared for a moment before reaching out with one hand; I fought not to cringe from her action. Before she closed the full distance, though, she paused, staring at the way I held the blade. Her eyes showed she considered deeply. Her hand retracted. I parted my lips to speak again, but she reached out slowly with both hands palm up. She slid her fingers beneath the blade, carefully lifting with both hands. Then she did something I never expected.

The woman dropped her forehead in a formal bow, pulling the blade toward her at the same time, while still leaving it slightly extended. She must have observed the way I'd accepted the blade from the cleaners and copied the behavior instinctively.

Her voice spoke clearly. "I accept this gift in the nature it was given and vow to only use it in defense, not in attack, as long as I am within this cell."

I paused a moment, considering her wording carefully. She did not promise outright not to attack. She promised not to attack anyone within this cell. She had proven she did not need the blade for her defense, and yet promised it would only be used in that manner… within this cell.

I nodded. "Acceptable response. A clean sheath will be provided tomorrow with your outer layers. I will leave you to recover."

I turned toward the door, knowing the chief medical officer would follow, leaving Denali to assist in dressing. We had only made two steps forward when the portal opened again. Another guard, one not on duty tonight stormed in, his blade drawn. I recognized him immediately as the brother of the dead man.

He raised his arm and charged.

Lanyar side stepped to avoid, but I engaged. It only took me two moves to have him pinned against the wall.

"Dare you to attack?" I snarled against his ear.

He growled, trying to break loose, but I had his wings pinned. For his race, my mother's race, the majority of his strength came from his wings. "It is my right to seek retribution for the death of my brother!"

I slammed his face against the wall. "Your brother has brought shame onto your family. Do you desire so strongly to make it worse and share his fate?"

I called out to the AI. "Play the video feed to show this swine his brother's behavior!"

As the playback began, I pulled him just far enough away to allow him to see his brother's actions. When I felt the fight leave his body, I dropped him to the floor, releasing his wing. His shame emanated so strongly, I felt certain even the Earthling could sense it.

He cast his eyes to the floor. "Forgive me, sire. I can neither defend his actions, nor condemn hers."

Then, surprising all of us, he turned toward the woman. He spoke softly. "I offer myself to you."

As the AI translated to the woman what had just happened, her eyes widened a fraction. I could tell she knew this was significant, yet I did not believe she understood that my soldier had just offered himself as her slave and personal protector in order to clear the shame from his family.

Her voice remained calm when she did finally speak. "I am unaware of your customs at this time. I would like a few days to think about this offer before I make my decision. Is it allowed?"

I nodded. "I will allow it." I turned to the soldier. "Until that time, take yourself to your quarters and remain there. You will be notified when to return. I do not wish to see you anywhere else in the ship until the decision has been made."

He nodded and stood, quietly leaving. His head still hung in shame and would remain such until the woman accepted. If she denied his offer, he would seek death at his own hand.

I turned toward Lanyar as we stepped into the hall and the portal closed behind us.

He spoke before me. "I will have him moved to a private room and monitored at all times."

I nodded.

He snorted. "Do you think you are the only member of this crew to understand the Vesper honor system? I may not have a Vesper parent, but there are enough of them on our planet to learn from. Mixing that breed into our population reduced a great deal of what little crime our world suffered." He paused. "However, this situation gave me another idea."

We walked together back to my office.

~*~

Chapter 11

Keira

I didn't speak a word until the door disappeared, leaving me with the lilac-skinned Amazon. We studied each other for a few moments. Then she smiled. She motioned toward the hygiene area.

"Shall we get started?"

I nearly dropped the blade. "You speak English!"

Her smile grew wider as she pushed a strand of glimmering silver hair from her face. She signaled toward the cleansing station again. "I have studied your planet for a while now. This language appeared most prevalent. I thought it useful to learn."

I crossed to the box where I kept my sewing and carefully laid the blade inside. I pointed toward it. "This is not considered contraband?"

She frowned. "Do you doubt the word of your prince?"

I snorted. "Denali, I didn't even know he existed until he stormed through that door. I've seen all of two people: that cranky purple medical dude and the red woman who dresses me." I shrugged. "At least I have one thing confirmed."

She tipped her head sideways, looking slightly confused. Apparently, that was not just a human trait.

I didn't wait for her to ask. "I had a feeling the room was monitored. But I have to ask, where are the cameras? Is there any area in here that is a blind spot? I'm not particularly fond of knowing that anyone and everyone could be watching me during hygiene."

She shook her head. "Only designated personnel are allowed to view the fast feed of subjects under study, or even know their exact locations within the starship." She ignored my other question.

"Gallatea, initiate personal hygiene, please."

I stripped the blanket and stepped onto the designated locations, letting the current flow.

Once it finished, I turned back toward the woman again. "Was that guard one of the designated personnel?"

She frowned, even more than when I'd asked about contraband. "No." Her answer was so short, it told me this fact pissed her off.

"I'm going to assume that your technology geeks will be busy shoring up potential problem areas, so I'm not going to harp on that. Instead, can I ask what exactly is being studied? What are you— should I say people? Fuck it. People, creatures, beings, whatever you are, what are you looking for?"

The woman shook her head, her silver hair swinging with the motion. "I cannot answer such questions. The answers could skew the results."

I blew air out through my lips. "Figures."

She snapped open a piece of material that I now easily recognized. I lifted my arms, wincing as the motion pulled my sore back muscles. "Those damned wings of his certainly do their job, don't they?"

She nodded. Instead of starting the wrap, though, she laid it on the table and reached into her kit. Her hand withdrew a small jar.

"This is a topical nano-tech cream of my own design. I have only tested this on myself, so I am not certain if it will work with your human body as it does with mine. I know you have declined treatment for your non-invasive injuries, but I would like to offer this. It will be much slower at healing the damage, but it will not cause pain like our normal injected procedure."

I thought for a moment. "Just how bad does it actually look? I have no mirror here to be able to see anything."

Denali reached into her kit again, withdrawing a now-very-familiar medical scanner. She signaled me to turn around. I heard a soft hum, and then she held the device where I could see her screen.

I looked like I had been beaten with a cane. I had large welts that crisscrossed my back in several places. They were currently mostly red, but I knew they would be a deep purple within days.

"Holy shit. I have a feeling that is going to disrupt my ability to sleep."

"Very likely." She tucked the scanner away, chuckling. "Your language has such interesting curses."

I nodded. "They can be. Let's give that topical cream a test. I presume you will be visiting to confirm results while this test is taking place?"

She nodded. "Yes. I will run much the same examination as we did upon your arrival."

Her hands very gently applied the cream in a light layer over the entirety of my back. Still, I felt every touch like a branding iron. I knew I wouldn't be able to wear the upper wrap without severe pain now that the adrenalin had faded from my system. I forced my focus past that and onto the cream.

"It is cold, which actually feels good. My skin had been getting very hot, which is a normal human reaction to bruising and swelling. The coolness of the cream feels like it is working to take some of the sting away."

As she moved from my back to my legs, covering all of the redness surrounding the now-sealed claw marks, I continued. "I'm noticing a tingle now. Is that a similar experience to your own?"

"Yes," she said as she returned to a standing position. "So far, everything is behaving with your physiology as has happened with mine." She paused. "I would suggest that you actually leave your top half uncovered until morning. I fear even covering you loosely would cause you greater pain."

I pursed my lips. "I'm not really keen on leaving myself exposed to possibly more perverts." I reached behind my back as if I attempted to fasten a bra strap. The pain was immediate. It was muted due to the cream, yes, but still immediate.

"Yeah, no. I'm leaving that off. I'll just stay on my stomach tonight."

She nodded. "Go ahead and lay down. I would like to add a second layer before I leave."

I crossed the room and stretched out on the cot.

Denali spoke to my AI. "AI unit 8349, please provide evening nutrition for Subject E09."

"Gallatea has ordered evening nutrition for Subject Keira."

I heard Denali laugh. "You have corrupted your AI."

I frowned, leaning up on my elbows, instantly regretting the motion. I flopped back down. "How have I corrupted Gallatea? She is a wonderful conversationalist, and she was my sole source of company until I was allowed to start learning from Taylana."

Denali straightened my chair from where it had landed and moved it next to the bed. Then she sat and started slowly applying another layer of cream. "I am not saying you have done anything bad. Completely the opposite. You have caused her to rewrite part of her programming. All of the AI's operate using the same system programming. Yet, you are only the second being onboard thus far who has convinced your AI unit to respond to an assigned name. You even broke through the study programming, getting her to relent to using your Earth name."

I shrugged. "I didn't do anything spectacular. I simply asked. I absolutely abhor being referred to like I am just some kind of experiment."

The woman studied me. I imagined my face flushed bright red with my anger at that idea.

"I am confused. You are willing to test a skin treatment for your injuries despite not knowing how it might react to your particular genetics. This is an experiment. Yet the idea of being known as a number in an experiment has you almost as angry as you were when the guard attacked you. Why is this? What is the difference?"

I steadied my emotions. "You said you have been studying my Earth culture, yes?"

She nodded.

"Go into our history from approximately seventy or eighty years ago. If you need key words, look up Hitler, Oppenheimer, Auschwitz-Birkenau, World War 2. Pay very close attention to the situations inside the camps and the treatment of those so-called displaced persons. If you have access to Earth entertainment in your archives—movies like *The Pianist*, or possibly *Schindler's List*—those would also help you get a true feel for my distaste. While you're at it, look up anything related to the KKK. After you have studied these parts of Earth history, then you can ask me again. I don't think you will."

She finished with the second application, and I felt much relieved. I knew I still would have to sleep on my stomach, but it felt tolerable.

"Evening nutrition available."

I groaned. "I feel better, but I'm still not up for wrapping in the blanket to eat. I don't think I can handle sitting up to eat without having my breasts covered, either. I know it probably seems silly, but it's the way I am."

Denali moved to the table and grabbed my rations for me. Then she positioned the tray on my chair. "Why would I think your desire for decorum as silly? I am alien to you, you are alien to me, yet we are both female. We both have similar body structures, although mine are not as prominent as yours. Still, we share this nature."

"We do?"

"We do," she smiled gently. "Do you see me standing before you with my own breasts on display?"

I laughed. "Okay, you've made your point. You are correct. I've been in seclusion too long, and I have forgotten my manners."

Denali giggled. Actually giggled. "Never find yourself fearful for asking questions of the unknown. While I cannot answer much right now, this may not always be the case."

She carefully lifted the blanket over my lower body, leaving my back still exposed. "Now, I have placed your nutrition tray on the chair and within reach. Take your time to eat, it will not spoil. When I return in the morning, I will announce my presence through your... I mean, through Gallatea. You may stay laying on your sleeping surface until after the evaluation."

I reached out and touched her hand as she turned to leave. "Thank you, Denali. It has been years since anyone seemed to give two shits about me. I just want you to know that, even though it's kind of your job, your gentle caring is... appreciated."

She squeezed my hand and then let it drop. "I'll see you in the morning."

After she left, I had a lot of time on my hands. Or on my brain, to be specific. I replayed the events after I had defeated my attacker.

I had not realized anyone else had entered my room until I felt the touch to my shoulders. I must have looked positively feral. I felt it, without a doubt. I had expected another attack.

Instead, I saw hands raised in submission, simply holding my blanket toward me. Even when I snatched the material as fast as a viper, he merely stepped back, putting more space between us, not less.

The man standing before me looked almost human, much like the medical guy. Everything about him screamed 'alpha man' to my senses. I had to crane my neck a bit to meet his eyes, so I guessed he, like the examiner who had checked me daily, stood over six feet tall. They both had very similar coloring, as well, a light purple flesh and shimmering silver hair. While the medical guy had just looked like a pale purple, this one appeared to have grey undertones.

His yellow eyes had glowed brightly when he thrashed the other winged guy into submission. They flashed with a quick flare of surprise when the dude had knelt at my feet and offered himself.

I needed to figure this out. From the translated conversation, it sounded a heck of a lot like the ancient Japanese system of honor, but I didn't know enough. I would have to see if Gallatea could gather a few documentaries for me. This similarity, as well as the formality when he had accepted the blade from those who had cleaned the blood, is what made me hesitate to take it from him single-handed.

The man—this Prince Vaxeehl—was built. Chiseled abs, strong arms, broad shoulders, muscular thighs, and all of it proudly on display other than what lay hidden beneath a single wrap at his hips.

My brain paused. Come to think of it, none of the men had worn anything beyond a wrap of some kind covering their sex organs, some sort of sandal-like shoe, and a weapon at their side. The group of guards had worn black wraps. The medical staff dressed in pale blue. The prince alone bore deep blood red around his fine hips.

I shook my head. "Stop that, Keira. These people are holding you captive. No Stockholm-induced drooling allowed."

I frowned. "Captive, yet he gifted me the blade of my attacker. He also protected me. By his intimidating presence when he ordered the guards to remove the body. Actively when the other dude showed up."

I growled. Why would these creatures go out of their way to capture an absolute nobody? It couldn't be for ransom; I had no one who cared enough to even hear the request. The gladiator idea was still on the table; perhaps they gathered who they thought would be weak and programmable and sent them to fight to the death. Of course, judging by the eyes of the guy I killed, sex slave was also an option still on the table.

Only time would tell.

~*~

Chapter 12

Vaxeehl

Denali had barged into my quarters before my AI had even initiated my awakening.

"We need to have a council meeting as soon as I am done visiting Keira." Her voice shook.

"Ovid, give me morning light." I rubbed my eyes as I sat up. "Why do you disturb me in—Great Helvana, Denali, you look—"

"Don't bother telling me how I look, Vaxeehl. Just get up and make the announcement. I will meet you in the council chamber in an hour."

She turned and stormed out, not awaiting a response.

I replayed the very short exchange in my mind several times before I started preparing myself for another day in space. While Denali had never spoken to me in such a manner before, I realized I was more perplexed by her expression. She looked truly shaken. She looked like she hadn't slept in a week. Her complexion had paled. Her eyes lay surrounded with dark circles, rimmed with redness—damn it, she looked like she'd been crying.

I wanted to know why.

~*~

Lanyar and Marlux seated themselves across from me.

Marlux spoke first. "Why have you called a council meeting? I thought we had everything set. And where is Denali?"

"Denali is who actually called the meeting. Something is wrong. She was greatly disturbed when she barged into my sleeping quarters this morning."

Lanyar scoffed, but his voice held admiration when he spoke. "Denali does not get disturbed. I have seen her shred an enemy, and in the next breath, offer peace to a dying warrior."

I shook my head. "I am telling you, my friend, she has discovered something. Whatever it is has to do with E09. Did any of you review the feed from after we left last night?"

Marlux shook his head. "Denali locked the feed as soon as the portal sealed behind you two last night. She reported that she is testing one of her product designs on E09's injuries. She said that until E09 is healed enough to be clothed, only she will have access to any feed concerning this particular subject. We are not even allowed the thought scan transcripts."

Lanyar nodded. "Until tech can track down how Gundar ended up in there, I feel that is safest and agree with her assessment."

"Speaking of, Gilnax is meek as a baby lumfin right now. How long do you intend to allow E09 to deliberate?" Marlux asked.

"Since we are having a council meeting, whenever Denali arrives, we will discuss Gilnax after."

As if I had spoken her into being, Denali stormed into the room. She no longer looked pale, but she remained emotional. She did at least look slightly calmer.

I cast my gaze to Lanyar. "Did I not say?"

He blinked, clearly stunned at the visage before him. The man then ignored me and addressed his assistant. "Denali, what happened with E09—"

She slammed her hands on the table, interrupting him. "Her name is Keira!"

No one said a word. I didn't even twitch. Denali must have reached a critical conclusion that was possibly detrimental to the whole program.

Lanyar's brain clearly was not functioning at full capacity yet, because he completely missed the signal.

"She is Subject E09 until such point—"

Denali barked at him. "No! You do not speak this morning. None of you. *I will speak, and you will learn.* Afterward, Prince Vaxeehl, should you deem me in need of punishment for my behavior, I will submit. But until I am done, you will *keep your fucking mouths shut.* Am I understood?"

The severity of her emotional uproar, including human curses, struck all of us the same, even her supervisor. We merely nodded.

"I know that we have a specific protocol designed for our selection process. We have used the same protocol with small or moderate success on a few planets. Your brothers, my prince, have followed this same protocol on their own acquisitions, also with only small or moderate success. Do you agree?"

I nodded. "I agree."

She turned toward Lanyar. "You told me you studied this planet's history. You said that women have been treated much the same way throughout their history. Yes?"

He nodded.

"You said you had techs assigned to determine whether the lack of cross-color breeding was societal or genetic. Yes?"

He nodded again.

"Did you get an answer yet?"

He frowned. "No."

"Useless bastard. Him, not you. Although I am not happy with your data presentation either."

She tapped the table, opening a dialogue box. I noticed an upload sat ready.

"I would normally take the time to explain what I learned last night, but I am tired. I did not sleep. Could not even *consider* sleeping. Therefore, I am angry, I am tired, and I am disgusted with the male leadership of this planet, as well as the idiocy of our researchers missing something of this nature. Hands on the table. I am going to upload some very important information that we *all* needed to know before we ever grabbed the first Earth female, yet our researchers ignored...." Her voice trailed off, and she pursed her lips, clearly struggling to contain an emotional tirade of monumental proportions.

This made me curious enough that I absolutely had to know what Denali had learned from her brief conversation with the human that had led to such a reaction.

I rested my hand on the table.

The other men followed suit, albeit at a much slower pace. I did not blame them. As Lanyar had said, Denali survived the virus, she fought with the best of my warriors, she treated their wounds after battle, and she helped calm the fatally injured as death welcomed them home. She did it all without ever losing control of her emotions. If she felt so strongly affected by what she had learned, I dreaded my own reaction.

She tapped the image, and data and graphics flowed into our brains. The sheer volume of information caused my head to throb. I reached my other hand to my temple and pushed, trying to sublimate the stress. Then it all began to unfold in my sight.

I slammed my eyes closed as the images played, speeding through like lightning. Flashes of numbers compiled in my thoughts. When the upload finally finished, the playback started over, slightly slower to allow our minds to process it all.

I gasped. I heard both Marlux and Lanyar vomit. I swallowed several times, trying to keep my own nutrition in place. The horrors, the atrocities, the sheer quantity of wasted lives, tattooed numbers… and the experiments. Great Helvana, the things this species has done to each other based on pigmentation and religion… I would have nightmares of this myself, and I did not live on that planet.

"May Helvana forgive us," I choked out.

I lifted my eyes to Denali. Her tears flowed unchecked. I realized just as quickly that I shed my own for this species.

I nodded to her and spoke softly. "Go rest, my warrior. We will reconvene tonight after you have rested, and we have had time to understand what you have found."

She sniffled. "She *will* pass. I have no doubt."

And then my strong, unshakeable warrior and medical researcher quietly exited the conference room, leaving three men behind with equal shares of shame and dread filling their souls.

As the portal closed, I spoke just one sentence before dismissing them to their other duties. Or seclusion. I knew I would spend much time in meditation for Helvana's guidance. Surely, our goddess would view this a great failure.

"We have made a shameful mistake."

~*~

The room felt much subdued when we gathered later that night.

Marlux had arrived alone once again, although Taylana had been welcomed to the council after their union.

"I do not want her to learn of this ghastly information, my prince. She carries my young, and this would destroy her compassionate heart, putting our child at risk."

Lanyar had led his assistant with great gentleness. He feared, like the rest of us, that she might fall apart again. He also recognized that she had spoken true. I think it had awoken in him the latent protective dynamic.

Denali looked only barely rested. I imagine she had no dreams, only nightmares to greet her every time she closed her eyes. I had removed the upload as soon as I returned to my quarters, but many traces of it remained. She had not learned through an upload, though. She had learned through research. She could not remove any of the information from her mind.

I requested tea delivered and then dispersed it to everyone. Once I had returned to my seat, I reached across the space and grabbed Denali's hand.

"As your prince and commander, I am *ordering* you to make use of one of your own experiments tonight. When you return to your quarters, you will grab a dosage of that dream blocker you have been working on."

She locked her eyes to mine just briefly before nodding. Her fingers squeezed before releasing, and I knew she would come through this.

Her voice sounded stronger, yet she still spoke with calm deliberation, like she had to consciously maintain her control or risk succumbing to her emotions again.

"The remaining eight women must be returned to Earth. We need to design an entirely different protocol if we are to have any chance of real success."

Marlux agreed. "Without question. Where do we start?"

I gazed at Denali.

She met my eyes fearlessly, not blinking, her head held high with confidence.

I spoke. "You said 'the remaining eight women'. We have nine currently in holding."

She gave a single firm nod and returned to her tense posture. "I did. We are keeping Keira. She will be ready to test within three days; the cream is working exceptionally well with her physiology. Although, I would argue that the collective is nothing more than a formality at this point, and you all know it. Once she has passed, I want her on the council. I want Keira in here to help us design our Earth-specific protocol."

She paused to open a screen on the projection where she had already started detailing items.

"I am honestly amazed that we only had one of the ten who completely lost her mental function. After I returned to my quarters, I could only sleep in fits, so I checked E04's history. She is directly descended from survivors of that *camp*." She spit the final word with ferocity. "To awaken in a strange place, and then to be assigned a number... it was all too much for that poor woman. I took the liberty of finding her and transferring her closer to her own people. I planted a memory of her travelling there on her own so that she did not suffer any further. I can only hope this makes up for the horror she felt from our actions."

"Thank you for correcting our error," I said softly.

"I spoke with Keira very briefly this morning when I evaluated her response to the cream. I could not understand how she could possibly agree to allowing me to test an untried product on her. Not after—" She paused, swallowing hard. Then she continued. "Apparently, she had two reasons.

"The first was simply because I let her choose. She explained to me that the freedom to make certain choices has led to a great many civil wars. I believe her. I have no more room in my head for such horror and refuse to research deeper."

I heard her stifle a sniffle. I never wanted to see this strong woman cry again.

"Her second reason, unfortunately, is the same reason we have taken any of the women lately. She said that in the long run, she did not matter. She had no one to notice her absence. She had no one on Earth, on an entire planet with a population of eight billion, who cared whether she lived or died. To her own government, she is nothing more than a number and a source of tax currency. At least here, with us, she felt wanted, even if she did not know why."

Lanyar swore. "Great Helvana, we will never get enough females at this rate. How many other historical events did we dismiss on other planets that caused unnecessary failures?"

I shifted my eyes from face to face. I saw no opposition, only guilt at having missed such a momentous detail.

"Lanyar, finish the last details for the collective. Marlux, I know your wife has demanded that she be allowed to participate with E0—Keira's trial. I would meet with her and the other Borkanian woman, Reganda, to discuss this. Denali, begin the process of returning the remaining eight women to their homes. If you can, find better homes for them, as you did with the first release. It could be possible that they end up back with us after revisions, but we are not going to hold any of them at this time. I am going to contact my brothers and see if their researchers have made the same mistakes. We have visited more than fifteen planets between us. It is time to stop until we can fix this issue."

~*~

Chapter 13

Keira

The morning after the attack, I had not moved a muscle until Denali returned. She told me in no uncertain terms that only she would view my feed until she declared otherwise, and I finally relaxed a bit. Her voice held so much anger, I almost feared her touch would reflect it. Yet her hands remained extremely gentle as she completed her scans, took a blood sample, and then applied another thick coat of cream.

She instructed me to wait half an hour before standing to give the cream time to soak into my skin. Then I should move about as freely as I desired until she returned to apply another layer before I slept.

She also tried to speak about what she had learned. Instead, I had stopped her and told her that I could see she understood. I could see how the information haunted her. She had not spoken further about the specifics, but she acknowledged that she had found my vecmāmiņa, my adopted grandmother's name on one of the camp registries from directly before she moved to the United States with my soldier grandfather.

I think I broke the beautiful giant.

Once she left, I waited an hour just to make sure. Then I stood and began my exercises. I made it through part of the martial arts and most of the yoga, but I skipped my push-ups, sit-ups, and kickboxing, feeling the skin stretch too tight across the injuries. A few days to heal would not cause me to lose any muscle mass or ability. As long as I could still manage some of the routine, I would be fine.

On the third day, after Denali applied only a thin layer of the cream, she finally declared me healed enough to handle clothing. She even took the time to explain how the wrap did not just circle back around. It crossed, twisted, and looped back like a chain link fence before coming forward under the arms. Then she lifted her silver hair and turned her back to me so that I could see it.

Before I could ask, she explained. "All females, or their mated male, assist each other with dressing. It is common on Volitar to wear the same wraps for several days unless you exert yourself or get dirty. And if you work a job where filth is common, a suit is provided, much like your Earth hazmat suits, although much less bulky."

Throughout this time, Taylana had not visited, either. Of everything, this saddened me the most. Denali had told me that my companion had other duties this week and would not be available, even for just a few minutes. She also assured me that this was not meant as any kind of punishment. She understood that I likely still felt that way, although this was not their intention. Just that the timing on my perceived exile fell horribly in line with something else of great importance.

Her explanation helped, but it did not take away all of the sadness.

I spent my silent evenings finishing the work on my wrap. It had taken a lot of careful stitching and color selection, but when I held it aloft, I felt great satisfaction at the work I'd done. There, on my own personal wrap, I had crafted a phoenix rising from its ashes on what would be my right hip. Over the rest, I had managed a particularly unusual interlocking thorny vine set in mostly deep blues. I tucked it safely into my box, unsure when I would chance wearing it. I ached to be able to see Taylana's eyes when I could finally show her what I had done from her lessons.

Denali returned one more morning for a final round of scans and blood. As she removed the device from my arm and peered at the screen, she smiled.

"I see no changes to your base physiology, and the results are fantastic. The visible discoloration is greatly reduced, although I believe it will take another week to fade completely. You have reported no lingering pain. It will need further testing to make sure the results are not a fluke, but between you and me, I hope I never have reason to find out."

I smiled. Then I did something very unusual for me. I reached out and pulled the nearly seven-foot tall, sexy as sin, soft purple-skinned, silver-haired Amazon woman into a hug.

She hesitated briefly before circling her long arms around me and drawing me against her. She held me tight for several minutes.

Finally, we parted. Denali stepped to the door. Then she looked back over her shoulder with a mysterious smile.

"I will see you again. Very soon."

The portal closed behind her, and I sat down at the table.

"That wasn't cryptic at all, now was it?"

~*~

I heard water running. Real water. Like a stream or a river. I opened my eyes. Then I closed them, rubbed them, and opened them again. I lay under a tree. I'd never seen a blue tree before, but it was still a tree. I extended one hand, softly resting it upon the bark, or what I assumed to be bark. The smooth texture and slight peeling made me think of a birch tree.

I pushed myself upright and looked around. Trees of various shades of blue and orange grew in tight clusters, leaving very little space to pass among them. From the branches of some, I noticed masses dangling that reminded me of the fruit item from my daily rations.

The light in the area appeared similar to a sunrise, but the totality of it made me think of how my room lit without a light source.

I shifted my gaze to the ground. Red grass—no—moss. Or maybe some kind of moss-grass hybrid. I ran my fingers across the ground, letting the tiny blades tickle my skin. Then I leaned my face down to the soil and drew in a deep breath. It smelled just like the woods on Earth. It let me imagine that most places in the universe had that smell.

I found a small pack bundled beside me. Inside held three large pieces of that filling dried meat, a decent-sized water skin, and my blade tucked inside a gleaming sheath on a chain.

I pulled the blade out and studied the sheath first. It had no locking mechanism, yet the weapon did not slide out without intent. I even shook it upside down and smacked it against a tree. The blade remained firm.

Then I studied the chain. Beautifully crafted, it appeared the perfect length to circle my waist with no excess. It also looked more fragile than it truly was. I hooked the clasp and pressed it beneath my foot. Then I pulled as hard as I could, trying to damage any part of it. It held strong. Satisfied, I fastened it in place.

I stared at the pack a moment before breaking the pieces of meat into easily handled strips. This would allow me to eat while moving. Then I packed all but one piece away. That bit, I nibbled. I lifted the water skin and realized it felt light. I opened it and tipped it up for a drink. It contained only a few swallows of liquid. I closed the skin and returned it to the pack. Then I threaded the draw string under the chain and tied it securely.

I studied as far as I could see in either direction. By sight, everything looked similar. I saw five possible trails that all led through lots of those powder blue trees. The foliage stood so thick that I could not see through the top.

So, I closed my eyes and listened. I had heard water as I woke, and I needed to fill the skin. I had no idea how long I would be in this new location. Judging by the amount of food in the pack, it could be days. I needed water more than I needed food.

There. I found it. I turned toward the direction of the softly moving liquid and started walking. I reached the stream after about twenty minutes of careful steps. I did not want to move too quickly and perhaps startle some form of wildlife that I could not recognize. Instead, I moved my feet cautiously, my eyes sweeping from side to side before each step, my ears continuously listening for the water to make sure I stayed on track.

I cupped one hand in the stream, testing first the feel of it, and then lifting a small amount to my tongue. It wasn't just cool, it was absolutely frigid, like a mountain stream in Colorado fed by melting snow. It had no unusual taste to it that I could recognize. I took a large mouthful, swishing it around a few times before swallowing.

Then I waited.

I waited nearly an hour to see if my body reacted to anything in the clear stream. When I felt I had waited long enough, I forced myself to wait just a little bit longer. Finally, I filled the skin, drank enough to quench my thirst, and filled it again.

I walked a few steps into the stream, testing the water depth. I could cross it if I needed, but I would risk hypothermia in the process. I quickly climbed back onto the bank, rubbing my legs and feet to ward off the chill. I decided I would follow along the bank until I found either a bridge of some sort, or some other trail.

I stared at the water flow, casting my eyes for a short time in the upstream direction while I thought back to my days hunting with my dad. I was an only child born to an only child, who had been adopted by a Holocaust survivor. Because of what my grandmother had survived before moving to America and meeting my grandfather, Dad and Grandpa had made absolutely certain I could survive without relying on government handouts, even if that meant I ate squirrel and snake. I turned around and started following the current.

The stream began to narrow about half a mile down. I also found another trail at the same time, steering away from the water. I stood there, staring back and forth between the other bank and the trail for several minutes.

The decision ended up made for me when I heard a blood-curdling scream. I raced along the bank, hunting for the source. It echoed across the water again. Then I saw her. The young woman who had dressed me almost every day for well over a month cowered against a boulder on the other bank. Growling at her, teeth bared and huge claws glistening in the light, stood an animal that terrified me on sight.

It looked like a horrible science experiment gone wrong, like a hybrid cross between a wolverine, a Komodo dragon, and an angler fish, and stood as high as a pony. Its wolverine-like head looked soft, yet the mouth extended much further, almost bulging from its skull. The lips lay peeled back, exposing a massive row of astonishingly long, pointy teeth in varying sizes. The scale-covered body meant it would be profoundly difficult to injure, despite the patches of wiry hair sticking out at odd angles.

It reared back on its hind legs for just a moment, the front extended like a bear, displaying almost talon-like claws. But it also exposed a very fur-covered underbelly. I saw no scales in that area.

I needed to get closer. I had to make it rear back if I had any hope of defeating the creature. Between the talons and the teeth, however, I held little hope of actually killing it, more likely to get mauled in the process. Yet, that beautiful girl, while we had not actually spoken, I had become comfortable with her. She had served me faithfully and without malice for the entirety of my captivity. I couldn't just leave her to her own fate.

I gritted my teeth and took my first step into the icy cold water.

With the narrowing of the stream, the current had strengthened, as well as deepened. I would have to swim, rather than just walk across as originally planned. I gritted my teeth against the biting cold and jumped forward at an angle, letting the current carry me. I would have to back track a bit to return to the girl, but it was safer to let the water help me.

My muscles ached by the time I could touch dirt again. The cold had sapped some of my strength. I could hear my teeth chattering, but I forced myself to stand. I started walking carefully, my footsteps sure, but as soft as I could make them. I needed the creature to not hear me.

As I closed in, I could see just how small the spaces between the scales grew. The hairs barely had room to slither between them.

The girl spotted me as I approached. Unfortunately, when her eyes shifted, the creature noticed. It spun around, peeling its lips even further back, growling loud and angry. As soon as its attention shifted to me, the girl tried to move, but it spun back to her again.

I thought quickly. I reached to my hip, ready to wield the dagger as best as I could. Instead of my blade, however, my hand landed on the pack. My pack full of meat. My gaze jumped quickly between the beast and the meat pack while my brain calculated the risk versus reward. It was worth a shot.

I kept my voice as gentle as I could. "I don't know if you can understand me, ma'am, but I am going to try to distract this… thing. If it works, move slowly in my direction." I met her eyes but saw no recognition. I just had to hope she could think like me.

I pulled out a small strip of meat and held it up, showing it to the large, almost black eyes. The snarling stopped. It tipped its head to one side, seeming to evaluate whether I teased it. Not wanting the thing to charge me, I tossed it gently, like I would a treat to a dog.

The maw opened wide and snatched the dried meat from the air, gulping it down with no hesitation. A lizard-like tongue licked out, wiping every crumb from each miniature sword in its mouth.

I reached into the pack and grabbed another small piece with one hand, signaling the woman to come toward me with the other as I tossed the meat forward.

Again, the creature snatched it out of the air with laser precision. The girl crept slowly, one careful step at a time, giving the animal a wide berth.

The eyes shifted toward her again, and she froze.

"Hey! Over here, ugly!" I yelled at the creature, waving another piece in the air. I'd fed it nearly a day's rations already; I hoped we would not be in this collective too long.

It whipped its head back toward me again. The confusion on its face disturbed me. It actually looked offended that I had called it ugly, yet it wanted the meat.

I blinked several times, taking in the odd expression. Then I reminded myself that I did not walk in an Earth forest here. This was alien to me, as was everything in it. The chances that this creature could understand my words... I couldn't even attempt to calculate them.

I went with my gut. I tore a smaller section from the large piece in my hand and tossed it softly toward the gaping, frightening teeth.

"You didn't like me saying you were ugly, did you?"

It seemed to consider me as it chewed my latest offering.

I moved one step closer, prepping another section. "If you let the woman come to me unharmed, I'll give you the rest of this." I held up both hands, showing the larger pieces I held.

Shocking the both of us, the creature yipped like a dog, then sat firmly on its haunches, its tail thumping.

"Are you freaking kidding me," I asked aloud.

I looked to the girl, her face showing the same confusion as mine. Instead of waiting for her to come to me, I carefully crossed the distance. I handed her one of the meat slabs. Then I walked close to the animal, close enough that it could likely kill me in a single swipe or bite. I held out the offering, my palm open.

I trembled with adrenalin. This was probably one of the stupidest ideas I'd ever had, but I knew I could not judge this place like I would my home planet.

As gentle as a butterfly, that tongue slid across my skin, carefully taking the food and leaving me unscathed.

Acting on impulse again, I allowed my hand to inch closer and closer until I could stretch my fingers and touch under the jaw. This put me only slightly bent at the waist due to the creature's height.

Those dark, piercing eyes closed, and I felt a rumble.

The woman behind me finally spoke. "It hums?"

I kept scratching and looked back at where she stood statue still behind me. "What?"

She repeated herself, pointing at the animal. "It hums!"

The words in my brain said, 'It hums.' But the way her lips moved looked more like she'd said 'Bobo fay."

I blinked, thinking I might be hallucinating. "Repeat that one more time for me. I want to make sure I heard you correctly."

She locked her gaze to me, and I watched her lips move. The motions very clearly said 'bobo fay,' and I could hear just the slightest whisper of that in my ears. Then my brain shifted the sounds to clearly tell me, "It hums."

Interesting development.

I set aside that thought for now and just nodded. "I think it was just hungry. An animal's nature is to find the easiest food source to reserve as much energy as possible. It will always seek the least fight for the most food. This…" I glanced at the creature. With my hand so close to its teeth, I did not want to offend it again. "This particular animal is clearly either a carnivore or omnivore. It also seems to understand me, though I refuse to spend too much time thinking about *that* right now."

I pointed toward the meat in her hand. "Come here slowly and hold out your hand. It needs to see that we are not a threat. Once its belly is full enough, I have a feeling it might leave us alone."

She crept forward, all six of her hands shaking.

"I'm Keira," I said as she stepped to my side.

I caught her acknowledgement as she slowly opened her hand toward the animal. "I am called Reganda."

She giggled as that tongue slid across her palm. "It tickles." Then she reached above the animal, carefully stroking its head.

It actually arched upwards, showing signs of thoroughly enjoying the attention.

I leaned over, meeting its gaze, and could have sworn the thing smiled at me. I laughed. "You're not wild at all, are you?"

That tongue shot out and licked from my neck all the way to my forehead.

I closed my eyes, feeling sliminess spread. And probably a couple pieces of food remnants. I sighed. "Listen here, you," I spoke sternly. "No face licking. That's just gross."

I swear the thing pouted.

I shook my head and stood to my full height again, turning toward my new companion. "Seeing as we can understand each other—and I have no idea how that happened because we are clearly speaking different languages, yet hearing our own—anyhow, seeing as we can understand each other, how about we do some walking and talking at the same time."

She agreed, wiping the slobber from her hand onto her waist wrap. I noticed then that she did not have a pack, a weapon... she only had her clothing. On her clothing, though, I recognized the pattern stitched on her top. It matched my own back in my holding cell. Hers hung larger on her torso, covering what looked like four breasts.

I gave the creature one last pat on the head. "Alright, buddy. We're going to head out on our own now. Do you think you've had enough to eat to leave us alone for a while?"

It yipped excitedly. I took that as a 'yes.'

We turned away from the animal, looking around. "I have no idea which way to go." I glanced to the woman to my left.

She pointed back toward where she had met the beast. "I came from the woods that way. I heard the water."

I nodded. "Same here, but on the other side of the stream. Have you need of a drink? I notice you have no supplies."

She frowned and hung her head. "I had a pack. When the beast startled me, I dropped it. I think it went into the river."

I opened my pack and pulled out my water skin and a piece of meat, handing them both to her. "Here. We need to keep our strength up."

While she ate, I explained my original tactic. "My grandfather taught me to hunt. He also taught me that if ever I found myself lost in the woods, my first task was always to find water." I pointed at the stream. "Once I found it, follow it. I was heading down stream. That way, if I needed to refill the skin, I could make sure the water was not fouled."

She furrowed her brow at me. "How do you know if the water is fouled?"

I pointed into the stream. "Where I first came out of the woods, I tested a swallow to make sure it would not make me sick. I don't have a purification kit, but I had the choice to take the risk or get dehydrated. Dehydration is a horrible way to die. It's been about two hours now, and I have still not had a reaction, so I'm guessing the water is safe. As long as we don't see a dead animal laying in the water, it should still be safe to consume. If we do find a dead animal, or dead body of any kind, we must fill the skin upstream before we pass it. After we pass, we do not dare drink from the stream again for at least fifty yards. Personally, I'd rather go at least a few miles. It just gives me the willies."

I kept the river to my right and Reganda to my left. We both kept our steps cautious, watching for other life forms.

We'd travelled another hour at least before stopping to drink more water and refill the skin. As I leaned cautiously over the stream, I heard a twig snap. My head whipped toward the noise, then I laughed.

I pointed and spoke to my companion. "We have a new friend, Reganda."

The skin full, I tightened the lid again and stood, signaling to the creature we thought we'd left behind. "Alright, you big bully. Come on over here. If you're going to travel with us, I'd rather you did it without sneaking. That's just creepy."

I heard the tail thump briefly before it joined us.

I shook my head. "Well, my friend, what are you? Boy or girl?"

The strange amalgamation flopped onto its back, showing us the soft underbelly. And proudly displaying that it was, by my knowledge of Earth biology at least, very much a boy.

Reganda laughed outright. "He truly does understand you. How strange. There are no animals like this on my home planet."

We both knelt down and gave the happy boy a belly rub. I gazed at him sternly, saying, "You are no different than the males on Earth, are you? Think you can just display your goods and have all the women in the area fawning over you?" I patted one last time and stood, the burgundy woman following my lead.

"Alright, boy," I said. "Do you have any idea where we are supposed to head next?"

He bounded and yipped like a puppy. It made me laugh. Still, rather than leading us in any direction, he seated himself at my side. Directly at my side. The heat from his body radiated outward with his hum, entering my skin and finally chasing away the chill from my water crossing. I dug a piece of meat from the pack and gave it to him.

"Thank you. I needed that." I turned to Reganda. "Let's keep going."

So we set out, continuing to follow the stream. A human female carrying an exquisitely crafted blade, a burgundy skinned woman who reminded me of one of the Hindu goddesses, and one of the strangest looking puppies I'd ever seen in my life. Whoever watched us must be having the laugh of their lives at this ragtag pack I'd managed to form.

~*~

Chapter 14

Vaxeehl

We all stared at the screen, anxiety filling the council chamber from each and every one of us. We desperately needed Keira's input to design a new protocol if we wished to gather any women from her planet, yes. However, this collective had become even more important than our own success. This female held each of us in some form of thrall.

For Taylana, she had become a friend. The Borkanian woman still harbored anger that I had not let her be in the collective with Keira, but she had relented when Reganda stepped forward. Reganda had been the young woman I had questioned during the mating ritual, the one who had first recognized Taylana as her matron. She had also been the first to volunteer for assisting with the new acquisitions. She was proving herself a bold creature, willing to step up to be the first for many new experiences.

Lanyar sat weighted with guilt still. He had confronted his researchers. Because the deaths had been aimed at a general population, they had ignored these major events in Earth history, much to our detriment. My chief medical officer had reassured me that they would never make that mistake again. He wanted Keira to succeed so that he could fix the program. He also wanted to offer some sort of apology, despite Denali's assurances the woman would find them unnecessary.

Denali sat more confident than any of us that Keira would surpass our expectations. She had formed a strong bond with the human during their few days of interaction, a bond that seemed stronger than even her own brother shared with her. She had not bonded with any of the hundreds of women we had collected, despite spending such lengths of time helping them assimilate. This human, though, captured my warrior's loyalty.

Marlux wanted to right our wrongs, but mostly, he just wanted his wife happy. She had been upset at not being allowed to speak to her friend for nearly a week already, and she had made her anger known. The captain of the guard had whispered to me that if the human woman did not pass, he was likely to need a secondary sleeping quarters, as his wife had not allowed him in his own since the attack.

For my own concerns, I still felt drawn to this human. I had fought the obsession many times, but I failed just as often. However, I found I did not want to read her thoughts on a screen anymore. I wanted her to communicate directly with me. I wanted to stop scanning her mind and have her soft voice tell me what she wanted me to know.

I wanted her children to be my heirs.

I sat forward when she dove into the water.

Lanyar swore. "What is she doing? Her body temperature will drop too quickly. She recognized that on her own when she filled her waterskin."

Denali raised her chin and smiled. "She is not thinking of herself at this moment. She is thinking of the strange female on the other side of the water, facing a snarling creature she has never seen before."

Marlux laughed. "Snarling, my ass. I don't know why you insisted on bringing those hideous creatures. They are great for battle when properly trained, but are seldom of use on the ship. That one in particular shows signs of attack when they are trained to defend."

I glanced to my chief medical officer. He shot me a quick wink. He knew I had instructed the slognip to feign viciousness, and he kept that news from the rest of the council.

I smiled as I watched the slognip drag his tongue up her face. "Right there is why. The woman first assumed it to be a feral beast, yet she did not attack. She earned his trust and now has a devoted protector."

Lanyar scrolled through some stats. "Her body temperature is still dropping, despite the activity. Why did we not include a blanket with her supplies?"

"It would have served no purpose," Marlux replied. "She is not to be in the collective longer than one day."

I waited and watched. I could see her shivers, watch her rub her arms occasionally for warmth. When the slognip sat against her and started humming, and the readings showed her temperature increasing to a safe range again, I released a breath I hadn't even realized I held. "I think our battle mounts have kept a great secret from us all these years."

Taylana tapped the screen and played back part of the feed, highlighting the thought scans. She pointed to the set of scans regarding the language barrier. "I think we have also proven true that Keira is intuitive as suspected." Another tap and the feed returned to its real-time location.

The small troupe neared the clearing. They spoke softly, Reganda telling Keira of her life before being taken. Thankfully, the woman kept the knowledge of exactly why they'd been taken to herself.

"So, you are hopeful you can find a mate among our captors," the human asked.

The woman nodded as she knelt to inspect a bush. "They are a very beautiful species, even if they only have two arms. They are larger than the men at home by half a head. Very trim, very muscular. Tell me you have not ignored that fact."

Keira snorted. "How could anyone ignore the sheer size of these goliaths? Even you are taller than most people on my planet. But how one appears is not as important as how one behaves." She pointed to her back. "I have not had the best experiences so far in my few direct interactions. They have been too impersonal, too scientific."

Reganda agreed. "Still, it gives me more hope than I had at home. I had surpassed my opportunities. My only purpose remained as a nurse for someone else's young." She raised her eyes. "I would rather raise my own, have them learn important things like your survival skills. I would be honored to have my young learn from one such as you."

Keira frowned. "Even if it means becoming a slave to your potential mate?"

The Borkanian woman stood, pressing all six of her hands to the human. A faint glow began, much like the mating ritual, yet subdued in its intensity.

"A true mate will never treat our kind like a slave. Our touch allows us to see deep within the being of another. It leads us to find the one who is destined solely for us. When our two souls collide, the magic reveals our potential futures to them. If they would have that future, they must actively choose it, choose us. In exchange for that choice, they gain a touch of our gift, and we gain their protection. Any who would choose to harm us, to take us against our will, would receive horrors in their minds."

I saw a tear slide down the pale woman's face. Her expression reminded me of Marlux after the searching ritual. I wondered what the Borkanian magic had shown her.

She spoke, sounding emotional. "That is an amazing gift. Thank you for sharing a sample of it with me."

The red woman bowed slightly. "You have protected me. It is only honorable."

They continued on their path, so I turned from the screen and stared at the matron. "Did you plan this? Is this why you relented when she volunteered to take your place?" I frowned.

Taylana visibly bristled. "Sharing of our gift is always an equal exchange. It could not have happened by design. You told the secrets of the collective to neither me nor Reganda, only that it would be real rather than a joint upload. We could not know she would feel so strongly for Keira's actions."

I felt wrong-footed. "How will this affect the collective evaluation?"

Taylana studied the playback several times before she answered. "The link made was familial. I believe Reganda has adopted Keira as a sister. It will have given her a sense of belonging. Such is normally reserved for our mate's families. Reading the thought scans, Keira does not realize the totality of this link yet. She currently believes it was simply a demonstration; she does not understand how to access the gift for her own use yet. Not being Borkanian, she may never develop that ability. I do not believe this will affect your results."

Denali scoffed. "It has *no* bearing. It is little more than another unforeseen circumstance. *Everything* is different with this human," she reminded the room.

I thought on her statement for a while. Denali knew more about the humans than any of us, even though her personal research had only started a week ago. I had trusted her judgement thus far. We had removed a great portion of the collective testing already due to the revelations Denali had uncovered, as well as the attack.

Reganda had only known that she would meet up with the human woman. She had not known she would be cornered by a hungry slognip, nor that the creature offered her no true danger. She had no knowledge what setting we would use. Her own evaluation had been nothing more than an upload while she slept, with the thought scans providing us with results.

This time, we had dropped them in the middle of our onboard park. After learning of the human history, Lanyar had refused to risk damaging the tiny woman's mind. The only upload he felt willing to perform without her consent pertained to the languages so that the women could communicate.

Her observant and curious nature had already recognized that something had happened to her to allow her to exchange words with her companion. Instead of letting the strangeness rule her, she had determined it acceptable.

Had Keira attacked the slognip to protect the stranger, she would have been bitten. Slognips injected hallucinogenic venom, paralyzing their prey. It would not have killed her—he had been trained to restrain himself—but she would not have enjoyed the nightmares that would have flooded her mind with the venom. Had she drawn the blade before the meat, he would have assumed she aimed to injure the other woman and would have attacked her before she had the chance to strike.

Her scans, however, revealed that she knew she could not judge the creature based on visuals alone. She needed to see behavior. Exactly as she spoke regarding us, her captors. By befriending and feeding the animal, she had removed herself as a threat, allowing that not everything acted as it appeared.

Normally, we would have also included a situation requiring the subject to act without having time to think. This usually presented in some form of attack, be it from a random creature, or from images of some of the species we have fought in the past. This, especially, was done with an upload, as we had no wish to harm the subject; we only wished to determine how they would react. Keira had already demonstrated her ability to think fast and creatively, even in battle, when she had fought Gundar in her cell.

If we could gather one hundred women with abilities like her, I would consider this planet a great success.

Two tasks remained for Keira. She had to find a safe place to bed down for the night. At that point, the women would be transported out of the collective.

The final task, Keira would face alone. She had to give Gilnax her decision regarding his offering. Gilnax had always been a good soldier. His brother had made a tremendous error, and the honorable nature of the Vesper drove him to make his offer. While the human had lain in her cell, healing from her injuries, she had called on Gallatea to seek information about an Earth-specific culture. I had followed her path of investigation and realized this culture she sought shared much of the views of the Vesper. I felt secure she would make the right decision without influence from us.

I heard a scream. My eyes shot back to the projection.

Reganda had tripped over a rock and fallen in the water. The current pulled her downstream quickly.

Taylana gasped. "She will drown! Do something!"

Marlux barely stood before I shot out a hand. "Wait. Look!"

Keira had taken off running, the beast easily matching pace. As we watched, the slognip dipped his head, scooping the startled woman from her feet and onto his back. She quickly adjusted, holding to his neck. They thundered as a pair, gaining ground on the struggling female.

A large log crossed the stream about a foot above the waterline. Keira spotted it, her plan forming on the projection as fast as the thoughts crossed her mind. She leaned toward the beast's ears and whispered to him. The slognip huffed, clearly not liking her plan. As he turned toward the log, he reared back, dumping his rider. Then he clambered onto the fallen tree, digging his talons deeply into the wood. He stretched his head down, opening his mouth wide. The venom teeth folded back, keeping only the smallest of points for grabbing.

His teeth clamped onto the red woman's hand just before she slid beneath the current. She cried out in pain but did not struggle. One clawed foot at a time released and moved on the log, slowly reaching the safety of shore.

Keira stood ready, grabbing the other side of her weakened companion.

Lanyar flipped through several screens fast as lightning. "No signs of venom, but she is dangerously cold."

Denali smiled. "I've never seen it before. I knew it was possible, but I've only ever seen them in battle."

Marlux signaled his impatience. "Do I intervene?"

I glanced at Taylana. Tears shimmered in her eyes. "I give you my word, Tay."

One of the tears escaped, and she grabbed her husband's hand. "Sit, my love." Then she turned back to me, anger and promise in her gaze. "If you lie, I will destroy your heart."

Having seen two demonstrations of their strange gift, I did not doubt.

~*~

Chapter 15

Keira

I finished pulling my new friend back to the grass, thankful that her extra appendages did not make her too heavy to maneuver. Once she was fully away from the water, the beast released her hand from his jaw. Her normal burgundy pallor had a purplish tone now. I pressed my hand to her skin, feeling the cold emanating from her. Her eyes drifted closed.

I patted the ground with my other hand, fighting back the panic. "Alright, boy. Lay down here and snuggle up. She's freezing, and she needs warmed."

I picked up the arm my new 'pet' had clamped in his jaw, expecting to see a mangled stump from all of his teeth. I only found four tiny holes on either side. They bled freely, but not overly much. At least, not much based on human biology.

I raised my eyes back to the odd creature and asked, "Just how did you manage to only puncture four tiny holes on her arm with all of those monster teeth of yours?"

As if bored, he stretched his jaw into a large yawn. I watched as the large fangs that had scared me on first sight rose from a folded position. Then they folded back down as he snuffled his nose against Reganda's cheek.

He snorted at her chattering, dropping next to her with his belly exposed. I shifted the woman closer to his soft fur, practically draping her over him. I heard the soft hum and drew a deep breath, hoping his heat would be enough.

I gazed at the blood flow again. "I need some moss. Or something like the moss on Earth." I tucked her hand close to the fur, trying to get as much warmth into her body as I could. Then I stood. "I'm going over into those trees a few feet to see if I can find what I need. You will protect her?"

He answered with a puff of air through his snout. I got the distinct impression that he felt I had insulted him by asking.

I rubbed his head quickly before scrambling toward the trees. Just a few feet inside the foliage, I found what I wanted. That soft red moss had wound its way around the trunk of one of the blue trees. I carefully yet quickly pulled a large clump from the bark and rushed back to where my companions lay. The beast had shifted so that Reganda now lay fully on the ground again, cradled against him.

I extended the moss toward the beast. "What do you think? I'm not exactly from around here, so I'm not sure what is safe."

He sniffed it a couple of times before resting his head across Reganda's chest, humming louder.

"I'll take that as approval." I kept speaking while I worked, peeling the moss into a network of vegetation I could wrap around the wounds. I didn't know if I was talking to myself, the creature, or my injured companion. "My dad loved learning. He had wanted me to go to college, but after the virus hit, education just felt a lot less important than survival. He used to watch all sorts of documentaries, especially on things like early medicine. In all sorts of so-called primitive societies, they use moss to wrap injuries. Apparently, it absorbs the blood like a bandage. I never paid close enough attention to get a grasp of what plants could be used for medicine, and I doubt the knowledge would serve me here, but I at least know how to wrap a wound to slow the bleeding."

I tucked the ends of the moss together. Then I turned her arm over a couple of times. "Looks like it's working."

I flopped to the grass.

"I've had just about enough excitement for today. Don't you agree?"

The creature yawned wide.

I petted his head. "You did very good today, boy."

Reganda stirred. A small groan slid between her lips. I leaned closer, pressing my hand to her forehead again.

"You're warmer. Good. How do you feel?"

She licked her lips. "Cold. Tired." She forced her eyes open. "Are you well?"

I chuckled. "I'm just fine. You spent way more time in the water than I did. Our unusual friend, here, pulled you out, but he did bite you to do so. All I've done is order him around and wrap some moss on your arm."

"Good friend," she patted the head on her chest.

He huffed on her, ratcheting up his purr another notch.

"Mmmm," she moaned. "So warm. Ferocious on sight, friendly in action."

She fought another yawn.

I ran my hand over her hair, smoothing it away from her forehead. "Rest, my friends. You are too exhausted to continue any adventuring right now."

She struggled to stay awake a little longer. "Are we safe?"

I smiled down at her. "Between me and our little beast friend, I dare anything to come close. Now sleep, Reganda. You'll feel better in the morning."

As night fell around us, I listened for the noises of nature. The air seemed eerily still. I was used to the sounds of wildlife, even wolves howling. This unnatural silence bothered me.

Halfway through the night, the beast lifted himself from his position. He shook like a dog, making me chuckle.

I reached over, checking my friend again. She felt warmer than normal for a human. I hoped her kind simply ran a warmer base temperature than mine, hoped this was not a sign of a fever.

Our strange defender stepped next to me. I wrapped both arms around his neck, hugging him. "Thank you for saving her, friend." I leaned away and yawned.

He pushed me with his snout, almost knocking me over.

"Hey now. What's that all about?"

He pushed against me again, then shifted his head toward our sleeping companion, then back to me again.

"Are you telling me to sleep?"

He huffed, sounding almost like a sneeze.

"Are you going to stand guard over me, then?"

Another sneeze sound.

I stretched my muscles. They'd grown a bit stiff. Between swimming across an icy stream, miles of walking, charging along the bank, and the absolute emotional turmoil of the day, my body was exhausted, and I knew it. I didn't want to wake Reganda, not if she'd finally gotten warm enough for her sleep to be healing in nature. Neither of us had any idea how long this evaluation would last. She would need her strength.

As would I. I watched for a moment as the beast seated himself facing toward the trees. "Wake me if there is danger, boy." I laid down, resting my head on folded arms, and closed my eyes.

~*~

Soft light filtered through my eyelids, stirring me from my sleep. I felt fully rested. I heard no nature noises. More importantly, I no longer heard the gurgling of water nearby.

I grumbled to myself. "I'm getting really sick of shit changing while I sleep. It's disconcerting."

I forced my eyes open. I had been moved again, back into some sort of room. It did not look like my original room; it looked more… medical. I shot upright in a rush, my hand reaching for the blade at my hip. My fingers closed on open air.

"You are in no danger here."

The deep rumbling voice sounded familiar, although I couldn't remember hearing it speak my own language before. I closed my eyes only briefly, sorting through the faces in my mind, searching for the face that went with the voice. I had heard it fairly recently, I felt sure. *Fuck it*, I thought, not wanting to wait for my brain to awaken to full functionality. I opened my eyes again and turned toward the source of the sound.

The prince—Vaxeehl, my mind supplied—sat in a nearby chair. He looked relaxed, fully at ease. His silver hair draped over his lavender shoulders. My fingers twitched, wanting to find out if those strands felt as soft as they looked.

Stop that, I yelled at them internally. *Focus on gaining information, not Stockholming.*

"Where is my blade," I demanded.

He pointed to my right side. I glanced in that direction and saw the blade, sheath and chain, all laying neatly within reach.

I darted my eyes around the rest of the room. Me in the bed, the small table with my blade, and the chair holding the prince.

"Where is Reganda?"

"She is awaiting her turn to see you, as are a few others. You have one last task you must complete before I reunite you with your companions. Gilnax awaits your decision."

I frowned. I did not recognize the name, but I knew who he meant. "The big guy with the wings whom you slammed into my wall? His name is Gilnax?"

He nodded at me. "That is correct. Only the handful of guards who answered my summons know the nature of his brother's shame, and they will not speak of the event. The offer was not his to make, as the shame did not belong to Gilnax. However, once the offer has been made, it cannot be retracted."

I shoved the blanket off and turned, swinging my legs over.

The prince stood, his silver hair swinging with the motion. "Why do you move? You still need rest."

I scoffed loudly. "I will not address something of this magnitude sitting down like some invalid. I will look him in the eye when I speak to him." I looked down at the dirt stains on my legs. Then I lifted my hands, which still had dried flecks of blood on them. Red moss stained under my nails.

"Good lord, I look disgusting. Can I not have privacy to cleanse first?"

I met his eyes. They remained firmly golden.

"You will be cleaned and repaired after your final task. Then you will also learn. But this must take priority over your comfort." He bowed toward me. "I apologize."

I rolled my eyes and caught the hint of a smile on his beautiful face. I stood, steeling my resolve and preparing to face the strangest situation yet. And coming from the aspect of having been kidnapped by aliens, that was saying a lot.

"Let's do this."

"You must call him to come to you. Until your decision is made, he will answer to none other."

I counted to ten in my head. Twice. The oddities among the inhabitants upon this vessel would never cease to amaze and aggravate me. I drew a deep breath. "AI unit?"

"Good morning, Keira."

My eyes shot open, and I knew a huge smile graced my face. "Gallatea?"

The prince nodded. "Your AI goes where you go, Keira."

I felt suddenly much more cordial toward the large man standing so close.

"Gallatea, please instruct Gilnax to come to me. I assume you know where I am, since I have no idea."

"Opening portal."

I whispered through gritted teeth, "He's been waiting outside this whole time?"

Tiny nod.

"Wait, did I magically learn his language as well?"

Another quick nod, and another small smile. I suddenly wanted to smack that smile off his snide face.

The light faded, revealing the tall, winged creature. He stood rigid, his head still down.

I glanced toward the prince, but he said nothing. Great. On my own to run on instinct again. I cleared my throat as silently as I could. "Enter, Gilnax."

The man stepped forward, dropping to his knees as soon as he neared. Even his wings drooped with his apparent shame.

Still, something did not sit completely right in my head. I had questions that needed answers before I gave a ruling.

"You will look at my eyes while I speak to you, soldier." I kept my voice soft, yet undoubtedly firm.

I watched his wings tremble slightly as he slowly lifted his face and met my gaze. Dark chocolate, almost black in their intensity, he fought himself to maintain the contact. He bore more guilt than just familial shame. I could see it in those eyes.

I stared hard as I spoke. "I understand honor, Gilnax. And although my only remaining family died in the pandemic, I also understand familial honor. My grandmother had nothing left except her sense of honor by the time she escaped Hitler's death camp. Your shame goes deeper than familial honor. You will tell me, now, the true reason behind your offer."

The intensity of emotion flowing from his eyes to mine staggered me. The depth of contact grew with every breath, every blink. I thought he would remain silent until finally, at long last, my refusal to look away or speak won over his determination to hide his own shame. Tears tracked from his eyes as he parted his lips at last.

The words seemed forced from his mouth. "I saw Gundar watching the feeds of all of the subjects in 2B. He fixated on your daily routine. I should have reported him, but he swore he would stop watching."

I still did not look away. "How did he access the feeds? They were restricted."

"He found a small gap in the security program. He admitted using it to spy upon all of the prior prospectives, looking for the woman he wished to mate."

So, these aliens wished for mates. That meant my assumptions based on the word 'nesting' were likely true. However, I would ask those questions of the prince, rather than of the guard. I squared my shoulders, continuing my questions. "Why did you not report either the gap or your brother?"

"If I reported the gap, I would have needed reveal how I knew."

I watched another set of tears roll down his face. "And your brother was all you had left, correct? The virus took everyone else?"

Finally, he could bear my eyes no longer. He jerked his gaze away, looking down and to one side.

I reached down, lightly touching his cheek and turning him back to meet my eyes one last time. "He was all you had left."

"Yes, my lady. I did not protect you when I should have. My shame is my own, and for that reason, I made my offer."

I stood tall, moving my hand to rest atop his dark hair. "Your offer is accepted."

~*~

Part Three:
Helvana's Blessing

Chapter 16

Vaxeehl

As I relaxed my shoulders, I realized this Earth woman had me holding my breath more than any creature yet. She had picked up on the strangeness of the soldier's offer quickly and had gotten the admission out of him. She had used neither intimidation, nor force. Just her sheer will as she stared into his soul until he cracked. I made a mental note to pass on the information about the security gap, although I suspected that Denali's crew had already found it.

During his confession, though, Gilnax had mentioned the seeking of mates. I had expected Keira to display more anger, or any reaction. She had paused briefly, as if considering the words, yet she had not questioned further on that line. I wondered if she had missed the comment, or merely disregarded it.

I opened my mouth to dismiss the soldier, but the tiny creature beside me spoke again.

"Gilnax, you look as if you have not slept in days. I command you to return to your quarters. You will eat, you will rest, and you will report back to me no sooner than tomorrow. Today, I have things I must do and figure out." She nodded. "After that, we'll take it one day at a time."

The Vesper male rose to his full height, easily towering the tiny woman. Then he bowed to her. "As you wish, my lady." He turned in the manner of soldiers throughout the universe, sharply and with an efficiency of movement, and left the room.

Keira chuckled once the portal closed again. "At least he didn't call me 'mistress.' I don't think I could have kept a straight face if he had."

I shook my head. "You are a force to be reckoned. Are you ready for your next visitor? You have many, each awaiting their turn."

I signaled toward the wall where another portal now formed.

She groaned. "You promised I would be able to see Reganda—and bathe—after I dealt with Gilnax. If anyone other than Reganda—" She stopped when the wall faded, revealing a burgundy-skinned woman with a large man behind her.

Keira smiled at first, but as the new visitors came more into view, that expression faded. She squinted toward the woman now entering. She studied the features closely, seeming to make note of the differences. She spoke hesitantly. "You're not Reganda."

The woman shook her head. Then she smiled. "This is true. I am not Reganda, but I pulled rank as matron of our tribe."

Keira gasped. "Taylana? Is it really you?"

The Borkanian matron smiled. "I have missed you, my friend."

Without another word, Keira darted across the floor, wrapping her arms around the other woman, almost knocking her over. They would have fallen had Marlux not stood directly behind his wife.

As Taylana's arms closed around the pale woman, blinding white light exploded in the room. It lasted only a moment, not even long enough for me to shield my eyes. Just as quick as it had formed, it faded again, soaking into their skin. Both women staggered under the weight of the magic.

I rushed forward, catching Keira as she fell while Marlux swept his wife into his arms.

My captain stared at me with eyes wide. He voiced what I thought. "What in the name of Helvana was that?"

~*~

Marlux laid his wife on the bed while I sent for Reganda. The young woman had been a great source of information before; we both hoped she would be again. We also sent for Lanyar and Denali. This room would soon be crowded.

With the bed occupied, I sat in the chair, holding Keira gently on my lap. I looked down, realizing that her head hung awkwardly from how I had caught her. I carefully rearranged her body, settling her legs to one side and resting her head against my chest. The weight of it felt right.

The portal opened and all three summoned individuals entered. They stopped barely inside, staring at us.

"Get in here and seal that wall," Marlux barked at the gaping creatures.

I turned to Reganda. "We need to ask more about your Borkanian gifts. Something happened, and we have no idea what it was."

She frowned, taking in the condition of the other females within our proximity. "What has happened to my matron? And why do you hold my friend as an intimate?"

I growled softly. Then I called out to the AI. "Gallatea, show playback starting with Taylana's entrance to this room."

The section of wall normally reserved for the portal shimmered into an almost life-sized view screen. Even on the video feed, the light glowed bright enough to hurt our eyes.

Reganda gasped, "The legend." She walked close so that she could almost touch the projection. "Playback again, quarter speed."

As soon as the light swirled around the women and started settling into their skins, Reganda spun. "Quickly! We have no time to lose. We must get them to the Borkanian women's quarters immediately."

Gallatea's voice interrupted. *"Emergency message from the bridal guard."*

I authorized the connection. Marlux's second in command looked stunned. "Sir, I—" he stumbled over his words. "Something is happening with all of the women."

He swallowed before continuing. "There are orbs of light bouncing all over the room, sir. The women are shrieking and singing, some are dancing—"

Reganda stomped her foot. "We must go now!"

Marlux scooped his wife from the bed and commanded the portal to open directly to the women's quarters.

I grumbled under my breath. "I really don't like all of this surprise magic." Even so, I gathered Keira into my grasp again and followed my captain of the guard. I trusted the man to not put his wife and child at risk, and he still had not shared with us what he had seen or felt during the mating ritual. Nor even what it meant when a portion of their gift became shared with their mate upon completion.

By the time we traveled the short distance, the floor space had been transformed. The women had cleared their beds, shoving them against the walls in haphazard piles. They all gathered in two rows with a clear path to the center, bowing at our entrance. The glowing white orbs swirled overhead.

Reganda led us forward, instructing both of us to kneel, keeping the women in our arms. Her guidance put us facing each other, both of us with matching looks of confusion.

The woman guiding us stared at the floating orbs for a moment before crossing quickly to the entrance and pulling Denali forward into the group. I noticed as they neared that one of the orbs had settled over my warrior's head, circling slowly. Other orbs shifted as well, seeking out specific women. As each ball of glowing energy met with its apparently intended individual, a look of joy encompassed that woman as she joined us.

One by one, the lights brought the entire group together, seeming to guide them to a specific position. Reganda raised her hands high, letting the light caress her fingers. She nodded toward Denali, who did the same. The crowd copied.

Then they all knelt, and I felt dozens of hands touching me, saw more as they rested on Keira, Taylana, and Marlux.

A tingling current trickled through my skin where each hand touched. It gathered within me into a single stream, flowed through my skin where flesh touched, into Keira and beyond, circling through the entire comb. I leaned my head back, seeing a ball of power circle above me. I closed my eyes. The feeling of rightness was too strong for vision.

The current grew stronger and stronger, moving a tiny bit faster with each circuit as it swelled to new heights that made me question our ability to survive whatever this was. My muscles trembled with the force of its flow. It seemed to spark within the space between us, judging our worthiness.

Scenes flashed in my mind, much like an upload, but scenes of events not yet come to pass. I saw beautiful children, running and playing, much laughter and joy. I saw Reganda clinging to one of my brothers, her belly heavy with child. Marlux holding two toddlers, while his wife cradled an infant. Keira as she fed a pale purple baby girl, a light tan boy looking on in adoration. I saw great crowds of human women, even some children, staring in awe as they took their first steps on Volitar.

Then the current coalesced into a single stream before bursting bright and cascading upon the room in a soothing blanket. I opened my eyes. My chest seared and tingled, and then it pulsed with warmth.

I gazed down at the woman in my arms as she stirred to wakefulness. Her eyes fluttered like wings before opening, revealing the sparkling blue I had grown accustomed to seeing only on a screen. This close, I could see tiny flecks of a deep yellow near the center.

I knew the moment she realized I held her. Panic, fear of the unknown, slid into those eyes, narrowing the black centers to tiny pin pricks.

I raised from my kneeling position and gently eased her so that she could stand, not removing my hands completely until I knew she would not fall.

"There is legend told on Borkania," Taylana whispered as her husband raised her until she stood next to the human woman. "Legend of a great winged bird that flew from the mountain to the plain, searching for her home. Although, she had no mate, no nest, no family to care for or to care for her, she was known as the Great Unifier. She slowly gathered the misfits, others like herself, bringing them together in one place. Misfits of all kinds, all forms of life, joined together under the banner of the great bird. She gathered the unwanted from everywhere, accepting them to her heart as her own, asking for nothing in return."

The dark-skinned woman stared at the inner wrist of her top-most left hand, the fingers of her right gently caressing it. "One dark day, a clan of warriors appeared on the horizon. They did not recognize even those who were taken from their own clan; they only saw a group of many kinds, and they judged them unworthy of life. On the eve of battle, as the warriors grew restless, the Great Unifier gathered those she had rescued. She reminded them all that no matter how different each looked from another, they all stood united under her banner.

"The misfits defeated the approaching warriors, yet not without much loss among them. The Great Unifier had been injured. Her bright feathers had been ripped from her body during battle, blood draining from each papilla. As she lay dying, her chosen clan gathered around her, each pricking their finger and giving her a drop of their own blood to replace that which she had lost. As the last drop of blood touched the great bird, flames burst from her talons, engulfing her body.

"The remaining warriors lamented and cried out as the fire raged until, with a great explosion, ash rained down upon them and darkness fell. A small ember flared where the wounded bird once stood. In her place, they now saw a woman of astounding beauty, marks of flames aglow on her chest. She raised her arms, casting out orbs of light which settled over all those gathered, blessing them with a touch of her magic. She chose a queen to take her place, vowing she would return one day, when at last her mate had been found. Then she returned to her bird form and flew away toward the sun.

"Through many hundreds of years, a glimpse of her fiery feathers in the distance would cause great uproar among the people, hoping and praying that their queen had at last returned. Yet she never came. She had given us the gift of her magic that we might find our own mates, yet did not keep the magic for herself.

"Every Borkanian woman who has been cast out has prayed to the Great Unifier, begging the queen to collect us and give us her mark. Take us to a new home, a new future."

Taylana finally looked up and met Keira's eyes. She held up her wrist, displaying a mark that had not been there before. A perfectly round golden circle with two half circles facing outward on either side, a straight line extending from the center of the open halves. There, in the middle of the full circle lay a bird made of flame.

I noticed motion from everyone surrounding us. Each of the burgundy women extended one arm, displaying the same mark. I turned my head toward Denali, seeing her stare at her own wrist in shock.

She finally turned her attention toward me and gasped. Her eyes darted between me and Keira, back and forth.

I cast my eyes to Keira, seeing for the first time what held my warrior enraptured. Spanning the width of the human woman's chest displayed a large, glowing image. The colors glimmered with each breath she drew, the flames dancing across her flesh. The same bird that graced the wrists of the crowd now lay seared into her skin.

Her eyes did not meet mine, however. She, in turn, stared at my torso. I glanced down, seeing a matching mark upon myself.

My voice held awe. "Helvana's blessing."

Keira's hand reached toward me slowly, the very tip of a single finger dragging along the bright flames on my chest. "A Phoenix." When her finger crossed directly over my heart, I felt a gentle warmth flood my body.

I reached my own hand, tracing her 'feathers' carefully. Her eyes followed the motion, seeing her own flames dance and move with my touch and her breath. Like with her, when my finger touched over her heart, that warmth flowed again.

Her eyes shot up to mine.

Taylana's voice echoed through the room.

"The mate has been found! The queen has returned!"

Still, I gazed into her eyes. Those flecks of gold I had seen before now danced, just like the flames upon her chest. Her chest, where my hand remained.

I blinked, breaking whatever spell held us, and slowly removed my touch. "Forgive me," I spoke softly. "I did not gain permission to touch you so intimately."

As she lifted her hand from me, I felt its absence acutely, as if a part of me had stolen away.

She shook her head a moment, as if clearing away confusion. "I am… completely out of my depth right now. How… What…" She seemed unable to put her thoughts into words. Then she glanced at her hands. "I still have blood on my hands, and I yet await the promised explanations. But right now, I am very overwhelmed by this… whatever this is."

I couldn't help it. I laughed. Then I took her hand and raised it to my lips, pressing a light kiss to her knuckles. "You are not the only one."

I turned toward Taylana. "Are there any other mystical events I should anticipate, matron? We found no record of any of this in the history of your people."

The woman shrugged. "This I cannot answer, my king. Tales of the queen's return have long been told only as children's stories, entertainment to aid our young ones in pleasant dreams. None for many generations believed the legends true, no matter our prayers."

I shook my head. "My father is the king, Taylana."

She raised her chin in defiance. "The magic has spoken, sire. The mate of our queen is therefore our king, regardless of what you call yourself."

I sighed. I had the distinct feeling I would gain no ground on this argument. The Borkanians put much of their faith into their magic, at least with pairing.

I returned my attention to the woman who would be their queen, and my mate, if their magic speaks true. I felt desire flood through me, and I knew if I did not part from her, I would act on it. I found myself wondering if she saw the same images.

Yet, while I knew much of this woman, she knew very little of me. Her eyes showed her confusion and perhaps a bit of distrust.

I stepped back slightly, creating space between us to show her that I would not act. "I will leave you to be pampered by your new family, Keira. Denali will bring you to the council chambers later."

~*~

Chapter 17

Keira

My eyes felt drawn to watch until the portal sealed behind Vaxeehl and his men. Even after the wall closed, desire to follow engulfed me. I drew a deep breath and forced myself to look away, seeing a veritable sea of women with similar burgundy coloration. They still kneeled with their arms raised.

I turned to Taylana and whispered. "Why do they not move?"

"They wait for you, my queen."

I shook my head. "I have no idea what to do or say. How can I possibly be the queen of a people I never knew existed until so recently? How did I see flashes of a possible future with a man I just met? And how the hell did I end up with moving flames tattooed on my body?"

I stopped my own rambling, pressing my hands together and touching my nose to the tips as if in prayer. I drew a deep breath, and then another, centering myself. Just for good measure, I allowed one more breath before I finally raised my eyes to the room again.

"Please, ladies, rise. No one need kneel before me. I am just like you. I am merely another woman in the room."

I saw the sea of dark red around me, the serious volume of appendages, and I laughed. "Okay, maybe not *exactly* like you."

Tittering giggles echoed as bodies rose from their positions of genuflection.

I noticed the face rising directly before me. "Reganda!" I pulled her close, hugging tightly. Then I stepped back again. "Please, may I see your injury? I had absolutely no idea what I was doing, and I have to know if I hurt you worse."

My new friend raised her hand to show me, turning side to side. "Not a trace of injury, my queen. You did well. Once we were retrieved from the collective, only minor treatment needed done."

I rolled my eyes. "Please, you called me Keira yesterday."

She bowed slightly. "Of course, Queen Keira."

Taylana leaned over and spoke softly. "I would not argue, Queen Keira. The magic has named you. It would be disgraceful of us to address you differently."

I released a large sigh. "Okay. I accept. I have no idea what I am getting myself into, but I accept."

Reganda smiled. "Your things were delivered here this morning. Would you like to bathe and redress?"

I released a breath of relief. "Would I ever. Don't get me wrong, my friend, I happily accept that we now share a bond, but I hope I never have to wear your blood on my hands again."

Another figure stepped close, this one a shade of lilac. I recognized another new friend. Her face still echoed shock, but I could tell she fought to overcome it.

I took her hand in mine, admiring the gorgeous marking as it flickered on her inner wrist. "Denali, my friend. I see you have been honored by this magic as well."

"I am overwhelmed with the images I saw." She cleared her throat. "It has rejuvenated my hope for the survival of my home planet."

I hugged her to me, speaking in her ear. "Does this mean I finally get to learn why I was taken in the first place?"

She nodded. "It does. I will explain it while you prepare."

I turned my eyes to the room of waiting women once again. I felt the need to address them, yet I remained unsure what to say. "I look forward to learning all of your names over the days to come. Please, return to your normal routines for now."

Then I glanced at Taylana. "Show me where the hygiene unit is located. I am absolutely disgusting."

She laughed. "I will show you the hygiene unit. After that, we have a surprise for you."

"I don't think I can handle any more surprises," I spoke honestly. My mind already worked hard trying to sort through everything that had already happened.

Denali looped her arm with mine, leading me toward an open doorway on the other end of the room. "I think you will like this one."

~*~

Inside the other room, Reganda aided in removing my dirty wraps, casting them toward a familiar looking table. I recognized the circles for the hygiene unit and wasted no time. When I faced them again, expecting to be draped in another set of grey wraps, Taylana grabbed my hand, tugging me toward another archway.

"The surprise is in here."

I let her lead me. The sight that met my eyes made me giddy. Set into the floor before me lay either a small pool or a large tub. Either way, it was water.

"Oh, ladies, this is amazing!" I stepped forward, dipping my toes to test the temperature. I nearly moaned as warmth seeped through my body. I did not hesitate to walk down the few steps into the large basin and find a seat along one side.

I leaned my head back, letting the heat soak into every inch of me. "I have missed being able to soak in a bath. I love the efficiency of the hygiene protocol, but there is just no substitute to soaking in a tub of hot water for feeling both relaxed and clean in one swoop."

Denali knelt near my head. "We may not use water much for washing, as it really is inefficient, but Volitar has pools like this in every neighborhood. They are kept warm using something like Earth's geothermal system. They are difficult to build, so they are shared, the only restrictions being men and women may not bathe in the same pools publicly, and all must pass through the hygiene unit before entering the water."

I smiled. "Like the ancient Romans."

She tipped her head, studying me. "Did our researchers miss other information?"

I shook my head. "I will happily talk, Denali, but I refuse to stare at you upside down. Join me. All of you."

While my friends cleansed themselves, I dipped my head beneath, letting the heat warm my scalp. As I rose above again, I heard giggles. I wiped the water from my eyes and saw Taylana slowly lowering herself.

She pointed at my chest. "I have never seen flames dance under water before."

I looked down, seeing what she meant. It really was a sight to behold. The flames churned and swirled on their own, much like watching a log burn in a fire pit. Yet, the rocking of the water with each movement accentuated and exaggerated those leaps, making it look like writhing, fiery snakes beneath the surface.

Once the other ladies had settled in, I asked the one question I most desperately wanted answered.

"Alright, Denali. Talk. What was the purpose of taking me from Earth?"

~*~

My tears fell and joined the water of our shared bath as I listened to the devastation caused by Virus 442-C and how Vaxeehl and his brothers now searched the entire universe, trying to find life forms on another planet capable of reproducing with the variety of species on Volitar.

"This is not just a breeding program, like your thought scans have shown you believed a possibility. We are searching for life-mates. On Volitar, women are treated equally, yet they are also revered. Many life-mates only produce one or two young. We were already outnumbered by men before the virus wiped out so many of us."

I frowned. "Why so much secrecy? I understand the need for quarantine. I watched people die from the virus. Hell, I lost my own parents to that invisible killer. So, yes, I understand the quarantine. But why the secrecy? Why assign numbers?" I shivered at the memory.

Her face fell, showing her distress. "We did not realize the mental damage it could cause. We had not encountered a planet with a history so traumatic as yours. At least, our researchers did not mention anything. They have since been retrained about important historical events."

She dipped her head under briefly, continuing after she rose up. "Seclusion sickness can strike down even the most stalwart warriors. We will be aboard the ship for a long time yet to come. If those collected fail evaluation, and we have to return them to their home planet, we do not want to risk damaging their minds. The more they know, the more we have to erase and rewrite. It gets tricky."

Then she told me about the women who snapped and started killing. That was when they changed the collectives into uploads.

"So I really *did* magically learn new languages? Seriously? That is so cool!" I paused. "Wait, are you telling me that beautiful forest was constructed only in my mind?"

She shook her head. "No. After I learned what I did, we opted to have your collective be real. Even Lanyar, that stubborn ass, refused to risk damaging your mind. With the knowledge of what your kind has endured, he feared what your thoughts might create."

I smiled. "Good, that place was beautiful. I would love to see it again, now that I know I won't die there."

"I am sure Vaxeehl will gladly escort you for a walk in the park." Her eyes filled with mischief.

I blushed. "Stop that. This whole 'mate' business has my nerves bustling. Earth men are sometimes large enough to be scary in that department. Every man I've seen so far is at least a foot taller than the average I'm used to seeing. I'm a little terrified that his lower half will be just as proportionately larger."

Taylana grinned. "I cannot speak for an Earth woman's expectations, but if they are all designed like Marlux, the rest of the Borkanian women will be *extremely* happy when they find their mates."

We all burst out laughing at my admission and Taylana's rebuttal. I couldn't remember the last time I'd engaged in naughty girl talk. It felt good.

When we finally settled, I looked to Denali. "So, I'm going to go with my instinct again and say that I am called to the council chamber to discuss how to *safely* recruit more women from Earth?"

She smiled. "Taylana was right. She said you were intuitive." Her silver head bobbed. "Yes, we need help figuring out how to gather Earth women without damaging their minds. This planet has so much disastrous history, yet it also has the best genetic compatibility. Not to mention that our initial scans picked up so many that we could simply pluck from the surface that we could likely call the other two ships to handle overflow."

I thought about this for a while before standing and moving toward the steps. "Alright, Denali. Let's get dressed. We have a battle to plan."

The lilac woman froze. "You want war?"

I realized what I said. "Sorry. That's a human figure of speech. I mean that we have a plan to design."

As soon as both feet touched the last step removing me from the water, I felt that familiar gentle current course through my body. I glanced downward, seeing all of the water had evaporated. I shook my hair forward; it, too, was dry. I chuckled. "Ladies with extremely long or thick hair are going to absolutely *love* that feature. Although the ones with curly hair might have an issue if it gives them frizz."

Reganda approached with a slightly embroidered set of wraps. "I have seen your curious looks when I come to dress you, trying to figure out how we manage to place the wraps so securely over our numerous breasts and arms. Would you like to learn?"

I agreed without hesitation. Taylana stepped before us.

"Just so that you know, this will likely be the most difficult adjustment for any of the women we gather. It's not exactly public nudity, but—outside of a few nudists—Earth women sometimes have difficulty baring themselves in front of their husbands, let alone other women. We tend to be extremely hurtful, and easily swayed by media telling us we are all ugly. The fact that every woman onboard I have seen so far is absolutely gorgeous will feed those insecurities a bit."

Reganda guided my hands as we carefully wove the material.

Denali clicked the clasp on her own lower wrap. "Your women have suffered greatly for useless reasons. Much of your body variances are caused by the inequality of nutrition and medicine. These things are shared among our people without malice."

I snorted. "So you're telling me that not a single female on Volitar is heavy?"

She frowned. "I meant no such thing. Our genetics are so similar that it is almost as if we had originated from the same species. We have—or had, rather—the same variances in sizes as your own planet."

I smiled. "Good. Because I refuse to include discrimination of any kind in this plan."

I fastened the clasp on the lower wrap and laid my hand flat to pass over and check the fit. My fingertips tingled as they fluttered near her abdomen. A flash of light passed before my eyes. With it, I glimpsed an image similar to what I had seen during the magic that named me their queen. I jerked my hand back.

Taylana looked at me in confusion.

I pursed my lips and nodded toward her belly again. "I am running a hundred percent on intuition here, but may I?"

My friend did not speak, just nodded.

I rested my hand directly below her navel and closed my eyes, concentrating on the tingle. As the images flashed, I knew I smiled. Although I had never experienced anything like visions before, I felt in my heart that what this *magic* showed me would come to fruition.

I opened my eyes, feeling a few tears slide along my cheek. "Congratulations, my friend. What is your husband's name again?"

"Marlux. He is anxious for the first scan, and no one knows how well the genetics will mix in our babe."

"How common is multiple births among Borkanian?"

She gasped, her hand flying to her abdomen. "I suspected, but our magic has never let us confirm. It only hints through the mating vision... Is it true, my queen?"

Reganda answered my question, her smile huge. "Twin births are rare, but not unheard of. They are an omen of good fortune to our kind."

I bit my lips. Literally, bit them. My cheeks hurt from how much I smiled.

I turned to Denali. "How about among the varied people of Volitar?"

She signaled me to stand and turn so that she could dress me. "Not unheard of, but also not common."

"Okay, so the first thing we need to do is address that issue. If what I saw is true, there will be a multiple birth aboard this vessel. I want to know that everything will be ready." I paid little attention to the process of dressing, my mind racing about my friend's pregnancy.

Denali finished smoothing down my wrap, yet her hand remained. "How did you craft this design?"

I glanced down, realizing I had been dressed in the wraps I had sewn. I shrugged. "It just came to me. Why?"

"If Vaxeehl is awaiting any further sign that you are his mate, this is it." She traced her fingers over the careful knotwork. "I will let him tell you."

She stood, offering another cryptic smile.

I shook my head and grabbed her top wrap, carefully smoothing it into place. "I really hate not having all the information. But I'll wait. We have bigger fish to fry."

"What does fish have to do with gathering women both willing and capable of producing offspring?"

I laughed. "Another figure of speech. We'll have to work on those, seeing as we are looking at how to populate your planet with what is likely to be some heavily outspoken individuals."

I paused, the scope of my duties starting to sink in. The women likely to be recruited are all going to have some heavy emotional baggage. I would shelf that until we were in the council chambers. That topic definitely needed more attention than just this group.

Going back to our previous topic, I started tossing questions out. "Talk to me about your scanning tech. How soon and how often it can be performed? Do you have medical personnel present who are capable of handling a simple birth, let alone multiples? What about emergency situations? Do you have anything like a c-section?"

Denali frowned. "I cannot provide these answers. I work primarily in development and battle healing."

I nodded. "Alright then. Let's head to the war room. Of all the battle plans we need to layout, dealing with Taylana and Marlux's children takes top priority."

Chapter 18

Vaxeehl

Lanyar's eyes kept shifting to me. He would stare for a moment, then quickly turn his gaze away.

I could find no fault in his behavior, though, so I left him to it. I let my own mind play over the variety of planets and people we had approached, searching for other signs of failure in our methods.

I frowned. "You realize that thought scans are no longer enough for selecting our targets?"

He growled at me. "I have, sire. I have spent much of the last week doing my own research to correct this horrendous failure. Taylana and Denali are both correct, though. We need your human to assist us."

I hiked one eyebrow, but said nothing, at his naming Keira as *my* human.

He continued. "There are too many pitfalls to navigate on this planet. I have never seen such a torn history. If the science did not support that they stood the best chance of saving our people from extinction, I would suggest abandoning this place and searching elsewhere."

Marlux grunted. "Such talk is pointless. The failure was not on only your shoulders, Lanyar. The shame falls on all of us. Your assistant made great strides in correcting the damage done to the first group. We can only move forward." He paused. "We all want mates."

He turned his attention to me, pointing at my chest. "You know what this means, sire. Helvana herself has marked you to rule Volitar."

I frowned. "I will not challenge my father. The crown remains his until he decides differently, even if that means I must begin covering my upper body to avoid starting a civil war. Or even remain in space, where the issue is a moot point."

Before our conversation could continue, Denali, Taylana, and Keira arrived. My gaze roamed the features of the last to enter the room. Her eyes still danced with flames, but they showed signs of determination. I also saw hints of sadness.

The flickering flames on her chest hovered perfectly above the traditional Borkanian stitching on her upper wrap. It pleased me to see the work she had crafted during her seclusion. It also pleased me to see a blush stain her flesh as my eyes caressed her.

Lanyar cleared his throat and pointed at the woman's lower wrap, causing my eyes to shift below. "How did you get that kilnat, Lady Keira?"

She lifted her chin as if expecting battle. "I made it. This is what I worked on during my evenings. I'm sure you watched me painstakingly place each stitch during your monitoring."

He nodded. "Yes, but I did not pay attention to the image. How did you gain access to that design?" His voice echoed with a brashness that I did not particularly like him using toward my potential mate.

She rolled her eyes. I loved watching that particular human expression. It said so much without speaking a word. "That's what Denali asked, and I will give you the same response I gave her. It just came to me. I loved the look of the top pattern, which I now know is Borkanian. But for the lower, I wanted something that I had designed myself."

I interrupted, speaking in a much softer tone. "What made you choose this specific pattern?"

She blushed as her eyes met mine. "I started with the phoenix," she pointed to the small golden bird near the top. "I've always liked mythology, and the story of the phoenix drew my attention more than most. The phoenix is a magical bird that bursts into flame at the end of its life cycle, only to be reborn from the ashes once again. It seemed fitting, as I was undergoing a rebirth of my own when I designed it. The rest just seemed to flow on its own."

Her brow furrowed. "Why is this design so intriguing? I received a few strange looks from some of the guards during our walk here. I thought maybe it was just my unusual coloring and height, or maybe the magical tattoo, but seeing as I now have a tribe containing over thirty women with six arms and additional mammary glands, I find it doubtful that my external features caused the stares."

I inclined my head toward her, a smile gracing my face. Then I signaled behind me toward where my home banner hung. "You have wrapped yourself in the emblem of the king of Volitar."

She stared at the image a moment, seemingly taking in the significance of what she had unintentionally done. As I watched the thoughts play across her face, I wondered if Helvana had guided her hand while she worked.

This woman drew my attention even more in person than she did on the projection, and that is saying much.

I stood and crossed the room, offering her my arm. "Come. Allow me to seat you so that the meeting may begin. We have much to discuss."

Once she draped her hand atop my arm, a tingle spread outward from her touch. I led her to the seat next to mine. I wanted as much time next to this woman as possible, regardless of what any strange ritual dictated. She had held my interest for many weeks already, and the fact that she now wore my banner on her body, put there by her own hands without knowledge, stirred my attention. I wanted to be near her when Lanyar started asking her questions. I wanted to feel her emotions, not just read them on her face.

Once she had seated herself, I took my place next to her.

The chief medical officer wasted no time. "I assume Denali has already enlightened you to our situation."

Her head tipped forward to acknowledge.

"As with the Borkanian women, we must determine whether our data is supported by reality. It is your decision whether you become impregnated in a traditional manner, or by medical intervention, but with the length of the estimated gestational period, it is imperative that we start immediately. I would like to return home before we hit the ten-year mark."

She scoffed, and I almost cheered. "You are such a clueless scientist with a one-track mind."

The colorful, descriptive language tickled me, and I was glad I had studied it outside of just the upload.

He bristled. "Excuse me?"

"Neither I, nor any of the women I intend to help you recruit will agree to be treated as brood mares. I may not be pitching a bitch fit over having been taken from my planet, but that is simply because I had nothing. To be successful, these women will need offered safety and security without breeding being held over their heads. None will respond if they think that their only worth is their uterus."

"But the data—"

She shot forward in her chair. "To hell with the data!" Her tone made me smile while stopping his tirade. "Data is nothing but numbers. Denali told me that she uploaded the horrors we have faced as a people when someone treated us as little more than numbers. Do you need to have that repeated, with greater details? My own grandmother lost her ability to bear children because of that treatment."

Keira then leaned back again, calming herself. "We have a much more delicate situation to deal with before we start worrying about how and when I choose to get pregnant. And this situation *will be* dealt with, or I will choose *decidedly not*."

Lanyar opened his mouth to argue more, but I raised my hand, stopping him. I wanted to know what her concerns were.

"Please continue, Lady Keira. I wish to hear your concerns."

She nodded. "Taylana, may I have permission to reveal what I learned?"

"Of course, Queen Keira."

Keira rolled her eyes at the royal address, but I sensed nothing harmful in her expression this time, more like she had argued against and lost the battle.

She lifted her hands slightly, staring at them a moment. "This… magic, this gift that was bestowed upon me is revealing itself in stages. To be truthful, I am running on pure instinct, as even the Borkanian women seem to have a lack of information."

She paused, turning toward Denali. "I would like access to all of the Borkanian history for personal research. If this was a legend, I want to find the rest of the legends and study them. Legends clearly were dismissed by your researchers, and I am not faulting them for this, because the majority of humans disregard anything mystical at all. But I would like to do some checking of my own. Lots of legends have basis in facts."

"Yes, my queen," Denali spoke.

Keira returned her attention to the room in general. "Taylana carries more than one child. I need to know how you intend to handle multiple births, and if you even have the proper capability. If not, I need to adjust the plan I'm already forming, and I'd rather do that sooner than later."

Lanyar started raising projections. "Twins have been very rare on Volitar lately. We do not actually have a birther, or midwife aboard the vessel. However, if we place a call to one of the other ships, they could bring one." He frowned. "I am unsure whether they could arrive in time, though."

Keira released a large sigh. "How long are we talking?"

I answered. "The travel time just from Volitar to our current coordinates is almost four lunar cycles utilizing every worm hole available to shorten the time. My brothers are all scattered throughout the galaxy, awaiting news from us regarding the redesigned selection program so that they may continue searching for other compatible life forms. By our data," I tipped my head toward Lanyar, "we know that Vesper, Volitar, and Borkanians share similar gestations. Approximately five cycles. I think this is around twenty Earth weeks. The matron is currently just over one lunar cycle since conception."

She swore under her breath. "Fuck me all to hell and back." Then she spoke louder. "So, the first thing we need to accomplish, long before we even come close to considering getting me up the duff—sorry, Earth idiom that means getting pregnant—is finding an Earth doctor to bring aboard. Allowing for quarantine time, that gives us a maximum of three months to find, convince, and transport a doctor aboard."

Lanyar bristled again. "We have all of the knowledge available. We could ask for one of my staff to volunteer for medical upload."

"Absolutely not. There is more to medicine than just knowledge. There is gut instinct and compassion. So far, doc, you aren't giving off the gut instinct vibes. I don't mean this in any sort of mean way, but your reliance on technology has made you mentally and emotionally lazy."

She held up a hand to stop any response. "I apologize for speaking so brashly, doc."

He gritted his teeth. "I am Lanyar, the chief medical officer aboard this vessel."

She hiked one eyebrow but continued in a calm tone. "Lanyar, I do not mean to speak ill regarding you or your staff. You have grown accustomed to working with data, and I have great faith in science. I respect what you do."

He seemed to visibly calm, allowing her to continue.

"On Earth, multiple births regularly need surgical intervention due to the mortality risk to both mother and child. They are also commonly premature, requiring equipment to help the young breathe for some time after birth.

"Surgical intervention requires a lot of knowledge, yes. But it also requires practice, confidence, and a shit-ton of gut instinct. Sometimes the knowledge says to cut in location A, but to do so could cause the patient to bleed out. We have specialty clinics on Earth that are dedicated to handling high risk pregnancies. One famous instance even dealt with a woman who gave birth to eight children at once, although that is such a rarity as to have made worldwide news."

I watched the color drain from Lanyar's face. "Eight? In a single pregnancy?"

She turned toward the captain. "Marlux, your wife currently carries four. Do you want to take the risk of allowing an untrained doctor to oversee her care?"

Even during battle, I had never seen Marlux so pale. His normally dark complexion appeared nearly as grey as his wife's kilnat. He turned toward his wife. "Four?"

Taylana smiled. "I suspected more than one, and Queen Keira confirmed this with the vision she received while aiding me in dressing. But this is the first that my queen has openly said precisely how many."

Keira smiled. "Two boys, two girls. And one of the boys displays your Vesper heritage." She paused, turning toward Denali. "How the hell do I know he has Vesper heritage?"

Denali smiled softly. "I uploaded some basic information while you slept after your collective. Access in your mind was allowed once Vaxeehl declared you completed."

After mulling over the revelation that he soon would have four children, Marlux set his jaw. "How do you propose we find a doctor able to handle such a situation who will not trigger a manhunt upon disappearance? Based on what you have said so far, it would seem that those doctors are well tracked."

She nodded. "Very much so. Multiples occur in around three percent of human births, I think was the last number I heard. With the judicious use of fertility treatments, that number is on the rise." Keira paused. "I have an idea—one gleamed from a few pop culture movies I've watched, so I'm not one hundred percent sure if it would work—but it's the best I can come up with, and I'm concerned about your reactions."

"Present your idea. I want my wife and children to survive," Marlux commanded.

"Gallatea," she called to her AI. "Gather course of study information regarding Earth veterinary medicine and present it to Doctor Lanyar, please."

In moments, the projection screens changed from data to lots of medical jargon and strange anatomy drawings.

Lanyar frowned. "You want to bring aboard an *animal doctor*? You think we are no better than beasts?"

She raised one eyebrow, ticking off points on her fingers as she spoke. "You locked me in a non-descript metal box. You assigned me a number. You put me through tests like a lab rat. And you're trying to get me knocked up like a cheerleader on prom night. If anyone has been treated like a beast, it was me. But that actually has nothing to do with my thoughts.

"We need someone who is willing to look past human biology. One of these babies has wings. A human doctor trained for delivering babies won't have the slightest idea how to handle a child with wings and claws. And just how well do you think that human doctor would react to seeing six arms? All of this defies their science. For them, seeing six arms means they either have to start looking for corrective surgery to remove the extra limbs, or the baby has such genetic defects that it won't survive. Veterinarians study human biology as part of their class requirements. Then they also have to learn the anatomy and biology of a great number of other species.

"Even still, they have to use gut instinct when they are faced with an unusual combination or situation. If you have a doctor used to dealing with cows who suddenly is faced with a horse, they have to be able to research fast and think even faster. They have to know ten times more than a human doctor in order to bring their variety of patients through alive. Plus, they deal with multiple births way more than humans."

She turned to me. "I'll be honest with you, Vaxeehl. I'm pulling this information out of my ass and just hoping that I'm right. I have no idea if this will work. But Taylana is my tribe. I would have nothing happen to her.

"I'm creating the plan as the words are flowing out of my mouth. I have nothing but intuition pulling me forward." She turned back to Lanyar. "Your original idea of uploading medical training to your staff *is* a solid one, and one that I feel you should proceed with right away. But I think we need to have that emergency option available."

I found no fault in her plan. "Marlux?"

He knocked on the table. "If my wife agrees, I agree."

"Taylana?"

"I trust my queen."

"Denali?"

"I find no error in the logic."

I turned to the final member of the council. "Lanyar?"

He frowned, clearly angry, yet at the same time mollified by Keira's concession to the training upload. He stood, circling the table to stand next to Taylana. In his hand he held a scanner. "May I?" He waved toward her abdomen.

With a nod from her husband, the woman stood. Lanyar held the scanner in position, transferring the data to the projection. There, on the screen, we all saw confirmation of four small lives, one of which showed the first nubs of wings.

He sighed. "I find myself still facing great concern. It is a lot of risk to undertake without knowing that the humans are capable of reproducing. But we have never dealt with more than two babies, and definitely never aboard a starship. We should proceed, cautiously, with Lady Keira's plan."

Keira nodded. "I agree. I think caution would be wise."

He returned to his seat. "So how do we get started on finding a veterinary doctor?"

Keira stood and started pacing slowly. I spun my seat so that I could watch her thinking process. "It's going to be tricky, that's for certain. I need to know how you ended up selecting me, and I think we can tweak the protocol to help pinpoint where to start." She stopped near my chair, one hand reaching for something to steady herself, the other flying to her head.

I grabbed her outstretched hand, standing at the same time, pulling her against my body for support. "Are you unwell?"

The small woman blushed, refusing to meet my eyes. "I have not eaten since the collective. I think that between the stress and excitement, my blood sugar is low. Could we possibly take a short break to allow me time for nourishment?"

I frowned. My finger settled beneath her chin, forcing her to look at me. "Why have you not eaten?"

She rolled her eyes. Directed at me, I did not find the motion as entertaining. "Woke up, accepted Gilnax's offer, met my friend, magical binding ritual that apparently named me queen of the Borkanian women aboard as well as your potential mate, finally bathed while learning everything I could about why I was brought from Earth, and reported here. When exactly was I supposed to take time for myself in that delightfully busy schedule?"

"I instructed you to eat after your hygiene."

"Sue me. I forgot."

"Gallatea, provide enough meals for all present, please."

"Nutrition order placed."

She frowned. "You just steamroll over anyone who disagrees with you, don't you?"

~*~

Chapter 19

Keira

I'll be damned if my heart rate didn't shoot through the roof when that beautiful man wrapped his arms around me and held me to that rock-solid chest of his. He made it hard to think just being in the same room. I'd felt my blood sugar dropping during the walk to the council chambers but had dismissed it as just anxiety about all of the information now swirling in my brain and the monumental tasks before us. I should have asked the ladies to detour. But my head was so stuck on worrying about Taylana giving birth safely, I hadn't thought one second about myself.

This queen stuff and new magic weirdness was going to make me need a damned full-time nanny. For myself. I needed to figure out how to manage all of this before it reached that point.

Speaking of new magic weirdness, the way he held me allowed my cheek to touch his flaming phoenix. I could feel the flames writhing next to my skin, as if they reached toward me. Honest to goodness arousal shot through my nerves. Arousal, I'd dealt with, but never to this strength. I fought hard, both mentally and physically, to keep control of the reaction, although I know he could hear the increase in my breathing.

That strong body led me back to my chair. Before I could move away, though, Doctor Lanyar ran that damned scanner over me.

"Elevated heart rate, increased respirations, temperature increase, decreased blood sugar, increased adrenalin. I see no sign of illness, but the readings—"

I shoved out of the strong arms holding me only to get pulled back when another wave of dizziness struck. I growled. "Put that stupid scanner away. This is exactly what I mean about relying too much on tech and not enough on instinct."

"I am the chief medical—"

I reached out and pushed the scanner away. It still beeped in alarm. I heard my friend giggle.

I tried to turn to look at her but felt absence as soon as my cheek moved. I rested it against Vaxeehl's chest again and spoke. "Taylana, would you like to explain to the good doctor why he has not found an 'ailment'?"

Her smile grew. "My queen is touching her mate."

Lanyar grunted. "What is that supposed to mean?"

I shook my head. "Good lord, save us women from clueless men."

Marlux started coughing and laughing at the same time, clearly unable to contain his mirth. Frankly, I couldn't tell if he figured out the situation on his own, or if his wife explained it to him. And I didn't care.

The rumble of his chest when Vaxeehl spoke ratcheted my desire even further. "Put the scanner away. Lady Keira will be medically well once she eats." I felt every vibration as yet another tingle. The high-pitched beeping on the medical device dinged faster and louder, matching the increase in desire.

I balled my hands into fists, pressing my fingernails into my palms. My blood thundered through my veins so loud, I could no longer hear even the scanner, nor the argument I knew had to be taking place. That idiot doctor was so stuck in his data and not using his senses.

I couldn't *hear* the words, but I felt each one uttered. My knees grew weaker. I felt Vaxeehl lift me into his arms. My god, it felt so right. Of course, the change in position released my arms. Despite my brain telling them to stay balled, my fingers opened, laying against his chest. Heat from the flames spread faster now. I had to make it stop, or I would end up acting on the instinct, regardless of an audience. I knew I whimpered.

There was just no way out of this embarrassing situation without putting the problem to voice, and I did not have the strength or willpower to push myself away from the source.

I gathered what little energy I had and used it to power my vocal cords. "Vaxeehl, please help me to my seat and put space between us. I refuse to lose control in a room full of people I've mostly just met." The words came out huskier than I had intended, and I barely suppressed the moan trying to exit my throat. I forced my eyes open, but refused to look at his face, just knowing it would be my undoing if I saw my own passion reflected in him.

Instead, I turned my eyes toward the doctor. Lanyar's face turned red; I could see that he finally understood why my readings were increased. He powered off his scanner and returned to his seat, refusing to look at us. That was fine by me.

My whole body trembled, and it wasn't just from needing food anymore. The more I kept in contact with Vaxeehl, the more my flames wanted to join with his. I could feel them reaching and seeking. I kept trying to not be driven by hormones or magic, but every instinct in my body wanted me to push him down and go for the ride of my life.

My flame mate lowered me to the chair before returning to his own, flattening both hands on the table. I leaned forward, resting my head on my arms, letting the coolness of the table surface seep into my overheated skin. Out of the corner of my eye, I watched Vaxeehl's fingers twitch and flex, and I realized he felt the pull just as strongly. I forced myself to take several deep breaths to bring those effects under control. To be honest, it didn't help much.

I felt Taylana's many hands start rubbing along my neck and spine. The effect was almost instantaneous, but I was so tightly strung, it only calmed in increments. Slowly, through her careful manipulation, the nerves started to relax, allowing my body to come back under my own control. She leaned down, whispering in my ear. "The longer you deny the connection, the harder it will be to ignore. It will be worse when your body is ready to conceive."

My breath stuttered with tremors. "I don't even know when that is anymore. My last birth control shot should have worn off over a month ago, but I haven't had a period yet. I don't want to jump in bed with someone I don't know anything about. I did that already; it didn't work very well."

She nodded. "I think I understand."

Several more minutes passed as the flames receded. Taylana explained what she could, and she did so with more decorum than I expected under the circumstances.

"The mating magic ensures that we end up with our mate. It provides an immediate passionate link to that mate. On both sides. Normally, the heat of the flame mate allows the pair to learn about each other, while slowly simmering beneath the surface. The longer the pairing delays mating, the stronger the flames grow. Most of the time, the pairs already know of each other and seldom resist, consummating their union within a very short time of the ritual selection."

The food trays arrived. I patted the hand on my shoulder and pushed myself upright. "Thank you. That helped greatly. At least I think I have stopped shaking enough to be able to eat without someone having to feed me."

She returned to her seat and continued. "According to the legend, the queen shared just a tiny piece of her magic with us. I can only assume that means the flames that we feel, despite being already powerful in their intensity, must be much more so for Queen Keira."

The tray before me lay heaped, considerably more than I normally consumed, even at the height of my seclusion while they worked to bring my body into balance. However, as soon as I took the first bite, I felt overwhelmingly ravenous, as if I hadn't eaten in a week. I forced myself to go slowly rather than just shove my face in the plate and eat like a dog. Even with the control, I finished my entire tray and still hungered. It made me wonder of the flares of magic caused my body to burn more energy.

I felt Vaxeehl's eyes wandering over me again, but I tried to ignore them. He grabbed my hand briefly, shoving a portion of his meat ration into it, then stood from the table. I watched as he crossed the room, laying his hand on a small square on the wall. A tall, rectangular portal opened, and he brought out two large bottles. When he returned to the table, he placed one directly before me.

I raised one eyebrow, silently asking him to identify the bottle.

"Drink," he pointed at it. "It's a high energy nutrition drink. Despite having eaten nearly double your normal portion, I could sense you were nowhere near filled."

I furrowed my brow. "How?"

One finger stroked his dancing flames. "I think we have a connection through this. I could feel your depletion as if it were my own. I also suspect this gift drains a lot of energy, as I, too, consumed more than normal and still hungered. We will have to compare our observations. Later."

My body shivered with the way he said that word. *Later.* I nodded, opening the lid and drinking half the bottle right off. Thankfully, I started losing the hollow sensation in my belly. A glance to my right showed me that he had done much the same. It made me relax to know that I did not deal with this strangeness alone.

While the rest of the group finished their trays, I started questioning Lanyar about their selection criteria, figuring out if I could just toss in some more refined options, or if we would have to start from scratch. A lot of it sounded like it should have worked without fail. Unfortunately, the history of my planet had proven itself the issue. We started brainstorming, getting suggestions from all quarters and talking the good and bad of each one.

When they started talking about how humans had better immunity against the virus, I scoffed. "I don't understand how that happened, nor do our scientists. The damned thing showed up riding the back of a small asteroid or large meteor, depending on who you talk to, and now we have strange animal sightings on the news all the time. Who knows what else is going to happen to the human population over the next few years as the rest of whatever entered our atmosphere starts to mutate?"

Vaxeehl nodded. "True. We should scan the area struck to see if we detect anything of use scientifically. We might be able to find a hint as to why the humans are more immune than our own people, despite the similarity of our genetics.

"But that will come in time. We have been working half the day, and we have many suggestions to research. Let us end this session and resume in the morning. We must not rush the process, as that caused harm in the past."

Denali and Taylana left with Marlux trailing behind, Denali asking all sorts of questions about the mating magic. I intended to do the same, even though my mate had already been selected. I still planned to take the time to learn everything that I could about this gift.

First, I needed to get some information from the good doctor. Once I had spoken the words aloud to Taylana, the thought had not left my mind. Foresight or not, I needed to know whether my body worked properly.

Lanyar had just reached the portal when I called out to him.

"Doctor Lanyar, if you would stay for a moment? I have a few questions I need to ask you about my scan results to date."

He hesitated, and I realized his pride still stung for not realizing what the data represented. "Would you not be more comfortable speaking with Denali, as she is a female?"

"It is true," I conceded. "I *would* find much more comfort speaking to a female. However, when I spoke with Denali earlier, she explained to me that her expertise lay in the realm of product development and battle medicine. I recognize that you are the more knowledgeable for what I need to ask. I also recognize that I could ask my AI to retrieve the data, but I still need help interpreting it as I do not have medical training. I am skilled in resource management and survival, but I have no higher education. I worked in a grocery store, not a hospital."

He seemed mollified and returned to his seat, waiting for me to speak.

I turned to Vaxeehl. "I understand that you have been selected as my mate, and I am working to come to terms with this information. My parents raised me to not keep secrets in a relationship. However, we do not actually know each other yet, so what we have is an attraction, not a relationship. I would like to ask you to let me meet with the doctor alone this time."

I had expected an argument, to be honest. Instead, the man bent over my hand, pressing a light kiss to the knuckles. "As you wish, Lady Keira." He turned and left without hesitation.

I sat blinking for a moment. I really had expected him to go all alpha male on me, demanding to stay. Instead, when I asked for privacy, he gave it to me. I definitely had a lot to learn about these strangers.

When my eyes met the doctor's again, he seemed perplexed.

"You did not expect freedom," he said, his voice relaying a combination of statement and question.

"No, not really. Earth men, particularly those in clear positions of power, tend to be much more controlling. And very territorial. Are all Volitar men so respectful?" If they were, it would certainly make the adaptation of human females much easier.

Lanyar nodded. "For the most part. There are always those outliers to the norm. However, any male found to be deliberately abusive toward a female is either reeducated or removed."

The way he'd spoken 'removed' brought to mind images of men being dragged through the streets, publicly humiliated, before being hanged or otherwise killed for their behavior. While I didn't know whether that mental image was correct, I nodded, deliberating this new information. "That is important to know. I suspect that a good portion of the women we will be able to recruit will have history with abuse. They will be very mistrustful of male companionship, and your men may need to dedicate a substantial amount of time to earn the women's trust."

He frowned. "This saddens me. I have seen signs of this in the scans but did not think it would be so prevalent."

I huffed. "I wish it weren't. Women have been fighting for fair treatment and stiff penalties for domestic abuse for years, but it is difficult to even keep the safe houses truly safe." I set that thought aside. "This is not why I asked to speak with you, though."

"Of course, Lady Keira. Please proceed."

I drew a breath to steel my resolve. I needed to talk about female stuff, and I did not really know this creature before me. Yet, Denali had assured me he would be my best source. "Here's the thing. On Earth, the main control women have available is the use of contraceptives."

He looked confused. I wondered if the word did not translate well.

"We have medications we can take to stop us being able to conceive."

His face relaxed. "Ah, yes. Now I understand. We also have something of this nature, although it is not used very often. Our women are typically only fertile a few times a year, thus reducing the need."

I wanted to growl. Instead, I said, "Well, that's just not fair. Human women are fertile, on average, twelve or thirteen times a year. Without birth control, we would spend more time pregnant than not. I remember reading on one of the social media sites somewhere that there was record of one woman who birthed only multiples, ending up with over sixty children. And pregnancy is hard on our bodies. That is something you can continue studying as it becomes important."

He agreed, but his fingers already flew over the screen, probably searching for that history fact. I knew he found it when his eyes grew to massive proportions. "I did not realize human females could produce in such a prolific manner."

I snorted. "Thankfully, not all, or we would have overrun the planet even worse than we already have."

Getting back on topic, I continued. "One of the effects of long-term contraceptive use is that some women find they have difficulty conceiving once they stop their medication. We also have a portion of the population who are born with the inability to conceive; it is suspected by some scientists that the prevalent use of birth control is a possible cause."

I felt my face heat up. "I have been receiving regular injections so that I did not get pregnant from an unsuitable male, or being so young. Thing is, judging by my body's response every time Vaxeehl gets near me, when I finally give in, we are going to be going at it like rabbits."

There was that damned confusion again. "That does not translate well. Can you word it differently?"

I closed my eyes as my face heated even more. Then I opened them again and locked to his. "I mean that this magic flowing through us will have us mating every chance we get."

I found it very entertaining to see the flush spread beneath his lavender skin. "I see. You are concerned about bearing a child every seven lunar cycles."

I gawked. "Seven? Human gestation is nine months."

He nodded. "Yes, but Volitar gestation is only one hundred fifty days, five Earth months. The data suggests that the combination could possibly result in either a five or seven month gestation."

"Damn. And here I was more worried that the long-term birth control use could have made me infertile."

Lanyar tapped the table surface. I watched my file open. He started pointing to sections of the screen.

"When you first arrived, the hormone suppression was found. However, the levels declined at a steady rate throughout your quarantine. I have not checked recently due to the trouble we had with the other women we were observing."

"That makes sense." I tried to calculate when I had received my last full scan. "My last injection was at least five months ago, which means the suppression should have worn off two months ago. Last I knew, it could take up to six months before I cycle."

"Explain this cycle, please."

I wanted desperately to bury my face in a pillow or hide behind a curtain. "Human females shed their uterine lining once a month when they do not conceive."

"How do you know this shedding occurs?"

I flushed with jealousy this time. "Your women don't bleed every month? That is seriously fucking unfair!"

The doctor's eyes grew wide. "You bleed?"

"From our woman parts. And it lasts anywhere from three to seven days, possibly more, depending on the woman. Sometimes, it is exceedingly painful. That is how we usually know we are pregnant. The bleeding stops."

Lanyar looked like he would be sick. Or maybe pass out. I wanted to feel sorry for the guy, but damn it, he was the one in charge of the medical side. He clearly had not done *all* of his research.

"And you are concerned because you have not bled yet?"

I almost clapped. "Now you get it! Plus, how will the human women deal with this issue? Your waste system is cool as hell, but it does not provide us with the means of soaking up the blood. It took me several days to understand how it cleansed... um... my backside after pooping."

I wasn't sure I was going to survive this conversation. But it was information I needed to know if I was going to help other women assimilate into this new tech.

He must have gotten an idea, because his fingers started flying over the surface again, and screens flickered so fast that I couldn't even hope to keep up.

When he found what he sought, he just scanned the screen. And scanned, and scanned, and scanned. "Here it is." He tapped once and a list popped up in front of me. I could read the words, but they made no sense to me.

"Sorry, doc, the language upload has allowed me the ability to read, but my lack of medical knowledge hinders my understanding."

"Of course. I apologize." He moved from his seat and stood next to me, pointing to certain things. "Your waste cleansing system recognized the shedding process as needing removal. It simply disintegrated the waste cells when you cleansed about three weeks ago."

I laughed. "*That* is going to be the best selling point you could have told me. But that means my ovaries have started working again, right?"

He retrieved his scanner. "May I?"

I stood, letting him place the device against my abdomen. He followed with a blood sample. Then he frowned.

"Your fertility hormones still appear suppressed. They have increased slightly, but not enough to aid toward procreation yet. I would like to monitor you to track this. I do not know enough yet to determine if intervention is necessary." He paused, then he seated himself in Vaxeehl's chair, motioning toward me to join him.

I did.

He did not meet my eyes, but I could see he struggled with trying to put to words what he wished to say. I kept myself silent, letting the doctor speak when he was ready.

"I know you view me as a bit of an automaton, more like an AI unit than a living being."

My mouth fell open. "No, Lanyar. Not at all."

He shook his head, so I stopped talking.

"I understand why you would think this. The woman I wish to mate also sees me in this manner. The task set before us has taken all of my energy, and I have failed greatly. With the troubles the Norvaxian women have experienced, conceiving, yet not being able to carry to term, I have refused to act on my desire for this woman. Science is safe. It does not have emotions. If we do not succeed in finding a suitable species, I may be forced to share my mate in the hopes to keep our population from extinction. If she willingly chose to do so is one matter, but to do so by force is simply wrong."

I laid my hand on his. "And you should never be forced to share something like that. Ever."

He slowly raised his bright green eyes to mine. "I cannot. Just as you have stated, no female should ever be treated as just some brood mare. This program has to succeed if I am to save her from such a fate. The king has already asked for the few females still alive on our planet to volunteer for this. Only a small handful have done, but I fear he will make it an edict before long. If she were not here, aboard this vessel, I am sure she would have felt obligated to volunteer."

The man may be clueless about signs of arousal, but he truly had a heart. Every aspect of his being had been dumped into the program, driven to keep the woman he loved from bearing children until her uterus fell out.

"I promise you, Lanyar, that I will do everything in my power to help you protect Denali."

His eyelids rose all the way to his forehead. "Did your magic tell you this when you touched me?" His gaze darted to where my hand still held his.

I chuckled. He had essentially hung a glowing sign over Denali with his words, since she had been the only female Volitar or Vesper that I'd seen onboard, but I figured I'd keep that information to myself. "I didn't need magic to see how much you care for her. This is just my intuition. But I'm not wrong, am I?"

He hung his head, looking shamed. "No, Lady Keira. When she showed so much heartbreak over your planet's history and the psychological damage it had left you with, all I wanted to do was remove her from the council and protect her from such knowledge. Seeing her so close to broken, when I have seen her so strong in battle... I knew I had failed *her* worse than I had failed the humans."

I nodded. "I worried I had broken her, myself. So listen, big man." I almost laughed at his expression when I called him 'big man.' Instead, I gathered my resolve. "You and me, we're a team in this project. I have a gut feeling about this magical weirdness, that it is

183

going to help us tremendously, but I need time to understand how it works. Regardless, though, I will help you figure this out. Once I had set my mind to accept that I had been abducted by aliens, and that this was my new life, your people essentially became my people. Even more so once I figured out you had no intention of turning me into some sort of slave."

I stood up and offered my hand. "So, we're in this together. Got that?"

He stood to his full height, making me crane my neck to continue meeting his gaze. He accepted my hand, but instead of shaking, he bowed over it, touching his forehead to my knuckles. "You truly are a suitable mate for my commander."

Well fuck me sideways. The final hold-out just accepted me.

"Okay then." I glanced at the door. "How do I find my way around this spectacular star ship? I would like to explore my new home a little."

A few minutes later, my head spun with new information. Lanyar had instructed me to lay my hand flat on the table surface, and he had uploaded the layout of the ship, as well as more details on how to use Gallatea to get portals linked, order specific things… seriously, I had a small headache from how much information my brain now struggled to process.

~*~

Chapter 20

Vaxeehl

When I left the council chambers, my feet carried me straight to the park. The mating flames had reduced, but they still flowed through my body in great swarms. Once inside the park, I found a trail and started walking. I had to burn off some of this energy. Holding Keira, and feeling her response, had brought my passion to the forefront of my mind. Unfortunately, every time I thought of her, the flames traveled my nerves again.

She was right, though. She needed time to learn about me. I had to find a way to control this desire so that I could give her that time.

All of the species blended on Volitar had some form of mating sense. However, nothing so strong. It seemed to pull us toward our mates, allowing us to find and learn of each other. This... this blessing from our goddess combined with the magic of the Borkanian queen, seemed determined to drive me insane with lust. I had enough trouble trying to smother my obsession with the human woman *before* the magic interfered.

I also needed to process this other aspect I had found while we ate. I could sense her needs. I could tell without asking that my lady needed more nutrition. Gallatea had clearly picked up on the energy depletion, since she had provided larger rations than normal. Yet, it still had not been enough.

Even as I walked, I could sense her discomfort. I also knew not to react to it. Somehow, I just *knew* that her discomfort was not due to the presence of my trusted friend, but to her topic of discussion. My heart warmed at remembering her words to me when she requested privacy to speak to Lanyar. She did not desire to hide from me; she simply had not reached a point of comfort yet.

I wanted her to find that comfort.

I had reached the stream and looked around, realizing that my feet had carried me to the place Keira had met my slognip. It had been dangerous, for both of them, to use him for her collective. I had instructed him, but he was still relatively young. If she had attacked, his defensive instinct would have kicked in. The venom works quickly. Had she found the willpower to fight through the venom, he would have gone for vital organs.

A shiver wracked my frame at that thought.

Another sensation traveled along my nerves, too. A sense of homecoming, of nearness. I raised my eyes, seeing a familiar form walking my way.

"Thank you for trusting me alone with the doctor." Keira approached, her beautiful body moving with grace as she drew near. I noted with pleasure that she no longer walked barefoot.

"I have spent a good portion of the last week learning as much of your history as I could. I understand how trust might be something with which you struggle." I closed some of the distance between us, remaining careful to not get too close. I wanted this woman to want me beyond the magic.

She tipped her head slightly sideways, a sign of thinking for both of our species. "My history, or the history of my planet?"

Fair question. "I will admit to studying both. Unfortunately, your personal history is little more than data. It tells me nothing about the woman before me other than her ability to learn, and what sort of tasks she performed in service."

She nodded and said, "I think Doctor Lanyar and I have reached an agreement on that topic finally." She studied me again.

"Lanyar and Marlux are more than just my crew members. They are trusted friends. Lanyar is still young. He studied genetics in the hopes to aid in bringing outside food sources into our environment for safe use without damage to the ecosystem. When we were quarantined onboard, he ascended to Chief Medical Officer based on his education and ability to blend disciplines. He is doing the best he can, relying on a lot of uploads to learn. As you have pointed out, he still lacks a certain element, but I feel certain he will get there."

We both turned when we heard a yip and thundering footsteps. My slognip slid to a stop at my feet and rolled onto his back. I knelt down and started scratching his underbelly. "Pangou, my friend. How do you fare?"

He yipped again and then let his tongue hang between his teeth.

Keira came closer and knelt to scratch under his chin. "Well hello, my friend. It is nice to see you again." Her eyes lifted to mine. "I gather this overgrown puppy is yours, then?"

I laughed. "This slognip is my battle hound, Pangou."

Her brow furrowed. "Slognip," she repeated. Her lips formed the word several times as she petted the beast, cementing it in her mind. "They are battle hounds?"

I smiled gently. "Do not let his friendly countenance fool you. In battle, he is much more ferocious than he displayed during your collective. Slognips have a strange ability to understand language, as well as interpret intentions through unseen signals. We have trained and worked with them for many decades, yet they had never revealed that they could aid with warmth. Of course, we seldom spend time in areas with extremely low temperatures. We also do not normally treat them like pets, as you had done. That might have changed his behavior toward you."

She glanced slightly toward me, a sly smile upon her face. "You appear to do this, sire."

I laughed silently while shaking my head. "And I have also given my AI unit a name. Something else we appear to have in common."

She shrugged. "Humans are known for trying to befriend or make pets of even the most dangerous of the species on our planet. Even inanimate objects. We have a pack mentality, is what I believe it is called. There is an old movie about a man stranded on an island after a plane crash. His only friend for years was a face he'd drawn on a volleyball. He named it Wilson. When Wilson got washed away during the course of their escape from the island, the man's spirit broke to the point where he finally gave up and was ready to die."

She stopped scratching Pangou and stood. "Shall we walk along this beautiful stream and get to know each other?"

We kept a very sedate pace as we talked. I learned how she felt her strength came from her grandmother, how the stories of the death camps had helped teach her to find a way to survive. She spoke more of hunting and fishing with her grandfather and father. She even spoke of how she packed everything and left after the loss of her parents to the virus, and the difficulty of being suddenly alone. I sensed more to that story, yet the sadness emanating from her made me hesitate to ask.

I shared much of my childhood with her. Being raised to take over the crown at some point, a bit of how each of my siblings and I handled our mother's death. It felt right speaking with her, sharing our histories.

She let me speak, just listening.

"Being aboard this vessel for eight years now is the closest I have ever come to being an only child. I have three brothers, all younger than myself. I and the next two brothers all took after our father's Volitar genetics. The youngest, Raklin, inherited mother's Vesper genetics. It made playtime and fighter training much more interesting when he finally learned how to use his wings. After the virus killed our mother, Raklin flew off into space. He has not responded to any calls, and we have been unable to track his ship. We fear he has fallen, either to attack from another advanced life form, or to great sadness. He was always closer with mother than the rest of us. My brothers and I have made a great many requests to Helvana that she keep our youngest safe until we may find him again."

"Tell me about Helvana," she asked.

"Helvana is our goddess, the keeper of our people. She guides with honesty and compassion. No one really knows when she came into being. She simply has always been spoken of through the generations. The people of Volitar used to be nomads, wandering the planet, following the growing season and the game.

"Many centuries back, my ancestor spotted a strange bird while hunting. Its bright feathers sparkled in the sun, yet the colors allowed it to hide among the sparsely fruited trees without notice unless it moved. As he drew back his arrow, poised to strike, the bird raised its head, beady eyes staring straight into those of my ancestor. It is said that he saw visions, both great and terrifying, of things to come."

I paused, meeting her eyes. "My ancestor, at that time, was merely a member of the tribe, a young man on the brink of adulthood. His father had fallen to a raging beast, and his family relied upon him for sustenance. He'd had very little success in finding food recently, and the family sat on the verge of death. While they did belong to a tribe, the sparsity of sustenance left each family concerned only for their own survival. A great mountain had sent much ash into the air, causing the weather to change, and many animals to die. Much of the people on the planet suffered hunger. The bird was the first animal he had seen in many days.

"Yet he could not bring himself to kill it. He released the tension on his bow, lowering it out of sight. Then he dropped to his knees, crying freely, begging Helvana's forgiveness for his failure. He felt his family was sure to die if he could not find something soon for them.

"While he knelt in the dirt, tears coursing down his face, his muscles rigid with defeat, he felt talons close upon his shoulder. He raised his eyes, blinking away the moisture. The bird took flight, guiding him, pausing to make sure he followed.

"She led him away from the mountain, away from the trees, out to a wide-open plain filled with brambles. Even though the thorns stabbed at him, he followed her. Suddenly, she dove beneath the brambles. He heard scuffles and a high-pitched squeal. Then the bird rose again, holding a creature in its mouth, much like your lizard. It swooped over, dropping the creature at my ancestor's feet. As he bent to examine the beast, others swarmed over him, coming from all directions within the brambles. He did not have time to notch his bow. He simply grabbed an arrow and began stabbing the animals, spearing them upon the shaft. By the time the attack ceased, he had four arrows full of these creatures. Yet, he saw many other eyes peering at him through the vines. The creatures thrived among the thorny foliage.

"He loaded the carcasses into his game bag. The bird once again drew his attention, leading him back the way they came. When they returned to the trees where he'd first spotted her, he gutted one of the creatures, offering the innards to the bird. She took them, flying up to a nest. He realized then that she, too, had a family to feed. Had he killed her, the young would have died.

"When he cooked and tested the meat, he felt rejuvenated. He realized that a small portion gave him great nourishment.

"Our people had never searched for creatures among the brambles. There did not appear a means of survival within those vines. The large thorns could pierce even the hardest of scales, such that we only neared them to harvest the spines for use on our arrows. Yet there, in an impossible place, lay an abundance of animals who seemed able to survive the barren times.

"He finished gutting the rest of the creatures, leaving everything behind as an offering of thanks. When he returned to the camp, he spread his gains among all of the families, telling them the tale. The elders scoffed, claiming he had been hallucinating from hunger. Yet, they could not deny he had brought home enough game to share. Even in this, they denigrated him, claiming him foolish for not keeping it for his own family.

"The younger tribe members, however, thanked him for his selflessness and began asking him for guidance. Over the next weeks, more and more of the younger members followed my ancestor's lead, learning where and how to hunt the creatures. When a water source closer to the hunting ground was found, the younger members wished to move the camp, hoping to reduce the amount of travel needed to feed their families. The tribal elders refused until the small pond nearby began to dry up.

"As the clan travelled slowly across the land, one of the elders motioned for all to stop and remain silent. The elder raised his bow, aiming into the trees. My ancestor realized where the arrow would land just moments before the elder fired. He sprinted forward, placing himself between the hunter and his prey just in time for the arrow to pierce his chest and embed into his heart.

"The elder ranted at my ancestor, berating him for getting in the way, doing nothing as the young man dropped to the ground. Yet, from up in the trees, a beautiful melody arose. The mother bird drifted down, alighting upon the bleeding chest. She tipped her head side to side, studying him as the life slowly faded from his body. 'Thank you for helping me save my family,' he said to her. 'I have repaid your kindness. Go now, and live.' With the last words, his breath escaped from his chest.

"The bird did not leave, though. She wrapped her talons around the arrow and spread her wings to her full span. As those majestic wings began to thrash, and the arrow slowly pulled from his body, a torturous scream erupted. Smoke billowed from the wound as the flesh sealed itself. The bird flew over, dropping the arrow at the feet of the hunter. Then she returned to my ancestor, landing upon his rising and falling chest. There, she burst into flames, leaving only a pile of ash behind, and a mark upon his skin in her shape."

I drug my fingers along the dancing flames upon my own skin. "Much like this, only appearing of ash. As he moved to rise from the ground, much surprised at still living, a shrill peep could be heard from the remains of the great bird. There, he found another similar creature, now young again. He carefully rose, lifting the small bird, and traveled away from the clan. He climbed among the branches until he found the nest, placing it gently where it belonged.

"With little else spoken, the clan continued, reaching the new encampment just before nightfall. That night, the tribal council determined that my ancestor had been chosen by Helvana herself as our leader for his show of compassion and understanding."

I nodded toward her kilnat. "That is why our crest bears such symbols. Helvana enflamed, rising from her bed of ash, and the knotted vines are those from which we still collect our most prized meat, although we are careful to eat it only in moderation as to maintain the population."

With that, we continued, and I started pointing out the various forms of vegetation growing here, about the different types of fruits, vegetables, and animals on Volitar. This discussion caught her attention.

"If you have so much variety, is there a reason for the limited selection served at mealtimes?"

I smiled at her. My fingers itched to trace her face. Instead, I locked my hands together behind my back while I talked. "The selections grown on the ship are used for maximum nutrition and minimum waste. The ships are designed to be able to safely hold nearly five thousand, although most often only hold a few hundred unless we head to war. Most of the waste has to be recycled, and we do that successfully. At full capacity, though, bodily waste accumulates too quickly, and may need ejected instead of recycled into fertilizer for the orchards and gardens. Space rocks of any kind, including bodily waste, could transmit harmful microbes to any number of planets. We do not wish to cause undue harm to other environments."

Her face reddened. Without thinking, I stroked the back of my finger over the color. "I find this flushing endearing."

Her eyes fluttered, and she drew in a deep breath. At that same moment, I felt flames flicker along my arms.

I jerked my hand away, locking it behind my back again. "I apologize. I am trying very hard not to cause you distress, but I find myself behaving without thought." I turned away from her, trying to give us both time to calm.

I spoke to distract myself. "I must admit, Lady Keira, that I studied your quarantine feeds with an unnatural obsession. I felt drawn to you from your first day aboard. The strange magic that has joined us has only enhanced what was already present." I turned back to see her face, see her condemnation that I have behaved no better than Gundar, only without trying to take her by force. "But I understand your need to learn of me, and I am trying to give you that time."

I noticed her hands trembled as she brought one up to touch her cheek where my fingers had stroked. "I know you are not acting with intent. I thank you for respecting my desire to learn about you."

She thought for a moment again. This woman spent much time thinking before she spoke. I found I liked her moments of silence just as much as the sound of her voice.

She seemed to come to some decision. "Would you show me your quarters?"

My heart slammed against my chest. "Great Helvana, Keira. Are you testing my resolve? I am unsure that I could withstand the temptation of having you in my quarters and not act on it."

She smiled. "I can barely withstand the temptation just walking beside you. We need to be able to focus on revising the selection process, yet I can barely focus on anything except your existence. It seems to me that we have the rest of our lives to get to know one another." Her pale hand reached toward me, barely grazing my own cheek as I had done to hers.

My hands unlocked from behind my back and shot out, pulling her against me before my brain could stop them. Despite the ferocity with which I grabbed her, I gently lowered my lips to hers, more than anxious for this first taste but not wanting it taken with force. I hesitated, waiting to see if she would pull away. Instead, she stretched upward and closed the remaining distance.

Relief soared through my veins.

As I had suspected would happen, the second our lips touched, the flames engulfed my body, sending wave after wave of pleasure soaring through every inch. I wanted to join with her immediately. Judging by her own reaction, she felt the same.

Keira's arms wrapped around my neck, her fingers tangling in my hair. Her soft moans stoked the fires between us.

I swept her tiny body into my arms and made my way to the exit by memory. As soon as I neared the portal, I forced myself to part from her delectable lips.

"Ovid, connect a direct portal to my quarters."

Having done this many times, it only took seconds for the door to open. While I crossed the few steps through the portal into the room, Keira's lips trailed along my neck and chest. I did not stop until I reached my bed. I lowered her gently.

When I tried to pull back in order to remove my kilnat, I felt her hands slide under the material and circle my shaft. Breathing became optional. I could only groan.

"Keira, little one, if you give me a moment, I will undress us. I want to take my time learning you." I forced the words from my lips.

She growled, her hands shifting and making quick work of untying the knot at her neck. She then stood, letting it drop, revealing her breasts.

I grasped onto her hips, lifting her high enough to suckle those beautiful globes. Her moan shot straight to my shaft, and her hands pulling tufts of my hair frayed the last of my control.

I lowered her back to the floor and pointed at her kilnat. "Strip." My own hands flew to remove my own. "Or I might destroy your beautiful hand-work, and I quite like you wearing my banner." The clasp released. Still, I nearly shredded the cloth trying to unwrap it from my lower body.

Her words at seeing me revealed broke through the fog of lust. "I am going to be many levels of sore by the time we are done tonight."

I froze, thinking about the differences in our sizes. My body was built for other Volitar females. Humans were quite a bit smaller.

"I wish not to cause you pain, Keira, only pleasure."

She must have heard my concern. Her own haze of lust cleared just a bit. "You misunderstand me, Vaxeehl. I do not think you will cause me injury. There are certain aches and pains that come from *great* sex, and I have a feeling you and I are about to have *fantastic* sex."

With that, she finished unwrapping herself and dropped the cloth to the floor.

My breath caught in my throat. I had seen her shape before, but only on a projection. The reality left me awestruck. Her breasts heaved with every breath she drew. My eyes caressed her belly, imagining it swollen with my young, and my loins burned. My gaze traveled further down, admiring the strong, shapely legs, picturing them wrapped around me.

I knew then with certainty, I would not rush even this first time with her. I wanted to hear her cry her pleasure to the stars many times this night.

I laid back on the bed, patting the space beside me. "Come to me, woman, so that I may worship every inch of you."

Her lithe body crawled toward me like a grown lumfin, looking just as predatory. She dipped her head, flicking her tongue across my nipple. I groaned, digging my hands into the bed to keep from grabbing her as I wished. She wanted to explore me, and I wanted to let her. But her touch was driving me to the brink of insanity.

She straddled my waist, her warm core touching just above my hardened member. It reached as far as it could, straining toward her.

Her hands settled over my heart, and she slid herself backwards, her body engulfing my own. Heat flooded my senses, stealing my breath.

When her eyes locked to mine, the tiny flames I'd seen before now filled the entire width, dancing from within. She rose slowly, dragging her inner walls along my shaft, caressing each inch, before returning just as slowly. As I watched her rise and fall upon me, the flickering wings of Helvana upon her chest grew and spread, snaking down her arms. Her breath came in shallow gasps as the flames caressed her skin.

Her speed increased, and she trailed her hands up my shoulder, along my arms, until she locked her fingers with mine. As soon as our hands joined, the flames rose from her flesh, forming Helvana's wings upon her.

"You truly are Helvana, my goddess made flesh. May I always be worthy of your presence."

The markings on my chest swirled to life, reaching toward her, caressing her where my hands could not. They slid along her beautiful form, worshiping her, welcoming her, tangling with her own until I could no longer feel any space between us.

The inferno grew stronger, the flames brighter until they glowed with pulsing white energy. Her body rocked on mine, drawing every spark of life to join the conflagration, until finally, the light burst, and I heard her scream her completion as my own shot deep within her body, searing us both from the inside.

Her spent body collapsed atop mine as the light burst to ashes, sprinkling the room with a fine coating of dust. I wrapped my arms around her, holding her tight to me, letting our heart rates calm.

"I have seen inside your heart," her voice whispered hauntingly between us. "My king's desires are also my own. Together, we shall save our people. We shall bring the lost home."

She yawned. Her eyes closed. Her breathing leveled out.

As I felt sleep claiming my body, I whispered against her flesh. "My queen."

~*~

Chapter 21

Keira

I woke to the feel of fingers sliding gently through my hair, carefully removing tangles. My body still hummed with a low level of the magic that had grown between us. It was the most amazing sensation, as if I could feel everything about him. I wondered if it would still be noticeable whenever we finally separated our bodies.

Most of me had no desire to figure that out. I enjoyed this closeness. This was passion. I had known its absence most of my life. Now that I had found its presence, I never wanted to let it go. Mentally, I commanded a flame to tickle along my lover's neck.

His sharp intake of breath caressed my scalp, telling me that the flames had obeyed. I felt him swell and realized he still lay buried deep within me. I moaned as the searing heat slid along my internal walls.

"Oh god, do that again," I pleaded, digging my fingers into his chest.

He began to rock slowly inside me. "As you wish, my queen."

I felt my body lubricate instantly, something that had never happened before without veritable *tons* of foreplay, smoothing the way for him. I cleared my throat to force words through the haze of lust. "I didn't mean to fall asleep on you."

He twitched again. "I found no fault in the action."

Those familiar flames stirred again. "Mercy! Is it going to be this powerful every time? We might actually die from pleasure."

His groan drove me wild. I wanted to move, but his hands held me securely, letting him lead this time. "I will die the happiest man in the universe."

I laughed, and then moaned at the friction it caused. Finally, I lifted my head to meet his eyes. "Did you actually sleep with your dick in me the whole time?"

Without warning, Vaxeehl rolled us, pinning me beneath him. "Even my wildest dreams could not prepare me for you, Helvana. Though the magic had wrung every drop of my life essence to seed your womb, my cock stayed rigid within your warmth, anxious to plant more."

My eyes rolled back in my head, his voice stirring along my spine while his rock-hard member wrought magic from within.

"You have been a beacon across the universe, slowly drawing me to you as we sailed the darkness. I searched for you among the many planets, never realizing that I searched for the one who would allow my goddess to take form."

He raised himself just enough to caress my face with the fingers of one hand. "You are strong, my Keira, my Helvana, my goddess, my queen. You carry within you so much hope and courage. In your many incarnations, you always draw the lost, give hope to those who have lost their own, taking command even when your heart lay broken in your chest."

I felt tears form and slide from my eyes.

"I see you now, in your human form. As our passion joins, I see your goddess form coalesce. You are supernal, you are magnificent. But most of all, you are mine."

He surged into me, coating me with his essence once again, and my body answered. I heard my passionate scream echo through the room as my orgasm washed over me, fingers of flames intertwining once again, drawing it out until I felt I would combust into a being of pure fire.

~*~

My stomach growled angrily, stirring me from sleep once again. I lay on my side. Vaxeehl curled behind me, holding me tightly. Curious, I squeezed my inner muscles to see if he had managed to sleep buried inside me once again. I felt the absence and sighed. It was certainly amazing to awaken with him hard and ready inside me, but I also felt relieved that he had pulled out after the last round.

I could find myself easily consumed with everything about this man. But I needed to focus on other things, as well. He is a prince, and the fate of his planet lay upon his shoulders. No single being should carry such a burden. Even had the magic not selected him as my mate, I would have been drawn to help him.

His words from last night played in my head again. Could I really be his goddess, Helvana, and the Borkanian queen, reincarnated in human form? Could this be why I so easily assumed command of the store with a pandemic tearing us apart? Is this why the people welcomed my leadership without argument?

I had to accept it as a possibility. The magic had shown itself real, despite my natural human doubts. And the way the flames writhed and combined when we made love, caressing us inside and out and pulling our passions to such heights, that was definitely not a human thing. From what I'd come to understand, it was not a Volitar thing, either.

My stomach rumbled and his echoed the sound, shoving those thoughts from my head.

I pushed the blanket from my body, not even caring enough to wonder when he took the time to cover us but appreciating the care. I sat up, feeling hungry but at least not dizzy this time.

"Gallatea, please provide nourishment," I whispered.

I cast my eyes around for something to cover my body and realized I needed to introduce the concept of robes to this species. The men had it fairly easy, as they could don their kilnats without assistance. The women had to rely on help, even to wander their own home.

I stood from the bed, letting my lover's arm slide over me. Even as he still slept, his touch ignited my flesh. I pressed my lips together, holding back the moan. The way he had rocked my world last night, he had to be exhausted. Somehow, I knew that if he heard my body respond, he would awaken and drag me back to the heights of passion again. I absolutely would not mind… but I needed food.

Seeing no other option, I carefully pulled the blanket from his body, wrapping it around me like I would a towel after a shower. Exposing him fully to my view almost pulled me to awaken him. Only the rumble of my stomach and the pressure from my bladder managed to pull my attention from the visage on the bed.

While I waited for the morning nutrition to arrive, I slowly and silently investigated my surroundings. Of course, I knew this time I could leave the room anytime I wanted, but I had a strong feeling this would be my new home. At least, it would be until we made it to Volitar.

I discovered his waste basin in a separate, closed off area after a few minutes, and I felt much more comfortable. Both for being able to relieve myself, as well as for not having to do so in front of him. Of course, after learning that the cleansing station kept me from dealing with the horrors of the human female monthly curse, I felt much more at ease with this particular advanced technology. If I didn't know the idiots in charge on Earth would twist it into some monstrosity of torture, I would consider convincing the Volitar to share this knowledge with our leaders. But our history proved itself over and over that those in charge, for the most part, could not be trusted.

I stepped out of what I deemed the waste closet and spotted the food trays on the table. My stomach made itself very loudly known again. I chuckled to myself and started toward the table.

Strong arms circled my waist, pulling me back against that warm, solid body I'd come to study so recently. I groaned as I felt his lips caress my neck.

"You taste wonderful, my queen."

I smacked his arms, pulling away as soon as he loosened his hold. My breath stuttered with arousal. "Go take care of your ablutions and join me for breakfast. I'm starving."

He laughed. "Yes, I heard your stomach announce it." He leaned down, placing a soft, tender kiss upon my lips before retreating to the closet himself.

I hummed in appreciation as I watched his backside disappear. Then I shook my head and crossed to the table. I seated myself and started working my way through the food with much less decorum than I had managed yesterday. Once again, I was ravenous, but this time, I didn't force myself to eat slowly. I practically inhaled the eggs, trying to satisfy the depth of my hunger.

I didn't even pause when Vaxeehl lifted me from the seat and onto his own lap. I heard him chuckle and growled, swallowing before I spoke. "Go ahead and laugh. I dare you to eat slow and steady like a normal dignitary. Your stomach was talking just as much as mine was."

He tried. Especially since he kept one arm secure around my waist, holding me as if he thought I would disappear if he let go. He took the first several bites slow and easy, but I could see his hands starting to shake.

"Gallatea, please provide two of those nutrient drinks."

"Confirmed."

The two bottles slid across the table just seconds later. I opened the first and raised it to his lips. He frowned at me. I frowned right back. "Yes, you are a big, strong man. You want to be known for taking care of your woman. Well, your woman also wants to care for you. Shut up and drink. Your energy level is so depleted that your hands are shaking."

He looked like he wanted to argue. Instead, he sighed and opened his mouth. I pressed the opening to his lips, tilting it carefully so that he could drink without spilling. Much like before, he consumed over half the bottle before showing signs of slowing. I drank the remainder of that bottle myself.

I glanced at his hands, happy to see the tremors abating.

"Much better." I nodded once. "Now, stop being such a silly fool, and eat that food. We have another planning session to attend."

He growled. "I'd rather stay here and fill you full of seed until you grow gravid." His hand spread across my belly, pulling me even tighter against him.

I rested one arm over the top of his, hugging it to me. "My fertility levels are still a bit too low for that. It could be a couple of lunar cycles before I get anywhere near high enough levels for anything to take." I shoveled another forkful into my mouth.

His fingers twitched. "Did something happen?"

I swallowed, trying to ignore the tingle from the close contact. Then, in between bites, I explained human contraception and its possible pitfalls, the suppression in my files, and how it was slowly going away. I breezed over the whole bleeding for a week part, though. We *were* eating.

He paused with a piece of meat partway to his mouth. "This is why you wanted to speak to Lanyar yesterday, isn't it?"

I nodded. "Yes. Although, I must say, had I known his reaction would have been so entertaining, I would have asked Gallatea to record it. The look on his face when I explained how human women knew whether they were pregnant was almost worth the embarrassment of the conversation itself."

Vaxeehl looked at me confused.

I shook my head. "Nope. I've had that discussion once already. You can just talk to the doctor. Then he won't have to feel so bad about his reaction to human biology." I smiled over my shoulder at him. "Of course, with my fertility levels currently down, we can have all sorts of fun figuring out whether the flames will respond every single time."

He nibbled on my neck. "You seem to have figured out a way to control them last night, using them to touch me instead of your hands."

I shrugged. "That was just me flexing my imagination, and it happened to work. Purely accidental, but I'm not complaining about the results."

The hand he held pressed to my stomach slid upward to my breasts. With his other, he pushed the food trays to the side.

"You're supposed to be eating to regain your strength. We have a meeting." Even to my own ears, my argument sounded weak.

Those strong hands gripped my hips. In a fairly smooth motion, he lifted, spun, and seated me on the table before him. "I am hungry, but I have something else I wish to feast upon."

~*~

"We're late," I scolded.

Vaxeehl just grinned as he smoothed my upper wrap around my body.

"Again," I frowned. Everyone would look at us, just as they had every single time we'd arrived late during the last three weeks.

He leaned forward, carefully crossing the material behind my back while I held my hair aloft.

"It's all your fault," I added.

"I didn't hear you complaining a few minutes ago," he said, his breath dusting my neck, sending shivers down my spine.

My own breath caught, as it did every moment we were within reach of each other. I smacked his shoulder. "Stop that."

He let his fingers drag along my body as he brought the material forward again.

I growled. "Damn it, Vax, stop it."

He pouted. My prince actually stuck out his bottom lip in a pout. He finished tying my wrap, and I let my hair fall. Then he pulled me against him, holding me tightly.

"You'll be transporting back and forth to Earth. I won't be able to see you except through a projection. What if you get sick? What if you get hurt?"

I slid my arms around him and settled my head against his chest. "I promise, my love. I will come back to you. This is for the good of our people. Gil will be with me the whole time. You even helped with my fight training, just in case."

I pressed my lips against his phoenix, his blessing from Helvana. "Besides, by the time we have gathered enough volunteers, my fertility levels will hopefully be working right, and we can finally start working toward producing you an heir."

His arms pulled me tighter. "If they never level out, I don't care. I know the mating magic has shown us having at least two children, but they matter less to me than you do. You are my heart, Keira."

Cue the waterworks. I reached up, pulling his face down so I could reach his lips. While I distracted him with my kiss, I let my hands drift to the clasp of his kilnat.

"I thought we were late?" He spoke against my lips, his own hands already releasing the clasp of my lower wrap.

"You're the one who said such sweet things to me. Shut up and make love to me, you damned sentimental idiot." I jumped up, wrapping my legs around his waist as he carried us back to the bed again.

His fingers reached for the upper knot.

"Oh no you don't. Leave the upper in place. It takes too long to keep redoing."

~*~

Almost an hour later, we finally entered the council chambers. Gilnax handed us each large bottles of nutrient drink. How he managed to do that without blushing, I wanted to ask, but I knew I could not without turning bright red myself. He'd seen more than his share of our moments over the last three weeks.

It was never intentional. Several times in the first week, as soon as the council meeting ended, Vaxeehl and I could barely contain ourselves. Our flames actually started reaching toward each other during the meetings. Taylana and Marlux found it hilarious. Denali and Lanyar appeared more embarrassed, as well as intrigued from a scientific standpoint.

As soon as the room emptied, Vaxeehl lifted me onto his lap, merely shoving his kilnat out of the way and spearing my already welcome body. By the time Gil had entered the portal, the flames had formed our wings, blocking us from view, but he had been frozen in shock.

Thankfully, we'd been too rushed to remove clothing. When the flames receded and I collapsed against my lover, the most Gil might have seen was the lower portion of my ass. Vaxeehl had calmly asked him to fetch us more nutrient drinks. By the time he'd returned, I'd put myself back together. That did not stop the bright red from staining my cheeks as I accepted the drink and downed it with barely a breath.

After him walking in on us for the third time, Gil arrived every morning with drinks in hand, announcing his presence through Gallatea, and awaiting invitation to enter.

The second week of meetings, I traded seats with Denali. I had hoped that by putting space between us, we could focus. It did help. A little.

I spent time every day after the meetings, and after my lover ravished me, speaking with each of the Borkanian women. I could now identify most of them with the correct names. I had three who volunteered as my personal crafters, adding the pattern I'd sewn into my first kilnat to the blood red wraps I now wore. Vaxeehl had insisted after a few of his men had eyeballed me while walking the corridor.

I thought this was overkill and relished it at the same time. This man wanted me identified to all as his, which added to the feeling of want that rolled off of him at every turn. But I also recognized that these men were awestruck at seeing what they considered the mark of their goddess. I tried to meet with some of them, yet many remained too stunned at what they saw to be able to hold a conversation. It made me feel thankful for Gil having seen me prior to the magic being bestowed.

My exercise routine moved into the training room where the warriors practiced. Vaxeehl had argued with me about that, in front of the warriors who were also exercising. He held concerns that my energy levels would deplete even worse by continuing my fight training. I reminded him that if he didn't jump me so often, my energy levels would be fine. When my lover finally admitted he was worried my magic would attract some of his men, Gil stepped up, reminding my secretly insecure lover that I was never without protection. He also convinced Vax to spar with me himself.

We quickly realized we could only spar together in privacy. Halfway through my hand-to-hand combat routine, Vax had thrown me over his shoulder and marched us back to our quarters. Even in combat, our magic had coalesced to passion.

He also tried to argue that I would not return to Earth, that we could send someone else. Denali had won that one, pointing out that everyone else on board either had skin colors that would draw too much attention, too many arms, or giant fucking wings. I felt really proud of her grasp of American cursing.

Of course, that also led to another argument. My lover absolutely refused to allow me to transport to Earth alone. Gil actually agreed, partly out of concern, and partly due to his vow to serve me. I didn't even attempt to argue my way out of this one. I knew that some of the areas I would need to travel through would hold some of the worst humans, ones who would not hesitate to attack a female walking alone, and likely as a group.

"Gil will be the best solution, even with his wings," I'd stated. Then I pulled up on the projection some Earth clothing designs that I thought could cover said wings. My personal crafting ladies had jumped on the opportunity to adjust the designs to work. Meanwhile, they had sewn a simple top for me to wear above the traditional Volitar wrap.

Now we sat in the very last meeting, finalizing my list of potential contacts. Denali would control the transporting. She would maintain scanners on each person on the list. Gil and I both wore com-links that looked like earrings, her most recent development, in conjunction with the engineers onboard. Bracelets gave us continuous direct links to each other just in case we got separated. Otherwise, we could use the earrings to contact a council member. No one else had access to these links.

Finally, we left for the transport room.

Denali handed me and Gil each a pouch of beacons. "Once they have agreed, and you think they are ready, just stick the beacon to their neck. It will feel like your Earth mosquito. This will immediately enact the transporter."

I laughed. "How the hell did you guys stick me with that? I remember thinking a mosquito had gotten inside my car. But there is absolutely no way you had someone hiding out, waiting to stick a beacon in my neck."

Denali grinned. "We had to transport the beacon and manipulate it from here. This will be *much* easier, believe me."

I hugged her. She whispered in my ear. "I have faith in my queen."

Marlux shook my hand. Taylana and her swollen belly, now nearing what would be about the fourth month of human gestation and the end of the second month of hers, engulfed me with all six arms. "Be safe, my friend."

Lanyar opened the door to the transporter unit. Ten large, lightly glowing circles on the floor lined up with another set on the ceiling. A large panel array stood to the side of the unit. I shook my head.

"What?" he asked.

"You really should gather every bit of Earth entertainment with keywords Star Trek. I think you would find it highly enjoyable that our fiction writers imagine a lot of technology that you actually have in use." I shrugged. "Actually, we might get a good segment of Trekkies from this task. It would be blasphemous to them if we didn't have that entertainment available."

He bowed his head. "I will make it so, Lady Keira." Then he stood tall again and grinned. "I'll even watch a few episodes while we await beacon signals. Maybe I can keep your mate distracted from trying to kill everyone in your absence."

I swatted his shoulder. "Goof ball. Now, give me a final scan. I'm really, really hoping to be Fertile Myrtle by the time I get back."

He complied, stating, "I thought you had no desire to be a brood mare?" When his eyes landed on the screen, though, he frowned.

My shoulders drooped a bit. "It went down again, didn't it?"

"I researched the various forms of contraception we talked about. The one you reported using can sometimes take up to eighteen cycles to fully clear your system. I'll start looking for a possible safe intervention."

I turned to my flame mate. My heart hurt at even the thought of stepping into that transporter. Yet, I knew I needed to do this.

I stared into his eyes. "It's not about just us."

He reached forward, caressing my cheek. "It's about the future of our people."

I stepped close, stretching up to kiss him. The flames did not consume us this time, but my wings burst into view, wrapping around him. They caressed him gently before slowly receding as we parted. "I love you, Vaxeehl."

He stepped back, restraining himself. His eyes screamed that he did not want me to leave, and for the first time in many years, I knew I would never be alone again.

His flames crossed the distance, dancing with mine just a moment. "And you are my heart, Keira."

He turned to Gil, his face taking on the true visage of a ruler in command. "If anything happens to my mate—"

My personal guard stood tall, his shoulders squared and chin high. "No harm will befall my queen while I yet live. Even if it means I have to press a beacon to her with my last breath."

Vaxeehl shook his hand, and then handed him a pack. "Keep an eye on her energy levels. She forgets how quickly the magic drains her."

I stomped my foot, more out of the frustration of knowing he spoke truth than annoyance. "I so do not need a nurse maid."

Both men turned and said, "Yes, you do."

"Fuck you, too."

With that, Gil and I stepped into the transporter and faded from view.

Part Four: Recruitment and Reconciliation

Chapter 22

Vaxeehl

Twenty-five days. Twenty-five days had passed since my heart faded from view. I spent my days much as I had before finding this planet. Of course, there were a few differences. I had asked Taylana and her ladies to modify some of the Earth clothing designs. I needed to uplink to my brothers, but I did not want them to see the mark of Helvana upon me without Keira at my side.

The first beacons had activated within just a few days. Keira and Denali had targeted something known on Earth as cults. Denali described them to me as places where women were reeducated to believe themselves solely as servants and breeders. There were many among them who wished to escape but had no means and no safe place to go without being found. Many in the past had tried and had been publicly abused upon being dragged back to their compounds.

Every time I learned of the atrocities on this planet, it made me wish to colonize. Instead, we would take these women away. Denali had started working with a few of the Borkanian women, uploading training gathered from many planets to help overcome this mental programming.

Within the first ten days, we had gained nearly sixty women and children. Keira had only reached her third set of coordinates. Now, the number topped one hundred.

I slid my arms into my special upper wrap, apparently called a tee shirt, and pulled it over my head. I did not like it, but I knew I could tolerate it for the length of my uplink. The ladies had stitched the part near my neck so that it felt like a rope strangling me; it took great effort not to rip it open. The part over my arms restricted my movement. If not for the nature of our natural fiber cloth, I would have felt smothered. It made me grin when I realized Gil was stuck wearing this restrictive clothing, as well as those trouser things Keira had ordered him to don.

"Ovid, provide a projection of myself, please."

"Self-view projection initiated."

The wall before me shimmered until I could see myself. The shirt fit like a second skin. More importantly, though, it hid the dancing flames.

I cancelled the projection and ordered Ovid to connect to my brothers. It only took moments before the two screens appeared.

"Hail, MeeKale. Hail, Arden. How goes your search?"

"Hail, Vaxeehl, what in Helvana's grace are you wearing?" MeeKale spoke, his green eyes twinkling. The maldron perched atop his shoulders blinked at me through the screen.

I shrugged. "This is apparently called a shirt. It is something the men of Earth wear. They are a repressed culture, determined that skin leads to sin. I decided to give it a try to see if it made the women more comfortable."

Arden guffawed. "It looks hideous. Take it off, so that I may take you seriously."

I shook my head. "I had a meeting with some of the Earth women that just finished, and another as soon as I am done here. It is a struggle to continuously remove and return the garment."

"What news have you, brother? Better than last we spoke, I hope."

I nodded. "The Borkanian woman has passed the crucial halfway point in her pregnancy. However, this raises another issue. She carries four young, and we do not have a birther onboard."

MeeKale hissed a breath. His reaction caused the sleeping maldron around his neck to complain with her own accompanying hiss "Four? Truly? This is fantastic news."

"And frightening, my medical staff tell me."

He nodded. "Very true. At best, I could fetch a birther and get there in three lunar cycles. That would be too late, would it not?"

"True, it would be late for the Borkanian. We have designated two medical staff for birther uploads, and Keira is currently searching on Earth for a viable specialist who might be willing to leave the planet."

I froze, realizing I had said her name aloud. I had not meant to reveal her involvement just yet.

Arden leaned close to the viewer. "And who is this Keira? Last I knew, the only female under your command was Denali."

"Fuck," I swore.

MeeKale piped up again. "Are you picking up curses from the women you gather?"

I laughed. "You will thoroughly enjoy the variety of ways the people of Earth curse, brother. Yes, Keira is a woman from Earth. She is the subject I mentioned when I had Lanyar send files to your researchers for revising the criteria. She has volunteered to personally recruit women from the planet."

"And how is that going?"

I smiled. "I currently house ninety-seven women of age, and fourteen young who belong to some of those women."

MeeKale scoffed. "Sure, but how long has she been recruiting."

My smile grew. I really *was* proud of her accomplishment. "This is day twenty-five."

Arden leaned closer yet. "And these women all understand already that we wish for wives? In the full sense of the word? Wives who will bear our young, and in return be cherished, yet knowing they may never return to their home planet?"

I nodded, but my smile faded from my expression. "The rulers on this planet, brothers... if I did not fear it would cost us too much in battle, I would destroy them. But we can help these women, and they help us in return. One of them actually told me she didn't care if we sprouted tentacles, as long as the sex was great and she never had to risk being found by her father. Apparently, Gilnax offered to kill her father, even if she did not agree to come. She called him 'sweet.' I heard him swearing through the com-link when Keira called to confirm the young woman had arrived safely."

MeeKale roared with laughter, causing his pet to hiss once again. "I wish I could have seen that. Gilnax is only 'sweet' when compared to that asshole brother of his. Aren't they both onboard your starship?"

I frowned deeper, both at the topic and at having to reveal information I had meant to keep silent until they had arrived. "Gundar has been fed to the waste pile."

Both of my brothers gaped. Arden spoke first. "I have a feeling that is a story best not spoken over com-link."

I nodded. I had no intention of ever speaking of it, but I would likely have to explain some when they arrived. So few reasons existed that would result in death as a punishment that I knew they had *some* idea what had occurred. Still, they would require a full telling.

Arden leaned back. "So, other than a birther, what else do you need? You could have called just one of us."

"If Keira and Gilnax continue recruiting at this rate, my holding areas will be pushed beyond maximum capacity by the time you arrive. Denali has already started changing the configuration to allow several women to room together for their quarantine period. We found it is best for those who were brought onboard together to stay together. Obviously, once their quarantine is finished, they can be moved to the general population areas, but with the new criteria, and the volatility on this planet, I think we may need all ships."

Arden sat with his hands steepled, fingers tapping while he thought. "The medical uploads Lanyar sent to father from this Earth have been helpful for the Voraxian women. It took some working to eliminate some of the harmful side-effects of their chemistry, but once that was done, father reported that three of the women have now made it safely into the third cycle without loss."

I felt an immense sense of relief sweep over me. It had been Keira's talk of contraceptives and monitoring her own fertility levels that had sent Lanyar back into the Norvaxian research. Like Earth, Norvax neared the point of over-population, even after the virus. Women outnumbered the men, but a great number of them had no desire for husbands or offspring. Lanyar had found that Norvaxian leaders tried to control their population by adding contraceptives into the food supply. Some of those chemicals had actually hindered the women's ability to carry to term, as well.

He had dragged me into the exercise room to spar that night. He gave as good a fight as usual, but I recognized his anger. When we both sat panting on the floor, bruised and sweaty, I smiled at him. "Keira would be proud of you, my friend."

I helped him stand. Then I sent him to clean up, heal his wounds, and rest. He sent his research in the middle of the night, refusing to sleep until he had finished.

"I will be sure to pass that information to Lanyar. He has blamed himself too much lately; I will enjoy showing him his success."

Arden visibly reached a decision. "I will start your way immediately. MeeKale, I assume you will fetch the birther, since you are closer to home?"

"I'm on it," he replied. "Already sent a message to father to have three ready, one for each ship, just in case. If nothing else, it will allow your medical personnel to com-link to them easier than trying to reach Volitar."

I watched him start to wave for screen dismissal, but I stopped him. "One last thing, brothers. I know it's likely foolish of me to hold out hope still but—"

Arden interrupted me, his voice dropping in sadness. "No, Vax-eehl. We have still not heard from Raklin. Even spread so far apart, not even a peep from a stranded pod."

My heart fell. I closed my eyes, praying to Helvana to keep the youngest of our number safe. I still had to beat his ass for disappearing. I drew a breath. "Thank you. I'll see you soon."

MeeKale's screen flicked out, but Arden's remained.

"You have chosen this brave human woman, haven't you, brother?"

My eyes rose. "Why would you think that?"

He scoffed at me. "You can fool MeeKale, but I have always watched you, Vax. I know you. I know you better sometimes than you know yourself. Your expression when you spoke of her gave you away, but only because I knew to watch."

I sighed. "She is my heart, Arden. Even if she never bears me a child, she is my heart. That is all I will tell you over com-link. When you arrive, you will see. Helvana has blessed us."

He pursed his lips. "I will withhold judgement. But brother, I will destroy her if she brings you harm."

I smiled. "The only harm will be if anything happens to her while she is recruiting for us on that horrid planet."

He seemed to take in my statement and nodded. "I will hail as we draw near."

Finally, the screen fell dark.

I pulled the shirt over my head and tossed it to the side.

~*~

I spent a lot of time in the holding area, speaking with the volunteers, making sure they fared well. Denali and the Borkanian women worked as a wonderful team, helping these humans learn to use our tech and adapt to their new surroundings. The holding areas were redesigned more like our normal quarters, separating the waste and hygiene areas for privacy. Apparently, the previous design too closely resembled prisons on Earth.

The young ones adapted quickly. The engineers had to write some new programming for the AI units to automatically deny access to certain information. One of them managed to find another security gap. She was only twelve, but smart as any of my onboard staff. I'd been cornered by half the engineering crew until I agreed to assign her to their group upon her release from quarantine. Her mother had cried at this news.

I thought I'd upset her, until Denali explained to me that these were supposedly happy tears. They had been taken from one of those *cults*. The girl had been denied education merely due to her being female.

I doubted I would ever fully understand these humans.

After many hours wandering through the holding area, and at least an hour in the exercise room, working myself to exhaustion, I made my way to my own quarters.

I'd never had trouble sleeping before, yet after a little over three weeks having Keira in my bed and at my side, I found I could not sleep without her. Instead of transporting back to the ship, she and Gil opted to just move directly from one location to the next to save time. They had returned with the first batch, but because of the quarantine, I could only see her through the new 'window' design Denali added. After that, she declared her heart couldn't take the stress. We could talk through the com-link, but she could not bear to see me and not be able to touch me.

I shared her thoughts, but I still didn't like it.

My rations disappeared into my stomach with little impression of taste.

Just as I settled onto the bed, my com-link dinged. "Hello, my love."

Her voice caressed my shattered nerves. I breathed her name aloud. "Keira."

"I miss you."

Gil's voice cut over the link. "Ask Denali to send another pouch of beacons and a jar of her bruise cream. Oh, and at least a dozen nutrient drinks."

Keira swore. "This is a *private* conversation, thank you very much, Gilnax. You could have called Denali directly for that."

I stifled a chuckle at her use of his full name. She only did that when aggravated.

"And not reassure your flame mate that you are being properly cared for?"

I pictured her rolling her eyes. "Is she being properly cared for? Why do you need bruise cream, love?"

She growled, although this one sounded a little less annoyed. "Gil, you're a tattle tale. It's just a sprained ankle. I stepped in a gopher hole. A little bruise cream, an elastic wrap, and I'll be fine. We got a lead on a vet who does some off-the-records human treatment due to not having a medical facility very close. Thankfully, this vet is close to where the scanners picked up lots of clustered signals for potential recruits. I really hate dealing with those backwater cults, but they *are* an easy-to-convince resource. Anyhow, with any luck, we'll have a possible doctor in a week or so."

I nodded even though I knew she could not see it. "I spoke to my brothers today. They'll be nearby in about three lunar cycles. MeeKale is stopping at Volitar and picking up three birthers, just in case."

I heard what I thought sounded like a sigh of relief. "Good. They'll be too late for Taylana, but it's always possible that we could end up with a few recruits who are already pregnant. Women get thrown out of their homes for all sorts of stupid reasons on this planet."

She paused. "Gil, please be a doll and either walk toward the trees to give me privacy or put the earbuds in and crank your music up. I really would like to have a few moments to speak to my mate alone, please."

She growled. "Is that really the best you can do?" She pouted. "Fine. But you only have yourself to blame if I embarrass you."

I laughed. "He has seen you ride me in the council chamber, my love. The only one getting embarrassed about some intimate talk is you."

"Bite me, Vax." She laughed. "I've been testing my magic, yes. I've learned several new tricks, including that I can actually burn something for real if I focus. Among other things. That's part of why we need more nutrient drinks. Tell me, flame mate, do you feel something?" Her voice turned husky.

"Other than an empty bed where I would prefer you—" I gasped. I could sense her flames trailing along my chest. "Goddess, how did you do that from so very far?"

"My thoughts of you are powerful, my love."

Gil's voice cut in again as the sensation faded. "Drink. Now."

"Spoil sport." I could hear her swallow. "Better?"

I decided that perhaps her protector could use a little assistance in convincing her. "You should conserve your strength, goddess. You'll need it when you return. The entirety of your quarantine will be done in our personal quarters, with me as your devoted servant."

Her groan filled me with anticipation. "I'm still not completely convinced that I'm a goddess, but the more I play with this magic, the closer I get to at least accepting that it's possible she has channeled herself through me. If I can make this go any faster, I will. I want that private quarantine." She sighed. "We won't be able to check in for a few days. We have another fairly sizable cluster of women to approach. Gil's presence has actually been really helpful. A few who thought we were full of shit about jumped for joy once they saw his wings. I hope everyone is adjusting well."

We spoke a bit longer catching up about the women she had already recruited. Just before disconnecting, she sent another fiery caress.

Chapter 23

Keira

Exhaustion spread through my limbs. Gil and I had been popping all over Earth for almost two months. I missed my friends, my tribe, and I desperately wanted to curl up next to my mate. I had known when we started that the women we were likely to gather would be damaged, but the extent of some of their horrors made me sick. Literally. I felt ready to vomit on an almost daily basis.

Realistically, I knew part of that could be simply from the constant transporting. Lanyar had warned us of that possibility. Thankfully, our current location had shown a very sizable cluster of potential recruits. We could actually travel between them on foot.

Some of these girls broke my heart. When we found Serena hiding beneath an overpass of the flood canal in Toronto, the girl was beyond terrified. It hadn't helped that she'd actually seen us materialize. She thought she was hallucinating. Her eyes kept darting between me and Gil, mostly watching Gil for any movement. Before we even attempted to get close, I removed my food pack and opened it where she could watch me. I pulled out a piece of the meat, tore off a section for myself, and tossed the pack to her. She watched me eat for nearly ten minutes before grabbing the pack and scarfing half the contents.

When I introduced myself addressing her by her name, she had scurried backwards, deep into the overpass supports, fear dilating her eyes.

"How do you know my name? Did my father send you? I won't go back! I won't!" She pulled a knife from her pocket and pressed it to her neck. "I'll die first, I swear it!"

I sat down on the angled wall and glanced back toward Gil. "Give me some time. I think your presence has her spooked."

My dedicated guard peeled off his jacket and draped it over my shoulder. "The air grows cold, my queen." He cast his eyes around, and I knew he sought a place to conceal himself from view yet stay close enough in case he needed to intervene. We'd done this routine a few times already. Then he turned his back and walked away, his wings in full view.

"That dude just called you a queen."

I smiled, gazing gently at her. The knife had moved away from direct contact. Good. "Yes, he did. Although, technically, my mate is a prince, but among my tribe, I am known to them as queen. It's still a little confusing to me, if I'm totally honest with you."

"A dude with wings on his back called you a queen."

"His name is Gilnax. I call him Gil. He is my sworn protector."

Serena frowned. "If he's your protector, why did he leave? I'm holding a knife."

I kept my voice soft. "You never threatened *me*, Serena. You only threatened yourself."

Her volume dropped so soft I could barely hear her. "Did my father send you to find me?"

I shook my head. "I've never met your father. I came looking for you in order to help keep you safe. I want to take you away where he can never find you again."

She pointed the knife toward me. "This is one of those sex rings, isn't it? I won't do it. Not even if you offered to actually kill my father *and* all of his men."

We sat in the channel, night falling around us, as I talked about Volitar and a new start, a place where she would have choices and protection, where she could learn to protect herself and kick someone's ass, even someone bigger. She scoffed at that.

"I've tried. All protecting myself ever brought was more pain."

Nearby, I heard Gil's soft growl. The wariness in the girl's eyes told me she had also heard it.

"May I ask Gil to come over for just a moment. He is near, as a protector should be, but I would like to use him to show you something."

She hesitated but did agree.

Gil floated down from above, his wings spread wide. I pushed myself off the ground and moved to stand directly beside him. He towered over me.

"Do you see how much taller than me Gil is?"

She nodded. I moved to stand directly in front.

"Do you see how his body structure is massively more muscular than mine?"

Again, a nod.

I turned to look at my winged guardian. "Gil, I would like to speak with Serena about how we met, but I would like this to not hurt you."

He frowned. I saw his head start to droop in shame again.

"Stand at attention, soldier."

He snapped upright. I could still feel his dislike of the situation, but he realized it would help convince the girl.

He nodded.

I seated myself again, looking to Serena. "Gil used to have a brother. He was just as large and also a soldier. Those wings," I explained, "are also weapons for the Vesper, which is Gil's heritage. And they hurt like a son-of-a-bitch. I know this because Gil's brother attacked me."

She gasped. "Did Gil save you? Is that why he is your personal guard?"

"Nope." I shook my head. I tapped my chest with one hand. "I saved myself, Serena. With just my hands and feet, and a lot of quick thinking, making use of everything in my surroundings."

She frowned, confused. "How did Gil come into the picture then?"

I drew a deep breath. "Gil came seeking revenge for his brother's death. I killed Gil's brother, Serena. The blood had barely been cleaned from the floor when this one came in, blade drawn, ready for battle."

She glared at him.

"This time, I had help. Frankly, if I hadn't, I doubt I would have survived a second battle. The first had exhausted me. When Gil learned what his brother had done, he offered himself as my personal guard. The Vesper and Volitar are honorable men. When one of their own behaves the way his brother behaved, they punish them."

Her face showed doubt. She stared directly at my guard. "Punish them how?"

He held his head high when he responded. "Had Queen Keira not beheaded Gundar, I would have ripped his heart from his chest while it still pumped."

Her eyes widened in shock. Frankly, I'm pretty sure my own were huge at his admission.

Serena opened her mouth to speak, but Gil held up one hand to signal silence. His head turned, staring into the foliage. His voice dropped barely above a whisper. "Seek shelter. I hear movement nearby."

The tiny blonde girl shuffled deep into the trusses, waving at me to join her. I slithered into the space, breathing softly. Gil's feet rose from the pavement as he took flight. Her small frame shivered beside me, and I knew it wasn't from the cold.

We stayed crouched beneath the concrete for nearly an hour before I watched the Vesper's feet drift back to the ground. "They are gone. Possibly just some hunters."

Gil extended his hand to help me climb out. In turn, I reached for Serena. She hesitated, but finally did accept. As soon as I closed my fingers around hers, the images flowed into my mind. Beatings, torture, being locked inside a dark room, rape, sodomy... gradually, even the faces of her attackers and how she had finally escaped. From my other hand, I saw through Gil's eyes. The men he had followed had been sent to find the girl. His rage encompassed me, and I sensed his need for death. Apparently, I'd transferred the images to him through that link. That was new.

He very gently helped us out from the safety of the trusses, his eyes meeting mine. We would discuss this new development later, but my need for blood was nearly as strong as his. He handed me a nutrient drink, and I nodded to him. He extended his wings wide and took off in a flash.

Serena watched until he disappeared from view. "Where did he go?"

I kept my face masked as gentle as possible. "He's going to circle around, make sure no one else comes near while we talk."

A few hours passed. I let her ask all the questions in her mind. She had to understand she would never be forced to do anything. Everything else, she could learn as she went, but that fact remained crucial.

Finally, as dawn rose, she agreed. "You really do mean a different planet, don't you?"

I giggled. "Have you ever seen an actual winged man on Earth?"

"Father could never find me. Never ever." She nodded. "I don't care if I have to scrub toilets for the rest of my life."

Gil landed nearby. I saw small blood streaks near his collar. He knelt in the stream running through the center of the channel, rinsing his hands. Rather than wipe them on his pant legs, he shook the water away. I pressed my com-link, calling to Denali.

"Beam down a fresh set of clothing for Gil, please."

A moment later, a pack appeared before me. I walked over, setting it next to him. I whispered, "I'll burn those once you're changed."

Then I returned to Serena's side, gently turning her so that we both faced away. I heard more water splashing. This canal water was not ideal, but it would have to do. We couldn't show up at our next target with one of us covered in blood. That would definitely make a less-than-stellar impression.

"You may turn, my queen."

He had tucked his soiled clothing into the pack. Unfortunately, they were soaked, and some of the fluid now leaked through the pack.

Serena noticed. "Ew! Is that blood?"

Gil nodded. "Those hunters looked for you. They will hunt no more."

I don't think I'd ever seen a person's eyes bug out quite like that girl did as his words soaked into her head. I held my hand over the top of the pack, sending my flames forward to destroy the evidence of his behavior. I noticed an itch on the back of my palm and made a mental note to ask for some kind of sanitizer during my check-in.

She blinked at him several times before she found her voice again. "You killed them? But how did you know they were after me?"

I sighed. "I try to keep a low profile. You saw those flames, right?" She nodded.

"The magic you just saw is part of a gift I received when I became queen. When you touched my hand, I saw everything in your head, the things that had been done to you. It also transmitted to Gil because he touched my other hand."

Her face fell. "You saw…"

Gil knelt on one knee before her so that he could look up and meet her downcast eyes. "This shame does not belong to you, and you should not bear it. I will kill your father and all of his men to remove your fear if you choose to remain on Earth."

When her tiny, trembling hand reached slowly toward my warrior's face to touch his cheek, I knew we had her. More than that, I knew deep down Gil had found his mate. It would be a few years before the match would be suitable; she remained quite young, and she had many things to deal with mentally. But when she felt ready, he would be waiting.

"You're so sweet. But that won't be necessary."

She turned excited eyes to me. "I'm ready to leave Earth behind."

I pulled a beacon from my pocket and pressed it to her neck. She faded from view just moments later.

"I am not sweet," Gil growled.

"Of course not. You're a trained killer. You measured out justice. There was absolutely nothing sweet about shredding two men limb from limb and scattering their bodies in the woods." I hid my grin.

That had been nearly five weeks ago. Serena had been just one of hundreds now, but she had made a lasting impression on my walking gargoyle. He tried to be sneaky about it, but I heard him regularly checking with Denali to make sure the girl was adjusting. She had started fight training almost immediately. Now that she had joined the general population, Taylana fussed over her, and Denali trained her personally. It helped strengthen my resolve to keep moving forward.

Many others like Serena still needed finding.

Despite the sanitizer, my hand continued itching. I tried to ignore it, but I would catch myself scratching at random moments. We had no

Earth money on us, so I couldn't buy any hydrocortisone cream. Besides, the itch wasn't really spreading. I didn't even see a rash. It just... was.

I spotted a small sign up ahead that caught my attention. It advertised a rural veterinarian who treated both small and large animals. Dr. Ruth Benton. The phone number was faded, but the address was clear. We were somewhere near Poplarville, Kentucky.

I glanced at my screen quickly. We had listed a number of thought scans related to children in trouble, mothers wanting to find a better place so that their children did not have to hide any longer. We'd seen this same scan pattern near each of the previous cults. I prepared myself to mentally deal with more brainwashed mothers and angry teen girls who just wanted the freedom to learn. The mothers were barely my age and had teen daughters themselves. They had been raised in these cults, forced to marry at only fifteen and bear a child right off.

These conversations seriously exhausted me.

We turned the corner onto the road with the animal hospital. I stumbled. Gil caught me, because of course he did. He thrust another nutrient bottle in my hand and ordered me to drink. I hadn't even used much magic the last several days because it drained me so much. I was beginning to wonder if my continued separation from both the tribe and my mate caused my magic to weaken.

I hadn't even mentally caressed my love for at least ten days. The most use of my gift came with a single handshake upon meeting new individuals. That touch graced me with a glance inside their minds, and a small glimpse of their compatibility with our goals.

Gil made me sit on a large stone off the road. "We should take a break. We've been beaming and walking all over this country of yours. You've done so much talking, I'm shocked you still have a voice."

If I weren't so exhausted, I would have argued with him. The damned fool would consider himself responsible if I collapsed, even if I insisted on constantly pushing forward myself. We'd visited several vet offices that Denali had flagged as possibilities based on our scan criteria, but just a handshake had proven most of them not worth wasting the breath. When we left those offices, the vets simply remembered putting to sleep a fatally injured animal, courtesy of a small hand-held inducer controlled by my guard.

"Let's check this animal hospital up the road here. She's close to where these large clusters are located, so it's not really out of our way. After that, I promise we can find a cave or a barn somewhere to just rest for a few days."

He frowned. "You must be more exhausted than even I thought, or you never would have agreed with me."

I huffed. "I am. I know we've argued before, and I've thrown the importance of success at you as motivation. But I really am worn out. We're not even halfway through the first list."

I drew a deep breath and pushed myself to stand. Based on the directions on my little phone-like device, our destination lay about two miles further up the road.

Before I could take a step, though, Gil hoisted me into his arms.

I protested heartedly. "What the fuck, dude?"

He ignored me and just started walking.

Despite the nutrient drink, I drifted to sleep in his arms.

~*~

Chapter 24

Vaxeehl

The recruitment program seemed to be working very well. We now had over two hundred human females of childbearing ages, another thirty who would reach a suitable age within a few years, and Lanyar worked with Taylana to set up what one of the new humans had referred to as an orphanage zone. This recruit had mentioned to them about a specific area of the planet where girl infants were regularly abandoned shortly after birth for no other reason than being girls. It then fell to their governments to care for these babies. Some were not even taken to these places; they were left to die in the wilderness. I recognized the description from Denali's earlier research, but even she had not known that children were being left to die.

Denali had quickly entered new search criteria into the scanners, seeking parents on the verge of abandoning their daughters. Some of the new recruits immediately stepped up to help when the children arrived, even getting multiple language uploads to be able to speak to any of them. We had determined we would transport every girl child in the orphanages at the last possible moment. A disappearance of that magnitude would cause a stir. We hoped their government would see their absences as a relief rather than a concern, but we wanted to be on our way far from this solar system before that happened.

The expression on Arden's face when I explained this plan to him would have sent chills down an enemy's spine.

"Every time I speak to you about this planet, it makes me more and more angry."

I agreed. "The better behaved on the surface are typically the ones they themselves call primitive. They have tribes who still live in huts or tents, and who share resources for the betterment of their tribe. We won't garner any from those groups, as they seem to value their women. Maybe not in the same manners we do, but they do not appear to cast out many."

"It astounds me your level of ease with recruiting. But then, you are not dealing with their government. Your female is dealing directly with the recruits themselves." He huffed. "Why did we not consider this approach in previous encounters?"

"As my mate has taught Denali to say, we are arrogant bastards who couldn't see past the end of our dicks to find our feet without women to give us direction."

He laughed loud. "Seeing her level of success, this Keira might be right about that."

"She and Gil are due to visit another potential doctor today or tomorrow. Gil has informed me that he has demanded she rest for a few days after this visit. He won't give me details, but I know Keira. She is stubbornly independent. If she has agreed to a break, either she thinks Gil is in need—"

"Not likely. He's a Vesper warrior. They can go up to a week with only minimal naps and still function well."

"Or she is barely able to function. It's been just under sixty day cycles, and we have nearly three hundred humans. Lanyar broke his vow of silence to her and actually reported she was showing signs of transporter sickness from being moved so often."

"Helvana send blessings. She swore your Chief Medical Officer to a vow of silence over her health?"

"I told you, brother. My mate has vowed to help save Volitar. She is as honorable as our own kind. She would rather suffer than fail to keep her promise."

He digested this information for a while. "I still am not fond of her manner of speech, but I think I am beginning to understand her. I look forward to meeting your future queen."

"What hails the news from home?" I wanted to deflect his attention, fearful I would speak of things best left said in person.

Arden studied me, and I knew he wished to discuss my mate more. Instead, he humored me. "The Voraxians continue to show improvement. Father is now agreed that these humans you have found, while still a primitive and war-hungry people, have given him hope. MeeKale has gathered the birthers and started our way."

Then he smiled. "I found a new worm hole that looks to reduce several day cycles of travel. I will be entering soon. By the time MeeKale reaches this point, I should be through and able to report success to him. If my engineers have calculated correctly, I should see you within another twenty days or so."

Thinking of how quickly we continued to gain recruits, I nodded. "That is very good news."

He leaned toward the screen. "And then you can tell me the real reason you keep wearing those shirts during uplinks, and much more about this Keira. If I may face against father for you, I need more than what you have given as of yet."

I frowned. "I have no intention of fighting against father. He is welcome to continue ruling Volitar."

Arden checked around him and his voice lowered to a near whisper. "Vaxeehl, the sharing program has led to unrest."

I growled. "Hopefully, this influx of suitable brides will aid in restoring order and canceling the sharing program. I cautioned him against it. As you did, if I recall."

He nodded. "We did. And he chose not to listen. Not all of the Norvaxian deaths were virus, brother. At least four were suicide. Father ordered them to take multiple mates."

Anger encompassed my entire being. Before I could react, I felt the flames encompass my flesh.

Arden's gasp told me they had become visible.

"That's new."

I drew several deep breaths, trying to calm my emotions and gather the power of the flames back to my body.

"I swear I will explain when you arrive. I have sworn that already."

"This has to do with your human mate, doesn't it?"

I nodded. "Yes. Plus the Borkanian females. Again, I must extract your word that you will tell no one. Not even MeeKale."

"We have never kept secrets from each other before."

The flames fully receded. "I have never been at risk of inciting civil war before, Arden. One glimpse of this development will have many of our people baying for father's immediate removal. I will not force him to step down. I can't. Your word, if you please. And lock down this com-link record."

He nodded. "You have it. But the explanation better be fantastic."

"Thank you, brother. I will see you soon."

The screen finally dark, I removed the shirt, carefully inspecting the material. I saw no evidence of damage, so at least accidental eruptions did not harm the material.

I left the council chamber and headed toward the general population areas to speak with more of the recent quarantine releases. It seemed to calm their anxiety when they realized they spoke with 'the prince'. It reminded me of my childhood. I would travel regularly with my parents as they journeyed all around Volitar, making sure to greet the farm hands in the same manner as the land holders.

However, when I entered the general population area, the women were barking orders. I spotted engineers redirecting walls, moving beds, piles and piles of blankets building up. Food carts arrived piled high with numerous trays.

At the head, directing every group like a seasoned general, stood Denali.

"Line up the transport crystals inside the quarantine hall. Belnic, I need that cleansing station attached from the transport crystals and straight into the large holding room the engineers are shifting. It's important that we keep all of this group together. Angus, two-forty-three, not three hundred. From the sounds of things, we won't have time to remove extras before they get to another potential area with at least a hundred more."

My head swirled a moment.

I felt a tug at my kilnat. A yellow-haired young one worked to gain my attention. I reached down, sweeping her into my arms. "Good morning, Janey. Did you get separated from your mother?"

She nodded. "Mommy is helping gather beds. She said the fire lady is sending lots and lots of new peoples to live here so they can be happy, too. I like the fire lady."

I chuckled. "I'll tell you a secret. I really like the fire lady, too. How about I take you over to the play area so that you don't accidentally get injured with all this activity."

"Okay." She started humming her favorite silly song about ants marching.

"Oh, thank goodness. I got so swept up in the excitement that I lost her." Mary, the mother of the adorable singer in my arms, came jogging over.

I smiled. "She's fine, Mary. I was on my way to deliver her to the children's area. It looked a little dangerous for her out here."

She stretched her arms out, but Janey refused to move. "Mommy, I want the Pwince to take me. I can see peoples up here."

"Go ahead, Mary. I'll see her safely across the public area." I watched all the activity. "What exactly is going on? I haven't gotten the report yet."

Mary bounced nearly as excited as her child. "The rumors were true! There really were safe houses. Lady Keira has found the first safe house. Denali said it would take quite some time to get everyone transported aboard, but she wanted to leave nothing to chance. She wants everything in place before the first one beams up."

I found myself glad I had let Lanyar bully me into watching the strange television shows my mate had suggested to him. It helped me understand much more of the unusual human terminology for our similar technology.

I nodded to her, bouncing Janey in my arms a bit so that she squealed with laughter. "Run along then. I'll drop the giggle factory with the other children and go see what else needs done."

It took another half hour before I could pry the young one from my arms. She had tried to convince me to stay and play games with her. I'd been forced to pinkie swear I would come back later.

Finally, I stepped up next to Denali. "I see we have a major influx coming in."

"Oh, sire, sorry. You were still in conference with your brothers when the call came through—no, Angus, count them again. The room isn't even finished yet, there is no way you have enough beds in place."

"Do you need me, or should I just get out of your way?"

She sighed. "Thank you for asking. Actually, can you make sure the medic trainee has everything he needs to check everyone in properly. I don't want to risk the records getting scrambled. Lanyar would be livid."

I furrowed my brow. "Why is Lanyar not guiding his trainee?"

Denali did not meet my eyes when she spoke. "He had to transport down to help. Apparently, there are some injuries that need treated before the transports can take place."

I glared. "There are possibly critically injured recruits in a safe house. Is that not a bit contradictory?"

Her eyes met mine. She parted her lips to speak, hesitated, and tried again. She pursed her lips.

"You want to tell me, but you have been instructed by your queen not to say."

Her shoulders sagged. "I vow that Queen Keira is not injured, nor are our people—any of our people—being put in danger. But she feared you would transport to Earth if you knew what she found. I beg you, sire. Please ask me no more. Just know that your mate is still protected. I would never put my queen at risk."

I stared at her for a while before responding. My mate was strong. She was used to being on her own, had been for years. She had taken on the task of helping to save a planet about which she only knew it had been devastated by the same virus that killed so many of her own kind.

I had to trust her.

I nodded. "I will check the medics."

~*~

Chapter 25

Keira

"Queen Keira, you must awaken."

My eyelids fluttered open. I felt at least a little bit better. Gil crouched over me, looking concerned. I pushed myself upwards, realizing he had laid me to rest under the shade of a tree.

I stretched, forcing myself to start functioning again. "Where are we? How long was I out?"

He handed me food and drink and waited until I started eating before joining me. "You slept for almost four hours. The destination is a short distance from here, but I did not wish to draw suspicion by approaching with an unconscious female in my arms."

My energy level still felt stifled, but I knew I had a vacation of sorts after we investigated this veterinarian.

"Wise choice. This is rural America here. People are a lot more mindful of strangers, especially with the return of so many drifters after the economy collapsed." I finished my meal and rose, testing my legs.

Gil stood, letting me take the lead. "You are still committed to resting after this visit. Yes?"

I sighed. "Yes. If I have to take a four-hour nap while you carry me two miles, then it is definitely time to rest. If I didn't want to risk the damned transporter sickness again, I'd return to the ship to recover."

I caught myself scratching my hand again. "Damn it. I wish I knew what the hell keeps causing this itch. I'm afraid I'm going to break the skin open with the constant scratching, then I'll be at risk for infection from who knows what we come into contact at all of these random sites."

Another weathered sign greeted us at the end of a long dirt drive. The drive angled and twisted through tall trees before finally revealing a building that looked more like a home that had been converted for use, rather than an actual office. A small barn stood behind and to the right. The dirt path continued past the barn, disappearing into a larger cluster of trees further back.

A small bell rang when Gil opened the door for me. An older gentleman stood by the counter talking to a bubbly young blonde in tie-dyed scrubs.

She glanced up, her eyes landing on Gil first, looking wistful as they traveled the entire length of him. When her gaze flittered my direction, those eyes opened wide. She had a look of recognition on her face. This confused me, as I knew I had never been near this region before, nor did I remember ever having met her.

She spoke to the gentlemen at the counter. "I'll be right back, Jim. Ruth has been expecting this couple, and I need to take them to her office. Ruth and Marianne are just pulling the stitches from Maisy's incision, and they'll bring her up."

She circled the desk, waving toward us. "This way, Mr. and Mrs. Johnson. Ruth is finishing with a patient, but she'll be with you soon."

Perplexed, I nodded hesitantly toward Gil. The chipper clinician didn't say anything else until she had led us to a room near the back of the building and closed the door. "Oh my God! I can't believe there really are more out there." She turned toward me. "And you're a royal! This is just amazing."

I never got a chance to answer. Someone yelled from the hall.

"Belinda! Finish Jim's bill so he can get going. He has his weekly date with his wife tonight."

The girl who I assumed to be Belinda darted back through the door, shutting it firmly.

"Ruth, the Johnson's are in your office." Despite the closed partition, we could hear the conversation clearly.

"The Johnsons?"

"Dude is tall as a church steeple, dressed in black, and that delicious chocolate skin. There's a woman with him, too. Dressed in their distinctive blood red. She has the same emblem as tall, dark and dreamy."

My eyes met Gil's, and I knew they had to be the size of saucers. Gil's certainly were. He opened his mouth to speak, but I shook my head. There was something very big going on, and I had an idea what it was, but if I could hear them speaking, then they could also hear us.

The discussion continued. "Once Jim has cleared the drive, lock everything up. If that son-of-a-bitch has been lying to me for seven fucking years, I don't want anyone close enough to hear me scream at him. He *swore* they were alone."

Footsteps drew near, pausing at the door.

The woman who entered carried herself with elegance and confidence. She stood near to my own height, had dark brown hair, dark eyes, and a medium brown complexion. If I were to guess, I would consider her of Mexican or Italian descent. She circled the desk, seating herself behind it, not bothering to acknowledge us or indicate we should sit.

"Alright. How did you know to come here?"

I extended my hand toward her. "You are Dr. Ruth Benton?"

She nodded, ignoring my hand. "I am, and I would appreciate it if you would answer my question. Belinda promised she had not recently posted anything on the darknet."

I retracted my arm and straightened my posture. "Dr. Benton, my name is Keira Sutton. This is my friend, Gil. I am unsure how to answer your question, though. I have no access to whatever darknet you speak of. We are just drifting through, and I seem to be having some sort of allergic reaction. I can't really afford to see a people doctor, so I was wondering if you might be willing to look at my hand."

The woman pursed her lips and rolled her eyes, mumbling under her breath. "Fucking foreign bastards can't keep their monster dicks in their pants."

I'm sure she thought she had spoken soft enough for us not to hear, but I gasped just the same. I narrowed my eyes and pointed at Gil. "You know something about my companion?"

She scoffed. "You could say that. Although, I have to admit that you have done a really good job covering his wings. We wouldn't have to deal with the biologists and government idiots snooping around all the time if the others would bother taking such care."

She stood up and crossed to a cabinet, grabbing a specimen container and handed it to me. I stared at it blankly.

She rolled her eyes. "How long has your hand been itching?"

"Five... about five weeks," I stuttered.

"Nausea?"

I nodded.

"Excessive hunger and exhaustion?"

"Yes. Why?"

"Idiots." She pointed toward a door. "Go pee in the cup. I'll grab some lidocaine cream."

The door closed behind her.

I blinked a few times before I turned to Gil. "I think we found Raklin."

"I must report—"

"No!" I practically yelled the word. Then calmer, I said, "Wait until we confirm. I don't want to cause an interstellar war by having a shit ton of you large bastards beaming down here to storm the castle. And what if Raklin isn't among the group? What if it's just other survivors?"

He frowned, but nodded. Then he pointed at the plastic jar in my hands. "Why does she want you to deposit liquid waste in a container?"

I shrugged, even though I had a *huge* gut feeling that I also knew what she suspected. The questions she asked were very similar to questions I would have asked myself had I thought of them together. "Let's find out."

I retreated behind the door the doctor had pointed to, filled the container, washed my hands with blessedly warm water, and returned to the main office. Ruth came back just moments later. She carried a large case in her hands.

Without speaking, she took the specimen cup and set it on her desk. Then she reached in the top right drawer and pulled out a very familiar package.

"Nuh-uh." Yep. I was real articulate.

She tore the foil packet open, pulled out the stick and held it in my urine sample. Then she laid it on the desk, took the remaining sample and flushed it.

I watched the liquid drift across the screen, seeing an almost immediate plus sign on the second window.

"Well fuck me."

She snorted. "Obviously, the big guy here already did that. Based on what you've said, the itching should go away in about three more weeks. The lidocaine cream will help numb the nerve endings until your hormones level out. I'm better with animal genetics than human, but my best guess is the itch is caused by the combined growth hormones. I would guess you about eight weeks right now, which means you have about sixteen more to go, since their gestation takes so much less time."

Gil ordered me to sit. I was so numb from the brain down that I obeyed without an argument. After a moment, I shook my head, trying to make it work again.

"I'm pregnant?" The words echoed through the room before settling in my own ears.

She turned to Gil. "Congratulations, you stupid idiot. I'm running out of room, but we'll figure out a way to keep you from being found. The bad news is that I don't have access to anything like an epidural or spinal block when she goes into labor."

Gil frowned. "The queen does not carry my child."

He turned his attention to me. "You must return to the ship. I will hear no argument."

My head cleared of confusion and filled with anger. "Excuse me, you overgrown bat, but I will do no such thing. The plan stays the same. I will not put Vaxeehl's heir in danger, but we are not finished."

"Did you say ship?"

Gil stomped, rattling the floor with his strength. "You had already agreed to taking a break. The safety of your child demands that the plan change. We can find someone else among the women you have already gathered to take over the recruitment process."

"Did you say ship?" Ruth's voice grew louder.

"Damn it, Gil. You've seen the shape some of these women have been in. Think of Serena! What if we hadn't found her when we did? Those men would have killed her!"

Ruth bellowed. "Hey! Can I please butt in a moment?"

Gil growled. "This conversation is not finished."

I growled right back at him. "Yes, it is. And if I see you reach for that com-link, I'll rip your ear off." I turned back to Ruth. "Did you have something to say? Other than being an absolute bitch without asking any questions? Because if not, I have a job to do. I can't afford to waste any time here if you can't help me. I happen to think that out of every damned veterinarian I've met so far, you are the most likely candidate, but you are so angry, I wouldn't let you anywhere near Taylana, or myself, with a fucking ten-foot pole!"

The woman deflated a bit. "I probably deserved that." She waved toward the chairs. "Have a seat, and let's start over. Did you say ship? They've finally arrived? Someone got the signal?"

I extended my hand. "Now that we're on the same page, will you please shake my fucking hand? You just told me I'm pregnant, even though my last exam scan before transporting back to the surface still showed my fertility hormones being suppressed."

She laughed. "Fine. Keira, I'm Ruth. Pleased to meet you." As soon as her palm touched mine, I dropped into the chair. The sea of faces that flooded my mind boggled it.

"Holy shit."

I released her hand, and Gil thrust a nutrient drink into my palm. I rolled my eyes, setting it down untouched. "I'm fine, Gil. That little bit of magic is hardly taxing."

I stared at the woman before me. "How many?"

Ruth stared at me confused, and I realized she had no clue that I had seen inside her mind.

"Between what I just saw in your head and what you've said since storming in here pissed to high heaven, you've been successfully hiding a pretty huge secret for seven years. Just how big is that secret?"

She sputtered.

I closed my eyes a moment, trying to gather my thoughts.

Ruth finally gained her voice. "There were twenty-one men who survived the crash, but we lost eight of them to the virus, the original one, not the new versions that spring up every few months. Thankfully, the protests take place in the metropolitan areas. It keeps the bio-engineered versions from making it this far. Somehow, these guys keep finding strays."

I frowned. "Strays?"

Ruth nodded. "Let's walk and talk. The golf cart broke last week, and I didn't feel comfortable calling the repair company to come out here."

She led the way out of the office. We followed her through a small kitchen and out the back door. Once we stepped off the wooden steps of the back deck, the bubbly blonde caught up with us. She opened her mouth to speak, but Ruth cut her off.

"Belinda, take the bicycle and ride ahead. Make sure they know we're coming. I'd prefer not to get shot."

The girl frowned, but she did as instructed.

Ruth sighed. "I apologize for Belinda. She's a good enough receptionist and an excellent lab technician, but she is completely enthralled with the Vesper males. The purple guys, not so much, but she has been flirting with anything with wings, begging them to take her with them."

I nodded. "Then you wouldn't be surprised to know that Gil's wings were a selling point for a few of the volunteers I've collected. How far are we walking?"

"It's about a mile and a half into the trees. I wanted it as secure as possible. You and I both know what would have happened had those fuckers in charge gotten their hands on an actual alien, and not just the virus."

"Why don't you start at the beginning? And pretend I'm dumb as a box of rocks, because I have a feeling I might be."

She laughed. "You know how the news has said the virus came in with an asteroid?"

I nodded.

She continued. "There was no asteroid, no meteor. It was a real life, alien-carrying spaceship. Melnon—apparently one of the pilots or technicians, I'm still a little confused on his job—said that was just the escape pod. Anyhow, some big disaster happened to their ship. Twenty-one of them survived and got into the pod. Then something went wrong with the pod. Earth was the closest planet with the right atmosphere and plant life for them to land.

"Being the *lucky person* I am, my sisters—that's Marianne and Belinda—and I had been over to Mt. Victory for a horse show and had the trailer with us." She pointed toward a large motor home as we walked past. "We actually saw the pod hit. We thought it was a plane, and we went looking for survivors. I may be licensed as an animal doctor, but I know more than enough about human physiology to handle trauma cases. I actually used to volunteer to treat miners whenever there's been a collapse or landslide."

I grinned. I couldn't wait to see Lanyar's face when he met Ruth. If she agreed to come, that is.

"We found injuries, alright. And a whole lot of purple and brown male flesh that clearly was not human. I went into doctor autopilot, assessing injuries and trying to figure out what I was doing. One whole side of the pod was burning. One of the dudes stumbled back into the pod and grabbed a tablet-looking device. He scanned my face, then his own. Then he asked me for a place to hide until they can figure out a way to call for a ride back home."

She laughed. "In English. And when I hesitated, he asked again in Spanish. Based on how I greeted you, you can imagine how I reacted when I finally found my voice. I went off about what would happen to myself and my sisters if the government found us hiding actual aliens.

Not illegal immigrants, actual freaking aliens. Meanwhile, Marianne started crying. One of the guys was bleeding horribly from a giant cut on his arm. The dude with the tablet thing knelt down next to him and aimed that scanner light. And right before my eyes, I watched the flesh knit back together.

"That's when shit hit the fan in my brain. I couldn't do it. I couldn't leave these guys to be found by the government. They'd have been locked up in some top-secret bunker for some jackass scientist to dissect, and their tech would be torn apart... I panicked. Somehow, in my insanity, I managed to get him to understand reality."

"Which reality is that," I asked.

"I realized that officials could show up anytime. If the tech on that ship fell into the wrong hands, it would be the end of life as we knew it. Dude scanned my face again while this panic-driven tirade flew through my brain, and whatever he saw on his screen got his attention. Or I started making sense, but I doubt that much. All I could picture was the start of another World War with weapons worse than nuclear. Dude could barely walk, but he stumbled back inside the pod, grabbed a few bare essentials, and came back out. As he walked toward me, I watched the whole thing turn to dust. The fire hadn't yet spread to the vegetation, so it faded out as the pod did.

"We had just enough room in the trailer to fit all of them. We loaded everyone up and got the hell out of Dodge. They've been holed up here ever since. Belinda has been keeping track of progress on the darknet. The government scientists know it wasn't an asteroid, but they haven't yet figured out exactly what it was."

The path turned a corner. My mind worked hard to take in everything the woman told me. "But the virus came from the asteroid."

Ruth's hands twitched. "Watching as it spread around the planet, I wanted to kill every last one of them, but the damage was already done. Marianne got sick first. She was the one taking care of them while I kept the practice going to keep suspicion away. She and I worked tirelessly, trying to figure out what was happening, hoping like hell that whatever was wrong with them couldn't transmit to us. Like I said, we lost eight of them—the worst injuries that the dude with the scanner couldn't fix. But then, Marianne got sick. Belinda and I got sick within two days of Marianne. These assholes kept us alive.

"The geologists who reported to the crash site caught it, too. That's how it actually spread to the rest of the planet. Once we got better, Belinda started digging deep into the darknet. I had blood samples from all of them, as well as us, and I improvised like hell to do my own research. Once I had the chemical fingerprint, Belinda managed to connect to a whistleblower and got her hands on so much information, it took me a while to read it, and even longer to believe it."

We approached a barn. A few horses roamed in a small clearing nearby. Ruth opened the barn. "Welcome to the worst possible safe house on Earth."

I stepped inside and met a sea of faces... the sea I'd seen in her mind. The details of her story flew from my thoughts as I scanned the crowd. A few tall males in various shades of light purple stood near the front, although they looked grey in the low light. Nearby, I noted at least three women with swollen bellies. I spotted a couple sets of wings spread toward the back. My eyes roamed from face to face for some time, almost overwhelmed.

"There has to be at least two hundred women here!"

Ruth shrugged. "I lost count. Belinda had foolishly posted a cryptic message on the darknet, and people started flooding this way. We had to recruit a trusted friend to house some of the overflow of women before Belinda was able to shut down the influx. Thankfully, the friend took in only women, and none of the alien men. They're located about nine miles away from here."

I stepped further inside to let my eyes adjust.

One of the grey/purple men stormed my direction, anger evident on his face. "You dare, human, to wear the sign of our ruler?"

Two things happened as his hand reached for me. Gil pinned him to the dirt beneath our feet, and my flame wings spread wide in full form instantly.

"Helvana has come," several voices whispered.

A heavily-accented female voice cried, "Analisa, no!"

I watched as a small girl child, maybe four years old, flew toward me at high speed. I opened my arms, catching her gently. Her fingers reached out, fluttering through my wings. "Yours are prettier than mine," she said, flaring hers out behind her.

I smiled. "I think yours are awfully pretty. Besides, I can't fly with mine. Maybe. That could change. I'm still learning."

A slightly younger version of Ruth came running over, looking terrified that I might hurt the child. The girl turned to her. "Mommy, the pretty lady said she likes my wings."

"How about I hand you to your mommy, sweetie. She looks like she wants to hug you really, really tight."

The girl giggled. "Mommy always hugs me." The girl jumped from my arms to her mother's.

Ruth addressed the woman. "Marianne, where is your husband?"

The young woman I now knew to be Marianne, Ruth's other sister, stared at my dancing flames a little longer before leading toward the back. She spoke in Spanish to Ruth. My language upload translated. "I think the wound is getting infected. He has a fever, and the skin is not closing."

I followed the sisters while they discussed what had been done. As we crossed the distance, I saw more Volitar and Vesper males surrounding a single Vesper male. He lay on a blanket on the ground. A large absorbent bandage covered his left chest, although blood and greenish fluid stained it. The woman, Marianne, knelt beside him, holding his hand.

"Raklin, my love."

Dark, cloudy eyes opened and looked at me. "Helvana has come for me." A smile spread on his face. "I have been forgiven my sins, and she has come to escort me to paradise."

I knelt on his other side, the men making space as I neared. I brushed his hair away from his sweaty forehead. "Even better, brother. We're here to take you home."

Marianne started crying. "No, please. He can't leave. How will I raise Analisa without her father?"

I willed my wings to fade. "Marianne, I would never take your husband away from you."

I looked to Ruth. "What happened?"

"Idiot went out flying again, despite the news reports of strange sightings. Thankfully, no one realized they saw something that looked human with wings, plus he keeps the hunting several miles away to deflect attention. He was trying to bring back a deer to help feed this lot and got his stupid ass shot. He flew in the opposite direction for a long while until he finally thought it safe to return. By then, the infection had already started to grow." Despite her harsh words, I heard the tears in her voice. "The scanner thing quit working a few months ago, leaving them at the mercy of human medicine. They'd been hoping a rescue ship would have arrived already, but that beacon stopped almost a year ago. I've done everything I can, but I'm almost out of antibiotics. The supply chain issues have made it difficult to get any of my orders filled."

I called over my shoulder. "Gil!"

He appeared beside me almost instantly. "Yes, my queen."

The men around the room mumbled at the royal address. "Oh for— I don't have time for this." I stood up, dusting off my knees. I raised my voice. "Men of Volitar and Vesper, Prince Vaxeehl has arrived. Ladies, I'm guessing by your presence here, all of you would be more than happy to get the hell off this planet?"

The whole freaking barn erupted into cheers. I turned back to Gil. "We need to figure out how many are here. I'm going to call for reinforcements."

I turned to Ruth. Her face looked crushed. "You're going to take my sisters away from me. I want to be happy for them, but I'm having a selfish moment."

I hugged her. "My god, woman. I didn't come here for *them*. I came here for *you*!" I pointed to the child. "I came looking for a doctor willing to help figure out how to safely birth cross-species children because we don't have one onboard the starship. You've already done it! You just need to catch up on Borkanian biology to help with that, but you'll have time during the quarantine to learn."

She froze. "What?"

"Listen," I sighed. "Gil and I were drawn to the area because the thought scans showed us a cluster of women looking to escape Earth, and a fear of keeping their children safe. We couldn't fully detect what was going on, just that it looked like an easy place to recruit a lot of volunteers in a short amount of time. When we saw one of your old billboards a few miles away, we decided we'd stop here on the way to these clusters, just to see if it was possible for you to be willing to learn."

I stopped myself. "There's too much to explain right now. I need a quiet place to make a call, but I need to stay close. I want whoever shows up to be able to transport directly here."

Her sniffles continued, but she led me out another door.

"Good luck getting a signal."

I snorted. "I'm not using Earth tech." I tapped my earring. "Denali and Lanyar, secure link, barring all others."

Back to back, I heard the connections. "Lady Keira."

"I don't even know where to start." I drew a breath. "Lanyar, is it safe to transport someone with an injury and possible infection?"

"It is not impossible, but it is highly risky. An open wound can be further split by the transport process," he answered.

"What about a pregnant female? What is the risk to a pregnant female during transport?" My gut clenched as I realized I was asking about myself, and I could have already caused injury to my own child.

"It would be best to scan each female before transport, but this has been done with our own people in the past. What in the name of the goddess is going on, Lady Keira?"

"I need this to stay silent. Not Marlux, not Taylana, and *especially* not Vaxeehl. I need one of you to transport down to my location with medical supplies. I have a wounded Vesper male with a possible infection who is not looking good. I mean not at all. I also have several pregnant females."

I heard Lanyar gasp and figured he'd already grasped my meaning.

Denali spoke. "Just how many are we talking?"

"I'm still awaiting a final count. But Lanyar, the answer to the procreation question is a resounding yes. It is one hundred percent possible for a human to successfully bear young to those of Volitar. And I have found a doctor who knows all about it, if she's willing to come."

He paused before asking, "How is that possible?"

I swallowed, finally prepared to speak aloud what he suspected. "Raklin lives, Lanyar. And if Vaxeehl finds out, he'll transport down here and put himself at risk unnecessarily."

"And the doctor?"

I stared at Ruth. "I'm working on it. You might be able to help with that."

Gil stuck his head out the door. "Two hundred forty-three, including the doctor and her sisters."

Denali swore. "Helvana be praised. Did he just say two hundred forty-three to transport?" She paused. "I'll be back in contact about logistics. I don't want to risk overloading, and I'll want to set up enough spaces."

I shook my head. "Try to keep them fairly close together, if possible. This group has been sharing a barn for a long time. We can work on splitting them according to their own preferences after we get everyone onboard and settled in. Apparently, there is a second location with even more women ready to move without much convincing needed, also."

Denali confirmed. Then Lanyar spoke again.

"I'll gather what I can and call you so that I have a fix on your location before I transport. I will aim to land directly to your left side, so keep that clear. I should be ready in ten minutes."

"Denali, I will start coaching now to prepare them, but I will await word from you that you are ready."

They both agreed, and I ended the call.

Ruth stared at the com-link. "You just made an interstellar call with your earring?"

I laughed. I laughed so hard I couldn't breathe. When I finally got control of myself, I patted her on the shoulder. "You literally stood beside me when flaming wings burst from my body, and *the com-link* is what shocks you?" I smiled. "I really hope you decide to come, Ruth. I like you, and I think I can trust you to help my friend. I've spent eight weeks beaming all over the country trying to find a vet who maybe dabbled in human medicine, who I could convince to help figure out alien biology to safely birth children. I have visited at least twelve, and I couldn't even bring myself to mention it."

My com-link dinged. "Keira here."

Lanyar's voice answered. "I'm ready to come down."

I looked to my left and realized I stood too close to the barn. I moved four feet, leaving space. "Bring it on, big man."

Ruth gazed at me, studying my face a moment. "Tell me about this Borkanian you mentioned."

I smiled and reached toward her. She startled.

"I can show you better than I can tell you. I figured out a few weeks ago that I could transmit as well as receive information."

She hesitantly stepped forward to be within reach. I pressed one hand above her heart and the other to her cheek. Then I closed my eyes and concentrated on sending her everything I could about Taylana. Once I sensed the magic had worked, I pulled my hands away and opened my eyes.

Ruth blinked a few times. "Holy Fucking Hell. Did I just see six arms?"

"Try having one of them be the first alien you see. 'Holy fucking hell' describes my own reaction pretty well."

Lanyar materialized beside me, and Ruth jumped backwards. Rapid fire curses in both English and Spanish flew from her lips. Her left hand held the exterior of the barn, her right lay over her chest. "Warn a girl before you do shit like that."

I started laughing again. "Sorry. I'm so used to Gil hearing all of the uplinks that I forgot you only heard my side of the conversation." I motioned between them. "Doctor Lanyar, Doctor Ruth Benton."

He acknowledged the introduction. Then he held up the instruments in his hands. "Where is the injured?"

Ruth led the path into the barn. I stayed out of the way, bringing up the end of the train. Lanyar almost tripped when he saw how many people crowded in the giant room. Hearing a number and seeing the reality of it were two different things. He quickly corrected and ignored everyone as he knelt beside the fallen prince.

"Raklin, you rotten son-of-a-bitch, you've had everyone scouring the universe for you, and here you've been camped out in a nice, cozy livestock shelter, soaking up the joyful companionship of hundreds of women? What the fuck, man?"

"Lanyar," I teased. "You've been watching Earth entertainment and picked up a human side."

He shot me a quick grin before he started scanning and staring at the screen. Then he turned toward Ruth, asking questions, getting answers. Soon, they worked as a team, only slowing when Ruth didn't recognize something he'd said. He would quickly explain or point, and they were right back to work.

I walked away, trusting in their conjoined training to save my mate's brother.

I spent the next two hours talking to the huge gathering of women. They stood or sat near the front of the barn, listening to everything I told them, occasionally asking a question. Mostly, they were all excited for this new chapter in their lives to finally begin after so many years in hiding. When I told them I had arranged for them to be quarantined together until we got everyone aboard and they could decide if they wanted separate spaces, I saw many happy faces.

At one point, one of the ladies handed me a tube of cream. I realized I had started itching again. I thanked her while applying a small dab to the back of my hand.

When Denali finally called, she informed me of all the changes she had put in place to accommodate my requests. However, because we were not using the actual transport room to bring them up, we could only send twenty at a time. She wanted to have each group decontaminated, changed, medically evaluated, and settled into their quarters before we sent another group. She estimated it would take two to three days to get them all received, allowing time for sleep.

I carefully explained the decontamination process to the crowd, as well as showing them the clothing they would receive. The hygiene units definitely took some getting used to. One of the ladies specifically asked how she was supposed to handle the monthly curse. When I explained how the hygiene unit made the blood go away with a gentle current, she cheered. "I'm sold for that alone."

I yawned. "Good grief. I took a nap just a few hours ago."

A large lavender form stepped up, tossing several packs into the crowd. "Plenty for everyone." He motioned to a bale of hay by the wall. "Gilnax said you need to sit." I noticed he had several scrapes on his face and a bruise coloring his left eye.

I glared. "You're the one who believes me unworthy of wearing my mate's colors."

He frowned. "I ask forgiveness for my error in judgement. I did not realize you were mated to Prince Vaxeehl. Gilnax has reeducated me."

I nodded. "Gilnax is a soldier of honor. He is sworn to protect me, and he takes his duties *very* seriously."

The man fought not to crack a grin. "I've noticed."

Gil approached from behind, clapping the man on the back. "It wasn't even worth the effort. I should have let the queen reeducate you herself." Then he glared at me. "If she were not carrying the heir, I would have. Sit."

I waved him off. "I'm fine, Gil. You worry too much."

"You passed out this afternoon."

"It's not about me," I began our very familiar argument once again.

He growled. "It's about the future of our people. A future you now carry in your womb."

The man laughed. "Is she this feisty all the time?"

"And then some," Gil replied, letting his frustration show through his voice.

I rolled my eyes, but I did cross the short distance and settle onto the bale. Gil sat beside me, handing me a pack. "Please, Queen Keira, reconsider. You are pushing yourself too hard. You now risk injury to the child."

I sighed. "I'll consider it, Gil." I opened the pack and split the rations with him. "We need to start separating everyone into groups of twenty."

He nodded. "I spoke with Denali as well. I have met with Raklin's men already. Each of them has mated to one of the females, and they wish to transport with their wives and children. They are arranging the groups on their own. I will handle distributing the beacons. All you need to worry about for the next several days is taking care of yourself and the young one. And perhaps convincing Ruth. Although, when last I stood near the two medics, she had already started asking Lanyar so many questions, I think he might be the one to convince her to come."

I frowned. "I wonder why she seems so hostile, yet her own sister has mated to Raklin."

He tipped his head, staring at me. "She feels she has dishonored her own people."

I stared, trying to figure out what he meant.

He continued. "She rescued Raklin's men, and in doing so, she feels she unleashed 442-C onto your planet."

The food in my mouth suddenly tasted like ash, and my stomach churned. I tossed the pack onto the hay and ran out the barn door. When I reached the trees, I leaned against one, heaving my stomach to the weeds.

~*~

Chapter 26

Vaxeehl

The first set of transports completed. I could see nothing. Denali had locked out my override. She even blocked all the AI's from accessing the feeds. So many nearly broken women came through the transporters recently, I feared what I would see if she went to such extremes for their protection right now.

The transport process was the easy part. Each person took fifteen minutes for decontamination and medical examination. Lanyar would likely have completed the process in less time, but he had gone to the surface to help treat injured.

I forced myself to see to my normal duties. Once the room was done and everything in place to begin bringing the crowd aboard, Denali had banished all except for absolutely necessary personnel. Those few personnel would be secluded in a separate quarantine room, ready for Keira's next call. Based on reports of a second safe house, it would be another large group of over a hundred.

The new blockade that had been built for the mass processing would remain in place. It completely sealed the quarantine section from the rest of the ship.

I spent a considerable amount of time with the children, helping them learn some of the easier technology. Every time I did this, I pictured teaching my own child. Then my mind would wander back to Keira's fertility issues.

Her beautiful face had looked so sad when the scan results showed lower levels. Lanyar had promised to look into a treatment for her, just in case. Since he would be in quarantine for the next thirty days, I determined that I would assign him this as a focus. I wanted to give my wife hope.

Just like that, anxiety gripped my heart. What if these humans faced the struggles the Norvaxians did? We neared seven hundred humans, once the current influxes were settled. If they struggled with loss like the others, I could not continue.

At the rate Keira kept collecting females, by the time my brothers arrived, we would have nearly a thousand, not counting the young ones we still planned to collect from the orphanages. Even being selective, we stood to gain several thousand young.

Every time I mentioned anything about this to Denali, she always answered the same way.

"I trust my queen. Do you trust your own wife?"

It angered me. Of course, I trusted my wife. "It's less about trusting my wife and more about trusting an image given to me by this magic. Magic that is mostly unknown to even the Borkanian women from whom it originated."

Denali frowned at me. "Trust in your wife, Vaxeehl. Nothing else matters."

I cursed aloud. "Nothing else matters. Everything matters. The weight of my entire population rests on my shoulders. The success or failure of this program depends on me putting the right people in the right positions, yet already I failed numerous times. I'm walking around with my dick in my hands like a youth who just discovered he has one."

Denali started laughing so hard at that comment, even I had to join her. It calmed me some.

She then patted my arm and sent me on my way so that she could return to her task.

The second day of continuous transports found me pacing back and forth by the wall. I had begged and pleaded to be allowed to see in the room. I wanted to check on these new people. I needed to do my duty and welcome them aboard. I wanted to ask them about my wife.

Denali ordered some of the soldiers to take me to the exercise area and kick the living shit out of me for several hours so she could concentrate. They followed her orders, and I felt better for it. Damned woman.

I tried approaching one of the engineers, far from the receiving area, and asked them to scan for Keira's thoughts. I needed something to show me she remained well. She was supposed to call me after speaking to the animal doctor, but all hell had broken loose. If I could not hear her voice, I could at least read her thoughts.

They denied my order, citing conflicting orders from Denali.

"I am your prince," I demanded.

The one closest to me spoke. "You are that, sire. And you may see fit to punish me however you wish. But Denali is way more frightening than you could ever hope to be. We've seen her experiments."

The third day, I stormed through the park.

At least, I stormed until Pangou knocked me over, drenching my face with his tongue. I rubbed his head, trying to stop his sliming me.

"Let me up, you crazy slognip."

He bounced backwards a few steps before sitting on his haunches.

Denali's voice sounded in my ear. "Vaxeehl?"

"Are they all aboard yet?"

"No. I just wanted to update you that those who have come so far are adjusting easily. Much preparation and the streamlined process eased the transition greatly."

I tossed a stick, watching Pangou thunder after it.

"Am I allowed to know anything yet?"

I could hear her hesitation. "Not yet. Soon."

"How soon," I demanded.

"The morning at the latest. It depends on whether the final grouping needs rest before they wish to speak."

I grumbled. "Do not bother me until I can actually be of some use."

Chapter 27

Keira

I felt soft hands touch my back, but I couldn't stop puking long enough to look. Tears streamed from my eyes. Sobs wracked my body.

Every face. Every friend, every coworker, every customer whom I personally knew to have died from Virus 442-C swam before my eyes, shredding my heart.

Janine who used to work the register beside me, tirelessly helping through the first wave without fail, only to fall when the second wave hit as soon as lockdown restrictions were relaxed. I heard her husband's broken voice in my ears as he called to tell me that they'd taken her body away.

Mrs. Borson who fed the neighborhood strays. She had collapsed at Janine's register while checking out. I'd fought to give her CPR, but our security guards had held me back.

Mr. Turnbull, my parents' neighbor and my former math tutor who constantly tried to convince me to start applying for scholarships to go to college instead of working myself to death to save up.

Marie, the stocker on third shift whose daughter had just given birth to triplet girls the night she started coughing up blood.

Mike, my former supervisor.

Frank, the corporate payroll who came to give me my promotion after Mike died.

Melissa, who had a rare disease and had stayed in quarantine to protect herself, only to get sick after her kids brought groceries to her.

The doctors, the nurses, the military, the police, the homeless…

My parents.

I'd done everything possible to keep them safe. As soon as the first reports made the news, long before the virus ever got near our area, I'd taken my savings and installed air purification and filtration units on the house. My former bedroom was filled with enough groceries and supplies to last two years. I'd bought a camper, parked it near the shipping bay, and moved the few things I needed for work into it. I talked to them only on the phone. I washed at work in the employee bathroom. I took my clothes to the laundromat and kept them in my locker at the store. By the time the first case entered our state, they were as safe as I could possibly make them.

The night my phone rang while the staff and I scrubbed the life out of every inch of the store after closing, my heart sank. Dad always stayed up until I finished at work, and then I called him. He never wanted to disturb me while I was working, "Because what you are doing is important, Keira. You're keeping your neighbors fed."

I dropped the scrub brush and hit the button to connect the call. "Daddy?"

His weakened voice flared my nerves. "You've done everything right, baby girl. You tried your best to protect us, and I want you to know that *you did everything right!*"

"What are you talking about, Daddy? What's wrong?" I already knew before he spoke, and I felt the panic rise.

"It's my fault. I insisted on ordering food to give Momma a break from canned stuff. One delivery, two days ago. That's all it took." His tears destroyed me. "Momma is in bad shape, baby. And I don't have much strength left. I'm going to do what needs to be done so that you don't have to. I just needed to say I love you one last time."

"Daddy, no!" I screamed myself hoarse.

The line went dead. I dropped my phone, and I ran. By the time I covered the sixteen blocks between the store and their house, the road was cordoned off. The heat from the flames tried to steal what little breath remained.

I charged through the police line, fighting my way to reach them.

Strong arms wrapped around my waist, holding me back. My vision blurred with my tears. I kicked and pulled, trying to break loose.

"They're not dead yet," I screamed. "You have to do something! Let me go!"

Those arms held tight. "It's too late, Keira."

The roof collapsed, sending embers high into the night sky.

The fight left my body. I let the arms holding me turn me away from the sight of my home collapsing to the ground, my parents inside, burning themselves alive to protect me.

Later, when I sat in the middle of the road, a blanket wrapped around my shoulders by one of the firemen, the tears continued to fall. The man who had stopped me sat next to me, offering what little comfort he could, knowing it wouldn't help.

I finally lifted my eyes from the ground and turned toward him. "Why didn't you do anything?"

Tears fell from his own eyes. "Your dad called me. They took cyanide as soon as the fire started so that they wouldn't have to suffer either the disease or the fire. They were dead before I ever arrived. He made me promise to keep you safe."

I glared. "I hate you." I'd known it wasn't his fault, and he had only done what little he had the power to do, but he was there. So, he received my anger.

He stared at the fire, looking nearly as broken as I felt. "I hate me, too."

~*~

Ruth sat next to me regularly, trying to coax me to drink or eat anything. It had been three days since the memories flooded my mind and made me sick. I hadn't spoken that whole time. Belinda and Ruth took turns caring for me while Gil stood watch. Even though I hadn't spoken, I had the strong sense that Ruth knew the thoughts running through my mind. Every once in a while, I could hear her speaking with Lanyar, namely every time he tried to get close with his scanner, trying to check my health.

Ruth kept him back. "You have to let her process this. You told me you guys have been collecting women to help repopulate your planet, and I get that. And she has been integral in making that happen. And she has now learned that the virus came here when your guys crashed. It's a lot to process."

I heard Gil reveal what I'd told him when I accepted his offer. "Her entire family died from the virus. Only she survived." ·

Belinda, bubbly, cheerful Belinda, scoffed. "Which one? The original wasn't that bad."

Ruth growled. "Not now, Bel. Gather everything you want to take with you. And don't forget all the surgical equipment. We won't be able to pop back for anything we miss. The last group needs to be ready in five hours."

The other voices faded away, leaving just Ruth near me. She plopped down, handing me a glass of water. "If you're not going to eat right now, fine. But you need to stay hydrated. Don't make me tell your secret to the purple people eater out there. I've had a bitch of a time keeping Gil from spilling the beans, but he has agreed to let me talk some sense into you."

The tears fell from my eyes again.

"Survivor's guilt is a bitch. I've been fighting my way through it every single day for the last seven years. I keep thinking that I should have left them to die, let them be captured by the government. Thing is, Belinda is right. This virus mutated faster than it should have. Faster than any virus in our history. But it never mutated on Volitar. My family is safer leaving this planet than they are staying."

She lifted my face to stare into my eyes. "Forget everything else and think of that. I hate them. And I hate myself for exposing my sisters to them. But I am giving up everything for the chance to keep my family safe. I've signed over everything I own to a neighbor, and I'm disappearing into the cosmos."

She stood then, dusting her hands. "If you don't eat by the time I come back, I'm knocking you out and planting one of those transport beacons on your neck."

She left, and Gil took her place. He didn't speak. He just sat beside me, pulling me against his chest, offering me some of his strength. I wanted to thank him and push him away at the same time.

Finally, I broke my silence. "How am I supposed to deal with this, Gil? My mate's brother indirectly caused my parents' death. Every time I close my eyes, I see the fire again."

He sat silently beside me while I told him everything, all the details of their deaths, the horror of watching the fire, everything I'd done trying to keep them alive. He listened to me rant about wondering if I could ever look at Vaxeehl or Raklin and not see the faces of my dead family swirl before my eyes. And yet, my heart still ached to touch my mate again. I missed him horribly. I wanted the arms holding me to be his.

I couldn't reconcile the dichotomy of my emotions.

Gil's talons carefully raked through my hair for a long while. He either couldn't give me an answer, or he worked long trying to figure out how to word it.

He stood to leave, still not speaking. Just before he walked away, he gazed down at me and spoke a single word.

"Gundar."

He left me alone, knowing he had said enough.

I cried again, this time because the strong warrior who I had come to think of as family had just told me with a single word that every time he looked at me, he saw his brother's face. *I* had killed *his* only family.

He had tried to protect his brother, and I had taken his life. Yet he now protected me. He comforted his brother's killer in his own arms, and he did it without malice, without any sign of revenge.

We were one messed up pair.

Several hours later, I stood from my pity party, resolved to do one thing right. I ate the food. I drank the water. I set my determination.

The last few people stood ready for transport, checking and double-checking that they had everything. Raklin, Marianne with Analisa in her arms, Belinda, Lanyar, Ruth and all of her equipment. Gil handed out beacons.

I stepped up beside him, waiting patiently. When he gave me his attention, I met his eyes with determination.

"I want you to return with them. I release you from your bond."

The Vesper stood tall, his strong jaw set firm in anger. "My honor is not your decision to make."

"Is your honor the only reason you choose to stay?"

His eyes flared with emotion. "No, Lady Keira."

I nodded. "Then release yourself from honor-bound service, and stay as family," I spoke softly. "I will accept no other alternative."

I held out my hand, the flicker of flames already forming over my palm. I nearly started crying again when he did not hesitate to rest his hand over mine. The magic swirled up his fingers, spreading in a faint layer over his entire form before settling above his heart.

When the light faded, he carefully opened the clasps of his shirt. There, just above his heart, lay a small flaming phoenix, similar to Vaxeehl's yet the size of my palm.

I heard Ruth speak. "That is some seriously next level shit."

Gil admired his new mark for a moment before concealing it beneath the sturdy material again. "Tell him."

I huffed. "Just because you are now my brother does not give you any more right to boss me around than you had before."

He crossed his arms and glared at me. "Tell. Him."

I rolled my eyes. Instead of addressing Lanyar, though, I addressed Ruth. "You spoke with the purple people eater about the effects of transporting during pregnancy, right? Give me the layman's version."

"As long as there have not been any signs of complications like bleeding or leakage, the risk is so minimal as to be almost non-existent. I'll be doing my own research to verify this, but he said he spoke with the birthers on the other dude's ship to make sure. Any bleeding or fluid leakage creates the same risk as moving a warrior with an open injury."

I looked to Gil. "See. Perfectly fine to continue as is."

Ruth shook her head. "You're even more stubborn than me, and that's saying something."

Lanyar looked livid. "And you are expecting me to keep this secret from your husband?"

I chuckled. "Finally figured out why they wouldn't let you scan me, huh? Here's the deal. I want to tell my husband myself that he is going to be a father. And this is partly your fault."

He balked. "Mine?"

"Oh, absolutely. You scanned me every few days, checking my fertility levels. You scanned me the morning before I returned to the surface. Even then, you said my fertility levels were still showing suppression."

He blinked. "The hormones would be suppressed during pregnancy, because other hormones take over. I didn't do a general scan, only a fertility scan."

I shrugged. "It wouldn't have mattered, doc. I needed to be the one to return to the surface. We discussed this in great detail during council meetings." Then I grinned. "And now, *you* get to be the one in quarantine. I'm going to have to ask Gallatea to save those video feeds for me. I might need the entertainment during my own quarantine when I'm done here."

He shook his head. "You get one more cycle, one month. That's it. And only transport when absolutely necessary. Stick to the large clusters of targets far from any city center. The quarantine and learning how to aid all these births will keep me busy enough to not tell your husband anything. But if he asks me a direct question, I cannot lie to him. You know this."

I narrowed my eyes. "Then you'd better pay very close attention to the wording you use to answer. If he asks how I look, you stick to a visual assessment of my appearance. No loopholes. This is *my* news. And you have no record of a new scan in your device."

He gritted his teeth, but he agreed. "Yes, Queen Keira."

Lastly, I drew a deep breath and approached Raklin. He looked much improved. The wound had sealed over. Small signs of infection remained, but it would take a few more days before his body cleared everything else. Even super space tech could only do so much to boost the immune system, otherwise they would not have been so harmed by the virus. But he could at least stand on his own.

"You brought the virus to Earth with you."

He nodded but did not look away.

"The virus killed my parents."

Tears slid from his eyes.

"You understand that Gil is now my brother."

"Yes," he finally spoke.

I motioned to the symbols on my kilnat. "You recognize this."

"Yes," he confirmed, showing himself unsure why I had jumped topics.

I poked him in the chest. "Vaxeehl is my husband, my flame mate. Because of my heart break, I could not find the strength to speak with you before now. Gilnax has accepted me as his sister, despite the fact that I killed his brother. So I must find the strength to forgive your part in my own family's demise. This magic of mine has bound Vaxeehl and me in ways even I fail to understand. I will know if anything happens to him."

Raklin's confusion was evident on his face. "I do not understand."

I forced myself to continue. I had to say this, for all of us to move forward. "You will refrain from hurting my husband."

"I would never—"

I let flames spark from my fingertip, zapping his chest and stopping his words. "My husband has been suffering greatly because of your disappearance. I have felt his hurt. Seeing you will help heal him. But you have to heal yourself, Raklin. By the time I return to that damned ship, you need to find a way to forgive yourself and become whole again."

He hung his head. "I do not know how."

"Figure it out," I spat at him angrily. Then I softened my eyes to gaze at Marianne and Analisa. "Your family will help. Because it's not about us, it's about the future of *our* people."

The final member of the party held a look that said she wanted to speak for fear of bursting. Yet, she held herself in check. Considering her boisterous personality, this took considerable control on her part.

I stepped to Belinda, studying her. Then I reached forward, trailing a finger along her forehead, letting her thoughts flood my brain. My lungs fought for breath, staggering under those thoughts. "Are you sure," I asked her through the mind connection.

She nodded enthusiastically, her blonde curls bouncing with the motion. "With every fiber of my being," she answered within the connection.

I dropped my finger away and spoke verbally. "Find a way to prove it. For the good of your family, find a way to prove it beyond every possible shadow of a doubt."

I stepped back.

Lanyar shook a finger at me like a grandmother scolding a child. "One month. That's it."

I conceded. "One month."

He cocked a grin and tapped his com-link. "Six to beam up, Scotty."

~*~

Chapter 28

Vaxeehl

The call had finally come. The last of the first large group of recruits had completed the decontamination process. They were ready, as a group, to reveal.

This news had spread through the entire ship. Everyone had worked together to make the transition as smooth as possible, but no one outside those few directly involved with the receiving process had any idea why this one remained such a secret.

I stood before the blank wall. Nearly all of the current group of humans, and any of my own crew who were not absolutely needed at their stations crowded behind me. Those still in quarantine had projections so that they might see.

Denali moved to stand next to me. "Are you ready, my king?"

I huffed. "How should I know? I don't know why everything had to be kept so secret."

She looked at me, though I kept my eyes on the wall, waiting for something—anything—to happen. "You would have insisted on transporting to Earth, putting yourself in danger."

I frowned. "Something worse than the camps?"

She took a half step forward, pressing her hand to the center of the wall. Then she moved away, giving me room. Slowly, the grey balkin nanite ore changed to a transparent window.

The blood pounded in my ears at the veritable ocean of faces. But when the crowd deliberately parted, my legs lost strength, and I dropped to my knees. I couldn't breathe.

I placed my hands to the window. My vision started turning grey.

The figure before me knelt, placing his hands directly against mine.

"Breathe, brother. Your wife would be very angry if you died while she remained on that wretched planet. She made me swear to your happiness."

At his command, my lungs obeyed, clearing the darkness from my sight. "My brother lives," my voice barely reached my own ears.

"I do."

I felt my heart swell, joy encompassing me. I leaned my head back and screamed to the cosmos. "My brother lives!"

Voices filled the background, and I heard Denali start crying.

"Children, my king. Look!"

I grumped. "We have a whole daycare center full of children. I haven't seen my brother in eight years."

Raklin waved someone forward. The person knelt beside him. He pointed with his chin. "I think she means our mixed-race children, you selfish bastard." He laughed, and I finally looked at the person next to him.

A medium-skinned young woman held a small child. A child with wings like her father. My mouth fell open.

"Analisa," he said. "This is your Uncle Vaxeehl."

The girl giggled and pointed at my chest. "Just like the pretty lady with the fire wings. She let me touch her wings. Do you have fire wings, too?"

I smiled at the girl. "I only seem to have my fire wings when the pretty lady is close to me. I haven't spent much time trying to see if I can do anything with them when the pretty lady isn't around."

I cast my eyes around the crowd for a moment before returning to Raklin. "Did my lady wife return with you?"

Raklin shook his head. "No. She and her brother continue searching Earth for more women."

"Brother?"

Lanyar stepped near. "He means Gilnax. I will explain later. As you can see, it is not only possible for the human women to conceive, but also to carry to term without intervention. Queen Keira spoke true."

I turned back to Raklin. Then I gave a short laugh. "She was right. I would have stopped at nothing to get to you."

"I would like to know how your wife ended up traveling *her* planet to recruit women to save *our* planet. I was delirious for a good portion of the short time in her presence. When my fever finally broke, she was… in seclusion."

I frowned.

My brother hung his head. "She had learned how the virus came to Earth."

Before another word could be spoken, a small bundle of energy shot forward, smacking Raklin on the back of his head.

Another woman reached to grab that girl's arm, but she shook free.

The tiny woman who had struck my brother spoke. "Shut up, Raklin. I have been trying to tell you for seven years, but none of you assholes would listen to a word I have to say."

"Belinda—"

"You too, Ruth. You even *know* I speak the truth, yet you've been so stuck in poor me mode that you refuse to let go of guilt that isn't yours. It's taken damned near everything Marianne and I could do to keep both you and this *moron* alive."

The yellow-haired woman pointed at me.

I realized I still knelt on the floor and stood.

"You. You're the big man on campus, right? You're Prince Vax-eehl?"

I confirmed.

"I'm Belinda. Keira communicated in my head. She *saw* what I know. She gave me a directive, and I need help to accomplish it."

The woman was tiny, but she was certainly a spitfire. "What is your directive?"

She started tapping her foot. "The original virus was practically harmless. I was on track for a double major in virology and genetics when everything went to hell. But I formed one very important con-nection who was feeding me top-secret information on the darknet. Marianne listened to me, but no one else would. If I can track down this guy, this scientist, I can get the rest of the proof we need to finally show that the original virus, what Lanyar said you call 442-C, would have killed less than one half of one percent of humans, and only those with severely weakened immune systems."

My mind boggled. "We lost so many on Volitar."

She rolled her eyes. "Because your immune systems had never been exposed to any variation of this particular asshole. But *we*," she waved one hand toward the human crowd, "have. For centuries. 442-C never mutated on Volitar, yet on Earth, new strains continue to pop up, and each is worse than the last."

I thought of the upload. I met Denali's eyes and could tell she also thought of what had happened at those camps. She nodded to me.

I looked back to the girl. "What do you need to do?"

She smiled. "You mean it? You're willing to take me seriously."

"I am."

"I need access to tech that can interact with the Earth internet. I need someone who is more capable than me to hack into some serious top-secret shit. And if what I think has happened actually has happened, I may need help breaking someone out of one of the most secure prisons in America."

Denali laughed. "Is that all? You ask for very little."

Belinda blinked. "Really?"

"I will create a portal that will allow you, and only you, to travel to another secure room. One of the transporter techs who greeted you can teach you how to use the tech. And there is nothing on Earth that can block our ability to transport. If the person you seek can be found, we can retrieve him." Denali said everything with a chuckle.

Belinda blushed. "Wow. Um. Is there anything I could offer in exchange for all of this? I feel like we are really uneven."

I tipped my head sideways, still studying the ferocious woman. "You are seeking a way to relieve my brother of his shame. I should be the one asking you if I can offer you some reward."

She shrugged. "I mean, it's only right. And it helps my sisters, too." She paused. "Just how many women are you trying to recruit? I mean, we could have had way more at the barn if we'd had more room, or any idea you were coming."

Ruth, or the woman I suspected to be Ruth, groaned. "Are you seriously going to start going off about your darknet shit again? That's how we ended up hiding over two hundred women in the woods, trying not to be discovered. Your 'aliens do exist' post could have been seen by any number of the wrong people and could have led to a raid!"

The girl rolled her eyes. "Um, hello, Ruth. *This is exactly* the situation that darknet post gave hope for. Melnon told you early on that they would willingly take anyone wishing to leave Earth with them. It's no longer about running out of room in the barn. These aliens actually *want* the response!"

Denali and I shared another look. She asked, "How many others are there that won't take in-person convincing?"

Belinda shrugged. "I don't know. At least a couple thousand replied to my initial posting. I had to almost immediately post a temporary closure when we ran out of space in the barn. The ones who are here were close enough to be able to travel to us easily. The queen's next stop is actually a secondary safe house we arranged when we ran out of room, and that happened in less than two weeks."

I nodded at the tiny girl. "You just became an important asset. Denali will set up the portal for you."

I turned to Denali. "I want a wall like this in the room so that you and I can participate. We shall meet in half an hour."

Raklin called out. "Am I slognip slime now that the blonde instigator has spoken?"

I frowned. "Speak no ill of me, brother. I carry the fate of every person on our planet. And unless you find yourself willing to share your wife with another, according to our father's recent attempts, I have work to do."

His wings flared out. "He did not."

"He's desperate, and he's tired. We have shown little success until we reached Earth. We would have had even less success had we not stolen Keira in the first test batch."

Raklin stood taller, one arm wrapped around the woman, holding her to his chest. "I no longer wonder why she is so determined to keep gathering. The strength of her compassion would not welcome such a thought of forced procreation."

"Unless someone else told her, Keira does not know of the sharing program. I only learned a few lunar cycles ago. I have not seen my own wife since she returned to the surface more than sixty days ago."

He stared at his wife, likely imagining what he would do without her in his life. "Because it is not about us," he said.

I nodded. "It's about the future of our people. She tells me this every time we speak."

He bowed to me. Slowly, everyone in the room beyond the window followed.

"Helvana has blessed you with a compassionate, caring, and wonderful queen, brother."

~*~

Through the next two weeks, Denali and I met daily with Belinda and the engineer, Eggar. The blonde woman had taken to giggling every time she said his name, mumbling something about a 'bug in the Eggar suit'.

The data retrieval portion had gone easily. Finding the human she sought took longer. Denali had altered the thought scanner again, using keywords from the man's research. It still took a full week of scanning to pinpoint a possible location.

The human male materialized beyond the transparent wall, screaming with shock.

Little Belinda snapped her fingers in his face. "Dr. Anderson, shut the hell up and listen. What was your screen name on the darknet?"

His screaming stopped. His hands travelled all over his body, taking inventory to make sure everything had come through. "Where the hell am I? And who are you?" His eyes landed on Eggar. "Dude, you're purple. Are you supposed to be purple?"

Belinda stomped her foot. "Pay attention. I'm Little Bo Peep, and I've just arranged your prison break."

He gasped. "Are you really?"

"Confirm your screen name, damn it. I won't say another word until you confirm your screen name."

He narrowed his eyes at her, as if doubting her sincerity. "RingAroundTheRosie. Finish this sentence: A bat wing…"

"Is much more than a stretched-out nut sack," she giggled. "That's still gross."

"It really is you!" He reached his hand toward her, but she jumped out of reach.

"Ew! Nasty. You haven't been decontaminated yet."

Belinda turned to the engineer. "Eggar, take him to decontamination and get him fed. Then return here. We have a lot to get done."

The man laughed. "Eggar? The bug in the Eggar suit?"

She tossed her hands in the air. "Finally, someone understands! I haven't been able to convince these guys to watch Men In Black yet."

I shook my head. This girl was more than a handful. "Welcome aboard Dr. Anderson. I'm sorry to tell you, you have been abducted onto what you would call an alien space craft. Unless you can give us a very good reason otherwise, you will never return to the wretched planet you call Earth. You were brought aboard at Belinda's request, and you will do everything she asks or demands of you."

He didn't seem phased. If anything, he appeared excited at the prospect. "I've been locked in a cell for the last two years because I refused to create biological weapons to kill my own people. Death is preferable to returning to Earth."

Belinda rolled her eyes. "Drama queen."

A portal opened to another room. Eggar led the newcomer away.

Belinda called after them. "And shave that disgusting beard. That's a serious germ factory."

I shook my head and turned to Denali. "I have things to do. I will leave the rest of this to you."

"Wait," the young girl flagged me.

I motioned for her to speak.

"Um, how long do you think until the other ships arrive?"

I mentally calculated the days in my head since my last conversation. "Arden should be here within fourteen days. MeeKale within twenty to thirty days after that, depending on the worm holes. Why?"

"I wanted to give the darknet contacts a rough idea of when we could start transporting them. I think we might need the extra space."

My eyebrows lifted. "You've had responses? Already?"

"Once I noted they didn't have to travel to us, that we would 'pick them up', the quantity doubled almost overnight. They are simply awaiting notification." Her voice sounded hesitant.

I bowed to the young girl. "I will hail my brothers to confirm. Denali, prepare instructions for them so that their crew may have everything in place and ready to accept transports as soon as possible. I will transmit those while we talk."

~*~

The door closed to the council chamber. I seated myself near the uplink station.

"Ovid, direct uplink to Raklin in Section 3B."

"Projection Active."

The screen appeared before me. Raklin rushed over, his daughter in his arms. "You're early, brother. We don't usually chat for another hour or two. Are you sure you have the time?"

"Hello, Analisa."

"Hi, Uncle Vax." Her dainty hand waved at me.

"I am preparing to call our brothers. I would like to have you and your family involved in the uplink." I pulled the hated tee shirt over my frame. I waved my hand over the covering. "This is to remain unknown for now."

He pursed his lips but nodded, calling Marianne over to sit next to him. While Ovid worked to establish the connection, he spoke softly to her, filling her in.

She started fidgeting.

"Easy, Marianne. You have no reason for nerves."

She frowned, turning to me. "What if I am too low class for them to accept? I would not wish to bring shame upon Raklin."

I smiled, hoping to quell her nerves. "You kept our brother alive and safe. That is all they will need for them to know that you are more than worthy to be his mated wife."

The screens blinked open.

"Hail, bro—Great Helvana!" Arden nearly tipped his chair jumping toward the projection.

"Fucking hell in a handbasket." MeeKale had clearly dedicated some time to studying the human entertainment he'd received during our last transmission.

Raklin bowed his head. "As you can see, brothers, the humans are viable wives. I would like you to meet my reasons for living. Marianne, my wife, and Analisa, our daughter."

His hand gently stroked her hair, making it very clear to all of us that she held his heart. I sat silent, letting them have their reunion. Raklin and I had spent several hours every day since his return, and I had learned of the events that ended with him stranded on this unusual planet. So, rather than participating, I simply listened as he explained it all again.

Mother's death had destroyed all of us in different ways. Being secluded away from each other had left us without the physical support of our family. Lanyar had kept me from potentially exposing everyone aboard our ship by sedating me until my mind could find a gap in the emotions to start thinking of those for whom I was responsible. Arden had spent many weeks in the exercise chamber, fighting all who were willing until he had cleansed the anger from his body. MeeKale had locked himself away emotionally, and it had taken nearly three years before his smile slowly started to return. Raklin had run.

No one blamed any of the others for how they dealt with their grief. Those who remained on the surface of Volitar had fared no better.

Raklin had wished for death. He pushed the ship too hard, worm hole jumping constantly to random points throughout the universe. When his navigators refused, he simply took control, overriding the system and locking them out of the computers. After eight lunar cycles of worm hole jumps, the power system failed, leaving barely enough to handle life support. The crew neared mutiny.

My brother realized he had put all of their lives at risk. He packed a few essentials into one of the pods. When he announced to the crew that he was leaving the ship so that they could repair it and return to Volitar safely, no one fought him. However, twenty men refused to abandon their prince.

Our pods were not designed for long-term travel. They have typically been used only for transporting large numbers to and from planet surfaces for war, moving supplies, or short dignitary trips to neighboring planets within our own solar system. They do not have worm hole capabilities, although they do allow faster than light travel in small increments.

Raklin had lost all will to live at that point. His navigator and close friend, Melnon, scanned for a planet with suitable vegetation, life forms, and atmosphere. By the time he finally spotted this large planet, the pod neared the end of its usefulness. They had no time to gather language details, histories, anything. Their survival depended upon the grace of Helvana.

Melnon found a place on the surface to hide the pod, hoping to be able to broadcast a distress signal long enough for someone to find them. Unfortunately, the outer shell of the pod faced stronger opposition from the atmosphere than he had anticipated. It started to separate and burn. They hit harder upon landing than expected, injuring many of them.

The landing target had not been nearly as void of life as the scan had shown, and they'd been spotted by the natives immediately. The blessings of Helvana began right away, as the ones who found them had gathered and hidden them. Unfortunately, the initial thought scans had revealed the females' fear of discovery. Melnon had conversed quickly with his companions, explaining to them the dangers of capture by the leaders on this strange planet. They had gathered their meager remaining medical and food supplies, the emergency beacon, and had disintegrated their only means of escape.

"Those early days were hell, both for us and for Marianne and her sisters," he said. "I still remained locked in my mind, wishing for death. Then the virus came. I couldn't understand how. We'd been away from contact for longer than the life of the virus. Still, we all fell ill. And despite the risk to themselves, these creatures cared for us."

He closed his eyes, tears sliding down his cheeks. "Our fevers broke, but to my shame, they fell ill. I went from patient to caretaker without a second thought. I decided then and there that if these females died because of my actions, I would end my miserable life. But they did not die."

He gazed at his wife, sliding his hands along her cheek, wiping away her own tears. "This beautiful creature became my salvation, brothers. She even protected us from her sister, who had the power to kill us, and who rightfully wanted to. Especially as news reports came in about the virus spreading throughout the planet."

Analisa, who had sat silently and very well-behaved through all of this talk, started squirming. "Is it flying time yet, Daddy?"

Not waiting for an answer, Marianne stood, kissing her husband softly before taking the young one so that she could play with the other children.

"Now that we have caught you up, brothers, I actually called for a purpose. We near a thousand females already aboard, Keira continues on the surface still, and Marianne's sister has another means of bringing a very large number of willing volunteers. Belinda's contacts are anxious. They want off Earth as soon as possible and are simply awaiting their opportunity. I would like to start collecting a few so that they may communicate to the others that they are not being played, as some of them have phrased their insecurities. We need to give them a solid time frame to allay their fears."

Arden leaned back. "My crew and I should arrive in about four days. The new worm hole shifted us faster than calculated."

I transmitted the files from Denali. "I've sent you instructions from Denali regarding how to prepare your receiving areas. I will ask for volunteers among the women already out of quarantine to help in the decontamination process. It will aid in the assimilation to see one of their own kind."

MeeKale chuckled. "I still can't wrap my mind around how a single female could make such a difference."

"Hah!" Raklin burst. "Wait until you meet Queen Keira. Her capacity for compassion and forgiveness is only overshadowed by her strong sense of honor."

MeeKale gasped. Quick as lightning, his pet fluttered onto the screen, settling on his shoulders. "You have claimed the crown?"

I realized Raklin's words. "I have not. I assume our brother has gotten so used to hearing my wife revered so often that he has lost the ability to think of her differently. The crown remains firmly in father's hands." I shot a look to Raklin, trying to still his tongue.

He hiked an eyebrow at me, but I could see his acquiescence. "His lady wife *is greatly revered* among both the Borkanians and her own people. She bears the blessings of Helvana to us in more ways than I can convey with words."

A short time later, the uplink ended, and I drew a deep breath of relief. I ripped the shirt off, hoping I would not need to use it much more.

Raklin chuckled. "I cannot understand your continued secrecy. Once we return to Volitar, you will be unable to hide the proof of your birthright. Our people will demand you take your position as ruler. Father will be forced to challenge you to retain the crown."

I finally gave voice to my concerns. "Our planet has been peaceful for so many generations, Raklin. Even with all of the interstellar gallivanting and welcoming of other races to live among us, we have remained peaceful. Looking at the history of Earth, even the current events, terrifies me of what could happen. Then I have Keira to consider."

He tipped his head. "How do you mean?"

I scrubbed my face with my hands. "Her fertility hormones have not stabilized. I can tell she wishes to bear me an heir, but what if she cannot? Will our people accept a queen unable to provide an heir? I will relinquish all rights to the crown for her, without hesitation. Tell me you would do differently so that I may call you a liar. I see how you look at your wife."

Raklin said nothing for so long that I almost demanded he speak. His eyes just kept studying me, his mind deep in thought.

He bowed his head a moment. Finally, he raised back up and parted his lips to speak. "Your lady wife is more worthy of her title than you know. And you have now proven yourself truly worthy as her mate."

He waved his hand. The screen went blank before I could respond. I tried for several minutes to get the uplink reestablished, but he had blocked me through his AI.

If he weren't still in quarantine, I would likely strangle him until he explained his words.

~*~

Part Five:
Homeward Bound

Chapter 29

Keira

I sat slumped on a fallen log. We had just sent a small group of five women up to the ship. I stared at the screen, feeling disheartened. I was so tired. Despite taking extra days to rest between transports, my body screamed at me. And the list before me held so many names and locations that I couldn't even attempt to touch.

I let the tears drift down my face. My brother seated himself beside me, pulling me firmly against him. "We can't even get near so many of these, Gil. They're located in busy city centers, places where new strains of the virus keep popping up. I feel like I'm failing both them and Volitar, yet I dare not consider putting Vaxeehl's heir at risk."

He rubbed my back softly. "Are you saying that you are finally willing to return to the safety of the ship and let someone else figure out how to move forward? That after all this time of thinking of every-one else, you are finally accepting that you are allowed to think of yourself, as well?"

I sighed, wiping the dampness from my cheeks. "I am. Call Lanyar and make the arrangements. He can scan me before I am reunited with my husband. I can't bear the thought of possibly exposing Vax to any of the germs from this planet."

He circled his arm around me, pulling me close. "When we began, we had only you. There are many among those who have now consented to join us who are also capable of making this journey. You needn't consider the task only yours any longer, my queen." He paused and then whispered, "My sister."

I nodded. "I've been alone for so long, had to take charge for so many years. And yet, convincing a lot of the women that I spoke the truth would have been much harder without your presence. It's going to take me a while to adapt to accepting help, but I'm glad I've had you with me for this journey. Go ahead and make our return arrangements, brother."

Gil's voice hovered barely over a whisper as he spoke with Lanyar. I let it comfort me, knowing that soon, I would hear my husband's voice rumbling again, through more than just a com-link. I forced myself to sit upright and eat. I had gained a very visible baby bump already, and I only neared the halfway point. I let my mind imagine Vax with his head resting against my belly. My hand absently caressed the burgeoning evidence of our short time together.

Gil ended the call and snagged some of the food pack. Between bites, he told me, "You should nap before we transport. Your energy level is extremely depleted."

"I have thirty days to nap, Gil. I just want to get home." My hand stopped halfway to my mouth. I no longer thought of this planet as home. I finished my last few bites while I digested that thought and realized it hadn't been home since my parents died. And I no longer cared the cause.

The Vesper chuckled, handing me another chunk of fruit. "You'd better eat more, then. I have a feeling your magic will flare the second you see your husband. You two could barely keep yourselves in check *before* you left for three lunar cycles."

I blushed deeply. Then I lightly smacked his shoulder. "You're not wrong," I laughed, stuffing the fruit in my mouth.

We ate until I felt completely full, which seemed more difficult to achieve as each day of this pregnancy progressed. We stood, holding hands and activated the beacons.

~*~

When I opened my eyes, I noticed an enormous crowd gathered. I blinked several times before realizing they stood behind a huge transparent wall. As a matter of fact, several transparent walls surrounded us with faces plastered to all of them.

"Denali warned she planned to make an announcement," I heard my brother whisper.

A hand at my shoulder drew me to one side, not letting me get a good look at the crowd. From what I could see, there appeared many more women than I recalled collecting. Gil caught my attention and pointed to a small, closed-off area where it looked like they had located the decontamination area. A smiling face awaited me.

I felt my heart swell. "Reganda, my friend. I would hug you, but I need cleaned first."

She bowed. "This way, my queen."

The whole decontamination process seemed much faster than I remembered, but, other than a single warm bath at Ruth's farm house, I'd been water washing in cold streams for months now. Reganda quickly dressed me, gently touching my extended belly when she finished. "You've been keeping secrets, my friend."

I glanced down to see how much the traditional kilnat exposed my current state. "Not for much longer." I saw the careful decorative stitching and felt tears well. "I've missed wearing this. And it really accentuates this life growing within me." It was the first wrap I had decorated during my quarantine.

Gil cleared his throat from the doorway. "You had best let Lanyar get the scanning done. I don't think Marlux and Prince Arden will be able to hold your husband much longer."

My heart raced at the mention of my mate. "Lanyar!" I yelled.

He appeared before me so quickly that I nearly ran into him. Only his quick reflexes kept us from colliding. "Let's get this going. He's about to... how do you humans say it? Lose his shit." He quickly began the scan process.

He tapped his com-link when he reached my swollen belly. "Ruth, is it coming through clear? Everything looks on target according to your data." He grinned up at me. "But as the queen is very fond of telling me, data is merely numbers if you do not have instinct to back it up."

"A tiny bit under sized, but I don't see anything that raises a flag." I realized he had included my own com-link in the conversation and felt warmed by his thoughtfulness.

His brow furrowed in confusion. "What does hoisting a banner have to do with the scans?"

I burst into laughter. "You are such a purple people eater, Lanyar."

Gil finished his cleansing and returned to the general area, but I did not have eyes for him. I scanned the walls. So many faces I did not recognize stared back, all clamoring for a glimpse of us. My eyes passed over them, knowing I would have plenty of time to get to know them later. Finally, I found my past, present, and future.

Vaxeehl stood near the center of the largest wall, his arms held tightly on either side by Marlux and another large man in a blood red kilnat who I had to presume to be Prince Arden. He looked ready to break both of them to get to me. Bits of fire flickered around him.

Love swelled in my heart. My magic flared instantly, my wings forming fully. Tiny tendrils of flame danced forward, pulling from my chest and reaching out to the other half of my soul.

The men released Vax's arms when his magic answered. I heard much murmuring at the display, but my ears could not discern actual words. Despite the partitions separating us, our flames met and danced in the middle.

Unfortunately, the burst stole much of the energy I had saved up. I staggered. Gil's hands caught my elbow, keeping me upright.

Vax cried out. "Denali, get me a portal right now! Keira's ill."

I shook my head. I whispered to my side. "Be prepared, brother. My husband is about to experience a spontaneous burst."

He nodded. He'd watched my magic change and grow during our time on Earth, seen a few of my own bursts.

I yelled across the space. "I'm not sick, you beautiful alien. I'm pregnant with your heir." I turned slightly sideways, my hand caressing the baby bump.

Less than a second later, I watched his flames fully engulf him until his form consisted of nothing but our magic. Like an arrow, he passed through the barriers, crossing the distance in a blink. A flickering cloud wrapped around me, enveloping me from head to toe, pushing Gil backwards. Then he reformed into his solid body, and I knew I'd come home.

His hands smoothed along my arms, my face. His misty eyes seemed transfixed. The mix of adoration and disbelief in his voice brought my emotions even higher. "You're here. You are truly returned to me. My heart has become whole at long last."

Three months of missing him, three months of wanting to touch this man, of hearing his voice in my ear but not feeling it, had finally reached culmination. I spoke in his own tongue. "May we never be parted again, my love."

And when his lips finally touched mine, I had no care for the faces around us, no concerns about whether we behaved like the monarchs they thought us to be. I wrapped my arms around his neck, pulling myself as close as possible while still remaining separate entities.

We only kissed briefly before he trailed his lips along my cheek and down until he could bury his face in my neck and hair. Still, his arms held me pinned to him. My own ghosted across his flesh, reassuring myself of his presence.

I heard Gil speak softly. "Restrain yourselves, you two. You are being broadcast to the entirety of at least two ships."

Vax swore against my shoulder. He slowly pulled away but kept me tightly against him. "So much for keeping a low profile."

His golden eyes glowed and danced as they met mine again. "I want nothing more than to sweep you away to our room and have Ovid and Gallatea lock down all access until our quarantine is completed. But we are leaders to a new blend of people. We have a few minor formalities that must be handled before I take you to our quarters for privacy, my love."

I reached up and caressed his cheek. "I've waited three months. I can wait a few minutes longer."

He swept me into his arms. Rather than argue with him, I reveled in his show of possession. Instead of insisting I could stand on my own two feet, I welcomed his strength and caring.

He growled lightly. "It had better only take a few minutes." He approached the partition.

I saw Raklin standing as close as he could manage in his quarantine space. The other one had shifted his position to stand next to him. Between them, I saw another smiling face on a projection screen, one whose eyes twinkled with mischief.

Vax noticed the projection about the same time. I heard him groan. "You uplinked MeeKale, too? I thought he was mid-worm hole."

"A little birdie called before the jump, so we delayed. I wouldn't have missed this for the universe, brother," the disembodied head spoke. "Now we know the true reason you've been hiding under that strange human clothing."

I tapped Vax's arms. "Let me stand, my love."

He frowned at me. "You are weakened."

I rolled my eyes, carefully pulling my magic within my body. "I'm growing a child; I'm not dying. Hold me if you wish, but please let me stand so that I may formally meet your brothers."

He carefully lowered my feet to the floor but kept his arms around me. His flames had also receded, although they still fluttered lightly across my skin. I tried to hide my smile.

Vax spoke. "Keira Sutton, formerly of planet Earth, recognized as Queen of the Borkanian tribe, may I present to you Prince Arden, Prince MeeKale, and I believe you have met Prince Raklin, my brothers." Each of them bowed their heads as their names crossed his lips. "Brothers, I ask that you recognize this woman as my mate, my wife, and my reason for living. I ask that you recognize the child she carries as my own. I ask that you protect Keira and my child as you would your own, as I would swear to you."

I forced myself to stand tall as he spoke, soaking in his essence to bolster my strength. This event felt huge, and I refused to appear weak.

Arden spoke first. "Prince Arden of Volitar welcomes Keira and her young. I, and all of those under my rule, recognize this union."

MeeKale echoed the words.

Raklin followed suit. Then he pulled Marianne and Analisa forward, repeating much the same oath.

After both unions had been formally confirmed, Vaxeehl spoke loudly, addressing the whole group. "Tonight, we celebrate these unions. We celebrate the rekindling of hope. When we have finished gathering the rest of the volunteers, we will make great haste to return to Volitar so that you may finally see your new homes. There, we will celebrate the future of our blended people. Helvana has blessed us all many times in this journey. May her blessings continue."

The deafening roar came from every angle. Humans applauded. Various shades of purple and dark brown winged men stomped or pounded their chest. Burgundy-skinned women danced and sang. I felt tears slide down my cheeks again, tears of joy.

I spotted my lilac friend waving and pointing toward a forming portal. I patted my husband on his chest, catching his attention and used my chin to point to it.

Vaxeehl swept me into his arms once again, not even bothering to bid his brothers farewell.

~*~

The portal closed behind us. I tapped my com-link. "Denali?"

Her voice held both a sigh and a smile. "You're off the broadcast, free and clear. I fully expect this will be the last I hear from either of you for a while."

"Thank you, my friend."

"One last thing before I go. Vax, the research is nearly completed. Should I allow a full broadcast with the findings, or do you wish to review them first?"

He slowly lowered me to my feet. "Are the preliminary results as expected?"

"They are."

His hands started loosening the knot at my neck. "Full broadcast. This information is as important to the entirety of the human volunteers as it is for my brother's sanity. Farewell, Denali. No interruptions of any kind for at least three days."

He pulled the com-link from his ear, tossing it toward the table. Right before his fingers removed the matching earrings from my own, I heard a giggle.

Then it was just the two of us.

Those strong hands slid gently over my flesh, carefully tugging the material away from my breasts. His fingertips caressed every inch of me revealed with such reverence that my heart ached.

The kilnat clasp released, dropping to the floor.

"I just want to look at you, to touch you. I worry this is all just another dream of longing, and if I close my eyes, I'll open them to find myself alone still."

I slid my hands over his chest, slowly down to release his clasp. With that done, I took his hands in mine and backed toward the bed. He laid down upon it. I stretched out next to him. We lay facing each other, breathing the same air, our hands upon each other.

"Close your eyes," I spoke softly. He did. "Pull your magic deep inside your heart, my love. Pull it back until you touch me only with your flesh."

Slowly, gently, the dancing lights faded. The flickering glow upon his skin reduced until only the embers on his chest remained.

I pressed against his shoulder, rolling him to his back and straddling him gently.

"Keep your flames held tight, my heart."

I raised my hips, angling our bodies to align and slowly lowered myself onto his shaft. His hands rose to my hips. Inch by glorious inch, our bodies joined. I cooed and coaxed him. We both breathed hard and fast, fighting to hold the flames in check. I trembled with my need. His hands grasped my flesh tightly.

When at long last he lay fully within my channel, I drew a deep breath. Despite being locked tight within my heart, I felt the magic guide me to speak, not in my own language but in his.

"Now open your eyes and look at me, husband." His eyelids flew open and his indrawn breath humbled me. "See me without firelight dancing between us. See that the eyes of Keira, the woman, shine with love for Vaxeehl, the man. The man who stole me from my aimless life. The man who charged in, ready to kill one of his own to protect a woman to whom he'd never spoken a word. A man who saw his mistakes and worked to correct them. A man who has carried the weight of his world, the survival of his people, on his shoulders for many lonely years. Know that you no longer bear this burden alone. Know that we are one, even without the golden power of the queen and goddess to guide us. Open your eyes and see *me*."

The love exuding from his gaze was only surpassed by his own answering words.

"I have always seen you, Keira. From the first morning you awoke in your cell, I saw you. The frightened and lonely woman who feared for her unknown circumstances. The curious and intelligent being who asked questions to find her way in this new world. The strong, independent warrior who taught herself to fight *for herself* as well as others. The pure heart who saw not color, nor shape, nor differences, but empathy and goodness in the strangest of beings, even in those who had held you captive and in isolation. I knew from the first moment I laid eyes upon you that you were my future."

He shifted, slowly withdrawing and returning, stirring the passions within us both. I felt us both trembling, the magic fighting to break free. But this was time for us, the man and the woman.

Our breaths came in gasps, our motions increased. And when we reached our pinnacles as one, the flames erupted from us, no longer able to be withheld, dancing together and merging into a single, blazing inferno that surged through our nerves, taking us to even greater heights than ever before.

~*~

As morning light slowly brightened the room, I stretched my muscles. Strong hands drifted around my body, pulling me against the warm flesh behind me. I hummed. "Good morning, my love."

His nose nuzzled against my neck as he wrapped himself around me. "Good morning, goddess."

"Gilnax requests communication uplink." Gallatea's voice echoed through the chamber.

I heard swearing and grumbling before the blanket covered us. Vaxeehl kissed me one more time before authorizing the connection. "This had better be important," he spoke toward the screen forming by the bed.

My brother sat calmly, hiking one eyebrow toward my mate. "I would not disturb you otherwise, my prince. I understand that you wish not to be bothered during your reunion, but with the burst of magic that took place last night, I felt duty bound to my Queen and sister to make certain you two had not combusted to ashes."

I blinked. "What burst of magic?"

He cleared his throat. "A short time after you retreated to your quarters, the glowing orbs appeared en masse in a bright burst. They started soaring throughout the ships—both ships. They circled and hovered over individuals for a while. Honestly, it seemed like they evaluated the people. It was... humbling to watch. Over the course of the next few hours, almost every single man, woman, and child currently onboard had an orb settle over them. There were a few individuals whom the magic did not touch, and I have requested that Denali's crew dig more into their histories."

I swallowed hard. "Do they all now bear our mark?"

He smiled. "The women and children all bear the tribal mark. The men," he paused. "The men have a different mark. Just a single thin line on their inner wrist, in the same position as the line through the tribal mark."

I furrowed my brow. "I wonder why the mark is different for the men."

"The Borkanian women spoke for many hours about this last night after the magic finished. They believe that the line shows the magic has touched them and found them viable, possibly even giving them a glimpse of their potential mate, but that the tribal mark will not complete until they have actually mated." He shrugged. "That is their best guess, my queen. They have stated that they would like to test a new theory they have regarding the ritual, but they wished to allow you time for yourselves before seeking permission."

I felt Vaxeehl chuckle. "And how did you get the joy of being the one to disturb us? Are you not also in quarantine?"

Gil nodded. "I am. Reganda happens to be nearby, and I heard her uplink conversation with the other tribe members. Apparently, while we were gallivanting on the surface, the Borkanian ladies have found their magic has expanded as well. One of the ladies, Seela, I believe, touched her hand to one of the crew members while they prepared for some of the recruits to arrive. It would seem that the mating ritual as they know it may no longer be necessary. Seela was able to sense her mate with that simple touch."

I smiled. "That is wonderful. But why would they feel the need to seek my permission?"

"You are the queen, the Great Unifier, our goddess in flesh. As far as they have ever known, you are the source of the magic, and they worried using it could cause you depletion, putting you at risk. And now that they know you carry young, they would do nothing to put you or your child in danger."

I sighed, my shoulders sagging. "I have no way of reassuring them, Gil. I had no magic until it was bestowed upon me. I have no way of knowing whether their use of it will affect me."

Vaxeehl tightened his hold again. "Their queen is currently safe and being monitored. I assume that Seela has avoided pursuing her potential mate without permission, seeing as I have not received information to record another pairing?"

Gil acknowledged. "That is correct, sire."

I felt Vax nod. "Tell her to test their theory. If Keira notices a drain on her magic, or if I notice her energy levels dropping drastically, you will be notified immediately. Otherwise, leave us be."

One hand raised, waving the screen into darkness before my brother could reply.

His lips caressed my neck once again. "Now, where were we?"

~*~

Chapter 30

Vaxeehl

Keira sat in my lap, humming. Her naked form pressed to mine as I fed her slowly. One week of our quarantine had lapsed, and we hadn't bothered dressing during any of that time. We ate, we made love, and we slept. Throughout that time, we talked, usually while she lay secure and sated in my arms.

Her trim form had softened, looking even more feminine. She blushed whenever I gave extra attention to those areas, and I could feel her emotionally fighting insecurities. She feared I would see these changes and find them unfavorable. I told her every day, both in word and in deed, that I worshiped every inch of her, not just superficial beauty.

Her fingertips danced across my lips as she placed a small piece of fruit on my tongue. I wasted no time in leaning forward to share it with her.

The projection blinked to life on the wall. Keira screeched, burying her body against mine.

"This is a public projection. For those of us from Earth, think of it like a special news bulletin you used to see on television."

My bride relaxed her form again, turning slightly so that she could view the broadcast.

Two faces appeared. I recognized them instantly as Belinda and Dr. Anderson.

Keira rested her head on my chest. "When did we bring aboard an adult human male?"

"He was collected to assist the young woman in your directive," I explained.

"Ah," she said. Then we both fell quiet to listen.

Belinda continued. "My name is Belinda Benton. I'm a virologist in training. My companion here is Dr. Daniel Anderson. He is a vaccine researcher who formerly worked for the United States government.

"All on Earth were led to believe that Virus 442-C, what we call Influenza B15, came to our planet when an asteroid or meteor struck near Mt. Victory, Kentucky, a little over seven years ago. As you have all learned recently, the reality is that Prince Raklin and his crew crash landed, and my sisters and I sheltered them.

"The virus had already destroyed their home planet, but it had been long enough that they should not have had any trace of it still within them. Unfortunately, one of them acted as a carrier, like Typhoid Mary."

The doctor took over. "Some of us will remember our history lessons, but I will explain anyhow to share the information with all. Over a thousand years ago, we had a disease called typhus. No one could figure out how it kept spreading to new locations after they thought it eradicated. Finally, through much testing, they realized that a single person, a woman who worked as a cook, carried the disease within her body. Despite multiple quarantines, she continued to infect those with whom she came into contact. She directly caused over fifty deaths, and indirectly led to thousands becoming ill. To avoid future infections, she was finally confined to a private island until her death.

"One of the men from Volitar acted as a Typhoid Mary, carrying the virus within him, unknowingly spreading it. The Volitar superior waste removal process kept the virus from spreading among yourselves while on the pod. Once you landed, you had to adapt your ways, which meant that the virus found the opportunity to spread to new hosts."

The projection enlarged with images as they continued.

Belinda pointed to the images. "This is the chemical pattern of the 1918 influenza pandemic." She pointed to another. "This is the blueprint of the 2009 H1N1. Their structural similarities meant that the majority of humans already had immunity, meaning it did not affect us as much as it could have."

A third image appeared.

"Virus 442-C, or B15, as you can see, shares the same similarities. Even though it spread quickly across the planet, very few actually died from it. This virus should have been nothing more than a small inkblot in our history because, as a species, our bodies were accustomed to dealing with the little beasty. Unfortunately, the population of Volitar did not have this immunity, and it devastated them, wiping out mostly young women of childbearing age."

Anderson's voice broke in again. "I am ashamed to say that I took part in some of the initial research on B15. My superiors told me that I worked to develop a blanket vaccine toward additional mutations. The reality is that they took my research and twisted it.

"The entire population of the planet had developed immunity within a short time of the first severe case being reported. But for some reason, new strains—stronger, more vicious strains—kept popping up. I used my connections to get blood samples from the infected, and I could not understand my findings."

Several more graphics appeared with portions highlighted. "These mutations should have taken decades, or even hundreds of years to achieve in nature. Not fully trusting of our leaders, I shared some of those findings to the darknet, where Miss Benton and many others agreed with me. As soon as I shared my findings with my superiors, I found myself arrested, locked away in an underground prison where I fully expected to stay until I died."

The images faded away, and their exhausted faces appeared again.

"Prince Raklin, Dr. Anderson and I have acquired information from every single hospital and lab on the surface, getting the chemical blueprint for every death in their systems since the crash. Thanks to the wonderful technology at our fingertips, I can tell you with absolute certainty that the original 442-C that came to Earth through you only killed a little over five thousand individuals. Worldwide. And while that may sound like a lot, humans deal with new strains of the influenza virus so regularly that we call it seasonal. Our seasonal flu kills over twelve thousand people every year, sometimes upwards of sixty thousand.

"You *did not* bring death to our planet. Our own leaders did. They have been releasing biological warfare into large crowds regularly, blaming it on the 'asteroid.' We have all of our research compiled and available for anyone to review. Much of it actually shows that the newer, more deadly strains are in no way related to 442-C at all. If you choose to look at the research and have any questions, either Dr. Anderson or myself will be happy to meet with you once our quarantines are finished."

With that, the screen fell dark again.

I held my wife to me while I absorbed the information we'd just seen. "We should check on Raklin."

She shook her head against my chest. "Give him time. He'll need to read all of the facts himself. He has carried heavy guilt for many years now. Both he and Ruth have blamed themselves for millions of deaths."

He agreed, and we sat silently cuddling for several minutes before Ovid's robotic male voice sounded through the room.

"Incoming uplinks from Arden, MeeKale, and Raklin."

I sighed, helping my mate to stand. "Looks like we have to cover ourselves, my love."

She giggled. "We knew our seclusion temporary. But we have the rest of our lives together, Vax."

I announced to my AI. "Tell them ten minutes so that we may make ourselves presentable."

A short time later, we sat side by side as the screens blinked to life. Anger suffused the faces that met ours.

MeeKale spoke first. "Those first uploads you sent to us were bad enough. But this! To do something like this with the full knowledge of their own history... This is horror," his voice echoed his outrage. The maldron around his neck hissed and grumbled, seeming to agree with him.

Raklin had both Marianne and Ruth seated beside him. Ruth looked both stunned and ready to commit murder. "Belinda kept trying to tell me, and I sort of believed her, but my head was so wrapped up—"

Keira waved a hand to stop the other woman from speaking. "This is what Belinda showed me right before you transported. This is why I gave her the directive to find the proof."

Arden growled. "How can we possibly abandon a planet full of people to such horrible world leaders? We should gather our forces and destroy them!"

"No," Keira declared calmly. "The risk to our own people is too high. There are other ways. Gallatea, uplink Denali."

A fourth projection popped into view. "How may I serve you, Queen Keira?"

"Bring up a world view of Earth, and I want you to see if there are any pockets where no additional outbreaks have occurred. We keep looking at just the big picture, the overall numbers. But logically, there has to be some populated part of the planet not being continuously bombarded with illness. I refuse to believe that every single leader on the planet decided to perpetrate the same atrocities all at once. Humans can be trash, but not all of them. That just doesn't make sense. Show me proof that there is at least one leader who works hard to protect their people."

I realized her intent and squeezed her hand.

Before long, the map appeared. I tapped the projection, bringing one area closer to view. My brow furrowed as I turned to look at my wife. "This area especially has not experienced any outbreaks beyond the first wave of illness. But I do not understand. Is that not the same area where those horrible camps once operated?"

I heard Ruth gasp. "I never even realized. Keira, that is amazing!"

Raklin turned to her. "Why is this significant? What are these camps you speak of?"

Ruth shook her head. Her eyes met Keira's. "I knew Germany had instituted a lot of travel restrictions and increased their border forces, but a lot of places did. It just became background noise after a while. I never even thought to look at the statistics in each location."

Keira nodded. "Raklin, Denali can provide you with the upload if you wish, but you might want to just speak with Ruth, Marianne, or some of the other humans in your quarantine area. Or even Lanyar or Marlux. Earth history is full of horrible events. This area," she pointed to the projection, "is where one of the most horrible took place. But when that war finally ended and the prisoners were released, the Allied troops *made* the people actually see the horrors that occurred. They marched them through the death camps and made them look at the bodies. Germany vowed then, and has obviously kept that vow, that never again would such atrocities ever take place at their hands."

She returned her attention to the rest of the group. "Let Belinda and Dr. Anderson get some rest. I'm sure they have worked tirelessly to put all of this information together, and they deserve a break. Once they are recovered, have them recompile all of the data to remove anything that mentions Volitar, aliens, the pod crash... all of it. Make sure it states with certainty to identify the virus as B15, and that the source was asteroid or meteor. Then convert it into files that will work on Earth tech."

Arden's face relaxed. "You mean to deliver the research into the hands of those willing to see the truth."

She nodded. "Earth history is full of war, and with a world so large and populations so dense, it'll stay that way. Even if you all were to band together and fight, even if you succeeded, there would remain pockets of resistance to your peaceful ways. That is, unfortunately, part of the nature of humanity. But if we put the truth into the right hands, it'll spread. Not everyone will believe it; that is far out of our control. We have to let the remaining people of Earth sort out their own problems."

Ruth agreed. "You can lead a horse to water, but you can't force him to drink. The best we can do is give them the proof of their leaders' misdeeds." She blew out a long breath. "It's going to get ugly, and fast. Releasing this information could lead to a new world war. Or at least multiple civil wars."

Keira's face showed that she knew the other doctor spoke the truth. "We should make certain to include detailed information about these pockets of safety, these leaders who continue to protect their people. That will provide others with hope and help these strong leaders rise above." Her expression appeared stunned. "Knowing what my vecmāmiņa, my grandmother, went through in the camps, I never thought I would actively work to aid Germany rising in power."

Arden and MeeKale still looked ready for war, but they appeared to realize we could not serve our own people while taking over another planet, especially one this size and so far from home.

Denali spoke up. "It should be more than just the data. As you have shown us through the redesigned collection process, this needs to have a face. In your Earth words, the information needs to be humanized. I will speak with Belinda and Daniel. If they are willing, we will record a projection similar to the broadcast from today. The evil leaders will try to target them, but since they are safely off planet, it will not matter." She grinned. "The search has already begun for Daniel, since he simply vanished from their prison deep beneath a building called the Pentagon. If we hack into the entertainment media and play the broadcasts while delivering the information to multiple sources for access, we can stop the leaders from being able to suppress it."

Keira nodded, deep in thought. "It *is* going to get ugly. But at the same time, we'll need to give the women aboard the choice to return. They may very well want to fight in this war, now that they know the truth."

~*~

I smoothed my hands over her rounded belly, dropping several soft kisses upon it as I slowly wrapped the kilnat around her. A thump struck my lips as I neared her navel.

She laughed, rubbing the spot. "That's enough abusing your father, little one. You're both going to have to learn to share."

I sighed. My fingers fastened the clasp, and I pressed my cheek to her. "This time secluded with you has been the most peaceful I have ever experienced. Yet, there is so much more to be done in preparation for our return to Volitar. Some days, I wish we could stay like this forever."

She placed a hand to my chin, raising it up so that she could press her lips to mine.

"I do understand, my love. But we have responsibilities to others as well. We have worked hard to reach this point, and we're a good team. We will continue to have time just for us, but we have to make time to serve our people."

I pouted. "Just because I know this does not mean I like it."

I forced myself to stand and offered her my arm. "Are you ready to meet several thousand new faces?"

"I'm ready to hold some babies. Taylana and Marlux's young ones are already three weeks old, and I haven't been able to kiss them yet." She glanced down at where our own still grew within her. "And I think I might need to get a little practice."

We stepped forward as the portal opened.

~*~

Chapter 31

Keira

I spent as much time as I could spare cuddling Taylana's babies and learning their names. I didn't even try to fight back tears; I just let them fall. None of this new generation would ever feel unwanted, outcast, or alone, and they would have the marks to prove it. A sense of relief also swelled within when I found that the young girl, Serena, and another runaway teen we had found during our time on Earth had quarters attaching to theirs so that they could assist with the babies.

After all, six arms didn't mean a single person could handle so many young by herself.

After that, I visited with the rest of the Borkanian women. Seela had mated to the crew member, and the rest of the women had been overjoyed to learn that it hadn't caused a draw on my magic. It amazed me that these individuals who barely knew me had all been willing to delay finding their potential mates for fear of risk to me. It would take me a while to come to full terms with their open acceptance of someone so visibly different from themselves.

A few had moved over to Arden's ship to help with transitioning the women over there. In addition to Belinda's darknet connections, several of the early recruits had picked up where Gil and I left off, returning to the surface in small groups to approach those I hadn't yet reached. Our numbers continued to grow faster than any of us had ever expected.

Reganda had, of course, volunteered for continuing the welcoming and decontamination work aboard the other ship. My chosen sister seemed ready to jump anytime a new opportunity arose. She visited me briefly before she transported, asking for my blessing.

I hugged the woman tightly to me. "Reganda, my sister, none of you need ask permission for these things."

Her dark skin turned slightly darker on her cheeks. Her eyes cast downward as she spoke. "I believe the younger prince may be my mate, Queen Keira. I feel a tingling flare in my mark whenever he is near."

I laughed loudly. "Well, sister, I wish you the blessings of the goddess. But I bid you make him work for your attention. It's up to us to keep these princes on their toes."

She nodded. "He, or should I say *we* will have to practice restraint, regardless. There are so many coming aboard every day now that it will take a lifetime to get to know them all."

I snorted at that thought. "If he is anything like his brother, restraint will be difficult."

My friend hesitated a moment.

I frowned slightly, reaching out and taking her hand in mine. I led her to a couple of chairs, waiting until we were seated before continuing. "Something bothers you, Reganda. Speak freely. You may always speak freely to me."

Her eyes closed for a moment. When she opened them, I saw a glimmer of tears forming. "I am frightened, my queen. I know that the magic shows us who our mate is. I have known this my whole life. And I see the happiness between those who have mated so far. But..." her voice faded off.

I reached forward, taking her hand in mine. My gift did not flare, thankfully. I had put lots of practice during my time on Earth into controlling it so that it did not show me images on its own every time I touched someone. At this moment, I wanted my friend to share with me at her own pace.

We sat silently while she gathered her thoughts. When her shoulders squared, I knew she had decided her words. "I have listened to a great many stories from the Earth women we have brought aboard. You had forewarned us that many of them will have suffered and would have fears to overcome before they would consider mating. This has shown true so many times."

She paused again. Then she sighed. "What if the mate my magic has chosen would behave toward me as many of these Earth women have experienced?"

When her eyes lifted, tears coated the lower lid, threatening to fall, yet being held back by her sheer determination. I released one hand, lifting it to cradle her cheek. I had taken so many factors into account when we designed and started the new collection process, but I had neglected to imagine the effects these tales would cause for such gentle creatures as my Borkanian family.

"My sweet, caring sister. You have been such a stalwart friend and companion, volunteering to take on the most dangerous of tasks aboard either of these vessels. I have seen so much strength from you that I had forgotten how even the strongest among us have doubts. I swear to you that I will allow no such horrors to occur among our new people, nor will my mate. Even the whisper of abusive behavior will bring our intervention. This gift from the queen and goddess allows both of us to see within a person's mind where we can find the truth of any allegations. Our people will always be protected, will always have the right to speak and to choose."

I engulfed her in my arms, whispering into her ear, "You need never fear. Any person who hurts someone protected by me will suffer great repercussions. I don't care if they are a prince or a pauper, a sister or a servant. I'll kick their ass without a moment's hesitation."

Her arms squeezed me one more time before she pushed away and discreetly swiped at her tears. "I'm being silly."

I shook my head, making sure she met my eyes before I spoke. I wanted her to see the seriousness in mine. "Not silly, sister. You're being cautious. There is nothing wrong with that. I knew the stories would have some effect, but I left you ill-prepared for this. For that, I can only offer my apology and swear to you that *you will always be protected.*"

A portal materialized. Reganda ducked her head, quickly wiping at her tears and composing herself.

Vaxeehl and Arden stepped through the opening. My mate crossed the room, bending down to kiss me gently. I raised my lips to his, welcoming the affection.

"Hello, love. I hope you have not been overtaxing yourself," he uttered as our lips parted.

I smiled, placing my palm to his cheek. "Only my voice, darling."

I let my fingers slide away as he stood back to his full height. Then I turned toward his brother. "Welcome, Arden. Are you and your crew prepared for the latest onboarding?"

The prince bowed slightly toward me. "Thank you, sister. I believe we are as ready as we could possibly be. I am extremely grateful that some of your recruits and crew have been willing to assist with the process to make the transition as smooth as possible."

His eyes coasted over Reganda. He bowed again. "Lady Reganda," he greeted, his tone dropping slightly.

She straightened her spine, folding her hands in her lap. "Prince Arden. The queen has granted me permission to join your crew. I should gather my things." She stood then, smoothing any wrinkles in her wrap before starting toward the portal.

As she passed, Arden's hand reached out, grasping one arm gently.

Reganda paused, glancing at where his fingers touched her. I noticed her breathing increase just slightly, but I saw no fear in her eyes.

Arden released his hold. He bowed his head toward her. "It would be a great honor, my lady, if you would permit me to escort you aboard my vessel."

My sister hesitated just a moment. Then she nodded. "I will return shortly."

Arden's eyes stayed affixed upon her departing form until the portal closed behind her.

I glanced at my husband and smiled. His return look told me that he knew as well as I that another of his brothers would soon be mated. Then I thought about what had been discussed prior to their entry.

I frowned. "I made an error in my calculations before we started recruiting."

Both men seated themselves, waiting for me to continue.

"I did not account for the secondary trauma that the helpers would potentially suffer."

We sat and discussed my concerns for a while, eventually calling in the rest of the council. Thankfully, among some of the recruits I had yet to meet, we'd managed to bring aboard a few skilled councilors. I felt relieved to learn that they had quickly stepped up, offering their services even while still in quarantine.

"Did one of these councilors volunteer to move to your ship, Arden?"

He nodded, while Denali responded. "Yes, Queen Keira. Once we understood the nature of their work, and realized the benefit, we requested that they partner into groups for each ship."

I released the tension in my body. "Good." Then I turned toward Arden again. "I would like to recommend that my sister and the other helpers be housed near them aboard your vessel. She has thrown herself into the fray at every turn, and I'm concerned that she is being negatively affected."

His lips turned down as he processed what I said. His eyes softened. He bowed his head toward me. "I will see it done."

Before the council parted, I also learned that the onboard medical team worked via uplink with the medical personnel on Volitar, developing their own forms of vaccines. Samples of all Earth-based inoculations had been collected and the historical data distributed for study. The onboard staff worked to have adapted the technology such that the whole of our people could be provided with the antibodies to protect them from potential mutations of Virus 442-C, as well as the risk of another Typhoid Mary situation with other Earth illnesses.

One medical minded recruit had suggested that someone return to Earth every few years to collect any new information and samples. By the time we dispersed the meeting, my mind felt overwhelmed at the thought of what we had accomplished.

Gil and I had collected nearly seven hundred women and another eighty or so children during our travels. Belinda's darknet connections, however, had exploded with volunteers who travelled, sight unseen, into a new, unknown future. After the broadcast coup, a few of them had asked to return to Earth, to fight for their planet, but we lost less than twenty to the potential rebellion. Surprisingly, those who opted to return had never been touched by the magical orbs.

That part had surprised me. I'd worried that many more would choose to return. However, the biggest majority of the volunteers were women like me, women who had no one left on Earth who would notice their existence or absence.

Those few who chose to return had some kind of family, even if distant and out of contact, for whom they wished to fight.

Including Dr. Anderson. He'd arranged a safe house, citizenship, and protection for himself in Germany, where he could continue his vaccine research to further protect the people on Earth. The German chancellor felt especially grateful to the doctor for including their innocence in the report.

~*~

Arden's ship neared maximum capacity at the last report, and both ships continued to double bunk in many places while we awaited MeeKale's arrival.

The day I learned about the plans to bring the orphans aboard, I started out hesitant. I knew that a great many of those orphans had been abandoned because they had defects of some sort. Lanyar had rolled his eyes at me through the screen and explained that most of those things were minor and could be repaired with the advanced medical technology they possessed. Denali and her crew had already started working on ways around some of the more difficult cases.

Of course, I cried at this. Stupid pregnancy hormones. Then I went for a walk, letting my brain rest from the information overload. I felt exceptionally grateful for the diversity of those coming aboard. Between their skills and experiences, I was able to let go of a lot of responsibilities and let the program run itself.

I found Ruth wandering through the park. Pangou nipped at her ankles playfully, a small litter of kits trying to copy him while their mother stood nearby, watchful that they did not face harm. Between my staying on Earth for the duration of her quarantine, followed by my own seclusion, it had been nearly two months since I'd last seen the veterinarian. Her features appeared relaxed. I hesitated to disturb her, but I also had questions. I approached slowly, not wanting to startle her.

Pangou spotted me as I neared, giving a playful yip before bounding toward me. He stopped just short of a tackle, choosing instead to nudge gently at my hand for scritches.

"How in the world did you manage to find time for yourself," Ruth asked. "As queen, I guess I imagined you holding court."

I laughed, shaking my head. "I'm still not one hundred percent sure about all of this 'queen' stuff. It would definitely not have been my first choice, had the Borkanian magic not seen fit to coalesce within my body." I paused, glancing at her sideways.

"So, Dr. Benton, do you still hate everything alien? You don't *have* to leave Earth, you know." I reached down and rubbed Pangou's soft underside when he rolled over—not an easy task with my belly extending so far. "Hello, Pangou, you crazy slognip. I see you've found your own mate and fathered a new litter."

He rolled back to his feet and sat on his haunches, clearly a proud father. I patted his head. "Yes, you are a big, strong slognip. And I'm sure your young will be just as big and strong as you are."

Ruth chuckled, scratching the beast behind his ears. "These creatures are fascinating. As soon as I was released from quarantine and Taylana's babies safely delivered, I begged for a place to find some peace. I've been living in the middle of nowhere for most of my life. Even with the barn full of people, I still had peace and quiet up at the house. I had the woods to walk in."

She raised her eyes to me. "You do realize I don't *actually* hate the bastards, right? I mean, yeah, I had my head up my ass and only half listened to Belinda when she tried to explain the shit show to me. But the real issue was that Marianne absolutely adored that winged jerk. We didn't even know he was a prince until a short time before you showed up. At that point, they had given up hope of returning home, and we were trying to figure out how to keep the children from ending up as some horrible science experiment."

She let out a long breath. "I have you to thank for that. You and Vaxeehl, and all of these assholes. I spent six months worrying whether my sister would safely deliver a child. Then the child shows up with wings, and I knew she could never have a normal life anywhere on Earth. That's what made me hate them. When these men find their mates, there is absolutely nothing that can stop them from laying claim."

Her eyes drifted around at the blue trees, red moss, and some seriously hot pink fruit dangling from vines nearby. "I go where my sisters go. We've always had each other, even if we didn't have much else on the surface. I'll give up everything I know, but I won't give up them. Even if I have to learn a whole new variety of animals."

Though I'd been raised an only child, the new family I'd formed here on this ship helped me understand her words. Taylana and Reganda were my chosen sisters, Gilnax my chosen brother. And Vaxeehl. I would give up everything to protect my new family, just as I had my former one.

"Queen Keira, your presence is requested on the receiving platform for Prince MeeKale's arrival."

I heard Ruth mumble, "Another arrogant prick. Just what we need."

I laughed and requested a direct portal. Then I grabbed Ruth's hand. "Come on. Let's go show them how human women treat arrogant pricks. These guys have had it way too easy so far with the mating magic."

We stepped through the portal and were instantly barraged with angry male voices. All four brothers stood arguing, pointing at something. Raklin had his wings spread, blocking whatever it was from getting near Marianne, who cowered behind him fearfully.

Ruth started running, and I released her hand to let her go. I easily understood the protective instinct that had kicked in at seeing her sister fearful. However, the best I could manage at this stage was a hurried waddle.

I could barely tell one voice from the next as I tried to make out the conversation.

"Why would you dare to bring a nesting maldron with you?"

"Are you insane?"

"That thing tried to bite my wife."

"She won't leave my side. What else was I to do?"

"Oh my god, she's *gorgeous*!" Okay, that voice was definitely Ruth.

I saw her carefully approaching something laying on the floor. She quickly lowered to her knees. The arguing stopped as the dark woman reached forward.

MeeKale tried to step in the way, but the creature snapped at him. "What the hell?"

I finally got close enough to see what the fuss was about. Ruth sat near what appeared to be a small dragon. Sort of. It had more of a salamander-like body, long and sleek, with shimmering scales of many colors. Except for one area that seemed swollen. Since I'd heard nesting, I assumed she either carried young or eggs in that area.

MeeKale stood frozen, staring as the maldron snuggled up to Ruth, rubbing her head on the woman's abdomen.

I stepped slowly close. The thing opened its eyes. It glared at me, but it didn't snap. I spoke gently to it. "You are beautiful, aren't you?"

It purred and let its eyes drift partway closed. Still, I could see its gaze drop to my belly and back up again. Something about that look spoke to me, creating a small sense of discomfort. I stepped backwards, giving them space.

Ruth must have noticed the gaze. Her hand lazily rubbed the shimmery multi-colored scales.

"Did you know," she spoke softly, "that there are certain species of birds on Earth who seem to have rankings. They won't let other nesting females anywhere near..." Her voice drifted off and her eyes rose to her sister. "Marianne, are you pregnant again?"

The other woman tossed her hands in the air. "How am I supposed to know? We don't deal with bleeding anymore, remember?"

I turned my head when Raklin gasped. He spun around, encircling the small woman with both arms and wings.

I made a mental note to talk to Lanyar about modifying the hygiene tech so that it alerts the women to their cycles. And to discuss birth control for those not wishing to spend their entire lives dropping babies. Hopefully, my pregnancy brain wouldn't make me forget before I could meet with him.

MeeKale cleared his throat. "This is all touching and special. But I did actually summon you here for a reason."

He addressed Raklin. "Brother, we found your ship on the way here. We got a ping right before that last worm hole. They had managed to keep the life support running, but only had enough power for the smallest of the thrusters. They've been able to travel, but not worm hole jump."

Raklin, still holding Marianne close, nodded. "I presume they are baying for my blood at this point."

He shook his head. "They're too busy trying to save their own necks right now. I haven't told them you're alive. The backup generators recorded the mutiny. It also recorded the fact that they were close enough to pick up your distress signal from the emergency beacon and refused to respond. They could have easily gotten within range to transport you off of a hostile planet. Under the circumstances, it would have been fully within their rights to lock you and your men away until they could return to Volitar, and they would have faced no charges.

Instead, they chose to leave you to your fate. Some of them, at least. A handful tried to battle for control and ended up in lockdown."

"You're all a bunch of swinging dicks, I swear. You lost your women, and then you lost your minds." Ruth mumbled just loud enough to be heard.

He spun around and glared at her. "Seriously, woman?"

The maldron raised her head and hissed at him. Ruth stroked her scales more. "Easy girl. Don't let the big, bad, barky guy bother you."

"Unbelievable. The mouthiest woman in the universe sits at my feet, stroking my pet, and still has the audacity to spit venomous words at me."

The moment the words left his mouth, he realized what he'd said. Unfortunately for him, so did Ruth and I. We tried to hold back our laughter in deference to the seriousness of the prior conversation, but it was a lost cause.

Between snorts of laughter and a huge grin, Ruth added, "I'll keep sitting here, stroking your pet. You boys go deal with the mutiny."

Marianne shrieked. "Ruth!"

She just shrugged and smiled. "You're the one married to a prince, sister. I'm still single, and I find the company of animals much more compatible."

My delightful husband, clearly seeing the way the wind blew, decided to speak up. "Then it is fortuitous that you should spend much time in the presence of another prince, seeing as he oversees the care of our creatures."

Before any further response could be uttered, he regained the men's attention. "We do need to address the situation."

Raklin shook his head. "I feel they deserve no punishment, brothers. Had our roles been reversed, had one of them taken control of the ship and flown like a raging fool until it nearly left everyone dead, we would not be discussing this at all. We all know we would have ignored the distress signal, just as they did. Or we would have ordered the person put to death, rather than allowing them to escape on a pod. They should face no charges.

"I was the one who put them at risk. If you must review their behavior, judge them upon their treatment of each other after I left the ship."

Vax stood tall. "You are adamant on this point?"

Raklin did not hesitate. "Absolutely."

MeeKale nodded. "It will be done." He drew a breath. "Of course, I'll have to edit out portions of this recording, but I had a feeling our little brother would put to voice such a point. I thought they should hear it directly from him."

Vax frowned. "For what reason did you summon our wives, then? This matter could have been handled without them."

He laughed. "Why else? I wanted to see in person the women who brought my brothers to heel. But I could not leave my maldron. She's not left my side for months." He glanced down at Ruth, who now had a long, spiky tail wrapped around her middle, his eyes narrowing in contemplation. "And she certainly has not let anyone else near her, either."

He sniffed the air a moment. "Is there a slognip wandering nearby?"

Ruth answered. "No, Keira and I were visiting with Pangou. His kits swarmed all over me."

MeeKale's eyes widened. "Slognips are mortal enemies to maldrons. I can't believe she didn't rip you to shreds when the smell got within striking distance."

Ruth just shrugged. "I'm good with animals. That's why I became a vet." Her eyebrows lifted and she stared at her hand where it rested on the lizard's body. "Um, do maldrons lay eggs or birth live young?"

"Live young," he responded. "The birth fluid is acidic."

She kept her voice steady, shifting as if to stand. "Alright, pretty lady. Your belly is doing a lot of squeezing. We need to get you somewhere safe for those little ones to be born." She yipped. "Okay, I get it."

Her eyes raised to MeeKale. "Find a cart that will hold both my weight and hers. She isn't letting go of me. She actually tightened her hold when I tried to move."

"But you could be injured," he protested.

"I've been kicked by a cow while she was birthing and had to finish with a broken arm. I'll heal. And if I scar, I scar. It won't be the first time. Now move."

MeeKale shot down the ramp.

Vax wrapped his arms around me and started leading me away. "Just in case, my love. Maldrons have been known to spit acid during birth."

I heard Raklin coaxing his own wife back toward our ship. I also heard Arden laughing. He, at least, appeared entertained by his brother's behavior.

I whispered to Vax, "Should we be worried about Ruth?"

He shrugged. "MeeKale knows what to expect. Last I knew, that particular maldron actually nests in his quarters. Frankly, I'm more worried about him when Ruth discovers she's stuck rooming with my brother for the next couple of weeks, at least. Perhaps much longer. Once the maldron chooses you, she will follow you everywhere, even if that means abandoning her young."

I gasped. "No! Someone should tell Ruth."

He shook his head. "She has access to the knowledge, and she knows how to ask. In your own words: Ruth is a big girl; she can make her own choices."

~*~

Chapter 32

Vaxeehl

Engineers and technicians from all of the vessels worked together to get Raklin's ship up and running properly again. Honestly, we needed every bit of space we could get. Once the craft was fully functional, several crew members from each of the other ships transferred over to assist.

And the humans... The changes to the onboarding process appeared to make their assimilation much easier. Of course, that didn't mean our differences stopped existing. For one thing, many crewmembers began approaching with random strange questions about things they'd noticed.

While entering the common area, one astute young woman approached me. "Sir," her timid voice gave the impression that she'd wrestled with her decision to approach.

I nodded. "Yes," I paused. "I must apologize. It appears I have fallen slack on learning all of the names, and yours escapes my mind."

She blushed, yet continued to meet my gaze, squaring her shoulders a bit. "I'm Micah, sire. I have an idea that I would like to pursue, and my mother insisted I needed to get permission before I could do so."

I waved a hand toward a couple of seats. Once there, I waited for her to continue. It took several minutes of her fingers fidgeting in her lap—something I'd seen several of the humans do when they appeared nervous—before she finally spoke. Of course, once she started, the words seemed to flow unchecked.

"Sire, I've noticed that the Volitar and Vesper onboard appear confused about some of our human behaviors. I mean, there's been a running joke on Earth that humans are space orcs, and it's highly likely we are. It really is a death planet. I mean, have you seen some of the things we've gotten up to in our history? And the creatures we've discovered on our own planet seem more like things we'd find out in space. It's hard to fathom sometimes how in the world we became the apex predator—"

I raised a hand to stop her verbal onslaught. Lowering my head and lifting my brow, I smiled. "Your idea, Micah?"

She blushed again. "Sorry, sire. I tend to ramble when I'm either excited or nervous. And I happen to be both right now."

The girl drew a deep breath. "I overheard some of the crew talking about how other races will react toward us. Or us toward them. I thought that—with your permission, of course—perhaps a guide of some sorts would be appropriate? I mean, obviously, it would have to be regularly updated as things are brought up, and maybe I'm not the best person to compile such a thing. But I also overheard that some ships from other planets in your galaxy may join in recruiting disposable humans."

Those words caused my thoughts to seize. I know I frowned.

The girl paled. She quickly lowered her gaze and started shifting in her seat. "Sorry. It was just a thought." She rose from her seat.

Before Micah could run off, I gently grabbed her arm, signaling her to return to her seat. She did, but she did not raise her eyes to me.

I released my hold on her and lifted one finger to her chin, softly insisting that she meet my gaze. I forced my face to relax. "I think it is a wonderful idea, Micah. My reaction was to your use of the word 'disposable'. While that may have been true in the past, on your home planet, that will not be the case anymore. I want you to understand that. None of you are garbage to be thrown out."

She swallowed hard, her throat flexing near my fingers. Her lip trembled, but she held her emotions tightly. "Thank you, sire."

I gave a firm nod before loosening my touch and shifting upright once again. "What do you need to make this accessible?" I paused, my gaze noticing a young human male standing next to a small group of crewmembers, grinning widely while my crew argued amongst themselves. "What is happening over there?"

The girl turned her head and chuckled. "That's Alex. Or maybe Jared. They're identical twins, and it's extremely difficult to tell them apart. They heard one of your science crewmen talking to their mother about studying Earth. So they came up with a game to introduce the guys to some of the wildlife. It's called 'Dog or Not Dog.'"

I nodded. "That much makes sense. What I am concerned with is, why my crew are so animated?"

Micah giggled, hiding behind her hand. "Sir, Earth animals are strange, to say the least. Matter of fact, I had an idea to consult with the twins when it comes to helping me detail human reactions to some of your own wildlife. I imagine there will be some that we have a visceral reaction to which are completely harmless, but the Earth version of a similar animal is deadly."

My head tipped, my eyes blinking. I shook myself mentally and focused back on her. "How do you mean?"

She shrugged. "I've only seen your slognip so far, and nearly had a panic attack, personally. They look like some sort of science experiment gone wrong."

As her words continued, describing a wolverine, a Komodo dragon, and an angler fish, and how all of those creatures behave, pulling up information from the Earth internet to show me, I understood better just how truly frightened Keira must have been when she first spotted Pangou. I realized then that this guide Micah had suggested would be necessary.

I whistled, drawing the attention of Garroth, one of the science crew. He frowned, not wanting to leave the discussion, yet did as bade.

"Yes, my lord?"

A short time later, the game of 'Dog or Not Dog' suspended for the moment, Garroth led Micah and Alex—Jared was apparently teaching another group about a place called 'Australia', where nearly every animal is capable of killing a human, and yet a large number of humans live—to find a space to use as an office and begin compiling the Helpful Guide to Human Behavior. It only made sense to have a human at the helm of such a thing, and young Micah seemed thrilled that her idea had been received positively.

Especially since, based on data analysis, MeeKale had contacted a few other vessels from some of Volitar's neighbors to begin traveling our direction, prepared to take on additional guests upon arrival. Even once our ships left the area and headed back to Volitar, recruitment would continue on Earth, allowing any individual who wished to escape their situation the opportunity. The additional ships might need any extra help they could get to understand the oddities among the varying human behaviors.

A few women from Keira's early efforts had taken over where she and Gil left off. This allowed my wife to relax, knowing that she had not abandoned the lost souls whose thought scans cried out for safety.

Gil had stepped up, volunteering to return with them as protection. A few of the other Vesper guards had also followed suit. Now that success lay visibly within our grasps, they felt drawn to do their best to aid it toward fruition. Gil took time to train the men as he had been trained, aiding them in learning to blend into the men of Earth.

Once these new teams transported to the surface, and my wife sat beside me, her burgeoning belly wiggling as our child rolled around within her, I felt my chest grow tight. The full reality of what we accomplished together settled over me, squeezing until I struggled to breathe.

Keira noticed. She stood from her chair and quickly settled upon my lap, her arms closing around me. One hand reached up, stroking my hair as my head nestled against her shoulder. I let my own arms circle her gently, always cautious of the miracle growing within her.

As my heart rate decreased and my breathing evened, I whispered against her neck. "I never thought we'd actually succeed. It's been years. I was ready to give up. I honestly thought Volitar, Vesper, and so many other planets would remain decimated with very little hope for the future."

Soft lips pressed to my forehead. "I know. It's overwhelming in so many ways. Realizing that so many women on Earth felt the same as I did, as if they could not possibly matter to anyone, was a hard pill to swallow. My first lonely month aboard was strange. I am thankful you were willing and able to adapt the onboarding process to remove the solitude and prison-like atmosphere."

I felt her smile against my skin. "You know, I still feel like I should have made you work harder, despite the Borkanian magic."

I tightened my hold a bit. "The more I learn about your planet, the more I realize how my behavior prior to our first meeting would have frightened you." I burrowed my nose against her neck, letting my lips caress her lightly and enjoying her shiver. "Father had told us we would know when we found our mates. He'd said that while much of our mating instinct had faded through the centuries, as long as we ruled fairly, Helvana would continue to bless us. But I was obsessed with you, even though we'd never spoken. I'd merely seen you on the projection."

She nodded. "Yes, Lanyar told me how he'd worried about your strong feelings. He thought he'd need to sedate you again, and he really didn't want to do that."

I raised my eyes to hers. "Do I frighten you with my intensity, my love? I'm trying to keep it under control, but it seems like if I am near you, I need to touch you."

She smiled so gently, her hand cupping my face. "I have long since forgiven you. While the mating magic may have driven you to the point of obsession, you never once let it overpower your actions."

Her eyes flared, the banked fires stirring within her. "Without the guiding hand of Helvana, I believe I still would have been drawn to you just as much, Vaxeehl. You are good, and strong. Your sense of responsibility mirrors my own, and we have both shouldered a great deal of guilt from the things that have happened. I am grateful that I have been able to help alleviate some of your guilt, just as you have done mine."

As her lips closed over mine, I bathed in the wash of heat, welcoming it through my entire being.

Chapter 33

Vaxeehl

Six pods touched down gently. The journey to Volitar had gone well, for which I thanked Helvana greatly.

I looked to Denali. She gave me the human thumbs up sign that the projections had connected across all.

"Ladies, young ones, when these doors open, you will finally get your first real glimpse of your new homes. All of Volitar has travelled to our capital to rejoice at your arrival. Please do not be overwhelmed by the number of faces you see in the crowd. They are merely curious to see those who have come to save our planet.

"Shelters have been established within the palace grounds so that you may have time to adjust. I want to reiterate that none of you are expected to select a mate right away. And if it turns out that you do not find a mate, you will still be cared for on this planet. None of you need ever concern yourselves again with seeking shelter or food.

"Your guides will bring you to the courtyard. There, the king will recognize you as citizens of Volitar. After that, you will be led to the housing areas so that you may select a dwelling. And tonight, at the setting of the sun, we will celebrate your welcome."

Denali signaled again.

I pulled the cloak around my shoulders, making sure it remained fastened. The collected females had made matching cloaks for all of the princes and their wives, all decorated to match the kilnat design originally crafted by Keira. My brothers had balked at first, but I had insisted. I wanted to give my father the chance he deserved. More recent communications showed him following our directives with less conflict, and it made me hopeful.

I had left Arden to handle all conversations with father. He quickly realized the importance of this move after Reganda mated to him. The tribal mark appeared the morning after their union.

Arden had finally convinced father to disband the sharing program and allow the women involved to select whether they wished to continue their triads, step away from both men, or choose just one of them as their bonded mate.

He had also dictated to father that he held absolutely no sway over the women aboard our ships. Together, we brothers had designed a new integration program, giving the human females their right to choose their own mates. Before the virus, that had always been the case on Volitar, and we vowed to return it to such. Keira and the other wives already planned to meet with the Norvaxian women to ascertain the status of their assigned relationships.

We had transmitted language uploads for the many Earth tongues so that our own people could welcome these new residents with understanding, strongly encouraging Father to upload all of them. Arden reported he had seemed strangely happy to receive the uploads, as well as the lack of responsibility.

The doors opened, and the ramps lowered to the ground. I double checked my cloak once more before extending my arm to Keira. She placed one hand gracefully upon my arm, the other gently holding our young son. We stepped forward, leading almost three thousand women and children from our pod, with my guards and crew scattered along the outer columns. A few hung back to make sure no one fell behind.

As we neared the courtyard, the six groups merged, appearing as an unarmed legion descending upon the grounds.

Father stood on the front step of the palace, a smile on his face. I hadn't seen father smile in so long that I nearly stumbled with my surprise.

As a group, we stopped. I glanced to my brothers. Raklin stepped forward, leading a now heavily pregnant Marianne and Analisa. Father nearly fell to his knees with joy, having missed our brother as much as we. He pressed a gentle kiss to both Marianne and their daughter's foreheads, welcoming them to Volitar.

He rested his hand on Raklin's shoulder. "My son, I find no fault in your grief. Had I not been saddled with the care of our people, I feel I, too, would have run to hide. I welcome you back with open arms and look forward to getting to know your lady wife and child."

Next, Arden stepped forward, Reganda at his side. In Reganda's arms lay one of the young orphans we had collected. The girl had been absolutely taken with the embodiment of Durga who cared for her, and Arden had insisted on adopting the child as their own, as a gift for his bride.

"My stoic son has found joy at last. I see great happiness upon your face, and I am sure these exotic beauties at your side bear much responsibility for that." He welcomed them with blessings as well.

MeeKale stepped forward, three baby maldron's riding his shoulders. Next to him, standing tall and proud, Ruth walked carefully, the mother maldron wrapped tightly around her waist.

Father laughed. "Not exactly the kind of grandchildren I expected, but I see that even my animal loving child has found a mate perfect for him." He leaned forward to kiss Ruth, but the maldron hissed at him.

Instead, he bowed slightly toward her. "I will offer you a different welcome, my dear Ruth. I hope you find no fault in an old man's caution."

Ruth chuckled. "She barely lets your son near me without an argument. I understand completely, sir. Hopefully, she will come to understand that she will have to share me with your actual grandchild in about five months."

"Splendid!" He cheered.

I heard my wife mutter softly, "That little sneak. She promised she would tell me."

"Come, wife. Formalities, and all that jazz." We climbed the steps slowly. I felt Keira's tremble. I wanted to send a surge of my magic to calm her, but she had explicitly ordered me against such an action.

She bent her knees in a regal curtsey as I bowed.

Father placed his hand gently beneath her chin, guiding her back to stand tall. "Lady Keira, despite all of my sons doing their best to hide everything they could about you from my eyes, even a king sometimes holds enough sway to hear a few secrets. I believe you may be the right person to help my son accept his future."

He gently kissed her forehead. Then he placed another upon our son. "His name?"

"Jasper," she said. "He's almost three months, born shortly before we left for our return journey."

He stepped close to me. "Vaxeehl, you have served our people well, stepping up to do what seemed impossible. You have succeeded beyond my wildest dreams, and you have helped your brothers become the men I always hoped they could."

His gnarled hands reached up, pulling the crown from his head. "Kneel, son, for I am old, and I wish to save my energy for chasing my grandchildren."

A lump formed in my throat.

Father paused, looking around him. He frowned a moment. "Take off those silly coverings, boys. The craftsmanship is beautiful, but for this, you must appear as the Volitar men you are."

As arranged, dedicated crew members stepped forward, aiding us all in removing the cloaks. The murmuring began immediately, though I ignored it.

I saw tears track down my father's face as he looked from me to Keira and back again. I dropped to my knees before him.

He spoke softly. "I see that the ceremony is just a formality, as the goddess herself has marked you." With those words, he settled the crown upon my head.

He turned to Keira while signaling someone forward. "Kneel next to your husband, Lady Keira." He reached behind him, bringing mother's crown forward and placing it gently upon her head.

Once done, he placed one hand beneath each of our chins, tilting our faces up. "Rise up and be recognized as the king and queen."

Keira looked to me. I nodded. She held our son toward my father. "Will you hold Jasper for us?"

The man looked thrilled, and I realized this truly was what he wanted. He was done ruling and wanted to simply be a doting grandfather. He happily snuggled the sleeping infant and stepped back.

Keira and I rose and turned. As one, we unfurled our fiery wings.

Father spoke from behind us, addressing the crowd. "King Vaxeehl and Queen Keira are truly blessed by our goddess, Helvana. May they lead us into our new future with her grace at their sides."

A wave of various colors knelt before us. I felt humbled by their faith, but I knew that with my goddess at my side, secure in the acceptance of our people, we would succeed.

As one, we placed our hands together as if in prayer. Then we flung them outwards, sending a blanket of mystical flames across the entire crowd. It soared all the way to the farthest reaches before slowly settling down, giving our full population just a touch of the magic we shared.

After all, everyone deserved the opportunity to find their flame mate, not just the royal family.

Acknowledgements

No book is ever written alone.

From my husband, who kept me fed when my head was so deep within the confines of these pages that eating was the farthest thing from my mind, to my friends who counseled me when I suffered what I call a writer's meltdown because I realized I had created a major mental issue that I had to find a way around. These are my support system, the people who helped me get this novel from concept to completion.

Ben, Glenn and Abigayle, my family who listened to me rant and rave, and bounce around when I finally got the details right.

Jessica and Spence, who helped me fine-tune the basic outline before I even wrote the first word.

Luis, Kendra, Dawn, Amber, and Cindy, who read through multiple drafts to help me catch missing plot holes, or even told me they couldn't bring themselves to like a specific character.

A special acknowledgment goes to TikTok creator @micahbriane, from whom originated the idea of the Helpful Human Guide with her #OrionsBeltInsurance skits.

Finally, to Christyn, who gave it that last touch, catching details that needed just a tiny bit of explanation as to not leave the reader confused.

While the idea starts in the writer's mind, and he or she is who puts the words on paper or screen, a writer never truly works alone.

So thank you, to all of you. Your support and assistance made the difference that took this story from concept to reality.

About the Author

Elura Coren resides in south central lower Michigan with her husband and numerous animals. She enjoys the quiet of rural life, which provides her with many colorful, panoramic views, as well as ample inspirational situations from which to craft her novels.